Babysitter

NOVELS BY JOYCE CAROL OATES

Breathe

Night. Sleep. Death. The Stars.

Pursuit

My Life as a Rat

Hazards of Time Travel

A Book of American Martyrs

The Man Without a Shadow

Jack of Spades: A Tale of Suspense

The Sacrifice

Carthage

The Accursed

Daddy Love

Mudwoman

Little Bird of Heaven

My Sister, My Love: The Intimate Story of
   Skyler Rampike

The Gravedigger's Daughter

Black Girl / White Girl

Blood Mask

Missing Mom

The Stolen Heart

The Falls

Take Me, Take Me with You

The Tattooed Girl

I'll Take You There

Middle Age: A Romance

The Barrens

Blonde

Broke Heart Blues

Starr Bright Will Be with You Soon

My Heart Laid Bare

Man Crazy

Double Delight

We Were the Mulvaneys

You Can't Catch Me

What I Lived For

Foxfire: Confessions of a Girl Gang

Snake Eyes

Nemesis

Because It Is Bitter, and Because
   It Is My Heart

Soul/Mate

American Appetites

Lives of the Twins

You Must Remember This

Marya: A Life

Solstice

Mysteries of Winterthurn

A Bloodsmoor Romance

Angel of Light

Bellefleur

Unholy Loves

Cybele

Son of the Morning

Childwold

The Assassins: A Book of Hours

Do with Me What You Will

Wonderland

them

Expensive People

A Garden of Earthly Delights

With Shuddering Fall

JOYCE CAROL OATES

Babysitter

4th ESTATE • London

4th Estate
An imprint of HarperCollinsPublishers
1 London Bridge Street
London SE1 9GF

www.4thestate.co.uk

HarperCollins*Publishers*
1st Floor, Watermarque Building, Ringsend Road
Dublin 4, Ireland

First published in Great Britain in 2022 by 4th Estate
First published in the United States by Alfred A. Knopf in 2022

2

A catalogue record for this book is
available from the British Library

ISBN 978-0-00-853681-7 (hardback)
ISBN 978-0-00-853682-4 (trade paperback)

Portions of this work originally appeared as 'Babysitter' in
Ellery Queen's Mystery Magazine (2006) and were subsequently
collected in *Horror: The Best of the Year 2006* (Prime Books, 2006).

Set in Minion Pro
Printed and bound in the UK using 100%
renewable electricity at CPI Group (UK) Ltd

MIX
Paper | Supporting
responsible forestry
FSC™ C007454

This book is produced from independently certified FSC™ paper
to ensure responsible forest management.

For more information visit: www.harpercollins.co.uk/green

For Dan Halpern

Things don't happen, it depends upon who comes along.

PAUL BOWLES

There is only one question: Of what am I capable?

Y.K.

I

She Asks Herself Why

Because he'd touched her. Just her wrist.

A brush of his fingers. A sidelong glance.

Because he'd asked *Which one are you?*—meaning *Which man's wife?*

Because it was a time and a place when to be a woman—(at least, a woman who looked like her)—was to be a *man's wife.*

Do Not Disturb

On the sixty-first floor of the hotel tower he awaits her.

No name for him that is likely to be a true name. Very little about him that is likely to be true. Enough for her to know—*he, him*.

She is the sole passenger in the elevator, which is a sleek glass cubicle rising rapidly and silently into the atrium as into the void.

Below, the crowded hotel lobby sinks away. Beside her, open floors and railings fly downward.

A sleek new way of *elevating*, so different from the larger, slower-moving, cumbersome elevators of her childhood.

In those elevators, often there were uniformed operators who wore gloves. In elevators like these, you are your own operator.

Lingering in the elevator a faint aroma, is it cigar smoke?

It is December 1977. Smoking in the public areas of private hotels has not yet been banned.

She feels a thrill of vertigo, nausea. Cigar smoke as faint as memory. She shuts her eyes to steady herself.

Her sleek Italian leather handbag, she carries not slung from her right wrist as usual but carried snug beneath her right arm, and steadied and supported by her left hand, for it is perceptibly heavier than usual.

Still, the handbag is so positioned that its gleaming brass label shines outward—*Prada*.

By instinct, unconscious, vanity's gesture even on this day—*Prada*.

Is this the final day of her life, or is this the final day of *a life*?

Of course she has memorized the number: 6183.

Could be a tattoo at her wrist. His claim on her.

Claim. Doom. She is not a poet, she is not a person adroit or comfortable with words, yet these words seem to her soothing like smooth cool stones laid over the shuttered eyes of the dead to bring them peace.

His room. In fact it's a suite, two spacious rooms overlooking the Detroit River where he stays when he visits Detroit.

Though it is possible that he has different rooms for different visitors. *She* would not know this, he has never confided in her.

At the sixty-first floor the cubicle stops with a hiss and a mild jolt. The glass door slides open, she has no choice but to step out. Something has been decided, she has no choice.

Gripping the handbag beneath her arm. *Has* she no choice?

Wondering is he awaiting her, near the elevator? Eager for her arrival?

She doesn't see anyone. In neither direction, any human figure.

You can still turn back.

If now, no one will know.

Facing the row of elevators, a glass wall overlooking the riverfront, the river, a fierce white sun. A foreshortened view of Woodward Avenue far below, soundless traffic.

Why isn't clear. *Why* she has come here, risking so much.

Never ask *why.* The challenge is the execution—*how.*

Making her way along a windowless corridor following the room numbers in their ascent: 6133, 6149, 6160 . . . So slowly do the numbers rise, she feels a thrill of relief, she will never arrive at 6183.

Underfoot a thick plush carpet, as rosy as the interior of a lung. The far end of the corridor has dissolved. Closed doors to the horizon diminishing in size as they approach infinity.

No reason for her to approach 6183 simply because the person awaiting her inside the room has summoned her, if she wishes she can turn back.

. . . as if you've never been here.

Never left home.

Who would know? No one.

Yet, she doesn't turn back. Feels herself drawn forward inexorably.

If you inhabit a riddle the only way to solve the riddle is to push forward to the end.

As the sleek glass cubicle ascended swiftly and unhesitatingly to the sixty-first floor, so she makes her way to the suite that is *his*.

A faint odor of cigar smoke in her hair, in her nostrils that pinch with nausea so remote as to be merely residual, memory.

What is she wearing? A costume she has chosen with care, white linen is always discreet, a silk shirt, red silk Dior scarf gaily at her throat.

Elegantly impractical high heels, Saint Laurent kidskin sinking into the carpet. If she must suddenly turn and run, run for her life, the tight-fitting shoes and the carpet will impede her.

One of those dreams in which she is a child again. She runs, runs. Her feet sink into something like sand, soft-seeming but not *soft*.

Never making any progress. Each time she has run.

Each time, *he* looms behind her. Daddy's strong hands threaten to seize her, lift her by her ribs . . .

A man's claim, a doom.

The room numbers accelerate. It is a fact of life to which we never quite adjust ourselves, how *out there* moves at its allotted speed, no matter our wishes *in here*.

Approaching 6183 she begins to shiver. It is always the same, she has been here before, that vibrating sensation of a vehicle that is being driven too fast, dangerously fast, in blinding rain, through deep puddles lifting like waves rushing over the windshields.

The nape of her neck rests against a very cold stainless steel table, there is a drain just beneath. Her eyes stare open, unseeing. Only when your eyes are unseeing do you see *all*.

Yet, she presses on. In the Saint Laurent heels it is still December 1977, she has not yet entered the room for the final time. She is determined that she will come to the end of the riddle.

The brass plaque on the doorframe is 6183, each time it has been 6183.

And the sign hanging from the doorknob, scripted silver letters on lacquered black—the identical warning sign:

PRIVACY PLEASE!
DO NOT DISTURB

I Am

I *am a beautiful woman, I have a right to be loved.*
I am a desirable woman, I have a right to desire.

When We Died

When we died, our (beautiful) (naked) bodies became inert matter.

When we died, our final, strangled screams were trapped in our throats.

(It would be said that, if you lay beside us in death and if you put your ear to our throats, and if you were worthy, you could hear a faint echo of this final scream.)

When we died, our torment ended. For mercy awaits us all.

When we died, none of you who had begat us were anywhere near.

When we died, we died alone, in terror. Because you were nowhere near.

When we died, ask yourself why did you have children if you don't love us.

Ask why.

But when we died, our bodies were prepared lovingly for death as none of you would have prepared us.

When we died, our bodies were carefully bathed, the smallest bits of dirt removed from every crevice of our bodies and from beneath our (broken) fingernails, and the fingernails cut with cuticle scissors, rounded and even; as our hair was washed with a gentle shampoo, combed and neatly parted in such a way to suggest that whoever had so tenderly groomed us postmortem had not known us "in life."

When our bodies were cleansed and as pure as our souls, we were lovingly "memorialized": photographed.

Where the human eye would betray us and soon forget us, the Eye of the Camera would render us immortal.

After days of captivity (the shortest, three days; the longest, eleven days), our bodies were transported from the place of captivity beside the northern lake in the pine woods to be displayed in public places in Oakland County, Michigan.

Three of us, in snow. Two of us, in the season after the snow had melted, laid on the ground on white terry-cloth towels.

Again, in our "resting places" we were photographed: a (tender) way of saying goodbye.

A casual glance, you'd think that we were large dolls or child mannequins laid on the ground, very still.

Our arms were crossed over our chests, our legs crossed at the ankles as an angel might cross his legs out of modesty.

Our eyes were shut at last in the peace that "passeth understanding."

(A gentle but forceful thumb on the eyelids—several times required before the eyelid remains shut.)

It would be said that unless you lay close beside us you could not see the blood-tinged ligature around our throats, so tight did it bind our throats.

Our clothing had been laundered and (here was a surprise) even ironed, neatly folded and placed beside our small still naked bodies as if the one who had perpetrated such acts had an intention to be magnanimous, to keep nothing in his possession that was not his.

Because you had been careless and undeserving of us, we were taken from you, and later, our bodies were "returned"—such acts so carefully performed, the one who perpetrated them would never be apprehended nor would you have any name for him that was not a foolish made-up name by a publicity-seeking newspaper reporter—Babysitter!

When we died, our (beautiful, naked) bodies would never advance in time—never age as yours will age. Always the eldest among us would be thirteen, the youngest ten.

And always we will belong to the one who loved us so much he could not bear such love like an avalanche or a flood that overwhelms and suffocates. And our gratitude will expand to infinity that through this love he has transformed us from children of no significance—about whom no one much cared, and whom no one much mourned—to become his.

Only This Once

H'lo, ma'am! Welcome to the Renaissance Grand."

Broad smile as *ma'am* enters the opulent seventy-floor hotel. Uniformed doorman, skin the hue of sandstone, exceptionally white teeth bared at the sight of the (white) woman beautifully dressed.

Recognizes Hannah, if not by name: rich man's wife from one of the (white) suburbs, or a guest at the hotel.

(The very doorman who will shoo away riffraff, any-color-skinned Detroit homeless-beggar riffraff not wanted in the Renaissance Grand or anywhere near.)

Graciously Hannah thanks the uniformed man without seeing him, rarely does Hannah meet the gaze of uniformed persons, hoping not to see in the corner of her eye the white-flashing smile fade as she moves past him, hoping not to feel the man's scorn for her, contempt. For surely Hannah is imagining this, must be mistaken.

Never look too closely into the motive of a smile.

And—*Never look back to see where a smile has gone.*

Hannah's father had been a joker with an aphorism for every life situation. Though you never knew if you were meant to laugh at his words or wince.

And take care, where you smile.

And so not even a furtive glance backward as Hannah makes her way through a corridor of bright-lit boutiques where her stylish high heels rap sharply on the marble floor, turns a corner, escalator, rising into an immense hotel lobby—a vast open atrium lifting out of sight, no ceiling within view, if indeed there is a ceiling for possibly the Renaissance Grand dissolves into the sky over Detroit ever shifting from hard bright blue to dreamlike and vaporous beset by storm clouds massing over the Great Lakes like brooding thoughts that come to no end . . . Harp music wafts through the airy expanse, an elusive Irish melody that quivers at the brink of recognition. Terraces of waxy-white Easter lilies sharply sweet-smelling, arterial-red tulips, blue hyacinth. At midday the lobby is moderately crowded. Guests displaying ID badges, a convention of computer programmers, another of hairstylists. Murmur of voices like those of an audience at intermission. Undertone of something pulsing, pumping like an artificial heart. The very air dazzles, blinds. A beautiful woman in beautiful clothes is so accustomed to being *seen,* her ability to *see* is impeded.

Except today Hannah doesn't want to be seen. Doesn't want to be identified. Dark designer sunglasses cover much of her flawless face.

Flawless is worth the price. Any price.

She vows.

Unfaithful to her husband, and to her children. Never will this happen a second time.

Of course: No one will know. Only her, and *him.*

Through the slow-revolving doors of the Renaissance Grand Hotel, which move of their own volition hastening the woman to her fate. A vast mechanism has been set in motion many millennia ago, she has no choice but to obey.

Approaching the concierge. Licking her lips to speak rehearsed words.

"Excuse me? There should be a message for 'M.N.' . . ."

The concierge looks blank, uncomprehending. Hannah must repeat her request in a more assertive voice.

". . . 'M.N.' A message . . ."

Hannah speaks with composure. Here is a woman certain that something very special is waiting for her, she has only to utter the proper words.

Thrilling to one so little practiced in subterfuge! Y.K.'s plan is to leave a note for Hannah with the concierge but not a note addressed to *her,* that's to say to *H.J.,* but rather to (fictitious) *M.N.*

In some quarters in Detroit, the name *Jarrett* is known: corporate wealth, philanthropy. Her husband's family, residents of Grosse Pointe. Not likely but still there's the very real possibility that the concierge would recognize the name, discretion is advised for an adulterous woman.

Since handing her car key to the Renaissance Grand parking attendant Hannah has been inhabiting a role not her own, initials not her own, and so a script not her own—but only this once. She tells herself.

Which one are you?—Hannah is eager to learn.

She'd expected a sealed envelope from the concierge but to her surprise, possibly her mortification, there is just a sheet of hastily folded hotel stationery.

M.N. scrawled in pencil on the outside of the note and inside, only the numeral 6183.

In that instant understanding that she is making a serious and (possibly) irrevocable mistake that will ripple, shudder, quake through the remainder of her life and (just possibly) the lives of her family though in a bright assured voice she thanks the concierge as if this perfunctorily executed note is exactly what she expects.

"Thank *you*, ma'am!"

Turning away, wounded. Another *ma'am*!

Ma'am is not how Hannah Jarrett considers herself. *Ma'am* is respectful usage but suggests a dowdy-matronly figure, a figure of stout middle age from which all romantic expectation/sexual desire has drained, not *her*.

Ma'am does not suggest the chic asymmetry of glossy scissor-cut hair, elegantly styled black cashmere coat, fine-stitched leather shoes.

Ma'am does not suggest hard, hot-beating furious blood.

Turning from the concierge's desk determined to betray no baffled expectations. Checking the note again to see if she has missed something. But no: No greeting for Hannah, no words of endearment or even instruction, simply the blunt fact of the room number, which is all the information she requires for the time being.

The man awaiting Hannah sixty floors above has no (evident) concern that the concierge might read the (private) message and know exactly what it means. But of course, there is no *private message*.

Hannah crumples the note in her gloved hand. No, she is *not hurt*.

Nothing so petty as personal feelings is relevant here.

"Ma'am? Elevators to the right."

(How does the concierge know that Hannah will want to use an elevator?—Hannah feels her face flush, indignant.)

But she has recovered, she is fine. The way children recover from sudden attacks of tears, spasms of raw emotion that overcome them but soon pass.

Not a sin, and not (even) a mistake. An adventure.

Who am I?—M.N. And just this once.

Her high-heeled shoes rap smartly on the marble floor as she makes her way across the lobby to a row of sleek glass elevators like space capsules.

Irish harp music, thrumming about her head. But where is the harpist?

She's aware of a figure moving fluidly, dreamily beside her, wraith-like, weightless—a reflection in a row of narrow vertical mirrors embedded in a mosaic wall—keeping perfect pace with Hannah.

Until it vanishes.

The Calendar

Suburban life in Far Hills, Michigan!—tyranny of the calendar. Weekday mornings, afternoons. Appointments.

Dentist, orthodontist. Pediatrician, gynecologist, dermatologist, therapist. Yoga, hair salon, fitness center, beauty clinic. Community relations forum, parent-teacher evening, public library referendum. Luncheons with friends: Far Hills Country Club, Bloomfield Hills Golf Club, Red Fox Inn, Far Hills Marriott. Meetings: Far Hills Historical Society, Far Hills Public Library Association, Friends of the Detroit Institute of Arts.

Indeed, this spring Hannah has been invited to be a cochair of the annual fundraiser for the prestigious Detroit Institute of Arts, the first time Hannah has been so honored, deeply gratified even as Hannah isn't so naïve that she doesn't guess the honor is linked to a sizable donation from the investment firm where Wes Jarrett is a partner.

They will acknowledge me now. They will see that I am one of them.

Suburban life: a (thrumming, warmth-generating) hive.

Family life: small smug hive within a hive.

In this, Hannah knows herself secure. She has defined herself—*wife, mother*. She is safe, nourished. She has ceased thinking about how, why she is the person she is. Her *hive identity* is secure.

Outside the hive, Hannah has little interest. Indifferent to "news" that doesn't touch upon the *hive identity*.

Rapidly she glances through the Detroit paper indifferent to most national news, all foreign news. Inner-city crime news: no. Hardly news. Increase of burglaries in the affluent suburbs north of Detroit, environmental issues regarding a "toxic" landfill not far from Far

Hills, those obscure crimes labeled as *domestic*—these snag Hannah's interest, but fleetingly. (*Domestic violence!* Women who marry abusive men, women who have not the courage to leave these men, foolish women, weak women—hard to be sympathetic with them.) The most frightening news, to Hannah the most distressing, is of a *serial child abductor, child killer, killer pedophile* in Oakland County since February 1976—Hannah looks quickly away from headlines.

She is secure, protected. *Her children.*

None of the abductions has been in Far Hills. None of the abducted children has been known to Hannah or her friends.

No room in Hannah's life for the unexpected.

Each day is a rectangle on a calendar. An empty space to be filled. Each space a barred window: Shove up the window as high as you can and press your face against the bars, breathing in fresh chill air faint with yearning, grip the bars tight, these are bars that confine but also protect, what pleasure in shaking them as hard as you can knowing that they are unbreakable.

This calendar day April 8, 1977, has remained empty. In a crammed week Friday remains blank.

Is that suspicious?—Hannah wonders.

Can't bring herself to mark April 8 on her calendar. Even in code.

Not because Hannah is afraid of Wes seeing a mysterious notation on her calendar and becoming suspicious: Nothing is less likely than Wes perusing Hannah's calendar unless it would be Wes searching through Hannah's drawers, closets. He is an orderly, fastidious person respectful of his wife's privacy as he would expect her to be respectful of his; if Wes has been unfaithful to Hannah, a possibility she has allowed herself to imagine as if to inoculate herself against it, he would not be so careless as to allow her to know: That would have been the cruel act, more than the infidelity itself. (So Hannah thinks.)

It's the risk to Hannah's pride, self-esteem, that she fears.

If he fails to meet her. If—nothing happens.

She most feels humiliation. Rejection.

So, better keep the date blank.

Even after his call, the perimeters of the meeting are vague. Will they meet for drinks at his hotel? Or . . . elsewhere?

As if (deliberately) putting an obstacle in Hannah's path. Asking her to check with the concierge when she arrives at the hotel.

Why, Hannah will wonder.

His motives, Hannah will always wonder.

She tells Ismelda that she will be gone "much of the day."

A suggestion that she isn't going far, she will remain in the vicinity, lunch with women friends at the Far Hills Country Club, might visit a friend in the Beaumont Hospital, possibly a quick trip to the Gateway Mall, should be home by five-thirty, which means that, today, Ismelda will pick up Conor and Katya at school.

Usually, Hannah picks up the children. This is important to Hannah: She drives the children to school in the morning and picks them up in the afternoon, most days.

Hannah carefully explains this variation in the schedule so that the Filipina housekeeper who sometimes has difficulty understanding English cannot possibly misunderstand.

Today, this afternoon: the children, at school. Yes?

Gravely Ismelda nods. *Yes, missus.*

Nothing to Ismelda about *downtown*. Not a word to Ismelda about driving *downtown*.

It's a journey: downtown Detroit. A pilgrimage.

Sixteen miles south and east on the thunderous expressway, not a journey undertaken casually by a Far Hills wife and mother.

Smiling to herself, self-astonished.

Why she is doing this, Hannah doesn't inquire. *How* is the challenge.

GOOD FRIDAY 1977, DETROIT MICHIGAN.

Chill of late winter, sunshine flashing like scimitars on the river, she is driving to meet him where he has summoned her. Wind sweeps in roiling gusts from the Canadian shore.

Driving in *her* car, a gift from her husband: gleaming white Buick Riviera.

At the horizon miles away her destination shimmers before her like a mirage.

Renaissance Grand Hotel, One Woodward Avenue, Detroit.

Seventy floors, the highest building in Michigan.

Sixteen miles from her home in Far Hills, Michigan.

Sixteen miles from her children, her life. What has been her life.

He'd looked at her, he'd touched her wrist. Between them passed something like an electric current, a sexual jolt.

Don't expect me to flatter you. All that in your life has been fraud, hypocrisy—the lies you've told yourself—ends now.

He hadn't uttered these words aloud. Yet, she'd heard.

He'd only touched her wrist, maybe he'd circled her wrist with his strong careless fingers. Yet she'd felt the jolt, and something like a rude caress, in the pit of her belly.

Don't look surprised. That's bullshit.

Rare for Hannah Jarrett to be driving on I-75: John C. Lodge Expressway. South into the great maw of Detroit.

At this time of day, nearing noon, what would be her purpose? Hannah tries to think of plausible explanations, her thoughts are swept aside like butterflies in the wind, wings broken.

Since she'd left the fieldstone colonial on Cradle Rock Road, Far Hills, half an hour ago, the mist-shrouded sky has cleared rapidly. Windswept cobalt-blue sky as depthless and unyielding as painted tin, so glaring bright it would hurt her naked eyes without the protection of dark (designer) glasses.

A journey into the city, Wes would be at the wheel. For safety's sake, Wes would be driving the Pontiac Grand Safari station wagon that is *his* vehicle.

In Far Hills, Hannah is a confident driver but her confidence has rapidly ebbed on the interstate. Motorcyclists in heraldic black leather, rough young faces obscured by tinted glasses, pass her slow-moving vehicle insolently on the right, cutting in front of her with deafening roars and expulsions of poisonous exhaust.

Wind! Fierce gusts from Ontario writhing and coiling like great invisible serpents.

As a child she'd seen wind serpents rush across open fields in the direction of her father's moving vehicle with the intention of sweeping it off the road. For her father had been angry often, driving: Hannah's mother in the passenger seat very still.

The wind serpents were to punish. Hannah shut her eyes tight, still *seeing* couldn't be avoided.

She'd tormented herself with such visions, knowing they weren't real. Yet possessing the power to frighten her.

Now in adulthood the struggle is not to see what isn't there.

Still, there is the very real threat of punishment.

Gale-force winds believed responsible for recent three-vehicle crash, John C. Lodge Expressway.

Trucks loom up behind the Buick Riviera dangerously close. Leaving her territory in the suburbs has brought Hannah to a hostile place where she is recognized, and resented: woman driver, white woman driver, expensive car, an affront to male drivers. No sooner does one rattling truck pass Hannah than another looms up behind her in the rearview mirror.

When it seems that a truck can come no closer to the rear of Hannah's Buick, it swings out to pass. Not fast but with excruciating slowness as a strangler might throttle his victim, taking his time.

A glaring face, blurred face in the high cab behind her, a jeering mouth.

Rich man's wife. Rich bitch.

These strangers don't wish to harm her, Hannah tells herself. There is nothing personal here, they don't know *her*.

Fate of the adulteress. Her punishment, even before she has committed the sin.

Sin! Don't flatter yourself.

He would laugh at her if he knew what thoughts she is thinking.

Almost, Hannah hopes Y.K. will laugh—he will dismiss her fears. Those times in a woman's life, as raw as an open wound, when the hope is to take comfort in careless male laughter.

Why do you think that anything we do together matters? It does not matter.

It will not be disaster, except (possibly) to you.

He's her friend. He's an ally. That was evident from the start.

The way they'd met—purely by chance. Recognizing each other at once.

Amid the festive cacophony of a social occasion feeling his fingers brush against her wrist. As if underwater, a predator fish gliding near.

H'lo! Do I know you?

Which one are you?

He was rude, but he was very funny. Not sure why Hannah is laughing but the memory is delicious.

Nothing delicious but it's secret, surreptitious.

If she has an accident at this inopportune time, in this place, traveling inexplicably south on I-75 into the city of Detroit, if Hannah dies mangled in the shiny white Buick, among those who'd known her or would claim to have known her it would be protested *But—what was Hannah Jarrett doing driving into Detroit! Why alone? There's nothing on her calendar to explain* . . .

Ismelda would have been stunned, baffled. For Mrs. Jarrett had taken pains to suggest to her that she *was not* going to be far away from home.

And Wes: astonished. Sensing himself betrayed, humiliated. So sure he knows his wife, as (he thinks) he knows his children, as familiar to him as the contents of his pockets, and of no greater mystery.

. . . that she'd had a (secret) life, an (illicit) life.

. . . a life beyond his reckoning.

It would be her first time—adultery.

Eleven years of marriage. A small lifetime. But whatever occurs today, or fails to occur, will be *out of time*. It will not factor in the *marriage time*.

As it happens it's the Friday before Easter: Good Friday.

Just chance. Accident. That *he* is in Detroit this week.

Guilt stirs in Hannah's soul like a rough-textured garment chafing the most sensitive skin.

She has been entering the city of Detroit, descending into a new terrain. Residential neighborhoods of small wood-frame houses in small lots, row houses, weatherworn tenements and commercial buildings, graffiti-scrawled walls. At the shoulder of the roadway broken glass, rusted hubcaps and fenders, shredded tires.

It has been a gradual descent southward from Far Hills to the sprawling city of Detroit: Her destination is the luxury hotel at the foot of Woodward Avenue, at the Detroit River, the boundary between the United States and Ontario, Canada.

Astonishing to Hannah: She will be meeting a man there, a stranger, who has told her to call him Y.K., at the Renaissance Grand Hotel.

His instructions, Hannah will follow.

All the while comforting herself—*Of course, I won't go through with it. How could I.*

That Leslie Caron voice of breathless sincerity, regret.

I'm sorry, I can't stay long. I will have to leave by . . .

Like an actress she will control the scene. Determining beforehand how the scene will play out.

. . . must be home by five-thirty.

How he will look at her when she tells him this! The desire in the man's face, that is enormously exciting to her.

He will be hurt, she thinks. For a moment, basking in that certainty.

But he may be unhappy in a way not flattering to her. There is *that* possibility.

Laugh in her face, shut the room door in her face.

No, he will be hurt. Hannah thinks so.

The woman, a married woman: coming to *him.*

Meaning that Hannah has the freedom to leave him, if she wishes.

You know, I think I can't stay. I think—this has been a misunderstanding.

Must try to explain to him that yes, she is attracted to him but her life is too complicated right now to commit herself to any kind of . . .

Wind, rocking the car! Hairs stir at the nape of Hannah's neck.

In the house in Far Hills wind sometimes whistles in the chimneys, rattles windows with a sound like something trying to gain entrance. Doors are blown open by the wind, or blown shut. Oh Mommy! Mommy! Katya cries. The ghost!

Don't be silly, silly! There is no *ghost.*

Yet Hannah hears the ghost, too. Hears something.

You don't want to think that, in one of these older houses, someone may have died. Marriages may have died.

Families, broken.

But Hannah hears the children clamoring for her. Her love for them comes in a rush, they so adore *her.*

Already her lover has laughed at Hannah, there's a certain stiffness in her, a kind of prudery.

Beneath the designer clothes, the anxious female.

I'm sorry. I guess I can't stay. Not today. Today isn't—isn't a good day.

Better to be brief, mysterious: *I'm sorry. Circumstances have changed, I can't stay.*

Y.K. has other women, Hannah supposes. More experienced, less awkward than Hannah.

Very likely some of these are women Hannah knows. Someone had invited him to the fundraiser evening. He wouldn't tell her, of course.

If you don't mind a married woman . . .

He'd laughed at her, he'd liked her frankness. She'd wanted to think that she had surprised him.

Not guessing how unlike Hannah such a remark was. She'd had a drink, or two. She'd meant to be bold, sexually provocative, in emulation of the chic black crepe de chine Dior she'd bought for the evening; yet she'd sounded, in her own ears, rawly wistful.

Leaving unspoken the deeper fear—*If you don't mind a wife and mother . . .*

A man who laughs at women. A man who laughs at women is likely to be a man who doesn't appreciate jokes from women. A man who sees through such jokes. Manly scorn, like one snatching away a frilly foolish article of clothing exposing the (naked) (female) body tremulous before him.

The children! If there is sin, if there is the possibility of a very bad mistake, it is because of the children.

She'd driven the children to school that morning. *That,* she is determined to do.

It would be said of Hannah—*She was an excellent mother, the children adored their mother.*

But they are quick to sense when Hannah's attention isn't focused exclusively on them. That morning in the car fretful, restless as Hannah only half listened to their chatter. Mommy! Mom-*my!*

Reproach in a child's voice, the heart is lacerated.

Needy, hungry for Mommy's love. Insatiable, exhausting. You wonder if any mother, any breast would do, to satisfy a child's hunger.

And a man's hunger: less personal and particular than in a woman. The curse of the female, to so badly need *love*.

The curse of the female, to *care*.

Mommy kiss-kiss! Mommy where are you going?

For they can sense: Mommy is going on a long journey, there is the risk that Mommy will never see them again.

No longer Mommy in the corduroy car coat but in a coat of soft black cashmere falling in loose folds about her legs. No longer the lace-up canvas shoes as comfortable as bedroom slippers but elegant impractical stilettos by Saint Laurent.

I would so value you as a friend. Someone in whom . . .

Must not seem to be pleading with him. If you plead with a man you have already lost.

How Hannah would cherish this man who is a few years older than Wes, and so much more *interesting* than Wes, as a friend!—*Whom I trust and can confide in.*

For she has no one. No one in her present life. Her friends in Far Hills are not intimate friends, no one whom Hannah could trust not to talk about her unsympathetically.

And Wes is not her friend. A husband cannot be a wife's friend.

Nor has Wes been faithful to her. Hannah is (almost) sure.

Look, you know you're coming. To me.

Bullshit your husband has anything to do with it.

Now the descent is more evident: tilting toward the river.

Exits rush past as in a dream. Street names cited often in local crime news—*John R., Cass, Vernor, Fort, Freud, Brush, Gratiot.*

Why hadn't she left home earlier! She will be late arriving at the hotel.

Her (female) pride in not having left earlier. Unable to decide what to wear. Changing her clothes (again). Pale rose silk shirt, impulsively she thinks—*Yes! This.*

And then precious minutes lost as she'd stood staring at a clock in the bedroom, mesmerized.

Must not let him guess how eager you are. How hungry, yearning.

No man wants a woman who wants him. Not in that way.

No man wants a woman who wants. That's the bottom line.

This bitter wisdom, Hannah's mother has imparted to her. Not in so many words, perhaps.

And now Hannah, poised on a precipice: thirty-nine years old.

Not *old*. Among their circle of Far Hills friends.

Still, it leaves Hannah just a bit breathless. And in a few months she will be even older: forty.

And how strange and unexpected, Hannah isn't much different from the person she'd been at twenty-six, nineteen, thirteen. The child self. The waif. Who this person is, she must keep secret from others.

This is new to her, this obsession with a stranger. Her conviction that, somehow, in a way that will become clear to her, Y.K. is not really a *stranger*.

If a woman is not desired, a woman does not exist. Help me to exist.

CITY CENTER
LAST EXIT BEFORE TUNNEL TO CANADA

For a panicked moment Hannah misreads this crucial sign, the very sign for which she has been waiting, then realizes that this is her exit.

A relief, to leave the thunderous expressway. She has been spared a spectacular collision, instant death.

And now, stuck in slow-moving traffic. Delivery vans, one-way streets. A maze of one-way streets.

The fabled *inner city*. Dreaded by (suburban) (white) citizens forced to drive through these blocks to the Renaissance Plaza at the river.

And all for *him*. Risking so much for *him*.

An impatient driver behind Hannah sounds his horn. At Lared and Fort the traffic light has turned from red to green, Hannah hasn't responded quickly enough.

Turning onto Lared, headed south into a dismal derelict block. Thinking this must be a wrong turn but then seeing, a quarter of a mile away, the towering Renaissance Grand.

Dazzling rows of windows rising seventy floors. Soft explosion of sunlight as filmy clouds part.

How thrilled Hannah is, to be *here*.

Out of her mounting anxiety, a sudden rush of joy.

Out of the ruins of the old Detroit, the new.

Very little remains of historic Detroit, demolished since the "riot" of July 1967. Wes's family had lived in Detroit for generations, in the exclusive residential neighborhood called Palmer Woods, now no longer, all have abandoned the city. Hannah has seen photographs of Detroit taken before 1967, rapidly receding into a sepia-tinged past.

Renaissance Plaza is the "new" Detroit: luxury hotels, spectacular new office buildings, high-rise apartments and condos, upscale restaurants and boutiques, a prestigious medical suite (specialty: cosmetic surgery), a theater/symphony hall seating two thousand people. Straight ahead, across the river, the merely utilitarian skyline of Windsor, Ontario.

Inner-city renewal, gentrification. Civic-minded corporate development.

Hope for Detroit's future!

Hope for the doomed city.

Hannah knows that Wes is among the investors in the Renaissance Plaza project but she has no clear idea how much money he has invested, nor even whose money it is, exactly—his exclusively, or his and Hannah's.

The project is (it's said) millions of dollars in debt and yet there has been some profit for investors. The vagueness of "some" profit is surely purposeful.

Hannah has only a vague idea of what bankruptcy is. In personal terms, yes; in corporate terms, no.

Her father had declared bankruptcy, in fact more than once. As a child she'd known nothing.

Wes has seemed bemused, explaining bankruptcy law to Hannah. For everything is a matter of "tax law": When it comes down to it, everything is a matter of "tax lawyers."

However, laws governing real estate differ from tax laws governing other sorts of businesses. It's possible—probable?—that investors in the Renaissance Plaza project pay no property taxes for it though the buildings have been built on the most expensive property in the state of Michigan.

Hannah had expressed bewilderment to Wes: Shouldn't they be worried about losing their investment? Isn't it a risk? And Wes had touched her wrist to comfort her, as one might comfort a fretful child. Saying, with a shrug, If you know what you're doing, there is no risk.

. . .

Hannah has reached her destination: the beautiful gated city within a city elevated ten feet above the street.

High smooth concrete walls, few entrances and none easily navigated by pedestrians; indeed, pedestrians are discouraged in this part of the city. Traffic entering the plaza is funneled into looping driveways where town cars and limousines, airport shuttle buses, private vehicles move slowly forward to be checked and greeted by security guards and uniformed parking attendants.

At once, Hannah feels at home. A relief to leave street-level Detroit and ascend to the gated city where she is recognized: *rich (white) man's wife.*

Uniformed staff are a comfort within the gated city. For what is provided is security: protection. Parking attendants, doormen, bellboys, a chorus of warm greetings for Hannah in the gleaming white Buick—*Welcome to the Renaissance Grand, ma'am!*

The Buick is taken from Hannah, gratefully she hands over the key to the ignition. Parking her car is a chore Hannah dislikes as she would dislike servicing or cleaning the car, vacuuming her house, scrubbing sinks and toilets, such tasks fall to persons who have been trained to execute them skillfully.

And how are you today, ma'am?

Is this your first time visiting us, ma'am?

Hannah is very well, thank you! And no, this is not her *first time* at the Renaissance Plaza.

Smiling at such greetings determined not to see that the uniformed staff despises her, of course (telling herself) they don't despise *her,* they have mistaken her for another (rich) (white) woman who may resemble her. In fact, the hotel workers must be grateful for Hannah Jarrett as for any visitor to the gated city in the very heart of the doomed city forestalling the inevitable day when the staff is given notice that the luxury hotel has declared bankruptcy.

Until that time, Hannah smiles upon the uniformed staff persons equally, when it's appropriate she tips them equally.

Always a cache of five-dollar bills in her wallet, to hand out like blessings.

Though *ma'am* is annoying to her, frankly.

Trying to smile through *ma'am,* with gritted teeth.

Impossible not to think of *ma'am* as a rebuke.

Rich (white) man's wife: ma'am.

Taking the parking stub from the uniformed attendant as if this has not happened already. How many times. That flash of teeth, staring eyes through the eyeholes of the smiling-mask face, of course they call her *ma'am,* in that other lifetime they'd slashed the throat of *ma'am* nearly decapitating the blond head.

You endured this once. All that lies ahead, you can't prevent.

Many times, again. For the first time.

First Touch

First touch felt like an accident. She would wish to think.

A stranger's fingers brushing against her wrist, claiming her attention. Sudden, surreptitious, a distinct sexual thrill.

As if underwater, unseen. Only just *felt*.

A predator seeking prey, perhaps. A shark propelling itself skillfully through shallow waters.

For this was a festive occasion, a gathering of several hundred guests in an opulent setting (Riverview Ballroom, Renaissance Grand Hotel, Detroit), an annual fundraiser (March Madness Gala) to benefit the chronically underfinanced Detroit Institute of Arts and so a kind of aqueous environment in which life-forms swim eagerly seeking other life-forms.

Without thinking she turned to whoever it was who'd touched her wrist, bright blind smile uplifted toward his face (he was tall, he loomed above her), the smile of a woman assured that in this environment she could make no fatal blunder for this was after all *her* environment—to enter the ballroom for the March Madness Gala you had to have a ticket, and each ticket cost six hundred dollars, and Hannah was herself one of several cochairs for the evening; and so Hannah turned expecting to see a familiar face, but no, this was a not-familiar face, a stranger's face, heavy-lidded eyes, prominent ridge of bone above the eyes, not a handsome face, not a face to give comfort, a singular face as if carved out of stone, yet—was the man smiling?—at *her*? Not in proper attire for the evening—not black tie but a necktie of some silvery-silky material, a lightweight woolen suit of dark pin-stripes, white linen shirt with onyx cuff links. His hair was thick and pelt-like, black, threaded with gray, brushed back stiffly from his fore-head and beginning to recede at the temples. Close-up his eyes were shinily black like marbles, the whites very finely veined; the heavy lids reminded her of the eyelids of hawks, or eagles—predator birds . . .

By this time the fingers had dared to encircle her wrist, seize and secure her wrist, as if indeed to give comfort, to assure, and firmly, out of sight of anyone who might be observing them; and whatever it was this person was saying to Hannah as he leaned confidingly close to her, bemused, ironic, inviting her to laugh with him, still smiling the blind bright smile Hannah strained to hear but could not hear, not clearly, though she heard herself laugh, with a kind of visceral shock, as if something protoplasmic, bacterial had been released into her bloodstream.

Which one are you?—she would recall him asking, though unsure if perhaps he'd asked *Which one of you?* or even *Which of you?,* possibilities that had seemed funny to Hannah, hilariously funny though (perhaps) none of it was funny but instead aggressive and insolent and in the exigency of the moment warmed by a single glass of white wine too quickly drunk, as by the excitement of the occasion for which she'd helped prepare for so many weeks, and would be publicly thanked for this effort from the dais and invited to stand with other volunteers to be applauded, Hannah Jarrett had been taken by surprise hearing her own startled laughter like the sound of a prairie bird's wild-fluttering wings as in panic it rises out of the protective cover of prairie grass into the air desperate to escape the hunters and the hunters' dogs bent on killing it.

But no. He was her friend. He would be her friend. *Her* friend.

Not laughing at her but in sympathy with her. As if indeed he knew her. In his manner a coercive tenderness such as an elder might feel for a child. As if they were old friends meeting by extraordinary chance amid a noisy throng of strangers.

Friends whose intimate connection is immediately resumed after years apart, that must be kept secret from others.

It might have been a scene in a film in which an *intimate/erotic/ fateful connection* is immediately established in the way the woman taken by surprise and the man who'd taken the woman by surprise regard each other: disequilibrium, wonder, and unease in the woman; sexual swagger, certainty in the man.

As in a film there was music in the background, jagged, occluded music: a jazz quintet playing an unidentifiable melody, musical notes like bright-flashing bits of glass whose primary effect was to make conversation, in the high-ceilinged ballroom with its hard polished uncarpeted floor, virtually impossible.

Difficult for Hannah to know what was being said to/asked of her.

Hears herself speaking lightly, brilliantly. Playful, capricious, witty, elusive—though providing, as she will recall later, her name, her identity, with a naïve sort of wifely pride or vanity, her husband's name, to the avidly listening stranger; nor could Hannah resist identifying herself as "one of the cochairs" of the evening.

His name was just initials: Y.K.

Enough for Hannah to know, for now.

She'd protested, faintly. Laughing—"But *why*? Does no one here know your name?"

Though seeing how he did not like to be interrogated. One of those men who gave up information about himself as if grudgingly, piecemeal.

Y.K. volunteered: He'd come to the fundraiser because someone had given him a ticket.

But also—he cared for the museum. For all museums. For *art*.

Also, he was staying in the hotel. His favorite hotel in Detroit, his usual suite on an upper floor.

He visited Detroit frequently on business. He stayed at the Renaissance Grand where there was a heliport. From Detroit he could be flown via helicopter to East Lansing.

Or the governor of the state might fly to Detroit, they saw each other for dinner sometimes, they had old connections. They'd been cadets together out in Colorado.

What did that mean, Hannah wondered—cadets, Colorado?

Later Hannah would realize that Y.K. must have meant the Air Force Academy, Colorado Springs.

She would calculate, if Y.K. was in his early forties (as he appeared to be), likely he'd been a pilot in Vietnam.

That bemused gaze, a look of distance. The pilot's gaze as he calculates when to release his bombs.

In a swooning sensation Hannah envisioned the man's body inside his evening clothes, ridged and riddled with scars. And a woman's hands, reading the scars like braille. Outspread fingers clutching at his sides, his muscled back.

The vision overcame her. And this, too, cinematic, in a flash.

Yet, strangely, not a vision so much as a memory.

All this while as they spoke—tried to speak, over the din—his fingers were gripping her wrist, at the level of her thigh. And pressing against her thigh. As if their speaking voices were disengaged from this strange intimacy established between them, an intimacy that preluded and occluded speech.

This is all that matters, this is real.

Don't expect me to flatter you.

All that in your life has been fraud, hypocrisy—the lies you've told yourself—ends now.

There is only one question: Of what am I capable?

Not one of these words was uttered aloud. Yet, Hannah understood perfectly. A flush rose into her face of excitement, unease.

She was standing very still, upright. How pleasurable, the rush of blood to her heart!

It would appear that they were speaking together, casually. Indistinguishable from the others. So many others, in the subaqueous setting. The din was deafening yet mouths moved without sound. Faces were contorted, grimacing as if drowning.

Hannah glanced about, would someone recognize her? Rescue her? She had many friends here, she had forgotten their names. A husband?

Glancing about, cannot see a familiar face. Where is the husband?

In secret Y.K. continued to grip Hannah's wrist. His knuckles pressing into her thigh.

From what he was saying, or implying, it appeared that Y.K. had money. Or was one of those who swam in the swift currents that money provides. If there is a distinction between a businessman and an operator in business, perhaps Y.K. was the latter, elusive and indefinable. Hannah would ask Wes if he knew him.

No, Hannah *would not* ask Wes if he knew Y.K. No way for Hannah to raise the subject without blushing, arousing suspicion.

Y.K. was saying that next time he was in Detroit possibly they could meet.

Have a drink, here in this hotel, would you like that?—Hannah laughed nervously, alarmed by the question, so blunt, yet (certainly) a casual and even harmless question. Not knowing how to reply yet unable to say *No*.

Was this a sexual proposition?—Hannah was stunned.

Or was it *not*? As Y.K. seemed to be laughing at Hannah's distress asking if there was a number with which he might contact her Hannah's mind went blank for a long moment as if her heart had ceased beating and in that moment her brain had ceased its functioning but then in the next instant she was fully in control again, of course she could remember her own telephone number, which was the household number, the family phone, adding, with naïve emphasis—"It's unlisted."

Unlisted—this struck Y.K. as funny.

Leaning close to her, laughing in her ear: "Hannah! There are no 'unlisted' numbers."

Ridiculing her, yet speaking her name.

Hannah!—the sound of his voice unnerving to her, so close in her ear.

Aggressively familiar, intimate. Pronounced with an equal emphasis on both syllables to make of it a dactyl—*Han-nah*. As a foreign-born speaker might enunciate the name, and not a native speaker of English.

Laughing together, excited. Both of them, Hannah wished to think, laughing—in delight . . .

I'll do that, then. Call you.

I . . . I'm not sure . . .

Yes.

It was settled. Nothing more to say.

At last: The cocktail hour was ending. Hannah was dazed with exhaustion, the exchange with Y.K. had been so intense, she wanted now to escape the man, and think about him.

(And where was Wes? Nowhere in sight.)

(Hannah felt a stab of sheer hatred of him, the husband who cared so little for her.)

The quintet of Black musicians had been playing jazz classics to which few in the (mostly white) crowd had been listening but playing with much animation and energy ending now with "Take the 'A' Train" so fiercely executed it might have been machine-gun fire aimed at the hearts of the oblivious crowd.

Hannah stared after Y.K. now moving away from her without a backward glance. Had he written down her phone number?—she didn't think so.

In an instant, he seemed to have forgotten her.

In an instant, Hannah's spirits were dashed.

As into the sea of men in formal attire, middle-aged and older, women with carefully coiffed hair, in gaily colored cocktail dresses and spike-heeled shoes, uniformed waiters winding their way through the throng with trays lifted above their heads like those heraldic figures on Egyptian tombs—Y.K. had vanished.

Like chattering geese five hundred guests were moving in the direction of the assigned tables bedecked with fresh-cut flowers and reproductions of classic artworks, not all of which the museum owned. Hannah stared resolutely before her, avoiding people whom she knew, or whom she supposed she might know, keeping near to a wall of the ballroom where she could move unimpeded like one who has been wounded, momentarily stunned.

He will never call of course.

I am in no danger—of course . . .

The Jarretts had purchased an entire table for themselves and eight guests, at a price of five thousand dollars; the artwork reproduced on the table was a panel of Monet's *Water Lilies*.

A favorite of Hannah's, she would have said, if asked. One of those pale blue dreamy impressionist paintings so popular with museum visitors.

Art that gives comfort. Art with no sharp lines, edges; art without shadows; art that doesn't mirror life but the undulations of life, shimmering color sensations like the most exquisite silk wallpaper.

Comfort, too, in the opulent ballroom setting: ivory-white walls, filigree of gilt ornamentation, chandeliers of gleaming brass and crystal. From overhead vents a continuous circulation of chill air stirred the hairs on the nape of Hannah's neck that felt too naked for so public a place.

Glancing upward, uneasily. As if there was only the ornamental ceiling to shield a view of the vast space beyond.

Wes was already seated at their table near the dais. Not *Table 1* but *Table 2*, which was a VIP table befitting Hannah Jarrett's status.

On the chair beside Wes was his briefcase, surreptitiously opened. Withdrawn from the festivities, Wes was glancing through a folder, making notations with a pen. How like him! At such a time! Hannah felt a pang of annoyance, hurt, her husband was clearly indifferent to the evening that meant so much to her.

Nor had he been missing Hannah for the past forty minutes or so. Oblivious of Hannah in the company of the man who called himself Y.K.

Whatever happens, then. It will be deserved.

Often it happened, Hannah and Wes drifted apart in large social gatherings. Almost, each forgot the other's existence until the mild shock of (re)discovering each other near the end of the evening: *wife, husband.*

Would they be attracted to each other now?—Hannah wondered. Twelve, or was it thirteen years after they'd first met . . .

Wes had been so young, so hopeful. That boyish enthusiasm, idealism; just slightly rebellious, determined to make his way without relying upon his father and the Jarretts. And Hannah had felt encouraged by his idealism, that she might, in her own way, free herself of the grip of Joker Daddy.

Things hadn't worked out in quite that way. No one's fault, but—no.

Aware of Hannah's approach, Wes quickly slipped the folder into the briefcase, shut the briefcase, set it on the floor beneath his chair. There was an exaggerated alacrity in the movement that irked Hannah: a suggestion that, discovering Wes working in this public place, Hannah would be displeased with him, like a chiding mother.

With mock gallantry Wes rose to pull out Hannah's chair beside his, a gesture expected of *the husband.*

Hannah ignored his play at irony and laughed, gaily: "Time for dinner, darling."

"Is it!"

"You look as if you've been bored."

"Bored! Never."

But why should she chide him for bringing work to the fundraiser?

For sequestering himself in a corner, as if hiding from the crowd? Wes was an adult, he could behave as he wished.

Hannah saw that her place card was beside Wes's. That was unfortunate: For Wes's sake she would have preferred someone else in that chair, with whom he might enjoy speaking more than with Hannah who he saw constantly.

At such formal dinners Hannah felt the strain of trying to hold her husband's attention. Wes liked to discuss politics, in the right company he was aggressively genial, argumentative; politics was essentially a joke to him, as to his father; a folly, in the service of business, otherwise of not much usefulness and not to be trusted.

"*You* look as if you've been having a good time," Wes said, "meeting your friends, being congratulated."

"I wouldn't go that far, Wes. 'Being congratulated' . . ."

"Oh, come on! You've earned it—that glow in the eyes."

Hannah smiled, uncertainly. Was Wes teasing her, or was he being sincere? With each year of marriage she was less able to distinguish.

Wanting to think that possibly she'd misread him, he didn't resent attending the fundraiser as her husband, after all.

To make the evening worthwhile for him, Wes had insisted that Hannah extend an invitation to a couple whom Hannah scarcely knew: a prominent General Motors executive and his wife, residents of Bloomfield Hills.

Harold Rusch was older than Wes by at least twenty-five years. There was an obscure business connection between the men, Hannah supposed; possibly a connection between Rusch and Wes's father.

Business interests are a kind of gigantic spiderweb, Hannah had grown to realize. Except the spiderweb isn't dominated by a single spider but by myriad spiders of differing sizes and statures, each connected closely with the others, though rivals, even enemies; each acutely aware of the others, hoping to exploit them or at least avoid being destroyed and devoured by them. So Wes, a small spider in this web, would hope to establish a connection to Harold Rusch, a much larger spider.

Hannah smiled at the thought, which felt mutinous to her, a betrayal of her husband. Exactly the thought she might share with *him*.

If not her lover, *he* would be her soul mate. The person to whom she spoke those thoughts aloud, she dared not share with anyone in her actual life.

How long it would be, the remainder of the evening! *He* was not observing her now, he'd passed out of her field of vision entirely.

Wide slow lava river that could not be hurried. For this was the *fundraiser:* to be endured.

Each table so lavishly decorated, guests had to peer across the table at one another, barely visible past the ambitious centerpieces.

Conversations had to be shouted, no one could hear amid the buzz of voices. Hannah tried to engage with Christina Rusch, who was but minimally civil to her as if having forgotten, or having decided not to care, that Hannah and her husband had paid for the Rusches' tickets for the evening; Hannah felt dismay, hurt, as a child might be hurt, at such a blatant refusal of gratitude.

Their tickets had cost six hundred dollars each. Hannah hoped that Mrs. Rusch knew that Hannah had paid for these, they had not been complimentary.

It *was* childish, to feel this way. Yet, Hannah could not avoid it.

Only when conversation drifted haphazardly onto the subject of northern Michigan and lakefront properties did Christina Rusch take interest, and began to listen, and participate; for it seemed that she had very happy memories of summers spent at a family lodge on North Fox Lake in the northern peninsula; the "first time, ever" she'd stayed overnight in a cabin in the woods, so close to the lake she could hear water lapping through the night and "mixing in with my dreams . . ."

How strange, Hannah thought. An adult woman in her sixties, wife of a multimillionaire, wistful and self-pitying as if such happiness was beyond her now.

Still a striking woman, Hannah could see, with some envy. No doubt, Christina Rusch's executive husband had married her primarily for her beauty.

Or her money. Or: both?

Curious, how Christina Rusch lapsed into a vexed sort of melancholy when she wasn't speaking, or the conversation didn't engage her. As if shadows of dark thoughts rose in her brain when she wasn't distracted.

Hannah saw that the older woman was expensively dressed, in

clothes Hannah had seen in the designer salon at Neiman Marcus: a dark red velvet sheath dress with elaborate stitching at the bust and a skirt to mid-calf. Her stiff, white-skinned face was neither old nor young, her glossy red-tinted hair might have been a human-hair wig. A great burden seemed to lay upon her thin, unmuscled shoulders, unjustly.

Canny Hannah waited for a lull in the conversation so that she might address Christina directly, daring to ask about her family, her children, and did she have grandchildren?—favorite topics for women of Christina Rusch's age who didn't have careers; but Christina stared coldly at Hannah, saying that they had just one living child, a son, who wasn't likely to be a husband or a father anytime soon—"Bernard is thirty-two and still 'searching.'"

One living child. Cryptic remark!

Such vehemence in Christina's words, Hannah supposed they were meant to attract Harold Rusch's attention as well as to put Hannah in her place; but Harold Rusch was laughing heartily, oblivious of his aggrieved wife.

Not knowing how to respond yet not wanting to appear to be rebuked, Hannah asked Christina what this son did and was met with the chilly reply: "I've just said—Bernard is *searching.*"

Now Harold Rusch interrupted: "My wife is being unfair! Or she is uninformed. Bernard is utterly absorbed in his work."

"Is he!"—Christina laughed sharply.

"Not everyone can be an engineer, my dear—not everyone can manufacture 'motor vehicles.' Bernard is studying to be a 'photo-journalist.' He intends to travel the world and photograph 'trouble spots'—'famines'—'droughts'—you've seen those photographs in *Life,* of Nigerian children—refugees . . . Possibly for the UN."

Rusch's presentation of the problematic son, to the table of strangers, might have been calculated to draw approval, admiration, applause, like the unveiling of a gleaming new-model automobile.

Rusch was a thick-set man for whom the adjective *porcine* might have been invented, but his eyes were alert and lively and shone with a sort of aggressive merriment. Hannah had heard rumors that Rusch was a brilliant but pitiless executive at GM who thought nothing of firing entire departments at the corporation and replacing them with hand-picked junior men.

As if there were a tired old quarrel between them which she couldn't be bothered to take up, Christina ignored her husband.

Awkwardly, the table fell silent. Then, a bright young man skilled in diplomacy, Wes changed the subject: the latest scandal in Lansing.

(Lansing, capital of Michigan.)

Hannah smiled in relief. How clever Wes was!

No need to listen to what was being said. Politics bored Hannah, but particularly state politics.

For what is politics but business under wraps: the buying of politicians, whose votes are essential in the ongoing drama of keeping business taxes low, lower. The only uncorrupt politician is one who hasn't yet been approached, Hannah knew. Or, Hannah had been told: Hannah knew very little firsthand.

Thinking what a strange ritual such occasions are, lavish fundraisers where well-to-do people are thrown together, seated at impracticably large round tables trying, amid a deafening din, to find something to talk about.

But really, there is nothing. Is there?

Nothing that matters.

Except: Which one are you?

Except: No "unlisted" numbers!

He'd been laughing at Hannah. Well, yes—her life . . .

Indeed, she knew. Her life was laughable.

But was life itself—*life*—laughable? She didn't want to think so.

"Ma'am?"—a waiter hovers beside Hannah, holding a silver tray.

"Thank you, no. Well—yes . . ."

Hannah has been pushing food around on her plate. Rapidly cooling food, not at all appetizing. Ironic how after months of preparation, anticipation Hannah feels so little interest in the actual dinner. The menu she and others had debated with the urgency of generals planning a military campaign: seviche with arugula salad, Chilean sea bass or filet mignon, rosemary fondant potatoes, julienne carrots, crème brûlée . . . So intense had the planning been, so high had feelings run, there'd flared up bitter disagreements, friendships annihilated in an instant. Bitter feuds that would never be forgotten or forgiven.

One of the women whom Hannah had quite liked, and who'd

seemed to like Hannah, had become particularly incensed over the entrée when Hannah had suggested the Chilean sea bass as an alternative to the more standard flank steak; later, they'd clashed over the dessert options . . .

Joker Daddy wryly observed: Women fight *small* because there's no *large* for them to fight about.

A fork slips from Hannah's fingers and clatters to the floor. A uniformed waiter hurries to retrieve and replace the fork.

"Sorry! Thank you."

"Thank *you*, ma'am."

Hannah's eyes are veiled, she does not wish to see if the young waiter is sneering at her.

He has left the ballroom. Hadn't cared to stay.

Why hadn't he cared to stay? To hear Hannah Jarrett singled out for praise in front of this vast gathering . . .

At last, Hannah's long-awaited moment of glory as the (male, gratingly jocular) master of ceremonies at the dais pronounces her name with exaggerated care—"Han-nah Jar-rett"—and asks her to stand and be recognized. Hannah feels a flurry of acute self-consciousness, a sinking sensation of despair, rises to her feet, head lifted, happy smile, suffused with happiness, basking in the moment, a beautiful woman in black crepe de chine Dior purchased for this occasion. Waves of warm and robust and sincere applause for "Hannah Jarrett" and the several other "fabulous volunteers" who've made "such a fantastic success of this year's March Madness"—in shy-giddy triumph Hannah feels a sea of eyes move upon her, wishing her well, not judging her harshly (as Hannah might judge herself), or as the bemused stranger with the heavy-lidded eyes might judge her, for Hannah has proven herself one of them in the pursuit of a common goal and they are merciful to one of their own.

And here is Wes Jarrett lifting a glass to salute his wife, smiling broadly as if Goddamn, no matter how silly this all is, he is Hannah's husband and he is happy for her.

"Thank you! Thank you—all of you . . ."

Abruptly then, the moment is past. The master of ceremonies has moved on, accompanied by laughter at a ribald remark of his which Hannah hasn't quite heard.

Hannah is seated again, deflated. Light-headed. Reaching for her wineglass, a solace.

So disappointed, *he* hadn't stayed to applaud her with the others. So that *he* could see who she is, and not just whose wife she is. And how valued she is, locally at least, among this elite audience.

I am a good person, I sacrifice for others, I deserve happiness.

That night, and nights (and days) to follow, the fever took hold.

Staring sightless bright and blind in the dark trying to recall the color of *his* eyes, very dark, shiny dark, Mediterranean dark. Reptilian coldness that made her shudder even as she drew irresistibly near.

Hearing again her name in his voice—"Han-nah."

Not the man's words but the intonation of his voice. There came a deep sexual yearning, distressful to Hannah.

After years of marriage, after two pregnancies, childbirth, the strain and distraction of young children, she'd somewhat lost that yearning, which returned to her only occasionally, unpredictably.

In bed with Wes, often very tired by bedtime, as Wes, too, was tired, and likely to be distracted . . . Making love had come to seem a preoccupation of younger selves who hadn't the responsibility that they had now.

Superficial selves, childless. What had they known of the consequences of sex!—in the throes of labor Hannah had recalled the heedlessness of her younger self, that had seemed to her unbelievable then.

Nothing like agony to annihilate even the memory of pleasure.

Hannah had never been a *sexual being*—not by nature. It was affection she craved, from any source—male, female. A sexual partner, a friend. For affection seemed to Hannah less injurious, if it went wrong.

Essentially, she didn't want to *feel*—not strongly. That a man might enter her body *physically* was repugnant to her, if she gave it much thought; that he might transform her by this act, and provoke her to *feel* powerfully, left her weakened, vulnerable.

Sexual sensation lingered longer in the woman than in the man, Hannah supposed, binding her close to the man, a leash around her throat. You begin in detachment, coolness. Then, the flame is struck, you are in thrall to the man. This is weakness, contemptible.

No more contemptible word: *needy*.

Recalling her father plucking her mother's fingers from his arm, a gesture of supreme contempt as he'd walked away from her, indifferent, bored.

In Hannah's mother, fading and frightened beauty. Love, devotion, fidelity to the husband, always defending the man against their children when there was opposition between them—Hannah had come to pity her weak, vain, flailing, needy mother, yet also to fear her mother's example.

For in the end, the woman is left with *caring*. In her physical being, encoded in her flesh, helpless, stricken, the woman will continue to *care* for the man after he has ceased feeling anything for her.

Hannah worried that Wes had essentially ceased *caring* about her. Of course he was her husband, he was not a rebellious or an unconventional person, like all of the Jarretts he respected routine, and was dependent upon the comfort of routine; he took pride in the property he'd acquired, at considerable expense, which included his wife and children—*his*. But *caring* on his part had faded over the years of their intimacy, so gradually, Wes was possibly unaware of the loss himself. But Hannah was aware.

So rarely now, Wes made love with her. To her. At such times Hannah sensed that his mind was elsewhere.

She did not blame him: the (bored) husband. That he took her for granted she understood, she was resigned to understanding. Only if she veered from her course, like a driver heedlessly changing lanes, would Wes take notice of her, but it would be a devastating notice.

But now, Hannah basked in her own secret. How *he'd* closed his fingers around her wrist.

How brazen he'd been, claiming her in such a way. Not gripping her wrist tightly enough to bruise it, but rather more playful, provocative. As if suggesting what he might do if he wished.

Still, Hannah imagined that, if she examined her wrist closely, she could see the faint imprint of his fingers in her skin.

Empty Ballroom

Today, Good Friday 1977. The Riverview Ballroom of the Renaissance Grand Hotel which Hannah remembers as deafening and festive, now deserted.

Such emptiness! Vast and graceless as a warehouse, unpleasantly chilly and smelling of floor polish and chemical cleanser.

The ivory-white walls are not pristine, as they'd appeared to be on the evening of March Madness. Grimy and scuffed at the baseboards, with a look of general wear though the hotel is only a few years old. At the high ceiling gilt ornamentation looks as cheap as foil. Chandeliers that had appeared to be made of brass and crystal are surely made of neither.

No elegantly dressed men in black tie, no women in dazzling cocktail dresses and spike-heeled shoes, no buzzing warmth of voices, laughter. No brassy jazz quintet, no festive decorations. No uniformed waiters making their deft darting ways through throngs of guests, trays uplifted. The small sea of tables covered in gaily colored tablecloths, bedecked with floral displays and reproductions of celebrated works of art—dismantled, merely utilitarian, stacked against the walls.

Which one are you?

Or was it—*Which are you?*

Hannah is disoriented, dazed. It doesn't seem possible that what happened to her in this vast soulless space could ever truly have happened. Amid the smells of floor polish, chemical cleanser like a whiff of formaldehyde . . .

She hadn't thought that *he* would call her. She hadn't thought that, if he'd called her, she would have agreed to meet him.

None of it has unfolded as she'd anticipated. A strange passivity has overtaken her like a narcotic. If the ballroom began to ooze befouled water, if a tide of filth arose about her ankles, legs, she'd have been paralyzed to move away from it, to save herself . . .

He awaits Hannah on the sixty-first floor of the hotel. Hannah has taken an escalator to the mezzanine, to (re)visit the Riverview Ballroom.

She tries to recall: the ballroom thrumming with life, voices and laughter, music. An aqueous environment quivering with raw creaturely appetite, desire.

She remembers being in a conversation of forced gaiety with persons she knew slightly, knew by name as they knew her by name, shouting to hear one another over the din, and the brush of someone's fingers against her wrist . . .

More than two weeks ago, by the calendar. So vivid in Hannah's memory it might have been yesterday.

Waiting for a call. Waiting, as one might wait for news of a medical test result. Telling herself—*Of course I am not "waiting."*

Lifting the receiver with the expectation that it was a call of no great significance, lifting the receiver without steeling herself for the shock of his voice—*Hannah? Hello.*

The actual call, the exchange, she scarcely remembers. But now it is the following day and she has returned to the Renaissance Grand Hotel.

Good Friday. The single day of the year in which there is no communion in the Roman Catholic Church.

No communion on Good Friday because there can be no consecration of the host on Good Friday.

No consecration of the host on Good Friday because Jesus Christ has been nailed to the cross, He has not yet risen from the tomb nor has He been carried lifeless to the tomb to await His resurrection on Easter morning.

Good Friday, so often a raw wet day in childhood. Cold rain laced with pellets of snow.

If you would just smile, Hannah! You would be pretty. At least try.

Made to walk from the parking lot behind the church to the front entrance of the church no matter the weather. Hard stinging rain, rain mixed with snow, hailstones. For Hannah's father refused to drop his passengers off in front of the church as others were dropped off— "coddling" was to be resisted.

Joker Daddy believed least of all in "coddling" himself. He had no patience for weakness. Hannah's mother seated beside him in the passenger seat wordless, making no appeal, head bowed as if meekly.

Don't be ridiculous. You can walk. We can all walk. What d'you think I am, a chauffeur?

Good Friday, not a day to *laze around*.

Hannah was determined at a young age: not to *laze around*.

But now it is years later. A lifetime later: Good Friday 1977.

No connection between that old, lost life and Hannah's life now. She is sure.

Retreating now from the Riverview Ballroom, its emptiness, vacuity. Vanity.

Nothing so desolate as a grand ballroom from which all human life has drained.

Why, where is everyone? Have we all died?

Silent as a morgue. Perhaps this isn't a ballroom at the Renaissance Grand Hotel at Renaissance Plaza, perhaps it is a hospital morgue. Windowless, because underground.

Faint whiff of formaldehyde. Hannah feels the shock of a fiery sensation up her nostrils, wires into her brain. She did come to him, like a fool she'd come to him, he'd strangled her with his strong bare hands, he'd disposed of her body and has already forgotten her name. Like a flash it had happened, and now it is happening again. Quickly, stepping out into the corridor and allowing the heavy door to click shut after her.

"Excuse me, ma'am? May I help you?"

A smartly dressed hotel employee on her way to the escalator notices Hannah in the corridor outside the ballroom, where she appears to be standing motionless as if stricken in thought or in some way entranced, and so pauses to address her in a Renaissance Grand–trained voice of friendly solicitude even as Hannah wakes from her trance, embarrassed, assuring the woman—"Thank you but no. I am not lost."

Lost

On the sixty-first floor of the hotel tower he awaits her.

Rapidly ascending in the sleek glass capsule like a vessel shot into space she feels a thrill of vertigo, she shuts her eyes.

A hissing sound like a sharp intake of breath. She is hurtled into time, she has been shaken free of gravity, such a curious sensation—*to fall upward.*

Sin

*M*y happiness is my children, my husband. My marriage. My happi-*ness is not myself but . . .*

In the glass cubicle rapidly ascending soundless and weightless rehearsing these futile words. Clutching between numbed fingers the folded-over sheet of hotel stationery she'd intended to crumple and throw away downstairs in the lobby.

. . . and so, I can't stay. I hope you can understand and will be my friend.

He will take pity on her, she believes. And he is dazzled by her, she has been led to believe.

The glass cubicle stops. Abruptly.

No choice but to step out. Finding herself standing before a plate-glass window facing the elevator. Many stories above the ground, disoriented. A fierce white sun impales Hannah like a spike through the forehead.

A blow of God. A stroke.

This is a mistake, this is sin, turn back.

Making her way to the room on a high floor of the hotel. *His* room.

With a part of her mind understanding that none of this is real. The familiar dream in which she is a child again. Trying to run, breathless and frightened. Not *again*, but *still*.

So many years we push forward. Always the effort of pushing against gravity, time.

It has been Joker Daddy who pursues her, has it?—Daddy longlegs overtaking frantic foolish short child legs.

That's a mistake, sweetie! Running from your daddy.

Not a mistake you want to make, sweetie. See?

Never struck her. Or—rarely.

Not sure where this place is. A windowless corridor. Rows of doors, shut and mute. Identical doors. A high floor of a high-rise building, just perceptibly tremulous in the wind.

Run stumbling along the corridor pounding on doors with both fists, no one will hear.

Before Babysitter

*H*ow're you doin' in a kindly voice. Important there was no threat implied for in truth, those days before Babysitter became Babysitter, there was not, or not usually.

Cass Corridor, East Warren, Gratiot. Cruising down Woodward and at the City Center exit of I-75, vacant lots heaped with rubble like wartime. In bodegas, on tenement stoops, in alleys, stairwells it was welfare mothers you'd approach. Sleepy-lidded eyes just barely lifting to yours, irises shrunk to a pinprick. Crack-cocaine glaze, soft-mouthed so just the right smile was the key, you could work it out so for a dime bag they'd give you their kid, that's to say *lend*.

At the Motor City Motel. Girl looking too young to be a mother sprawled in the backseat of the Olds, for a dime bag she'd lend us her kid.

You know, I could babysit for you. I'm, like, bonded.

It was a joke, even if you didn't comprehend you could see it was a joke and kindly meant with a wink. If your face was familiar to them, they didn't distrust you. Basically it was a small world.

Okay, man. Yeh.

Babysitter took only white children but before Babysitter there were Black children, brown-skinned, as well as "white." Depending on the mothers, on who came along. Weeks they'd be living on the street, then one day gone.

Life is what it is—who comes along. Tell yourself something more, you'd be lying.

By the exit underpass. Lucia, pronounced "Loo-*she*-a," would be missing anywhere from two to three hours to overnight. The baby was four years old but small for its age. Eyes not in focus but liked to be cuddled, hugged. Made a mewing sound. Anything soft it could eat like ice cream if not too cold. Melted was best.

Mister R__ would send us to deal with Lucia—"intermediaries." We had "bargaining power." Mister R__ was all we knew of his name but there were rumors he lived in a mansion in Bloomfield Hills. He'd pay you up front. "Cash and carry." You never had to worry about Mister R__ owing you and not paying like those others.

His friend rarely spoke. The Hawk, we called him. Tall, skin like parchment, heavy-lidded eyes but nothing sleepy about him.

The Hawk was the driver, Mister R__ would ride in the backseat in those days. They wore dark glasses and the car had tinted windows. The Hawk laughed at Mister R__ for the Hawk had no weakness for children. The Hawk could slap a child into submission as a snake might hypnotize its prey before swallowing it whole.

(My friend here tells me I am wrong, the Hawk had a weakness for some of them. A girl child, the Hawk might take for himself, you'd hear her screaming, then you'd hear the silence. You never needed to clean up after the Hawk, he took care of that himself. But Mister R__, he'd get drunk and need to be comforted.)

Years later, Mister R__ would kill himself. Single shot to the head, Glock revolver dropped at his feet. Brains dribbling down the broken skull. "Suicide note" left behind.

Evidence suggested that Mister R__ was (likely) Babysitter. Never proved.

For the record I am stating this now because all of this, Babysitter and all the evil he wrought, that was known to have been done, and attributed to him, and all that was never known and never attributed to him, as the sum total of all evil must be greater than the sum total of known evil, in those accursed years 1976 and 1977 in Detroit and suburbs, is "history" now passing into oblivion and the blamelessness of oblivion beyond even evil.

Conscience

They know! They will never forgive me.

That morning the children behaved strangely as if sensing their mother's mood. Nervous, anxious—like their mother, except Hannah knew better than to betray her feelings.

Hannah laid her hand against their foreheads that seemed slightly overwarm, damp. Fever?

Four-year-old Katya, usually so cooperative in the morning, had balked at being dressed, sulky-faced, tearful for no reason, and later, wincing when her hair was being brushed (by Mommy, not Ismelda) as if her scalp hurt. Usually Katya was sweetly docile, unresisting; there was a strange passivity in the child that worried Hannah, Katya so unquestioningly did what adults told her to do.

Conor, too, was irritable, uncooperative; daring to slap at Hannah's hand, not hard but petulantly, as if Hannah had slapped *him*. (She had not.) (Not even a feather-light slap against her children, ever.) Conor was complaining of bad dreams, his feet "stuck" in the bedclothes so he couldn't get out of bed in time to use the bathroom. (Ismelda had already dealt with a wetted sheet, quickly changing the bedclothes before Hannah noticed.)

It had become a curious complaint of Conor's that the bedclothes on his bed were too tight, or in some way confining, so that he couldn't move his legs or turn over without a struggle; the child seemed to fear that something was beneath the covers but when Hannah pulled down the bedclothes, proving there was nothing, Conor remained suspicious, uneasy.

Wes chided Hannah for indulging the children's fears. Allowing the children to sleep in the adults' bed when they were frightened was particularly not a good idea. All children are fantasists, Wes said; adults have to dispel their fantasies, or they will never grow up—they will be neurotics, weak-minded and fearful of life.

But life *is* fearful, Hannah thought. Especially the lives of children.

Hannah recalled a terror of sleep, in her childhood. For her the terror had been the paralysis that comes with sleep, that leaves you helpless, unable to escape if someone, or something, comes into your room in the night.

And suddenly in a rush, recalling the first abduction of Babysitter— a boy named Michel, thirteen years old—Hannah had seen his photograph in the paper without knowing what, who it was, staring at the soft-eyed sweet-faced boy looking younger than his age whose naked mutilated body had been found in a snowbank in a public park only a few miles away from her own children peacefully sleeping in their beds.

But Michel had been an orphan, Hannah recalls. A resident in a Catholic boys' home in Ferndale or Royal Oak, one of those suburbs just outside Detroit, he hadn't had parents to protect him . . .

There was Wes staring at her—why?

"Did you hear what I just said, Hannah?"

"I—I think so . . . Yes."

"You've been listening?"

"Yes of course. I—I'm in agreement with you."

No idea what Wes had said. No idea why he was staring at her.

At what point in a marriage, Hannah thought, do you begin to *see* the other? When does the other begin to *see you*? Wondering who this person is, why you are together?

A sudden chill, finality of a grate being yanked down over a store window.

Hannah thought, of the fretting children before her—*I will keep them home!*

She'd never thought of the (orphan) boy Michel again, since that morning. Never, no purpose, pointless, why?—not even the last name, no idea what the last name was, is.

Not her child. Not a child of anyone Hannah is likely to know.

Reports of colds, sore throats, bronchitis at the children's school.

For April it was such a raw wet windy disagreeable morning and the house was wonderfully warm. (When Wes was away, Hannah set the thermostat at seventy degrees; before Wes returned, the thermostat was discreetly reset at sixty-eight degrees.) She would keep the children at home and *she* would remain at home.

A call to *him*. A murmured excuse. Possibly, she could leave a message for him at the hotel, wouldn't have to speak to him in person.

Sorry. Can't. Not possible.

Not now.

Mommy would prepare Easter eggs with the children as they'd done last year. Already, Mommy's heart was lifting.

If Ismelda had purchased the bright colorful dye, the decals. If Ismelda had hard-boiled the eggs . . .

Yet: In the next half hour it happened in the confusion of breakfast, amid the daily morning task of feeding children who'd developed finicky appetites, Hannah was made to realize that yes, she was going to drive sixteen miles to Detroit along windswept I-75; and though she'd certainly intended to take the children's temperatures she did not take the children's temperatures (for that meant running back upstairs to get the damned thermometer) (she didn't want to send Ismelda on another errand for there was always so much for Ismelda to do in the morning), driving them to school as usual thinking (guiltily) that if they came home with colds, if they had fevers that evening it would be Mommy's fault.

She did like to drive them to school herself. Mommy in the bulky car coat! Waving at other mothers in their station wagons.

Mom-my! Strapped into their safety seats in the spacious cushioned rear of the Buick the children pleaded with her, no the children were angry with her, never would they forgive Mommy if she went away leaving them feverish, ill on Good Friday 1977.

But maybe: Ismelda would intervene. If something went terribly wrong.

If there came a call from the school. If one or the other child fell (seriously) ill.

Never (yet) any emergency in the Jarretts' family life.

A charmed life, you could say. Though Hannah does not like to say, for fear of, as it's said, *tempting fate.*

Explaining to Ismelda that she might not be back home in time to pick up the children at school so Ismelda should plan on picking them up: usual time, usual place.

Ismelda nodded. Yes, Mrs. Jarrett.

As if not surprised. As if, in fact, Ismelda had expected to pick the children up. Never any doubt that Ismelda would pick them up at the usual time, usual place. There was even a third car in the Jarrett household, a Ford Pinto, for such utilitarian purposes.

Maddening to Hannah: how Ismelda never expressed the mildest surprise when Hannah gave her instructions that, to Hannah, were out of the ordinary, a break in household routine.

For it was Hannah's conviction that she, the children's mother, drove the children to school and picked them up after school most school days.

Maybe not each day, but most. Usually.

Not that she didn't trust Ismelda's driving: She did. Both she and Wes were satisfied that the children's nanny was a good driver, and could be trusted. *Probably a better driver than Hannah, who was so easily distracted in traffic.*

Like Conor's bed-wetting. This appeared to be no surprise to the nanny who changed Conor's bedclothes without commentary but it was always a surprise to Hannah if she found out.

Was there not something insulting about this . . . secrecy? Something patronizing?

Possibly it was ethic, racial. The (brown-skinned) employee's lack of surprise when the (white) employer acted out of character. The nanny's *equanimity.*

As if they expect the worst in us. Never surprised when we are bad parents. Is that how they see us!

Hannah was becoming anxious that Ismelda somehow knew about Y.K. The new presence in Hannah's life, that so distracted Mrs. Jarrett.

Those sensitive nostrils in the petite brown-skinned woman could detect—what?

An odor of panic emanating from Hannah. Panic, and desire.

But no: not likely. Hannah spent even longer than usual in the shower that morning. Piercing-hot water, a powerful spray, the newly purchased ceiling-mounted showerhead in polished nickel, pounding delirium of water, hypnotic, punishing yet pleasurable, you wanted never to turn it off and step out of the shower dazed in the cooler, dull air.

And there was the creamy-white-gardenia lotion rubbed into the creamy-white-gardenia skin. Hannah, a supplicant in the worship of her very self, struck dumb with admiration, hope. Yearning.

Ultra-fastidious about deodorant: It must be odorless, but it must be one hundred percent reliable.

Mouthwash. First thing in the morning minty-green mouthwash gargled energetically for several seconds. Guaranteed to kill thousands, indeed millions of germs upon contact.

Cleansed of all possible odors, betrayals of the *body*. Free then to apply expensive scents of her own choice evoking flowers, fruits.

Still, Hannah was uneasy in Ismelda's presence. As Wes observed, you can't tell what *these people* are thinking.

Generally in Far Hills—as in Bloomfield, Birmingham, Grosse Pointe—you could not tell, you could not even guess, what *these people,* the brown-skinned servants who made complicated white lives possible, were thinking.

Born in Manila, eldest of ten children, scarcely five feet in height, can't weigh more than ninety pounds, Ismelda might have been any age between twenty-five and forty-five: one of those (undocumented? illegal?) immigrant workers who send all but a fraction of their wages home to their families.

One of those of whom their white employers say warmly—*We treat her just like family.*

Hannah invites Ismelda to sit with her and the children, at the children's meals, but Ismelda seems embarrassed, and declines. *We try, but they don't really feel comfortable with us. We try!*

Hannah feels less than complete, not entirely a devoted mother, in Ismelda's presence. For (surely) she would never work so hard, so diligently and without complaint, for modest wages of which most are sent home to a family thousands of miles away.

Well, maybe Hannah would sacrifice for her children. *Her* children.

But not other children, not nieces and nephews, siblings . . . No doubt the Filipino families are large, Catholic families. Hannah shudders. The hive life of family! She can only just bear her own, and sometimes scarcely even her own.

Of course, Ismelda is a devout Christian. That makes all the difference.

It seems that Ismelda belongs to a Catholic-related evangelical sect with its headquarters in Dearborn, where she and three other Filipino nannies in the vicinity worship each Sunday morning and each Wednesday evening. Hannah has never seen the church, has no idea of its size, even its official name—something like the Church of the Risen Christ.

In the small maid's room on the third floor of the house Ismelda sometimes plays Christian rock music late into the night, overheard by Hannah when Hannah is unable to sleep beside her slumbering husband, or unable to sleep because Wes is away on business and she has forgotten where he is, with whom he might be, tormented by the rhythmic thumping elsewhere in the house, near-inaudible, a sound as of sexual coupling, uneasily overheard, troubling, envied, resented, confused with the insatiable yearning of dreams.

If something happens to Hannah.

If (for instance) Hannah fails to return home to the house on Cradle Rock Road, Far Hills, on the afternoon of Good Friday 1977.

If (for instance) Hannah is missing for a day and a night, a night and a day, before her bruised and bloodied and naked body is discovered wrapped carelessly in filthy bedding and shoved into an obscure corner of a storage area on the ground floor of the newest luxury hotel in Renaissance Plaza.

If so, Ismelda will take over the Jarrett household at least temporarily, but capably.

Child care, meal preparation, housecleaning and laundry, sorting the husband's clothing, ironing the husband's dress shirts, overseeing the husband's dry cleaning, bringing in the mail and sorting it for the husband—most of these mundane but necessary tasks the nanny has already been doing since beginning to work for the Jarretts several years ago.

Certainly, Ismelda will be questioned closely by police. For Ismelda will be identified as the last person in Far Hills to have seen Hannah Jarrett alive.

"Give Mommy a Kiss"

Give Mommy a kiss—two kisses!"

Pulling them by their small mittened hands to the rear entrance of the school. At the door, just inside the door stooping to kiss Katya, stooping to kiss Conor, yes their foreheads feel mildly heated, yes it's too late to do anything about it, best not to think of it, or rather to defer thinking of it as the beautiful little girl surrenders Mommy reluctantly, the beautiful little boy pushes away from Mommy with a brave sneer, each with the gravitas of young children blinking back tears they must not shed in the presence of rowdier classmates.

Thinking—*But what if I never see them again? What if they never see Mommy again?*

Good Friday 1977.

PRIVACY PLEASE!
DO NOT DISTURB

In the corridor outside room 6183 of the Renaissance Grand Hotel Hannah has been trying to think! Hannah's head hurts, she has been trying so very hard to think.

Lingering smell of cigar smoke in the elevator, a passing sensation of nausea—she will overcome.

How to interpret the sign. If any interpretation is expected—if she is making something out of nothing.

The most obvious interpretation: The sign has no relationship to Hannah at all. Not a rebuke or a mockery of her, just a (routine) sign for the housekeeping staff.

Because (of course) (Hannah tells herself) a man expecting a woman to come to him, in the privacy of a hotel room, does not want a hotel employee intruding into that privacy. Hardly!

So Hannah reasons. Considering the sign hanging from the doorknob like a reproach, an arrow to the heart, *her* heart.

You should not be here. You are risking your marriage. Your children . . .

The sign is a rebuke. The sign is an insult. A special message for Hannah, to rouse her to her senses.

. . . the remainder of your life.

"Excuse me, ma'am!"—the voice is harshly male, impatient, annoyed, as unwittingly Hannah has stepped back from the door to suite 6183 colliding with a man passing closely behind her, murmuring an apology even as the man mutters, in passing, in contempt, "Stupid cunt."

So quickly this happens, so fleetingly, Hannah has scarcely time to register the incident, still less the insult. Vaguely she'd been aware of someone approaching, he'd been slowing his steps, then, seeing Hannah, he'd seemed to change his mind and quickened his pace, pushing past her, colliding with her and recoiling from her, in the same instant, as Hannah recoiled from him.

"Oh! Sorry"—Hannah's apology is a reflex.

The insult, the *cunt,* Hannah will pretend not to hear. The scowling face, Hannah will pretend not to see. Wisest strategy is to (always) turn away, avoid confrontation.

Her impression is of a man of about her age, possibly younger, roughened skin like sandpaper, untrimmed and unflattering mustache, steely ice-pick eyes behind tinted glasses. Detroit Lions cap pulled low on a low forehead, the sort of hat worn indoors by men prematurely losing their hair.

Upright rodent. Halfway metamorphosed into a man.

Hannah doesn't look after him: no. Waiting for him to let himself into one of the rooms farther along the corridor, assuming that he's a hotel guest, not wanting to knock on Y.K.'s door until the corridor is empty . . . But the scowling man surprises Hannah by not stopping at any door, continuing to the end of the corridor and disappearing through the exit door.

Hannah doesn't think: *Why?* The man in the Lions baseball cap, scowling, muttering an obscenity at her in passing, disappearing from her consciousness as from the hotel corridor.

For Hannah is very nervous, standing before Y.K.'s door. Like a diver poised on a high diving board. She does not want to make a mistake.

Still pondering how to interpret the sign hanging from the doorknob—DO NOT DISTURB.

It *is* a riddle. Like so much in Hannah's life.

The fact that her heartbeat is accelerating. Knocking against her ribs. A sign, a tell. *Excited, near fainting. A sensation she has not felt—if she is being honest—in a very long time.*

Well, she has come so far, and she is so beautifully dressed, what a waste, to turn away, flee like a coward!

Joker Daddy lights a cigar, amused. His favorite daughter's life has become one of those cruel fairy tales where whatever choice you make, you will regret.

Beautiful Clothes

But why, such beautiful clothes. On a weekday, midday.

To have come to *him*, who will tug them off of her, carelessly.

Scarcely seeing the rich man's wife, impatient, rough-fingered, amused by her alarm at what she has triggered into motion that cannot easily be stopped—*Oh!—don't. Wait . . .*

"Hello, Mrs. Jarrett!"

"How are *you*, Mrs. Jarrett!"

Beautiful clothes, elegant and understated. Not showy but casual, Neiman Marcus at the Bloomfield Mall, seventh-floor women's designer collection where Hannah is greeted with warm smiles.

Lighting up the faces of saleswomen, providers. Glowing faces casting a glow back upon Hannah.

How you know you are loved, cherished.

As a girl Hannah was trained in the art of self-presentation. Trained to understand that *first impressions* are absolute and irrevocable. If you fail the immediate test you have failed absolutely and irrevocably, except (perhaps) with persons (like yourself) of no significance, whose opinions don't matter.

Persons to whom failure is familiar, who don't even recognize failure. Such persons to be avoided like death.

Clothes, makeup. Only the most prestigious brand names. If it's a time in your life when you don't have much money know what your priorities are—fewer purchases but never less than the highest quality.

Why Hannah shops exclusively at Neiman Marcus, Bergdorf Goodman, Saks at the Bloomfield Mall, a small selection of boutiques in Far Hills. Prada, Louis Vuitton, Saint Laurent, Dior. Too insecure to purchase anything other than designer clothing, makeup. Ceaseless quest to find the perfect costume, the perfect face.

Before going out Hannah will require an hour examining herself in the mirror, in secret. Trying on clothing—"outfits." Tossing aside rejected items, pulling other items off hangers. Staring at herself as anxiety mounts like a vise tightening around her skull.

At the rear of the step-in closet is clothing purchased months, years ago, yet to be worn outside the house for it is never *quite right*.

Some clothing, still in its plastic wrappings. Discovered after her death with price tags attached.

A secret from the husband who would laugh at Hannah as if affectionately but go away disapproving.

The shallow soul. Who is this person I've married!

At a young age made to understand that clothing is *costuming*. You are the actress performing your own life, must choose the perfect clothing and makeup inside which to disguise yourself.

For God's sake try to smile at least, Hannah. A smile can perform wonders for a plain face like yours.

Trying on "outfits" is an interlude of such excitement and apprehension, Hannah's heartbeat quickens. Her breathing comes short and shallow as if she has been running up a steep flight of stairs.

Indeed, Hannah is frequently short of breath. She has been diagnosed with a mild case of emphysema, believed to have been caused by secondary smoke inhalation, years of Joker Daddy's Cuban cigars smoked in the house and in his car on those long trips to the summer place in Castine, Maine.

Those years!—when it was rude to ask smokers not to smoke, rude even to wave away smoke that was making you cough; when coughing was interpreted as a rebuke to a smoker, and prolonged coughing an insult, likely to provoke a reprimand if the smoker was Daddy and the cougher was his (favorite) daughter.

Hannah recalls that her mother never intervened with her father in the matter of smoking. Her mother did not (ever) intervene with her father in any matter of child treatment. She'd confronted the problem of her husband's Cuban cigars by insisting that the smoke didn't bother *her,* in fact she liked the rich dark smell of the cigars. Hannah has a memory of her mother shutting her eyes in a simulacrum of bliss as suffocating smoke drifts into her face, poor Mother trying with all her strength not to succumb to a fit of helpless coughing.

It would be years before sentiment would begin to shift away from smokers and toward their victims. When smoking was outlawed on airplanes, in hospitals, in public places. By which time it was too late, the cigar smoke had done its damage in the family.

Still, Hannah's very breathlessness has become one of her most charming traits. That air of girlish intensity, *sincerity.* Especially men are attracted.

Leslie Caron, Audrey Hepburn. That most gorgeous of quick-breathing beauties, Marilyn Monroe. *My models.*

Now that her parents have passed away Hannah has become her own most exacting critic.

With their sharp, always subtly disappointed eyes, Hannah sees herself. In the mirror is the tremulous child, prepubescent.

Their principles guide her. Elegance, simplicity, taste—never take a chance on appearing *common.*

In this phase of Hannah's life she has been a flawless performer. Only Y.K. has seen into her soul.

His (bemused) eyes penetrate her clothing, a mere costume won't deceive *him.*

Still, Hannah must try. Nervously she has rejected several changes of clothing and has decided to wear, for the trip into Detroit, for this (reckless, audacious) adventure, a pale rose silk shirt with mother-of-pearl buttons, light woolen trousers, a newly purchased winter coat, black cashmere with a mink collar. A belt that ties casually as if negligently at her waist which comes loose even as Hannah crosses the hotel lobby to the row of elevators feeling a presentiment of dread that she is trapped in a dream in which beneath the coat she is naked . . .

Run, run! Hide your face in shame.

No turning back. Too late. Ascending rapidly in the glass cubicle of an elevator.

Seeing, at *his* room, a DO NOT DISTURB sign hanging from the doorknob.

Reminding her: Joker Daddy never wanted to be disturbed. If the door to any room in which Joker Daddy was, was shut, never never turn that knob. Not ever.

Hesitant now. Not sure what to do.

Is DO NOT DISTURB a test? A test of Hannah? No accident for there are no accidents, there is only fate.

Telling herself: The test is whether she will behave as if she has no idea that the sign is a test, for she is not one for whom testing is likely; or will she acknowledge that yes of course it's a test, and an insult and a humiliation, for she is exactly the sort of person to be put to the test, and fail.

But Hannah has no choice, she must play out the scene. For she has so elaborately costumed herself: beautiful clothes, beautiful shoes, beautiful face.

If a woman is not desired, a woman does not exist.

Help me to exist.

Lifting her hand to ring the bell beside the door. And in an instant—done . . .

"Hello!"

Laughing at Hannah, the expression on her face.

His arms pull her inside. Quick before anyone sees, a roughness that might be interpreted as playful, or merely pragmatic, expedient—as the door is shut behind her.

Hannah's beautiful clothes—is there no one to *see* them? Calculate their worth?

Can't hear what the man is saying, a laughing remark, her voice falters, fails, all that she has rehearsed to tell this person, to inform him, to state clearly to him, yes and to apologize to him, her words she'd feared would disappoint him, none of this registers, no one is listening.

Pulled farther into the room, a sensation of something breaking massively about her like a landslide, an explosion of glaring-white heat—the realization that she has *crossed over* and cannot retreat.

Too taken by surprise to recall what name this man has given himself, or what initials. His face is coarser and blunter than the face she'd expected to see. His skin has the texture of parchment, his heavy jaws are unshaven. He isn't wearing anything like elegant evening clothes but rather beltless trousers, a damp undershirt against which wiry chest hairs press. Blunt bare feet, toenails discolored and clawlike; hair in damp dark tendrils on his forehead, which is lower than Hannah recalls. Heavy-lidded eyes, narrow, alert and shiny like the eyes of a predator bird.

She draws breath to protest. Or, simply to speak. With the palm of his hand he covers her mouth—*No.*

You Like This

. . . my happiness is my children, my husband. My marriage. My happiness is not myself but these others for whom I live . . .

Midafternoon, the tall windows are open to the sky. A spangle of sunshine like gold coins against the ceiling.

Something has been done to Hannah: her wristwatch, bracelet, rings have been removed and set upon the bedside table, as before surgery.

He returns from the bathroom, bare-padding feet, in his wake a crude sound of plumbing. The bed sinks beneath him as he kneels above her, straddles her without a word. The bluish eyelid, a hawk's eye. His skin slaps against hers like derisive applause. Her dilated eyes arouse him, he laughs into her face. His teeth are bared. She begins to plead *No, I don't think* . . . His fingers grip her throat, he hears nothing of her stammered speech. No words that Hannah has uttered has the man heard. None of her rehearsed pleas, her apologies, the boastfulness of her regret, none of this, he is indifferent to her except as the woman whose clothes he has removed from her without seeing, scarcely seeing her. His thumbs caress the arteries beneath her jaw. Beneath her makeup, her skin is wearing through. She begins to move in protest, she has become a beautiful scaly snake in his hands. As firm-fleshed as a snake, lithe and pained. The sensation between her legs is so sharp, it's indistinguishable from pain. She is having difficulty breathing, there is a shadow in her left lung. His weight increases on her prone and helpless body, a terrible annihilating weight, as blind and indifferent as the sun. Her eyes are open and stark and unseeing showing a mad rim of white above the iris. She is lost, unmoored. No idea where he has taken her. Her cries are torn from her, like blows. He is not squeezing her throat to cut off her breathing but there is the possibility that he will, he is only just teasing. He is caressing her forcibly, rhythmically. He is deep inside her even as his large hands hold her throat to secure her, he moves deeper, her body has no defense against him. He is unhurried, as methodical as a surgeon. A coroner. In an earlier lifetime he'd been a fighter pilot. At a distance he'd killed. It was not murder or slaughter but simply *killing*. It had been a task, such tasks stand between the pilot and the hours after sunset when he would eat ravenously, and then sleep the heavy blameless sleep without dreams. The bombings occur in daylight, the light of day is precious. Then, the oblivion of sleep. Such sleep is yet more precious. Truly you would kill for such sleep. A very young man, he'd been trusted by his elders to drop bombs onto the earth, onto cities. Trusted with death. Of course it had not been *death*, it had been a *task*. He had not performed these tasks alone, others had performed with him, a sky darkened by fighter planes like hornets tormented out of their hive, he'd been but one of an elite squadron though (of course) he'd been alone in the cockpit of the plane as he is alone now inside his skin. High in the air there is only *now*, there is never a time when there is *not-now*. Thrusting himself deep inside the female body like one intent upon evisceration, he is in the *now*. He inhabits no soul, he is a being generated by the random firings of neurons, yet there is bliss in such a being, animal grunts, guttural cries of pleasure. And as pleasure mounts and breaks, yet there is a reserve, more pleasure, confounding and annihilating. His thumbs release their pressure on the arteries in Hannah's neck, the relief in the woman is immediate, enormous. Breath rushes into the woman's lungs, she could have wept with gratitude. The wish to live floods into her lungs, her name has been forgotten as of no more consequence than the futile beating of a moth's wings against a window in a farther room for all that remains, all that breaks upon her like an explosion of the sun is her adoration for this man who has returned her life to her as negligently as a god that gives, takes, and gives again.

In the flat bemused reptile-voice staccato-grunting *You like this. You like this. You like this.*

. . .

It has been a long time, Hannah cannot move. Her eyelids flutter weakly, she cannot see. Her face is bare of makeup, her eyes smudged with mascara. Her mouth is bare, raw, swollen. Sensation has obliterated her, in the aftermath of sensation there is nothing. Her heartbeat, that had madly accelerated, is slowed now, almost imperceptible. A match had flared into flame, the flame had touched her, ignited her, exploded inside her, now the flame is extinguished, her body is numb, she can barely lift her head. The tender soles of her feet burn as if she has been walking on hot sand.

Her lips move, she must speak. She has been sobbing, now she must speak, helpless not to speak, for even the dignity of silence has been torn from her, hearing with a kind of pitying astonishment the futile words in a voice barely audible: *I love you.* These words uttered impulsively, unbidden.

As if a plea, an argument, a hypothesis—yet there is no one to respond, *he* seems not to hear as if sparing her.

She lies beneath the surface of shallow warm water. Sun plays upon the water, which is warm, unthreatening. She cannot drown in this water, it is too shallow. She is drifting into a stuporous sleep.

Jesus is condemned to death.

Jesus is made to carry His cross.

Jesus falls for the first time beneath His cross.

Jesus falls for the second time beneath His cross.

Jesus falls for the third time beneath His cross.

Jesus is stripped of His garments.

Jesus is nailed to the cross.

Jesus cries in a terrible voice, My God, why hast thou forsaken me?

She is kneeling, she has hidden her face so Jesus cannot see her shame, that He is suffering for her, she isn't sure why, could not have said why, though it has been explained that Jesus will die on the cross for her, whose name is Hannah.

For—*her!*

A game of adults. A game among adults. Joker Daddy pretends to believe. And so, the children must believe. The wife must believe. All must believe. And this belief includes also the understanding that though Joker Daddy does not (really) believe, yet it must not be acknowledged that Joker Daddy does not (really) believe, for it is Joker Daddy's power to make you believe what you know to be not-true.

Mommy? Mom-*my*? The child is Hannah, cowering before Joker Daddy, but no, the child is Hannah's daughter who has been searching for her, frightened, though Mommy is bending over her, leaning to her, the little girl stares through her wide-eyed; and there is the boy, his name, too, has been misplaced, a name chosen by the father of the boy, he, too, is searching for Hannah, he is anxious, fretful—*Mommy where are you!*—Hannah has become a wraith, they cannot see her.

Someone jostles Hannah awake, rising from the bed oblivious of her. He is barefoot, he is naked, he moves with negligent ease, no more self-conscious than an animal would be, or any naked man indifferent to being observed. Hannah calls to this person, his back is to her, he doesn't hear. Faucets are turned on, a toilet flushing. Hannah forces herself to move her limbs, lift her head from the warm slow-moving water as if she were lying in a stream in a trance of lethargy. *At the final station of the cross Jesus has died, His body is being removed from the cross.*

Her limbs are paralyzed, broken. Something as warmly sticky as blood between her thighs, on her belly and breasts, yet pale, milky-translucent.

It's clear, *he* wants Hannah gone. He has left the bedroom, he is in another part of the suite, still naked, making a phone call.

The body, left behind. He has murdered her with his bare hands, it is accomplished.

Like a sleepwalker Hannah makes her unsteady way to the bathroom, taking with her the sleek leather Prada bag. Even in such a state Hannah is canny enough to locate the bag on the floor near the bed, carry it with her.

Large, luxurious, white-tile-glaring bathroom, a place of refuge. Running water, as hot as she can bear, seeing the sallow swollen face and dilated eyes wraithlike in the steamy mirror.

How flimsy beauty is, a matter of pixels. Too close, magnified and as grotesque as enlarged pores. Too-small, collapsed, pinched features run together as in a bottle with a narrow neck.

Still, Hannah's eyes through the steam-scrim are beautiful eyes, appealing—*Love me, please help me!*

At a distance, a deep-guttural male voice. Easy laughter of a man laughing with another man. A man among men, *he* seems to her, unfathomable.

Despair of women, that men are unknown to them, essentially. The male with his brothers, exalting, in jubilation excluding the female.

Hannah manages to restore some of the damage done to her makeup, hair. A rash-like flush on her throat lifting to her jaw. That air of breathlessness. On the bathroom counter is a large black comb with thick teeth, a crude sort of comb, not entirely clean, which Hannah uses to tamp down her hair. She feels a stir of repugnance.

A man's deodorant, harsh astringent smell, applied to her damp underarms. Above all, she must restore the glistening-red lips. Survival!

Crucial to play out the scene. Not as a humiliated and ill-used woman nearing the age of forty but a naïve virginal breathless girl untouched by childbirth and the maulings of rough hands.

On the bedside table, Hannah's wristwatch, rings, bracelet—had she removed these herself? Had *he* removed them? But why? She feels relief that these possessions have not vanished.

Hurriedly dressing. Shaky fingers. Trying not to be repelled, her beautiful clothes have been sullied.

He has reappeared, phone between chin and shoulder. He is naked, indifferent, kingly. His eyes glide over her, the woman, as if in mild surprise that she is still here, or that she is here at all when his use for her has vanished. Murmuring into the phone *Sorry. Get back to you in five minutes.*

Hannah is on her way out. Hannah isn't going to linger. Hannah waves to the man, bravely smiling, mimicking a silent *goodbye* since Y.K. is still holding the phone.

With a sudden alacrity that suggests belated concern, even regret, or the pretense of such concern and regret, Y.K. hurries after her. He makes it a point to unlatch the chain lock.

"Hey: bye."

Gripping Hannah's chin to kiss her mouth lightly, playfully, as you might kiss the mouth of a child, a touchingly needy child, a boring child, a sweet-vulnerable child, to hurry her on her way.

The Adored One

Dusk! Hannah is stunned, it has become so late.

She'd told Ismelda she would be home by five-thirty, thinking that in fact she would be home much earlier (for certainly she didn't intend to stay in the hotel room with Y.K., whom she scarcely knew: they'd have a drink downstairs, discuss their circumstances, their feelings for each other, that would be *it*), but it is after seven by the time her car turns into the driveway at 96 Cradle Rock Road.

On the interstate, gusts of wind buffet the Buick. This raw wet Good Friday, lingering winter. Gigantic snakes rush invisibly at the vehicle but Hannah is too distracted now to be frightened. Her body aches, breasts, belly, between her legs burning. Headache, heartache.

As if she has been drinking but lacking the elation of drunkenness. Yet—*I have a lover. A lover!*

Forced now to recall Babysitter. As she returns home to Far Hills.

Fitting punishment: if Babysitter has taken her children, in her absence.

In the late winter/early spring of 1977 Babysitter is an (as yet unidentified) abductor and murderer of children in the suburbs north of Detroit who, in little more than a year, has taken five—six?—children between the ages of eleven and fourteen. The child victims are kept for days, allegedly fed and "cared for"; their bodies are then found in public places, naked, hands crossed over their chests in a position of repose, their clothes laundered and neatly piled beside them.

Cause of death: strangulation—ligature.

Rarely does Hannah feel the need to think of Babysitter for his victims have been older than her children. Abducted from public places where they'd been alone. *Her* children are never alone, not for one minute out of the sight of a responsible adult.

Yet thinking, as she approaches the Far Hills exit—*If Babysitter has taken my children, it is what I deserve.*

Approaching the house at 96 Cradle Rock Road.

Still the air is wet, raw, windy. At dusk the sun has vanished. Shadows rise vaporous from the earth like wraiths. Far Hills is notoriously dark at night: there are few streetlights. Outsiders are not welcome here, you must know where you are going before dark.

Cradle Rock Road, two miles from downtown Far Hills, is a particularly dark, twisting suburban road, a tunnel into the night.

Very easy to become lost on Cradle Rock Road if you don't know exactly where you are expected.

Is this Hannah's house?—suddenly.

But no: not Hannah's house, for there is a FOR SALE sign on the front lawn.

She drives on, another quarter of a mile. And here, of course: Hannah's house.

Seen from the outside, at night, her house is difficult to distinguish from other houses on the road. Warmly lit from within, set back into a partially wooded lot, a little distance from the road.

"Thank God." Hannah could weep with relief.

Turning into the driveway, approaching the (three-car) garage. A mild jolt seeing Wes's station wagon in the garage—(is Wes *home*?)—before Hannah remembers that of course Wes is away, on business.

As she has been away, undetectable on Wes's radar.

In the corridor leading to the kitchen, a fresh, fruity smell—Ismelda has prepared smoothies for the children: strawberry, banana, vanilla yogurt. From another room, comforting sound of TV cartoons. Children's uplifted voices, sharp-eared Ismelda calling *Mrs. Jarrett?*—quickly Hannah replies *Yes, hello, be right there!*—slipping away upstairs before the children can rush at Mommy.

Not ready to face the children. Not just yet.

Absurd fear that the children might smell *him* on her.

And Ismelda, certainly. A risk.

That oystery smell of semen. Wetting the crotch of her underwear, as she'd driven home on the freeway . . .

In her bedroom quickly stripping off the soiled clothes. Silk shirt, woolen trousers from Neiman Marcus, feeling anxious suddenly, dirty, befouled. She will throw out these clothes, she will never wear them again.

Needing badly to shower, she hadn't had time in the hotel, hadn't wanted to be seen by her lover with wet hair, flat-headed, unattractive to the man for whom female beautiful is essential.

Soaping every part of her body, near-scalding needles of water. Giddy with elation, guilt. *A lover! I have a lover.*

She feels a stab of guilty elation, she will love Wes less desperately now that she has become his equal.

Out of the shower, shivering with cold. A glimpse in the steamy mirror that is less harsh than the bedroom mirror—reassuring, Hannah looks younger, less harried than she feels.

Discovering that her breasts hurt, not unpleasurably. He'd squeezed her, pummeled her. Scarcely conscious of *her*.

Feeling that sinking sensation, the man's desire. Excluding *her*.

Examining her throat in the mirror. Have shadowy bruises begun to form? No one will suspect a man's fingers . . . Hannah is chagrined, excited. Wes has never touched her like this.

If bruises are more visible in the morning she will wear a turtleneck, long sleeves.

Wes would never notice, she thinks. (But Ismelda might.)

Downstairs, the children rush at Mommy, hugging her legs. She laughs at their ardor, their eagerness. She kneels with them, tears brim in her eyes. Like one who has returned from a dangerous journey hugging the little girl Katya, the little boy Conor.

Faint with relief—no one knows where Mommy has been.

Oh, what do they have to show Mommy? Easter eggs? Such colors!

Yes, the Easter eggs are very beautiful but didn't Ismelda understand that Hannah wanted her to wait until she returned home, she'd intended to dye the eggs with the children? Speaking sharply to Ismelda who is preoccupied at the sink rinsing dishes, seeming not to hear Hannah, and when finally hearing murmuring an apology, Hannah is doubly annoyed that Ismelda has disappointed her and is now apologizing in her soft-impassive way, forcing Hannah to raise her voice, making of Hannah an overbearing (white) woman employer, *exactly the person Hannah knows she is not.*

No idea how to interpret Ismelda. In a way, in awe of Ismelda: child-sized brown-skinned woman with the small fixed smile meant to communicate—what, exactly? Fear of her (white) employer?

Now that Ismelda has apologized, whether sincerely or not, Hannah is obliged to assure her that it's all right, of course it's all right, except that she is disappointed, just a little . . .

All this while the children are clamoring for Mommy, nearly knocking her off-balance. She laughs, flush-faced. *My life!*

Recalling the hotel room, tall narrow windows boldly open to the sky, raw wet April light, suddenly Hannah is there, with *him,* he might have suggested a drink out of the miniature bar while lying together naked in tangled smelly sheets but she'd caused him think she had to leave, why'd she suggest that she had to leave, a blunder, like blurting out *I love you* to embarrass him, how silent he'd been, how ashamed she is, wishing the children in bed for the night and Ismelda out of her sight upstairs in the snug attic room beneath the eaves listening to her Christian rock music so that Hannah can be alone, pouring herself a full glass of Chardonnay, giving herself over to an erotic reverie recalling her lover whose full name she does not (yet) know.

I am a murderer. I am the one. The children crowd about Mommy's ankles, adoring.

When I died, my body became inert matter.

    When I died, my beauty became a ruin.

When I died, my spirit did not rise from my body, there was only my body.

When I died, my body was pushed off a befouled bed and onto the floor of the hotel room and dragged by its ankles across the floor stark naked, dead weight with mottled arms, fattish upper arms of the middle-aged female outspread as in a mockery of crucifixion.

When I died, my body yielded its secrets: stretch marks in my abdomen, weblike creases in my thighs, bruises and welts in my white skin, and the imprint of a man's fingers in my neck.

Gaping lipstick-smeared mouth.

Enlarged nostrils, the terrible effort to breathe where there is no air to be breathed.

Wrapped in soiled bedding, clumsy dead weight pushed, dragged from the room and into the corridor by night in stealth and cunning, dragged to an elevator with no witness for it was very late in the night and the perpetrator took care to cover surveillance cameras' lenses with black tape in the corridor and in the elevator.

Dead weight gliding downward sixty floors to the ground floor of the hotel and there again the body wrapped mummy-like in soiled bedding was dragged along a windowless corridor through a double door marked EMPLOYEES ONLY. Lifted with a grunt, dropped into a filth-encrusted trash bin hidden from view by housekeeping equipment—maids' carts, vacuum cleaners, mops, gallon containers of cleanser.

On top of this bundle trash was placed, in a crude effort to hide it.

Styrofoam cups, plastic cutlery, wadded and discolored paper napkins, used tampons. Underground the vent-stirred air was cold as if refrigerated. The body wrapped in soiled bedding would not be discovered by hotel workers for forty-eight hours and in those hours, decomposition proceeded very slowly.

Eventually, an autopsy would be performed concluding homicide: death by asphyxiation/manual strangulation.

Evidence would suggest that the victim was believed to have been strangled over a period of time, a particularly gruesome torture death that involved choking the victim unconscious and then allowing her to revive, choking the victim unconscious and then allowing her to revive, and (again) choking the victim unconscious and (again) allowing her to revive, how many times repeated until the victim ceased breathing and did not revive.

Burst arteries in her eyes like exploded stars.

Infection

*M*rs. Jarrett—ma'am!

Upside down in the dark smelly receptacle in which she has been shoved, rudely headfirst, naked, contemptible, that least sexually desirable of entities, a *corpse*—yet (so strangely) at the same time she hears her name uttered, a name attached to her as if (yet more strangely) she is still alive—*Mrs. Jarrett!*

Teasing, taunting, a voice as familiar as her own but wrong somehow, in the wrong place, too close suddenly, begging—*Ma'am, try to wake up please . . .*

No no no *no*. Deep-sunk in sleep. Black-muck sleep. Upside down in the trash bin, black blood settled in her brain like wet cement.

. . . Katya has a bad fever.

With these terrible words, Hannah is awake. Her memory afterward is that after strangling her into unconsciousness *he* had wakened her by slapping her face.

But it is the Filipina housekeeper who is standing over Hannah, not Y.K. with the heavy-lidded eyes.

"Oh, Ismelda—what? What are you saying?"

Ismelda has dared to enter Hannah's bedroom while Hannah is in bed, or rather lies sprawled atop the bed, having fallen asleep the previous night without fully undressing or switching off the lamp beside the bed, and on the bedside table a lipstick-smeared wineglass and a near-empty wine bottle . . . Even in this moment of confusion and dismay Hannah feels a stab of shame, the other woman has seen and will not forget.

It is exactly as Hannah feared. But not Babysitter, Hannah herself is to blame.

Thinking, panicked—*My punishment is beginning.*

Ismelda apologizes for waking Hannah but since early this morning Katya has been coughing, and vomiting, and running a fever—"One hundred three point five degrees."

So high! Hannah is stunned. Trying to recall if this is even possible—such a high temperature in a young child.

And feeling a stab of guilt, that Ismelda has been taking the children's temperatures while the children's mother has been sunk in a wine-soaked stuporous sleep oblivious to the children's distress.

". . . tried to tell you, Mrs. Jarrett, when you returned home yesterday, that Katya was feeling sick after school, and Conor was coughing, so I gave them fruit juice and smoothies and a soup they like, and they ate some of it, not much but some. Before her bedtime I gave Katya a bath in cool water and she seemed to be feeling better, her skin wasn't so hot. But now, this morning . . ."

Through a roaring in her ears Hannah can hear only accusatory words.

"'You told me'—what?"

"Last night, Mrs. Jarrett. When you came home I told you it seemed like Katya had a fever, and her throat was sore. I gave her some baby aspirins. She didn't want to go to bed . . ."

"'Fever'?—no. You did not, Ismelda."

"Ma'am, I—"

"Last night? When I came home? No."

Stubbornly Ismelda persists: "Ma'am, I tried to tell you, when I picked them up, Katya and Conor were both kind of sniffling and acting sick—"

"No."

"When they were showing you their Easter eggs—"

"Ismelda, you *did not*. I never heard a word of—"

"—the Easter eggs, you were saying—"

"Stop! Never mind the damned Easter eggs. You never told me they were *sick*, if I'd thought that, I wouldn't have—just—gone to bed . . ."

Hannah's voice trails off weakly. She is frightened, appalled.

Truly she cannot remember. The children were chattering at her, and Ismelda may have been trying to tell her something, but Hannah's thoughts had been scattered, elsewhere.

With *him*. In the hotel room, trapped like a moth beating its wings against a shut window.

And now, in the only life that really matters to Hannah, the children are sick, it is *her fault*. And canny Ismelda knows and is blaming her.

Hannah does recall the children fretting, fussing. Easter eggs, Easter baskets. Competing for their mother's attention.

Why d'you have children if you don't love them. Ask yourself.

Hannah wonders if she should be offended, Ismelda has taken it upon herself to take the children's temperatures, presumably with the children's thermometer. As if Hannah might not do this herself. She wonders: Does the housekeeper do this sort of thing routinely? Has she, in the past? Monitored the health of *Hannah's children*?

It's like Ismelda, indeed it would be like Wes, to have recorded the exact temperatures: Conor, ninety-nine point seven; Katya, one hundred point two.

Low-grade fever, considered not so serious in young children as in an adult.

"A 'low-grade fever' is still a 'fever.' I—I should have been told . . ."

Trying to recover her equilibrium, her maternal authority.

Nothing more reprehensible, more shameful, than relinquishing her maternal authority to another person. If Wes knew!

If the other mothers knew, in Hannah's social circle. Those mothers who make it a (grim) point to drive their children to school in the early morning, faces pale and drawn without makeup, matted hair hidden beneath scarves.

Hannah tries to think: How long had she been unconscious in the bed? Blissfully *out*? Ten, twelve hours? Mouth fiercely dry, sinuses parched. Alcohol dehydrates, no wonder she feels like a cast-off corn husk.

He'd slapped her, had he?—vaguely she recalls the *smack!* of the open hand, the return *smack!* Trying to wake the woman-not-his-wife whose brain seemed barely flickering like a dying light.

Now her head is wracked with pain (shame, guilt) as if a vise were slowly tightening around it. Yet trying to retain calm, dignity.

"Yes, Ismelda—*I should have been informed.*"

Before Ismelda can summon a reply Hannah manages on shaky legs to cross the hall to Katya's room steeling herself for a shock, still she isn't prepared for the unmistakable vomit smell or for the sight of the four-year-old lying motionless with her eyes shut, flush-faced, in the little white cradle-bed decorated with cherubic bear cubs and pandas.

Kneeling by the bed. Clutching at the child. "Katya! It's Mommy!"— her voice rises, she is helpless.

How small Katya is. You never realize how small a child is until she is stricken motionless, lying in bed. No longer in motion, the flame-like energy diminished.

Hannah begs Katya to open her eyes. It isn't clear if Katya is awake, if she can hear her.

Her eyelids are puffy, the whites of her eyes blurry and discolored. She blinks, squints, stares as if trying to get Hannah's looming face into focus.

Sallow-skinned, dehydrated Hannah kneels over the stricken child. Trying to speak with her usual Mommy authority but her voice is a hoarse croak and her mouth is too dry as if she has swallowed sand.

His sand, gritty encrustations of *his* semen.

Hours of night sprawled on her bed unable to think of anything, anyone except *him*. Reveling in *him* and what he'd done to her while in the child's room a few feet away Katya's fever was steadily climbing. The infection had leapt from Hannah to Katya and was coursing now in Katya's veins.

No idea, I had no idea. It is not my fault . . .

Hannah is pleading: trying to explain.

. . . not my fault, I lacked the information.

Hannah's weak lung, wheezing, feels as if it has been punctured. Yesterday in the hotel room in the sumptuous sinking-creaking hotel bed she'd been unable to breathe for panicked seconds, flailing to save herself, on the edge of drowning.

Trying to clear her head. Focus on Katya. Sweet, frail, flushed little face.

And the little bed hand-built to resemble an old-fashioned cradle, though larger than a cradle, a bed that looks as if it might rock, though the bed doesn't actually rock . . . White headboard decorated with cherubic baby animals to give solace at such despairing times.

And the wallpaper in the room, charming pale pink flowers, cream-colored lambs, kittens cavorting in a world in which illness, pain, death do not exist.

Katya's eyes, usually bright and alert, are sulky-dull, opaque.

Pressing the back of her hand against the child's forehead, the skin is burning hot to the touch, astonishing. Katya winces, whimpers like a pained creature, the tender skin hurts.

Whimpering turns into a fit of coughing, dry wracking cough terrible to hear. Helpless! Mommy is so helpless! Oh God, wanting to hug Katya, hold her in her arms, reassure her, but hardly dares touch her, the fever-skin hurts.

Piteous to see the forehead of a child damp with perspiration, fawn-colored hair flattened damp against her scalp . . .

A mistake. Some persons are not worthy of parenthood. Hannah should not have become a mother, should not have *dared*.

Recalling that her mother had (evidently) come to the same conclusion. Not wanting to love her children, not wanting to be vulnerable, yet, in a time of crisis, terrified on their behalf, all defenses gone. As, confronted with the (evident) fact that her husband did not love her, the woman was broken, exposed.

Formerly a beautiful woman. If beauty is control: dominance.

But then, succumbing to the man, broken in the man's hands, dominance passes to the man.

Her children had seen their mother's dismay in those cold eyes. As of one who, at the wheel of a speeding vehicle, realizes that the wheel is not attached to anything—she is in free fall.

Once a mother—no turning back.

Once the love gushes like a burst artery—no turning back.

Hannah asks if Katya's throat hurts and Katya nods *yes*. Hannah asks if Katya's neck is stiff and Katya doesn't seem to understand.

"Honey? Your neck? Is it—*stiff*?"

Katya's head is unnaturally rigid on the pillow. Stiff head, neck, high fever—what could that mean? *Meningitis?*

Hannah feels faint. Meningitis!

A fatal illness, fatal for children. Punishment directed at *her*.

Yes, Katya's flushed face looks swollen. What does that mean—water retention? And the temperature—four or five degrees above normal!

Hannah looks about for the children's thermometer, intending to take Katya's temperature, for perhaps Ismelda made a mistake.

Trying to gently lift Katya's head from the pillow, resettle her in the damp bedclothes, make her more comfortable, but Katya shrieks with pain.

"Oh, honey! I am so, so sorry . . ."

Hannah looks to Ismelda, helpless. Her hands are badly trembling. Her head is pulsing, pounding.

She has forgotten entirely about the thermometer—taking Katya's temperature herself.

Useless! What a useless mother.

On the bedside table are a pitcher of (melted) ice water, a child's yellow plastic mug in the shape of a baby chick. Ismelda has placed these here, has been trying to get Katya to drink water, now Hannah tries, holding the mug to Katya's dry lips, but Katya winces, *no.*

Hannah begs Katya to try, please try, just a little swallow—but *no,* Katya squirms away. Water runs down her chin, wetting her pajama top that is already damp with sweat.

The pupils of Katya's eyes are the size of poppy seeds, not dilated as you'd expect with fever. And her breath short and shallow like a dog's panting.

On the bedside table is a washcloth Ismelda has been soaking in ice water, pressing against Katya's face, upper chest, bare shoulders to bring down her fever, and this, too, Hannah takes up, recalling having done this when the children were younger, hardly more than infants; the kindly grandfatherly pediatrician had assured Hannah that fevers in young children are "not uncommon," chest colds, coughing, loss of appetite, stomachaches, all common ailments that shouldn't throw parents into a panic, treatable with liquids, sponge baths, baby aspirin. Symptoms will usually subside within a day or two and if not, give the office a call . . .

Recalling the blithe assurance—*give the office a call.* How is Hannah to do this without abandoning the child?

Wakened by the commotion Conor enters his sister's room boldly. Stares at Katya in her bed. He's in rumpled pajamas, barefoot, thumb shoved into his mouth.

Smells in the room are wrong, Conor's nostrils quiver with repugnance. He is a lively cheerful child who, in the blink of an eye, can become a spiteful punitive child. Now frightened, somber, but (also) resentful, the "sick" baby sister has drawn all adult attention that should belong to *him.*

As years ago when they'd brought her home from the hospital one day, a tiny red-faced bawling thing, not just to visit but to remain, attention that rightfully belonged to Conor was lavished upon *her*.

Hannah tries to dissuade Conor from coming farther into the room. Telling him that Katya may have a "contagious" disease.

Of course, Conor ignores Hannah. That pleading in Mommy's voice, almost certainly the child senses weakness in the mommy, will not obey.

Boldly continuing to stare at Katya as if subtly repelled by her, resentful.

"Conor? Please stay back."

"Why?"—Conor makes an impudent face.

"Because—I told you. You might catch Katya's illness."

Conor laughs, in a kind of bliss.

Hannah recalls: Young children are said to hope for their younger siblings to die, disappear—to restore the happy equilibrium of an earlier time.

As, in a marriage, one might glance back to the earlier time—before children, and the lurching into a new, unanticipated reality that children entail.

Dissolution of love. Breaking into components. Not enough love to go around.

"Conor! I'm telling you . . ."

But Hannah doesn't speak sharply. There is no threat in her voice as there would be in Daddy's voice in such circumstances.

To discipline a child is to risk losing his love for you. Hannah can't take this risk, her children's love is essential to her, deeply gratifying, she hasn't the strength to resist.

Joker Daddy's grim strength, in *discipline*.

His children had come to hate him, as a consequence. Even Hannah, who'd been entranced by her father. Love for Joker Daddy riddled with hatred like a radioactive vein in a mineral.

Lovehate. Hatelove. Stronger than either *love* or *hate*.

Conor is sniffing loudly. His nose is running, he hasn't made any effort to blow it, even to wipe it. Now wiping his nose on one of his pajama sleeves until Ismelda comes to him with a tissue.

Hannah feels a stab of gratitude, the petite Filipina woman is so *capable*.

Amid so much, in the "white" Jarrett household, that feels *incapable*.

Between Ismelda and Conor there is some sort of rapport. Conor will disobey Ismelda gleefully but without disrespecting her as, gleefully or meanly, he will disobey Hannah as much as he can, testing Hannah's patience.

Ismelda tells Hannah that she'd taken Conor's temperature as well as Katya's and his temperature was *ninety-nine point seven* that morning. Which is near normal.

But Conor has a cold, he should not be barefoot.

"Then why *is* he barefoot?"—Hannah asks sharply.

Ismelda fetches socks and shoes for Conor but Conor shrinks from her, giggling. Ismelda approaches him, he dodges her, pushes at her, runs from the room giggling, coughing, with Ismelda in pursuit.

Hannah wants to call after them to chide them both but thinks better of it.

Thinking: *Meningitis.* Why has she not focused upon *meningitis*?

Should she call 911?—it looks as if Katya is struggling to breathe.

No: Better to drive Katya to the ER herself. She and Ismelda. She dreads strangers bursting into the house, rushing upstairs, carrying the terrified child away on a stretcher.

A traumatic experience Katya might remember all her life.

You weren't home, I had to make a quick decision, not the ambulance, Ismelda and I drove her to the ER.

That is, I drove her. Ismelda came with me.

Hannah has made a decision: tries to lift Katya, a hot, tense little body, heavier than Hannah expects stooping over her. Telling herself Katya *is not* a baby, she *is not* in danger of dying before her mother's appalled eyes.

But Katya whimpers with pain, her skin hurts. Hannah doesn't know whether to remove her sweat-soaked pink pajamas imprinted with tiny white kittens, to risk hurting her further, or to wrap her in a blanket and carry her downstairs . . .

No time to change the pajamas. Can't bear hearing Katya whimper with pain.

No time for Hannah to change out of her own slept-in clothes, still less time for Hannah to shower or wash herself. Her hair is matted, her makeup of the previous day has worn off, mascara smudges around her eyes, cheap pathos in the stark morning light.

Hannah does take precious time to use the bathroom. It's almost an emergency: Her bladder has been aching. In desperation she leans to the mirror, smears maroon lipstick on her mouth—otherwise can't face the world outside her house.

What a slut you are! But you are paying for it.

"God, forgive me. Don't punish Katya."

God in whom Hannah hasn't believed for thirty years. What a joke!

In haste, scarcely needing to communicate, Hannah and Ismelda manage to get the children into Hannah's car, to drive to the ER. For of course Conor must come with them, can't be left behind alone in the house.

Ismelda buckles the fretting uncooperative little boy in the child seat in the back of the Buick Riviera but will hold Katya on her lap, in the passenger seat, as Hannah drives to the Beaumont Hospital in Birmingham several miles away.

Behind the steering wheel Hannah is terrified. Her tongue has gone numb, the interior of her mouth has lost all sensation. At the same time Hannah thinks, with a thrill of elation—*I will do it. I am doing it!*

Daddy isn't here. Isn't home. Away overnight, Hannah thinks in Chicago. Of course. And so Mommy is driving the children to the ER.

Wes will be returning home soon—Hannah thinks. Not sure when, probably in the late morning. He would have taken an early flight.

In her haste to leave the house Hannah has forgotten to leave a note for Wes, to explain where they are. She will call him, she thinks. When she can.

It's Ismelda she depends upon, not Wes. Very hard to be a mother in Far Hills without an Ismelda in the household.

Such intimacy between the women, like sisters in their concern for the children. Much of their joint effort is without speech. Household routines, the children's schedules, baths, meals, the ritual of dressing, socks and shoes. Chattering children, linking the women to each other though (of course) they scarcely know each other.

As in a fairy tale one of the sisters is rich, the other is a beggar maid dependent upon the generosity of the rich sister. Looking for a housekeeper Hannah had interviewed several Filipina women who'd resembled one another so closely they might have been sisters; she'd decided to hire Ismelda, the one who'd smiled the most and was the least assertive, with fewer questions for her (white) employer, who'd been too shy (Hannah had thought) to actually look Hannah in the face. Often, Hannah has wanted Ismelda to "like" her—spontaneously, voluntarily; at other times, she wants Ismelda to be grateful to her, impressed by Hannah's generosity. (Christmas bonuses, impulsive gifts of items no longer wanted by Hannah, including cast-off clothing, Ismelda is free to mail home to relatives.) Over all, Hannah has begun to fear that Ismelda knows her too intimately, in unflattering ways. And Ismelda is "foreign"—it's a mild shock to hear her speaking on the phone in a language unintelligible to Hannah, reminded of this obvious fact as if it were an obscure insult.

Hannah had asked if Ismelda was speaking—*Filipinese*? But Ismelda hadn't seemed to understand the question; she'd smiled uncertainly, no idea how to reply.

You resent them, Hannah thinks. Because they know so much of *you*, of which you have no idea.

Failings as a mother, particularly.

Of course Ismelda noted: How Hannah took the children to school when they were running fevers. To meet her lover at the downtown hotel.

The man, Ismelda could smell on Hannah. That oystery smell, unmistakable.

And the drunken aftermath, Hannah sprawled on her bed comatose. All of this, Ismelda has noted.

But Ismelda seems to forgive Hannah, as one might forgive a reckless fool. For all that matters is the children: protecting the children.

That is Ismelda's task, essentially. And in emergencies, Ismelda is unerring. She is quick, determined, capable. For a woman with the delicate bones of a bird, she is impressively strong: She can lift Conor more readily than Hannah though she is inches shorter than Hannah and weighs twenty pounds less.

Now that she has become a mother herself, Hannah can understand

why her own mother felt overwhelmed with her life, resentful, stymied: Three children, only a few years apart. Two girls, a boy. Health
issues. Never free.

Basically, you dread that your child will die on you. And you will
be blamed.

Meningitis. That terrible word.

Virulent infection: viral or bacterial. One of the symptoms is muscular rigidity, a stiff neck. High temperature, brain damage. Does the
brain *swell*? Does the brain *boil*?

Have there been recent cases of meningitis in Oakland County? In
Detroit? Wouldn't Hannah have heard, if there were?

It is totally unnatural, that a child should die. In Far Hills, in the
affluent suburbs north of the city. So different from the mortality rate
in inner-city Detroit.

Rarely do white mothers die in childbirth. Much more frequently,
Black mothers.

Can't happen to us. No.

Yet, a cousin of Hannah's had died of meningitis when they were
children. Lizzie had been nine, Hannah six or seven.

Not that Hannah had been told at the time, none of the children
had known what happened to Lizzie, where Lizzie had gone—"Away."
Eventually, Hannah doesn't even know when, they'd learned that
Lizzie had *died.*

A terrible and mysterious *death: meningitis.*

And it is she, Hannah, who has brought this contagion into their
lives. *She,* the child's mother!

"Ma'am—I'll take her."

Gently Katya is lifted from Hannah's arms by a male attendant. Carried away into the interior of the ER.

Hannah follows behind stumbling, dazed. An olive-skinned young
woman, a very young doctor, possibly an intern, walks with her asking
her about Katya's symptoms, medical history. She is taking notes, she
is superbly professional.

Hannah tries to enunciate words clearly. Her tongue is so strangely
numb, she is having difficulty speaking.

Determined not to ask about meningitis, she will not utter the dread word.

In a haze of anxiety she'd filled out forms at the receptionist's desk. Looking frantically through her wallet for her medical insurance card, so distracted she'd misspelled her daughter's name—*Kayta.*

She perceives that "Katya" is a pretentious name, there's a faux-ethnicity to it, incongruous with "Jarrett."

Everything about you: faux.

Except the bruises on your neck.

Instinctively Hannah touches her neck, which feels slightly sore. But there are no visible bruises—are there? She'd seen none that morning.

By now the previous day is nearly forgotten. Might've happened months ago, years.

Now, nothing matters except the child—both children. Hannah's brain is close to shutting down.

"Mrs. Jarrett?"—a nurse escorts Hannah into the ER where Katya is being examined. Rows of cubicles, white curtains drawn around them for privacy, still you can hear a child cry. You can hear a child scream.

Hearing herself ask the nurse the very question she has vowed not to ask: Could it be—*meningitis*?

Waiting

Anteroom of Hell.

Hannah has failed to leave a message for Wes. Hannah has forgotten Wes almost entirely. In her panicked state having trouble breathing. As Katya is having trouble breathing.

Bargaining with God. Take *her* life, let Katya live.

"Mrs. Jarrett? Would you like me to call—?"

Ismelda asks her not once but twice, three times. Hannah says no, of course not, *she* will call. But, *she* forgets.

"Mr. Jarrett will wonder where we are . . ."

Hesitantly Ismelda reminds Hannah. Rouses her from her state of torpor. At last locating a telephone for Hannah, a pay phone, to call home.

How much easier if she'd left a message on the kitchen table. On the side door. Explaining. But of course, she hadn't thought, too much was happening.

It is 11:20 A.M. No answer, the phone rings in the empty house.

Evidently Wes hasn't returned from wherever he'd been on a business trip—Chicago?—he seems often to be in Chicago.

A relief, Wes isn't back. Hannah knows that he will blame her.

Trying to remember if Wes had called her the previous night. Yes? No? He must have, he always does. Her head feels hollowed out.

When Wes is away he will sometimes leave a voicemail: for Mommy, Conor, Katya. He will call, Ismelda will answer, he will tell her to hang up and let him call to leave a message.

So often this happens, Hannah has the impression that Wes prefers to leave a lighthearted little Daddy-message than to actually speak in person with his family. For Daddy is invariably in a hurry, on his way to—dinner with a client? a business associate?

Lighthearted as a TV Daddy but a bit harried. *Missing you! Love you!*

Hannah has heard. Some stories. Well, *rumors.*

High-priced "escorts." Provided by companies, for visiting out-of-town clients. VIP clients.

High-priced "escorts" in high-priced "luxury" suites in high-priced hotels but only for VIP clients.

She'd seen them, she is sure. Impossibly beautiful flawless young women at the Renaissance Grand, in the lobby bar. Approaching the elevators in stiletto heels as Hannah had approached on her way to her lover.

Avoiding each other's eyes. Avoiding each other.

The previous night, at about nine, when Hannah was lying in bed drowsy with migraine tablets, a glass (or two) of wine, to forestall a fierce headache, a call had come from Wes. Quickly she'd picked up the ringing phone warning herself beforehand—*Don't be disappointed, it will not be* him.

And so it was not *him,* it was her husband.

The children bathed, put to bed. Daddy had missed speaking with them, unfortunately.

A meeting had run late, or a dinner. Or, no—dinner came next.

A late dinner, at an exclusive restaurant. Or maybe Wes was already there, at the exclusive restaurant, a faint din of happy voices in the background.

Hannah listens sympathetically. These are not unfamiliar conversations.

"Well, we're all disappointed but we'll all be here when you return, Wes—as always."

Trying for the bright tone, sometimes you miss and it's brittle, ironic.

Not good: irony. Husbands do not appreciate irony.

Never reproach a man. Never criticize, or seem to be criticizing. It will only rebound to you, the man will come to detest you.

Never criticize a man, never say *no* to a man if he initiates lovemaking.

Never appear to be avoiding a man, he will take revenge.

When Hannah calls home again, half an hour later, Wes picks up the phone agitated, annoyed—"Hannah? Is that you? Where the hell is everyone . . ."

Hastily Hannah explains. Katya, fever, difficulty with breathing. ER, Beaumont Hospital.

"We left in a rush. We didn't think to leave a message for you. She's in the ER now, they're running tests . . ."

Hannah tells Wes that Conor is with Ismelda in the hospital cafeteria having breakfast.

No, Conor isn't ill—but he has a bad cold, he's running a mild fever, a nurse examined him.

Stunned silence as Wes absorbs this information.

"Just come here, Wes! We need you."

Hannah feels a deep throb of gratification, a grim sort of satisfaction, that Wes will be made to realize that their daughter may have become gravely ill in his absence while she, Hannah, the mother, the responsible parent, has been home.

Wes drives to the hospital at once. In the ER reception area they embrace.

A scene in a film, Hannah thinks: frightened parents, in each face a glimmer of guilt, and the secrecy of guilt.

They are waiting, Hannah says, for the diagnosis. But it's definite, Katya will not be going home today. She will be hospitalized for more tests. Her high temperature and rapid pulse must be treated immediately.

Hannah does not utter the fatal word—*meningitis*.

Wes surprises Hannah by not firing questions at her. Instead, he stammers an apology, for being away when this happened. For not having called Hannah that morning as he'd promised. (Had he promised? Hannah had forgotten entirely.)

Quickly Hannah assures him—No, no! This is no one's fault. Katya picked up some sort of infection at school that got really bad during the night.

How easily Hannah lies. Breathless little-girl-earnest lies. How much more fluent she is, lying, than she would be confessing the truth.

I was with another man. I neglected Katya, to be with him.

I did a desperate thing, there is no one to blame but me.

Waiting with Wes, in the ER reception. Anxious parents, gripping hands.

Feeling *young* again, the married couple. Helpless.

Wes glances about, looking for Conor. Or aware that there is someone else, another child, for whom he is responsible . . . Hannah explains that Conor is with Ismelda in the hospital cafeteria.

"*He's* all right?"—Wes asks anxiously.

Hannah assures Wes, *yes*. She cannot consider that Conor, too, might become ill.

In the early afternoon the younger doctor emerges from the ER to speak with them. Through a roaring like a cataract in her ears Hannah hears that Katya has something called *sinusitis*—"A viral infection in her sinus."

At first Hannah hears *a viral infection in her brain.*

It's a "severe" case, she and Wes are told. But the condition is treatable with antibiotics. As soon as a bed is free Katya will be moved to the adjacent Children's Hospital. She will be in the hospital for at least three days.

Katya's prognosis is "promising," the parents are told. Hannah listens humbly, the doctor's words seemed chosen to flatter, soothe. "You did the right thing to bring her in when you did. She is likely to make a full recovery."

You seems to be Wes, to whom the doctor is speaking, not Hannah. But Hannah isn't offended, Hannah is weak with relief. She'd expected so very different a diagnosis.

Wes, too, is enormously relieved. He has many questions for the doctor, he has assumed a father's authority, concern edged with doubt, a suspicion that he isn't being given the complete story. When can he see Katya?—he wants to see her as soon as possible.

Hannah feels herself begin to shrink, deflate. So tired! Wes will take charge, Wes is the child's father, the medical staff will defer to Wes Jarrett.

All that matters is: not *meningitis*—*sinusitis*.

Hannah will cling to this revelation as to a reprieve.

Ismelda returns with Conor, who runs to his daddy with a cry to be hugged. Hannah is surprised to see the boy's face light up with surprise and pleasure, she'd been thinking that Conor has come to resent Wes, away so often.

Conor is told that Katya is going to be all right, she will have to stay in the hospital for a few days but she will be all right; needy for attention the boy seems scarcely to hear the good news as Daddy squats to embrace him.

"How's my little guy! How's he doing!"

Excitedly Conor tells Daddy about something he'd seen on TV in the cafeteria—a nuclear-powered aircraft carrier. Conor has no questions about his sister, no curiosity. Hannah can see, the boy looks to Wes for protection, authority. Not to Mommy.

If Daddy is present Conor has no need even to look to Mommy. He has Mommy all the time, it is Daddy who is special.

Hannah, watching her husband with their son, concedes that yes, Wes is the more dynamic of the two of them. Wes is authority, certainty. One of those Matisse figures outlined in black, that never exist in life. Hannah lacks definition, a watercolor that has begun to fade.

When Daddy is away the children are possessive of Mommy. They are eager to be with her, disappointed when she leaves the house, relieved when she returns, chattering and excited. Hannah has basked in such childish attention, delighted to be so cherished, secure in the knowledge that, for the moment at least, they love their mother more than they love their father; but such moments don't last.

Absence, presence. It's no surprise, it should not be wounding to Hannah, children tend to take their mothers for granted. Mommy is the one who is always *there*.

I don't feel that I exist to them. I am not real to them.

With you, I feel that I am real . . .

She will tell *him*. If indeed, which is doubtful, she will see *him* again.

Not drunk but feeling drunk. Mouth twisting in a grimace of a smile.

" 'Sinusitis'! Thank God it isn't 'meningitis.' "

Why has Hannah said this, out of her mouth these unintended

words, no wonder Wes looks appalled. "Why do you say such things, Hannah? Christ."

"I—I don't say 'such things.' I was sick with worry . . . I mean, I'm so, so happy that it *isn't*."

"But why exaggerate? Expect the worst? That's just like you."

"It is?"—Hannah is hurt, apologetic.

Now that the news is good Wes isn't feeling so kindly toward Hannah. He has thought to ask her why she hadn't left a note for him at the house, what she'd expected him to think, arriving home to find no one there . . . "Like the *Mary Celeste,* d'you know what that was?"

"*Mary*—who?" Hannah is baffled, chagrined.

So quickly Wes's moods can shift. So quickly a conversation with him becomes adversarial.

"Not *who, what*. But never mind."

Hannah apologizes. She'd been distracted, anxious about Katya . . .

But why should she apologize to *him*, Hannah thinks. So far as Wes knows, he is the guilty party having been away at this crucial time.

Hannah recalls, her father had been equally moody, unpredictable. Jovial, smiling, (seemingly) delighted with Hannah, yet the most subtle intonation in Hannah's voice that suggested resistance, the most minute alteration of her facial expression that suggested opposition, even playful opposition, an aggressive Joker Daddy emerged to swat her down like an impudent fly.

But Wes is more easily placated, fortunately. Once Joker Daddy became enraged about something, he could not be approached for hours.

How rare this is, Wes and Hannah having lunch together. A late lunch in the hospital cafeteria. Hannah is light-headed with hunger but fears eating too much, too quickly. Wes had an enormous breakfast in Chicago but he's hungry as hell, he says, eating from Hannah's plate as well as his own.

A special occasion, an observer might think. If Hannah had foreseen the two of them seated side by side in a restaurant booth, intent upon conversation, as close together as conspirators, she'd have been disbelieving.

"There are some 'passing thoughts' it's best you keep to yourself, Hannah."

Wes speaks matter-of-factly as if pointing out an obvious truth. He will not let the subject drop just yet. In silence Hannah stares at the tabletop waiting for the ordeal to end.

"You have this habit . . ."

Speaking the truth? No.

I never utter the truth if I can avoid it.

Best to remain quiet, rebuked. Soon Wes will lose interest in chiding her, satisfied that Hannah has acquiesced.

Hannah thinks: Wes does have reason to punish her. But no idea what the real reason is.

Through the long day at the hospital the Jarretts remain stalwart, stoic. To the hospital staff they are a couple. Ismelda has driven Conor home in Hannah's car, it's a relief to be alone together. *The Jarretts together in the intensive care unit beside the bed of the sick child who drifts in and out of a fevered sleep. Into a heartbreakingly thin vein at the bruised crook of Katya's elbow IV fluids drip continuously.*

Hannah stares at Katya's flushed face. Scarcely able to look away.

Hannah vows—*Never again will I risk so much.*

She reaches out to take Wes's hand. Half in dread that he won't return the gesture, will ease away, instead he squeezes Hannah's fingers, he is looking fatigued, vulnerable. Of course, Wes loves Katya, too. Wes is Hannah's husband, the father of her children. *Their* children.

It seems to Hannah, her strength is doubled by clutching at Wes's hand.

At eleven it's suggested that they go home for the night and try to sleep. Their daughter's condition has stabilized, they must take care of themselves now.

Stabilized! Hannah tries to comprehend that this is good news.

Breathe

When I died it was not peaceful!
When I died it was in rage!
When I died it was a terrible struggle!
When I died I was trying to breathe!
When I died I was trying to breathe, trying to tear the wire from around my throat, trying to dig my fingers beneath the wire tightening around my throat to tear the wire from my throat, to breathe
to breathe
to breathe

BODY OF MISSING 12-YEAR-OLD FOUND IN BLOOMFIELD PARK
BELIEVED TO BE 7TH VICTIM OF "BABYSITTER"

"Isn't this—terrible! These poor, poor children . . ."

"Why on earth can't the police find whoever is doing this . . ."

". . . a monster, a pervert, someone must know who it is . . ."

". . . if you were this poor boy's *mother* . . ."

". . . from a foster home, probably doesn't have a mother . . ."

". . . from this Catholic orphanage in Ferndale . . ."

". . . Royal Oak . . ."

". . . not from here . . ."

". . . not from here, most of them, why are they being 'displayed' here . . ."

". . . 'psychopaths' they call them, not crazy, just *monsters* . . ."

". . . all our children are terrified . . ."

". . . *we are terrified.*"

Uplifted female voices with the sound of distressed, indignant birds, in the main dining room of Machus Red Fox Restaurant, Telegraph Road, Bloomfield Hills, on a Thursday in late April 1977. Most of the restaurant's patrons arc businessmen, the air is hazy with cigarette smoke. Hannah is one of eight beautifully dressed women at a large round table but Hannah is not involved in the vehement conversation, indeed Hannah is appalled, dismayed that one of the women has brought that morning's *Detroit Free Press* to lunch with her.

Trying not to hear her friends' voices. Oh, *why*!

Obscene subject of the Oakland County serial abductions, rapes, murders, "body displays" taken up at such a time, a time meant to be celebratory, a time for relaxation and laughter, before a waiter has even brought the women their drinks . . . Hannah doesn't want to see the front page of the newspaper with its glaring banner headline, photograph of the most recent child victim, photographs of previous victims, several articles devoted to the Oakland County Child Killer a.k.a. Babysitter, as Hannah had not wished to see the identical front page that morning when Wes was reading it in the kitchen, so rapt in attention he'd ignored the scrambled eggs cooling on his plate.

She'd asked Wes not to speak of the abductions when the children were within earshot. Above all not to utter the name *Babysitter* if there was a chance that they might overhear.

And please would he dispose of the newspaper when he was finished with it, don't just leave it in the kitchen for Conor to discover. Nothing more terrible, Hannah thinks, than photographs of smiling children in the newspaper above captions identifying them as murder victims.

As Joker Daddy used to caution: Never smile when your picture is taken.

Why?—you might ask.

Because the picture will outlive you and you will look like a God-damn chump, grinning when you're dead.

"And what do you think, Hannah?"—one of the women is asking.

Among her women friends Hannah Jarrett has a reputation for being warm, gracious, funny, smart. But not *too* smart.

But now, Hannah's mind is blank, they've been discussing—what? Still on the subject of Babysitter. Oh, why!

"I—I think it's—terrible . . . Tragic."

Hannah stammers, weakly. For what is there to say, in mere words? The last thing Hannah wants to be thinking about in the festive interior of the Red Fox is murdered children, still less murdered naked children displayed in public places.

Thursday lunches with women friends are supposed to be mirthful, lighthearted, and gossipy, not grim and fearful. Not so *serious*.

It turns out, all of the women at the table, excepting Hannah, have children between the ages of ten and fourteen—the age category of Babysitter's victims.

Unfortunate for them, to have to care so much. To feel fear, apprehension, while Hannah is spared, her children are too young for Babysitter.

Unless Babysitter changes his habits, and seeks out younger children.

". . . he takes them when they're alone, hitchhiking . . ."

"... hanging out at the mall ..."

"... unsupervised. Left to 'run loose' ..."

"... in parking lots, vacant lots ..."

Her children are protected at all times. Picked up at school, never alone in the house, always under the eye of an adult.

Playdates with other children have been curtailed, or halted. Conor and Katya are disappointed but Hannah is relieved. Being a mother is so much simpler if there are fewer choices.

"... something has changed! In America."

"Yes! Definitely."

"Since the sixties ..."

"... all those marches, protests ..."

"... assassinations."

Hannah agrees: Some sort of trust has been broken. Bitter cynicism in American life as deadly as a drop of anthrax in a reservoir.

Out of this, not surprising that Babysitter has emerged.

"... things the newspapers can't print, terrible details ..."

"... you'd never see on TV ..."

"... not sure what 'ligature' is ..."

"... 'sex torture' ... they can't print *that*."

"... 'rape' ... 'sadistic' ..."

"... you hear, I mean I've heard, he 'revives' them and—and chokes them until they pass out, then ..."

"... oh, stop! That's disgusting! Terrible ..."

"... such sick souls in this world. 'Perverts' ..."

"... *men*."

Hannah shudders, wishing she were elsewhere. Why are her women friends so obsessed with this lurid story!

As, not so long ago, you couldn't avoid hearing of Vietnam War atrocities. Those photographs of napalmed children!—victims of American warfare.

Hannah rises abruptly from her seat. "Excuse me!"—needing to escape to the women's room.

Making her way through the buzzing restaurant. Eyes light upon her, casually assessing as men do, half conscious, without intention, some of the men acquaintances or even friends, recognizing her as Wes Jarrett's wife, *which one are you* and the answer is: *His.*

A solace! A place to hide: women's restrooms in restaurants like the Red Fox, scent of expensive soaps, hand cream, linen towels, rosy wallpaper, and mirrors shrewdly lit to flatter.

Babysitter! Hannah shivers, her teeth are on edge.

As a child, frightened of fairy tales. *Once upon a time* is no-time, no-place.

Shadows on the ceiling. Daddy longlegs. The door to her room easing inward, ajar. *His* figure, very still.

The first abductions had been in the winter, in Oakland County. Since he displayed his small victims in snowy places, parks, wooded areas, municipal lawns the unknown killer came to be known as Snow Killer.

Always the children were discovered, early in the morning, lying naked in the snow, thin bare arms crossed over their chests, clothes neatly folded beside them.

With the passage of time, as the snow melted, and the killings persisted into spring and summer, the killer came to be known as the Oakland County Child Killer.

Eventually, a name devised by a local reporter that caught on immediately with the media: Babysitter.

Not a good name, Hannah thinks. A name that "normalizes" its subject. Trivializes. Blurs the borders of gender.

Seven children have been abducted. No (evident) connection has been found among the victims: The first was a resident at the Saint Vincent Children's Mission in the suburb of Royal Oak, Michigan, a Catholic group home for boys between the ages of six and eighteen; others lived with single mothers, or with some semblance of families, in more "normal" households.

It isn't believed that individual children have been targeted, rather the abductions have been random and "opportunistic": a child happens to be available, the abductor strikes. Babysitter is a predator on the prowl, seemingly tireless, with an uncanny skill at eluding detection. One of his victims is glimpsed crossing a parking lot but never emerging from it; a vehicle is glimpsed departing but too far away to be identified. Or, a young adolescent is hitchhiking on Woodward Avenue after school . . .

So far, Babysitter's hunting grounds have been limited to the suburbs north of Detroit. But there is no reason to assume that Babysitter is a resident of one of these suburbs.

Babysitter is a "white man"—"not old and not young"—"dark-skinned"—"light-dark-skinned"—"*not* white." He is "stocky"—"maybe has a beard"—driving "some kind of van"—"some kind of pickup"—"blue hatchback, maybe a Vega"—"dark gray four-door sedan, maybe a Chevy." By the spring of 1977 there have been more than fifteen hundred calls to local police from self-declared witnesses.

Most calls are useless, of course. Some calls are vindictive, "witnesses" hoping to incriminate relatives, neighbors, former spouses. But virtually no call, police say, can be disregarded.

Many leads, but just a few "persons of interest."

The child victims have been discovered within a circumference of approximately six miles. Those who discover them report that they thought at first they were seeing mannequins, or "angels."

Could not believe my eyes, what I was seeing! Had to walk right up to it—to her—even then, it was hard to focus my eyes to see. Right there on the ground, out in the open, looking like she was asleep, this little angel girl . . .

Of the seven victims only two have been girls. Short-haired, wearing clothes that could be mistaken for boys' clothes, so police have speculated that Babysitter may have mistaken them for boys.

. . . like whoever Babysitter is, he wants to show he takes care.

Bathing the children's battered bodies, after he has sexually abused them. After he has tortured and murdered them. As in a cruel parody of mothering, washing and ironing their clothing, including underwear and socks, folding the clothing neatly beside them.

As his mother had taken care, maybe. Or—maybe not.

Hannah has been regarding herself critically in the restroom mirror. In her face there is a new maturity, she thinks. Since her humiliation at the hotel. Since the nightmare of Katya's illness.

A face registering chagrin, humility. One who has had a *close call.*

Yes, but I have learned. I am no longer that person.

"Hannah?—are you all right?"

One of her friends has entered the ladies' room, smiling quizzically at her. Hannah is annoyed, of course she is *all right.*

". . . drinks are slow today. We've been here, how long . . ."

Hannah isn't keen on speaking with the other woman. Especially as the woman heads for a toilet stall.

Returning to the large round table in the buzzing restaurant just as smiling slim-hipped Mario is bringing the ladies their drinks, white wine for most of them, prosecco for Hannah, hardly what you'd call a *drink*.

"And you, ma'am."

"Thank *you*."

Giddy with relief also to see that the damned *Free Press* has been put away, is nowhere in sight.

"Children Not Loved & Not Deserved"

Next day, an anonymously sent message is received by the reporter at the *Detroit Free Press* who has been covering the Oakland County child abductions/killings for the past eighteen months, who'd coined the catchy name "Babysitter."

Hand printed, neat block letters in purple ink on a sheet of stiff construction paper the innocent hue of daffodils. The kind of paper kindergartners color on, with Crayolas:

BABYSITTER TAKES ONLY CHILDREN NOT LOVED & NOT DESERVED

Something mocking, derisive in the very color of the construction paper: pale, pale yellow. The color of hope.

For: Included with the cryptic message are three eight-by-eleven photographs of the fourth child victim, a ten-year-old boy abducted "in broad daylight" at the rear of a strip mall on Woodward Avenue, Birmingham. In the photographs the boy, lifeless, naked, hands folded across his narrow hairless chest, lies displayed in an Oakland County park several miles from the strip mall.

Soft-focus close-ups of the child, in neutral colors, blurry at the edges as in a dream or (as a local art historian will note) as in photographs of children by the nineteenth-century photographer Julia Margaret Cameron. A (deceased) child as an aesthetic shape rather than a human child, wraithlike, face peaceful in death, small mouth slightly parted.

Ligature marks visible, if the viewer looks closely.

It will be speculated: How brazen, how reckless, the child killer dared to linger in this public place to take photographs after he'd positioned the body on the ground where another would have fled; is there not, in Babysitter, a perverse sort of *tenderness, love* in such a ritual?

Forensics experts examine the daffodil-colored construction paper, the photographs, the purple-ink block letters.

The manila envelope addressed to *Hal Hornsby, c/o Detroit Free Press, Detroit, MICHIGAN* is meticulously examined but yields no clues.

Observers note: What is curious (amid so much that is curious) is that the child killer has now openly acknowledged "Babysitter" as if with pride; and, though much effort must have gone into the mailing, the envelope was received at the *Free Press* stamped INSUFFICIENT POSTAGE with only two first-class stamps affixed.

As if he'd wanted to save the price of an extra stamp. A compulsive personality, obsessive in details yet hyper-frugal. Prone to overplanning, hyper-cautious yet likely to overlook the most crucial matter: whether his message would be received at all.

Armed

L aying them out naked, that's pretty obvious: bare white skin."
     Wes's voice quakes with rage. Wes is certain that Babysitter isn't from one of the suburbs (as police seem to think) but from Detroit, showing his contempt for suburban residents by dumping (white) children's bodies in (white) communities like Bloomfield Hills.

"It's terrorism. 'Destabilizing.' Targeting white children. Can't be an accident that all of the victims have been white. He strips them naked and takes their pictures to rub it in our faces."

And: "Imagine how we'd feel, if one of our children was one of *them*."

Yes, Wes has purchased a gun. No, Wes doesn't want anyone to know about it.

Hannah is upset: Wes bought the Smith & Wesson Magnum in a Detroit gun shop without consulting her. Unknown to her, too, he'd acquired a Michigan homeowner's license for a gun, though not for a "concealed weapon"; his gun cannot be taken from the house.

Wes argues: If they ever need a gun, they will have it. And, if they never need a gun—"Better yet."

No one was prepared for July 1967—the notorious Detroit "race riot"—but he, Wes Jarrett, will be prepared for next time.

"It wasn't a 'race riot,'" Hannah tries to point out. "It has been called a 'civil disturbance' . . ."

"Ridiculous! It was all about *race*, and it was certainly a *riot*."

Wes isn't afraid of Babysitter, personally. Still, he's a husband and father, he intends to be *prepared*.

.   .   .

"No. Please."

"*Yes.* Take it, for Christ's sake."

In the privacy of their bedroom Wes is insisting that Hannah hold the revolver, at least. In her own hand.

"But—it's 'loaded' . . ."

"Just hold it. Take it. It won't fire if you don't pull the trigger."

"Wes, no. I don't want to."

The Smith & Wesson Magnum isn't as large as Hannah might have expected, with a short barrel, but it is heavy, Hannah dreads dropping it.

Dull blue-black metal, from a little distance you might mistake it for plastic, could be a child's toy. If you didn't look too closely.

"Just hold it. It won't go off if you don't pull the trigger."

"Wes, no. I don't want to."

"If you ever have to use the gun it's because things have gotten desperate and if things have gotten desperate, you'll be Goddamned grateful to have a gun."

But Hannah refuses, shrinking away. *No.*

"Hannah! Goddamn."

Wes relents, the gun will be kept loaded but it will be kept safely locked in a cabinet in the bedroom where the children will never, never find it.

An unloaded gun is useless, Wes says. He isn't skilled enough and in a time of excitement and fear he wouldn't be calm enough to put bullets into the gun's chamber, one by one, so best for a homeowner like himself to anticipate surprise, and panic, keeping the gun loaded at all times but securing it in a cabinet in their bedroom.

Loaded at all times. These words carefully enunciated so that Hannah cannot miss their meaning.

And the key to the cabinet is kept in the nightstand drawer on Wes's side of the bed.

"It will never be anywhere else, Hannah: that key. Take my word."

Happiness

My happiness is my children, my husband. My marriage. My happiness is not myself but . . .

Words of dignity, calm, precision Hannah has prepared to repeat to Y.K. when/if he calls her.

. . . better if we don't see each other again. I'm sure that you can understand.

A dozen times a day even while beside Katya's bed in Children's Hospital with a part of her brain rehearsing *My happiness is . . .*

But a week passes. Weeks.

Hannah doesn't really expect Y.K. to call. Nor does Hannah want Y.K. to call, she will take no pleasure in speaking politely, calmly, coldly to the man.

A mystery that their bodies had been "intimate"—yet Hannah knows little about Y.K. as an individual, scarcely any memory of him that isn't (merely) physical, sensual. Her body has been invaded as by a plunging and pitiless scalpel, a surgery without anesthesia after which amnesia has numbed her brain. The physical trauma, the invasion and the insult of the invasion, and afterward numbness, amnesia.

The forgiveness of amnesia. The solace.

Better not to think of it. No.

What is crucial in Hannah's life is that Katya has been discharged from Children's Hospital after three days, the raging infection has been countered by antibiotics. An air of enchantment lies upon the Jarrett household, everyone speaks in hushed voices, even Conor has become unusually subdued, somber.

Hannah is touched, Conor behaves differently now around his little sister. No longer boisterous, bossy, but gentle, tentative, thoughtful. Can a seven-year-old comprehend death?—Hannah wonders.

We have all had a scare. We will love one another more now!

The challenge is to coax Katya into eating normally. She is frail, weakened, tires easily, has little appetite. In the hospital she'd lost three pounds, a considerable loss for a child weighing only thirty-seven pounds. Her eyes are enormous in her face.

Hannah and Wes have been told by the pediatrician that Katya is seriously underweight, which brings with it a danger of weakened bones, stunted growth, even neurological damage . . . The clinical expression is *failure to thrive.*

Hannah has thought *failure to thrive* an expression of pathos, applied to the children of the inner-city poor. Not applicable to children in Far Hills, Michigan.

On good days Katya will eat the foods prescribed for her—nutritious, rich in vitamins and calories—at least in small portions. On other days she rejects such food, has to be tempted by Hannah and Ismelda to eat anything at all—sugar-coated cereals, jams and jellies, peanut butter, pizza, mashed potatoes, SpaghettiOs, Froot Loops, smoothies, chocolate chiffon pie, chocolate ripple ice cream.

In sympathy with his pale, wan sister, or slyly wishing to take advantage of the situation, Conor, too, has become a finicky eater.

Mealtimes have become Events. Patience is required, and a kind of adult cunning.

At least Wes is spared; he eats dinner late, with Hannah, often after the children are in bed, if he eats dinner at home at all. Which is good, Hannah thinks, since Wes hasn't the patience to deal with his angel children when they are behaving badly.

Thinking—*They are my responsibility. To keep alive.*

Often Hannah sees Conor watching Katya covertly, with a kind of adult sobriety unnatural in a seven-year-old, and to Wes observes guiltily, "It's as if Conor knows how we might have lost Katya. The way the poor child looks at his sister now . . ."

"We weren't going to 'lose' her, Hannah. Sinusitis isn't fatal."

"Sinusitis is *rarely* fatal. But if it spreads to the brain . . ."

"Well, it didn't! Katya was put on antibiotics immediately. We have first-rate medical care here, we aren't aborigines living in the wild."

Hannah hears the exasperation in her husband's voice. Wisest for Hannah to remain silent.

Wes says hotly, "If Conor acts strangely around Katya it's something you've put in the poor kid's head. He's seven years old, for Christ's sake. He isn't *you*."

How frail the vessel—*family*. How desperate to keep *family* from pitching into the rough, devastating waters of oblivion, a frail vessel held together by love.

And what is love but emotion. And what is emotion but a wisp of smoke, a motion of the air, invisible.

By the end of April Hannah has ceased thinking of *him*. Hannah has ceased awaiting a call from *him*.

Yet out of curiosity Hannah wonders if he has returned to Detroit, without having called her. Without her knowledge.

Y.K. has frequent business dealings in Detroit, Hannah knows. He has friends, business associates in Detroit. He always stays in the same suite on the sixty-first floor of the Renaissance Grand Hotel overlooking the Detroit River.

That suite. *That* bed. Hannah feels faint, recalling.

Hannah wonders: What *is* his business?

With the excuse of checking financial accounts for the March Madness fundraiser Hannah examines computer printouts in the office of the Friends of the Detroit Institute of Arts, in Far Hills, to which as a cochair of the event she has access; she spends nearly an hour scanning printouts of names, long columns of names, hoping to see a name that jogs her memory—the name of the person who'd given Y.K. a complimentary ticket to the event.

Unfortunately she'd failed to ask Y.K. who his friend was. Would not have dared ask, for fear of offending him.

The kind of man you don't interrogate. No.

Hannah has the vague hope that she might recognize a name if she looks closely. She doesn't even know if Y.K.'s host had reserved an entire table or had simply had an extra ticket on hand, there were relatively few tables purchased in their entirety, at five thousand dollars, most of these were corporations like GM, Ford, Chrysler, the reservations made by secretaries. Eventually Hannah discovers seven tables purchased by individuals of whom five are known to her personally; it will be no effort for Hannah to seek out these individuals if she happens to encounter them somewhere, greeting them in a friendly manner and then casually bringing up March Madness, what a success it was, and from there leading the conversation into specifics: who was seated where, who was at which table, until by chance, or nearly, Hannah learns from the wife of Wilbur Mears, a Birmingham attorney, that a "single, solitary bachelor" had been one of the guests at their table—not a friend of Connie Mears, nor of her husband, but of a mutual friend whom Hannah might know, Marlene Reddick . . .

Marlene Reddick. Hannah recalls that she'd been speaking with Marlene at the cocktail party when Y.K. approached her, seemingly out of nowhere.

His fingers, brushing her wrist. That immediate intimacy, she'd turned in an instant to see . . .

But Y.K. was Marlene's friend, before he'd become Hannah's friend. That seems likely.

Hannah asks Connie Mears if she can remember the name of the "single, solitary bachelor" who'd been a guest at their table and Connie Mears says no, she doesn't; Hannah asks if possibly his initials were "Y.K." and Connie Mears says she has no idea. Hannah hesitates before asking Connie another question, not wanting to arouse the woman's suspicions, but Connie volunteers that she and Wilbur never met Marlene's guest—"After Marlene assured us the ticket wouldn't go to waste, her friend didn't show up."

"He *didn't*?"

"Not for dinner, at least. He may have been at the cocktail hour but left then. So a seat was vacant at our table. *Rude.*"

Which means, Hannah thinks, excited, that Y.K. has to be that man, that absence at the table; and Marlene Reddick, whom Hannah knows socially, but not well, knows him.

Happiness. Katya is safe. Hannah's family is safe. Hannah herself is safe.

A full month after Good Friday, *he* has not called.

Sexual Rival(s)

Marlene! Hello."

The sexual rival. Hannah knows.

In an instant, Hannah is aflame. Her mouth is an ugly smile, she must refashion it, quickly.

At the Far Hills Country Club where Hannah is meeting her Thursday-luncheon friends, and Marlene is meeting friends of hers, in the open, airy, main dining room.

Hannah waves to Marlene, gaily. Marlene is caught, cannot turn aside.

Before her quarry can elude her Hannah tells Marlene that she has a question for her, she'd hoped to run into Marlene to ask: At the fundraiser, her husband, Wes, had had a very interesting conversation with a guest whose name he doesn't know, only the initials—"Y.K." Or Wes *thinks* those were the initials.

"Do you know his name, Marlene? Connie Mears thinks you might."

A glimmer of a shadow in Marlene's face. Inscrutable.

Shaking her head *no*. She does not.

"He's a friend of the governor's, Wes said. They'd gone to the Air Force Academy together. Wes thinks he's in real estate development. They were talking about something interesting and were interrupted—never got back together . . ."

Marlene frowns with the effort to recall something so plainly of little significance in her life. Explaining that yes, she'd received an extra ticket from Wilbur, he'd wanted to get rid of it, so it wouldn't go to waste—"But the person I gave it to, a friend, must have passed it on to someone else, this 'K'—maybe . . ."

"So you don't know who Y.K. is? You've never met him?"

Marlene's gaze shifts. Marlene reconsiders.

"I—I may have met him at the cocktail party, without knowing who he was. I met so many people that night—we all did—hard to hear names, the music was so loud . . ."

Hannah says helpfully: "Wes said he was—is—about his age, Wes's age, early forties. He's tall, with dark hair—a kind of thick, *stiff* hair . . . He seemed to have a kind of accent, but Wes couldn't describe it. And he wasn't wearing 'black tie' exactly . . . You don't remember him, I guess?"

Marlene seems to be avoiding Hannah's eyes. Politely shaking her head *No, sorry.*

She knows him. Yes.

Hannah feels a shiver of contempt for her rival. *She* is younger, and more beautiful.

Marlene's face has become solid, fleshy. Pale-peach cosmetic mask, poreless. Her mascara-lashed eyes are puckered at the corners. Her fingers are somewhat short, stubby; the skin on the backs of her hands is loose. Her leather handbag is larger than Hannah's, arguably more expensive. It is rumored in Far Hills that Marlene has become a *secret drinker.*

In Far Hills there are *social drinkers,* and there are *secret drinkers.* Of course, the two can overlap.

"You don't know what his business is, Marlene? This man Wes met."

"How would I know? I've just told you I don't know him."

This is a sharp rejoinder. Hannah's air of naïve curiosity has become grating to the other woman.

Then, in softer tone: "Really, Hannah, I have no idea what any of them do—I mean, what they *really* do."

" 'They'—?"

"Our husbands."

Hannah laughs, startled. This is unexpected.

Our—as unexpected as a nudge in the ribs, and not entirely welcome.

Hannah has but a vague idea of what Wes's business is *really*. She'd never known what her father's business was, nor had her mother known in any detail, she is sure.

She knows, or thinks that she knows, what Wes's company does, in a vague sort of way. Investments. Money management. She has a vaguer sense of what stocks—stocks and bonds?—Wes has invested their money in; she has been told the difference between stocks and bonds many times but would not have been able to explain. She'd assumed that Wes and Harold Rusch were involved in some sort of business deal—but Wes seems to have refuted that. Certainly she doesn't know what deals have been made to float enormous loans of millions of dollars for financial ventures in which Wes is involved, with others or independently. From time to time Hannah hears that someone they know is *declaring bankruptcy*—a business is *going under*—but how, why, what this entails Hannah isn't sure.

The few times she'd inquired about the distribution of their finances Wes had spoken so earnestly to her, at such length, spread out documents on a table for her to peruse, smothered her with details as if pressing a pillow over her face until her eyes had glazed over—*Enough!*

In a confiding voice Marlene is telling Hannah about a mutual Far Hills acquaintance who'd consented to a no-fault divorce from her husband of twenty-six years only to discover too late that the husband had been depositing most of his income in a Cayman Islands bank, inaccessible to the wife . . .

"Poor Catherine! Dwight has taken 'early retirement' and claims that his salary is something like twenty thousand dollars a year now—of which she can hope for half. She has no choice but to settle, her lawyer has told her."

Hannah murmurs how terrible. She is sorry to hear . . .

"And there's another woman, of course. A 'junior executive' at his firm."

Why are they speaking of these others?—Hannah wonders. Regarding her rival suspiciously.

Of course. He has made love to her, too.

Squirmed, gasped, shuddered, struggled to breathe as the man's predator fingers closed about her throat—relenting at the last moment.

Has she wanted to die, too?—extinguished by those hands.

After the women part Hannah feels a small mean thrill of satisfaction: *He* has ceased calling Marlene, she is sure.

"Stupid C_t"

And then, in Neiman Marcus, a chance encounter with Christina Rusch.

Hannah on an ascending escalator, Mrs. Rusch on an adjacent descending escalator, the dignified older woman oblivious of the younger woman staring at her, as she'd been indifferent to Hannah for most of the fundraiser dinner in March.

"Mrs. Rusch?—Christina . . ."

Hannah calls out the name even as Mrs. Rusch regally descends out of Hannah's range of vision, not deigning to hear.

A figure elegantly dressed, dove-gray clothing, pastel scarf around her neck, carrying a designer bag in soft creamy leather and a Neiman Marcus shopping bag. Aloof, indifferent, not the sort of person inclined to glance over her shoulder when her name is called excitedly/ rudely in a public place.

As soon as she can Hannah takes the descending escalator intent upon catching up with Christina Rusch on the first floor, but on the first floor Hannah can't seem to find her.

You take the risk, for the risk is worth it. Not helpful to ask *why*.

Christina Rusch seems to have disappeared. Hannah looks about, perplexed.

(Fortunately, no one has seen Hannah. *He* has not seen her making a fool of herself chasing after the auto executive's wife who, at the fundraiser, as Hannah's guest, all but snubbed her.)

After minutes of wandering about the luxuriantly wide aisles of the store like a stubborn child searching for an elusive mother, Hannah sights Christina on the farther side of women's gloves, headed for an exit.

Unabashed, undeterred Hannah follows Christina outside the store, along a walkway. Christina turns a startled face to her as Hannah calls, "Hello? I thought that was you, Christina . . ."

Christina. It's clear that Christina Rusch is offended by this first-name familiarity, frowning at Hannah without (evident) recognition; yet, as a prominent member of the local aristocracy, a woman whose face is likely to be well-known, Christina manages to smile, if stiffly. Though saying nothing as Hannah hurriedly introduces herself, chattering nervously, not above reminding Christina Rusch that she and her husband were guests of Hannah's at the art museum dinner . . .

Vaguely, Christina seems to recall Hannah. Yes.

But still saying very little as Hannah tells Christina that she'd wanted to ask her more about the lake in northern Michigan where her family has a lodge, Hannah and her husband are planning to purchase a summer place in northern Michigan also . . .

With chilling equanimity the older woman allows Hannah to speak at length, not encouraging her with the sort of social cues (small smiles, nods of the head) to which Hannah is accustomed in such circumstances; uneasily, Hannah is reminded of her own mother, indeed of her mother-in-law. Is Hannah being rebuffed, snubbed—*again*? But stubbornly refusing to acknowledge the other's coolness even as Christina shakes her head curtly *no*, she can't offer advice, she knows very little about "real estate" in northern Michigan, or anywhere. (The words "real estate" are given a quaint intonation, as if they are slang.) Her family—"Not Harold's family: mine"—has owned property on North Fox Lake for more than one hundred years, they haven't purchased anything in decades, and in any case North Fox Lake is "all built-up"—the entire lakefront is privately owned, no open land remains and no properties come on the "market"—they are likely to pass down through families, generation after generation.

"Oh. I see." Hannah smiles, foolishly. "I guess I—should have known."

Why do you dislike me! I am trying so hard, have pity on me.

Christina has been glancing about, distracted. Hannah sees a vehicle approaching through the parking lot.

Of course, Christina Rusch hasn't driven herself to the mall. She must have a driver, a chauffeur.

Relenting slightly, as if she does pity Hannah, or feels an actual surge of sympathy for her, Christina says, "There are plenty of northern Michigan properties, I'm sure. You might try a good realtor."

This most banal of remarks Hannah is grateful for, like pennies flung to a street urchin.

For a moment it seems as if Christina might recommend a *good realtor,* but no, Christina can't supply a name.

Approaching at a speed too high for the mall roadway, the silver-gray Cadillac de Ville brakes to a jolting stop at the curb. Impertinently the driver taps the horn as if Christina can't be trusted to have seen for herself that her car has arrived.

Strange behavior for a chauffeur, Hannah thinks. If that's what the driver is.

Without staring at him, Hannah sees that he is a (white) man in his mid-thirties, wearing a coat with oddly wide shoulders that resembles a uniform, but evidently is not a uniform; a visored cap is pulled low over his forehead. But he is slouch-shouldered, sulky; his face is oblong, partly obscured by dark glasses and a drooping, outsized mustache in need of trimming.

Beneath the coat, Hannah sees, is a black T-shirt with a stretched neck. The visored cap is a Detroit Lions cap.

Certainly not a chauffeur, for this negligent person doesn't climb out of the car to open a rear door for Mrs. Rusch, or to take her packages from her; instead, Christina prepares to sit in the passenger seat in the front, struggling with the packages until Hannah steps forward to assist her.

"Oh, thank you . . ."

The driver glares at Hannah, as at an interloper. He isn't grateful that Hannah has helped Christina but seems to be frankly annoyed by her.

The (unmarried) son, Hannah thinks. What's the name?—*Bernard.*

Hannah can see why such a churlish person, no longer young, in no way attractive, might be a topic of troubled conversation between his parents.

Christina is embarrassed, her face flushes with chagrin. She has no inclination to introduce Hannah to the glowering man beside her.

"Well—thank you! Please say hello to your husband for me . . ."

Hannah smiles brightly: "Please say hello to *your* husband for me."

Christina has forgotten Wes's name, very likely she has forgotten Hannah's name. But Hannah is determined not to feel slighted.

Hannah stands on the walkway watching the elegant automobile pull away from the curb, jerking forward. The driver seems determined to annoy his passenger, as an adolescent son might annoy a parent, accelerating the vehicle so that he is forced to brake again at the first crosswalk.

Hannah watches, considering. How does a mother live with such a hostile adult son! Beneath Christina Rusch's chilly reserve there must be (surely) a lacerated heart.

Bernard looked much older than thirty-two yet exuded an air of decayed adolescence, and the insolence of adolescence: an adult son with no evident income of his own. In the hire of his mother, as a chauffeur. A misfit, a disappointment.

And the Rusches are millionaires, many times over.

What has gone wrong?—Hannah wonders.

"Today in Neiman Marcus I met Christina Rusch," Hannah tells Wes at dinner that evening, "we shopped together for a while, and had a very interesting conversation."

Wes seems only mildly interested. He'd arrived home late, he is very hungry and is already on his second glass of wine.

"She's such a lovely woman," Hannah says. "She asked to be remembered to you."

"Did she!"—Wes smiles faintly.

Hannah is baffled: What is wrong? Wes had been so eager for a social connection with Harold Rusch, she'd thought. It had been Wes's suggestion to invite the Rusches, whom Hannah scarcely knew, as their guests to the fundraiser.

Something must have gone wrong between the men. Or possibly, nothing had happened, to Wes's disappointment.

Hannah persists telling Wes about her encounter with Christina Rusch. How oddly it ended: "A driver came to pick Christina up, I'd assumed he was a chauffeur at first but he turned out to be, I think, the Rusches' son Bernard." Though not encouraged by Wes, who isn't looking at her but at the food on his plate, Hannah says that Christina tried to introduce him but it was very awkward—"He isn't at all social. I wonder if he's—is it 'autistic'? *Not* 'artistic'—'autistic.' Though he's supposed to be a photographer, I think. He just glared at me, he didn't say a word. It was so strange, uncomfortable—he and Christina barely acknowledged each other as if they'd been quarreling and didn't want to start in again."

Still Wes isn't very interested. His expression is neutral, stiff. Even the topic of the hostile Rusch son has failed to intrigue him.

"I suppose they'd hoped their son would come to work at GM. Or work at *something*. People say that Christina is cold and distant but I haven't found her that way at all, she's very friendly. But she's very private. A private person. Before the car came to pick her up she said she hoped the four of us might get together soon. You know what would be wonderful?—if they invited us to visit them in northern Michigan this summer at North Fox Lake."

"Really!"—Wes shrugs, scarcely listening.

Yes, something has gone wrong. Whatever connection Wes had hoped to establish with GM top executive Harold Rusch has come to nothing, presumably.

As much in life comes to nothing, and is not likely to be acknowledged.

You fawned on Harold, I've fawned on Christina. At least show some interest in what I am saying.

It's a frequent disappointment in the marriage: Hannah hopes to impress her husband with a bit of news, a glance into her fascinating daily life apart from him, her casual mingling with Bloomfield Hills wealth, but Wes fails to be intrigued.

"He was strange, not very courteous. He has the sort of mustache you want to rip off, it looks so fake—dyed . . ."

"Who?"—Wes glances up from his plate, annoyed.

"The son. Bernard Rusch."

"Why the hell are we talking about him, Hannah? Why would you think that I have the slightest interest in someone's son whom I have never met, and never will?"

Hannah is confounded. She asks Wes why he'd insisted that she offer two six-hundred-dollar tickets to the Rusches for the art museum gala if he's so little interested in them and Wes responds coldly that *he* hadn't asked her, inviting the Rusches had been her idea entirely.

"My idea?" Hannah is stunned, this is so unexpected. "I—I don't even know them . . ."

"Well—*I* don't know them, either."

Hannah stares at Wes to see if he is joking. He is not.

.   .   .

Realizing, later: She'd seen Bernard Rusch before that day.

The sulky peevish face, glaring eyes behind tinted lenses, aviator sunglasses, drooping mustache . . . grimy baseball cap pulled low on his forehead.

Sallow skin, complexion like sandpaper. A weak chin. But what hatred directed toward *her* . . .

Not in Far Hills but in Detroit she'd seen him, this person, in the hotel corridor outside Y.K.'s suite: a stranger of no distinctive age but probably in his mid-thirties; stepping out of the elevator some distance away, turning in Hannah's direction and walking with quick strides as if he knew his destination, which room he was headed for; but then, seeing Hannah, and seeing the number of the room, he continued past Hannah even as, not entirely aware of him, Hannah stepped back, and collided with him.

Excuse me, ma'am!—he'd hissed at her.

Under his breath—*Stupid cunt.*

Remembering now. How quickly she'd forgotten him. Tried to forget.

Excised the memory until that afternoon. Abruptly then, in the Cadillac pulling up to the curb. Had to be the Rusches' adult son.

Why such animosity between son and mother!—Hannah wonders.

No: the son's animosity, directed toward the mother . . .

That angry stare, ice-pick eyes inside the tinted lenses. Contempt, revulsion. He'd glared at Hannah in the hotel corridor, as he'd glared at Hannah in the rearview mirror of the Cadillac when she'd set Christina's packages carefully onto the backseat.

Hannah had quite liked it, helping Christina Rusch into the car, taking packages from her. As if they were friends, intimates. As if, for all the hostile son knew, they'd been shopping together at Neiman Marcus.

Ignored the hostility in the man's gaze. That in other circumstances would have alerted her to the possibility of bodily harm.

A man who loathes women.

A man who could eviscerate a woman.

If a rat were becoming a man . . .

No reason for him to look at Hannah with such hatred, a stranger to him: *misogyny.*

Uneasily Hannah wonders if he'd recognized her, in his mother's company.

If, not knowing Hannah's name, he recalled her from weeks ago in the Renaissance Grand Hotel. A woman poised to knock on the door of Y.K.'s suite.

But what was Y.K. to him?—it seemed hardly possible to Hannah, the crude ungainly Rusch son would be acquainted with Y.K.

Of course, Rusch is the son of wealthy parents. And Y.K. is a "businessman"—of some sort.

Hannah lies awake for the remainder of the night, thinking.

Tormented as by swarming red ants: Can there be any connection between Y.K. and Bernard Rusch?—for (possibly) (surely) Rusch had been headed for Y.K.'s suite until he saw Hannah preparing to knock; he'd seen, he'd decided to keep on walking, walking fast, exiting at the end of the corridor.

Had he taken the stairs down to the sixtieth floor, and then the elevator down to the foyer . . . He'd been aware of *her*, but she hadn't been aware of *him*.

She'd forgotten him entirely at the time. As women forget men who've spoken obscenely to them, if they are otherwise unknown to them.

Hanging from the doorknob—DO NOT DISTURB.

But Hannah had summoned her courage to knock at the door. And the door was opened.

Rehearsal

So long she has rehearsed the cool, curt reply *No.*
   Cool, curt *No. I'm afraid I can't.*
Hanging up on him. As he is speaking.
Just—hang up the receiver.
Sorry, no.
No more.

Asks Herself: Why?

Kitchen phone rings, Hannah answers trembling, not a good sign, standing very still pressing the receiver against her ear speechless, scarcely able to hear his words through the roaring of blood in her ears.

But *his voice,* she recognizes.

Giving her instructions: place, date, time.

No explanation, no apology, as if they'd spoken just the other day, he's in good spirits, his voice is deeper than Hannah recalls, he's amused by her, he's laughing at her, he's delighted by her, the faint quavering girl's voice—

No. Cannot.

Telling her *Darling yes you can.*

Fumbles hanging up the beige plastic receiver, it slips off the hook, dangles at the end of the rubber cord like a writhing creature.

Never Look Back to See
Where a Smile Has Gone

Parks her car at the Far Hills Marriott, North Telegraph Avenue, 11:50 A.M., May 9, 1977.

Hands the keys to a parking attendant who hands her a ticket in return, scarcely notices the uniformed attendant, tall, broad-shouldered, dark-skinned smiling *Good mornin', ma'am!* as she would scarcely notice a robot attendant in his place, though polite, unfailingly polite, simulating a radiant smile—*Yes! Good morning to you, too.*

Slips the ticket into the Prada handbag, of course it will be "lost" in the bag's clutter.

The uniformed attendant who parks Hannah's car before lunch is the identical attendant who will return the car to Hannah after lunch.

Pure chance this individual happens to be Zekiel Jones—in news accounts to be identified as "Zekiel Jones, 31."

On this day Hannah is attending a noon luncheon meeting of the Far Hills Historical Society at the Marriott. And this, too, purely chance.

The Far Hills Historical Society is smaller and less prestigious than the Friends of the Detroit Institute of Arts, still it's an honor to be invited to cochair the society's annual fundraiser. Hannah Jarrett was eager to volunteer months ago; now, not so eager, polite but distracted, indeed very distracted thinking of *him*.

She hates him, she is fearful of him.

Fearful she will sabotage her marriage, and why?—for *him*.

Other men bore her, might as well concede. She is transfixed by *him*.

One glass of prosecco at lunch, scarcely finished.

So little alcohol in prosecco, hardly considered a *drink*.

Men (like Wes) laugh at prosecco. Christ! Not for me.

Telling herself *No.* Through the meeting in a private room at which Hannah picks at a crab salad plate, sips prosecco, possibly she'd ordered a second glass, certainly didn't finish the second glass if she had.

Christ *no.* Jesus!

Nine women at the meeting, including Hannah, earnest talkers, how seriously they take themselves, Hannah feels a vise tightening around her head, so passionately the women are discussing the menu for the September fundraiser—beef, seafood, fish . . .

Hannah is listening. Hannah is engaged. *Yes, yes*—all the suggestions are good.

Salmon, halibut, sea bass—all good.

Must be a fact of great gravity, that some husbands hate fish, some husbands will only eat steak, wisest to offer both, plus the (inevitable) *vegetable platter . . .*

Wanting to scream, she is so, so *bored.*

Without *him* in her life, so utterly *bored.*

One o'clock, and now one-fifteen: amazing to Hannah that she hasn't (yet) made her decision. Anxious, jittery, excited clammy-cold hands trembling. Will this woman turn left out of the Marriott driveway (in the direction of the interstate entrance at Maple Road) or will she turn right onto Telegraph (returning to the Village of Far Hills) like the good little wifey. Dry cleaner for the husband's suit, Village Cobbler for the husband's (resoled) shoes.

Stops at the pharmacy, grocery store. Always errands, a pleasure in errands, suburban errands like saying the beads of the rosary for the good little wifey.

Of course, Hannah will turn right. Not for a moment has she seriously considered turning left.

Yet: She is meticulously, beautifully groomed for this luncheon attended solely by women. She is elegantly dressed, there is calculation in the day's clothing, earrings, jewelry, a discreet touch of that old classic Chanel No. 5 . . .

The time *he* has told her is three that afternoon.

This time when, as he has promised, he will *be free.*

A curious usage: *free.* As if, just minutes before, he will have been bound.

Three o'clock is several hours later than the first time. But the room, the suite, is identical: 6183.

He has informed her beforehand of the number. No need to embarrass herself picking up a message from the concierge, like the last time.

Crudely scrawled message he couldn't be bothered to have secured in a sealed envelope . . .

Futile to wonder why, if he always stays in the same suite at the hotel, he'd left the message for Hannah with the concierge; why he couldn't simply have told Hannah the suite number when he called her . . .

He uses different rooms. Different purposes.

But no need to contemplate *why*. *How* is more urgent.

Considering: Should she, should she not. Like pulling the trigger of a revolver in which there's just one bullet—"Russian roulette."

He won't actually know if Hannah is coming, smug bastard is due for a surprise.

DO NOT DISTURB. Taunting sign on his door, he'd (maybe) not intended.

He'd intended. Certainly.

"And what do you think, Hannah?"

Hannah stares. No idea what she has been asked.

"Crème brûlée, poached pear, cheesecake, cherries jubilee . . ."

Hannah stammers an answer that seems to placate the other women. Face is so suffused with blood, heart so erratically pumping, she understands that a decision must have been made for her without her knowledge.

"Well, we've certainly accomplished a lot today!"

"We *have*."

After the luncheon Hannah doesn't linger to chat warmly with the others as she usually does. Hoping, always hoping, that one of the women will suggest to her an evening with their husbands, at the Bloomfield Country Club perhaps, or, better yet, at the woman's home; if not already a friend, there will be an exchange of telephone numbers, the heady pleasure of adding a new name to Hannah's address book.

Except not today. Today, Hannah excuses herself to hurry to a women's restroom on another level of the hotel, where (she assumes, correctly) she won't encounter any of the Historical Society members, then exits the hotel to the parking garage where, vexed, flush-faced, she rummages through the oversized handbag failing to locate the little cardboard parking stub she'd carelessly slipped into it—not the first time that Mrs. Jarrett has lost a ticket in an oversized handbag but no matter, the courteous parking attendant remembers Hannah, attractive older blond white lady driving the new-model Buick Riviera he'd parked on B-level. Roughly half of the (female) lunchtime patrons of the Marriott misplace their parking stubs in their oversized handbags, no point in becoming exasperated, or upset, or enraged, nor is Zekiel Jones likely to betray any emotion other than good-natured affability, he has lived his entire life within a radius of twenty dense-packed miles and most of these within the fabled "inner" city of Detroit ravaged by the construction of I-75 in the late 1950s and later by the "riot" of July 1967, smiling as he parked the white lady's white Buick for her and now as he retrieves it for her, wide boyish smile, as handsome as (a darker) Harry Belafonte, as Hannah, embarrassed, murmuring an apology, genuinely contrite (yet) not surprised that she has been so readily forgiven by the parking attendant, presses on Zekiel Jones a ten-dollar tip though the parking charge is but three dollars and twenty cents—*Thank you, ma'am!*

Calling after, as Hannah prepares to drive away—*You have a good day, ma'am.*

Predator, Prey

On the sixty-first floor of the hotel tower *he* awaits her.

Tall vertical plate-glass windows whose blinds he has yanked up brutally to open to the sky.

Glaring light, he loves it. As a fighter pilot he'd loved it. Full sun, all exposed, nowhere for prey to hide in such light.

Vacancy of blue, froth of clouds. For hundreds of miles no impediments to the predator's vision.

Cruising, soaring on wide wings that can appear languorous, lazy from a distance but you'd be mistaken: The predator is always on the hunt.

Below, the timorous prey. Weak eyes, dim brain. Heightened heartbeat and nostrils rapidly sniffing as if death came upward from the earth, not swooping down from above.

Glide of wide wings, a shadow passes over. Frantic scurrying for cover but—too late.

Flapping wings, razor claws, tearing, terrible scimitar beak.

Of what are you capable? You have no idea.

Is that Hannah? A figure comprised of pixels.

Watching herself entranced. On a monitor in the hotel lobby, in fact a sequence of monitors set in a wall at a height of about twelve feet, grainy blurred screens and on each screen a woman's imprecise figure, wraithlike, suspended, crossing the lobby of the Renaissance Grand Hotel.

Let him wonder if I am coming to him.

Already she has resisted: She is late arriving at the hotel. Fifteen minutes, now twenty minutes. Soon she will be a defiant half hour late.

Turning left leaving the driveway at the Far Hills Marriott was the decision. All that has followed, consequence.

Taking her second parking ticket of the day from a uniformed (smiling, courteous) young attendant at the Renaissance Grand, Hannah was careful to place this ticket in a zippered compartment in her handbag, doesn't intend to make the same foolish mistake twice in one day.

Nor does she pass by the concierge's desk in the hotel lobby. Not about to risk the portly jovial smiling uniformed man recognizing her in a squint—*Ma'am? M.N.?—no message for you today.*

The atrium lobby is crowded. Several conventions are being held at the hotel of which one is the Midwestern Radiologists' Association: a preponderance of women, attractive young women, plastic ID badges on their lapels.

She might have been one of them, a radiologist conferee having coffee in the lobby of the Renaissance Grand with other conferees.

A useful life. A life in the service of others. Medical science, knowledge. Maybe she'd never married . . . Only the weak fall in love, they see no way of living otherwise.

But her parents would not have approved. Wouldn't have paid her tuition. Service occupation, hands-on. No.

One of the radiologists, first name Linda, smiling at Hannah as if she knows her—"Hi!"—but in the next instant realizes her mistake, *doesn't* know Hannah.

Hannah in her beautiful clothes, steep-heeled Saint Laurent pumps. *Not* a radiologist.

Rich man's wife at the luxury hotel to meet friends. A friend.

In the row of TV monitors on the wall the solitary female figure reappears still wraithlike, imprecise. Face blurred.

At the row of elevators waiting with others who wear ID badges and chatter among themselves but when an elevator arrives, engorged with passengers, spilling out passengers, Hannah draws away, doesn't join the chattering women who step into the elevator, waits for another . . . She is becoming mildly anxious now, she needs to be alone.

An elevator at the farther end of the row of elevators, glass door slides open, no choice.

Pressing the lighted numeral—61.

Admiring her manicured nails, nails newly polished, pearly saffron, which is a new shade. Yes, and she'd had her hair rinsed, "lightened." Streaks of gray, silver-gray, at her temples, she'd seen in distress in the mirror, now vanished.

So very tired of sick guilt, Hannah is unapologetic caring (for once!) for herself. The fact is, Katya did not die of meningitis, was nowhere near dying in the hospital. In this, Wes is certainly correct.

Hannah's rings glitter with miniature fractals of light.

Hannah is newly vain about her hands, never gave her hands a second thought but concerned in recent months that blue veins will (soon) emerge in the smooth skin of the backs of her hands. And at the edges of her eyes, tiny white puckers like those faint creases at the corners of Marlene Reddick's eyes.

Stricken eyes, avoiding Hannah's.

Of course! He has been her lover, too.

Rising silently into the hotel atrium as into the sky.

Thinking of the stricken eyes of women: Hannah's mother was the first.

Closing the door to Hannah as the child hurried to her—*No. Go away. Not now, you are not wanted now.*

Rising into the hotel atrium as into the sky as her mother had never done, never dared.

And why?—because at the roadway at the Far Hills Marriott she'd turned the steering wheel of the Buick to the left. Of her own volition, she'd turned the wheel. Until that moment it had not been clear to Hannah which way her hands would turn the wheel.

Yet not certain if *she'd* turned the wheel or if the wheel had *turned* Hannah's hands.

Lightly sweating palms of Hannah's hands.

Then, as in a dream: south on the interstate into the sprawling sepia haze city of Detroit.

South, as the land slants toward the Detroit River. Pull of gravity, fate.

What were those smooth cool stones laid upon her eyes?—*claim, doom.*

Feeling slightly dizzy as the hotel lobby sinks away. All your life you fear fainting in a public place, losing consciousness—*falling.*

A struck, staring blond woman in the glass cubicle. White-faced as if bloodless. Entranced by open floors, railings, stretches of concrete wall dropping rapidly as the elevator rises. Glimpses of faces, individuals awaiting a *down* elevator, fleeting and gone in the next second.

A catacomb of the dead. Skulls' flat blank faces, empty eyes.

But *she* is not among the dead, is she? Hannah is certain, she is not.

On the sixty-first floor of the tower the sleek glass cubicle stops with a hiss and a mild jolt, the glass door slides open. No choice but to step out.

He will think that I'm not coming . . .

Now Hannah is feeling less defiant, more repentant.

. . . he may be gone. To punish.

(Wondering if *he* is waiting near the elevator—but no, no one in sight.)

(Of course. No one in sight.)

Even after the steering wheel of the Buick had turned left—(Hannah is beginning to recall distinctly, the wheel seemed to turn of its own accord: all she'd done was not resist)—it hadn't been decided *irrevocably*.

For at each of myriad exits along I-75 Hannah might have exited her vehicle and returned (home) on the northbound highway. Even after the white Buick exited the interstate for the Renaissance Center it had not been *irrevocably determined* that Hannah would proceed to park her car at the hotel, handing over the ignition key to a parking attendant; it had not been *irrevocably determined* that Hannah would pass through the revolving doors, cross the hotel lobby, linger amid radiologists having a coffee break from panels and presentations, and (at last) take the sleek glass cubicle to the sixty-first floor where *he* is awaiting her.

It's a fact: At each juncture Hannah is free to make a contrary decision that carries her away from, and not toward, *him;* a decision that carries her away from, and not toward, the devastation of lives which going to *him* will precipitate. Fascinating to Hannah, who has constructed her life as a means of exploiting her own passivity, to be forced to see how free she is: how alert, excited, aroused and aware and in a state of anticipation she *really* is, and not "fated."

Considering that she might bypass the Detroit City Center exit, continue on to the tunnel beneath the river and into Windsor, Ontario.

She might, for she has the option, continue into the northern wilderness of the vast province of Ontario, Canada, where she knows no one and is known by no one.

Where do the *missing* go, when they disappear?

For surely the *missing* are not missing to themselves, only to others.

Quickly, before she can change her mind, as soon as she stands before the door marked 6183, Hannah rings the bell.

A beat, two beats. No response.

Inclines her head to the door, listening. Does she hear Y.K. speaking?—on the phone? Thinks she can hear—something . . .

Can't breathe. The tension is so great, a vise around her chest, her weak lung about to collapse . . .

Poised on the brink. Precipice. Thinking—*But I can leave, none of this has happened yet.*

Then, the door is opened inward. Y.K. in the doorway, taller than Hannah recalls, more *heft* to his body. In her memory his features have blurred and softened but in person he's exactly as before—sharp-boned face, ridge of bone above the eyes, heavy-lidded eyes glistening with reptilian mirth. His hands grab roughly at her, a kind of playful roughness, mock-playful roughness pulling the woman into the room, at once the door is shut behind her, safety chain secured.

Stumbling in stiletto heels like an ungainly long-legged bird, forced smile, terrified eyes.

Did you think I wasn't coming?—Hannah has rehearsed a brightly flirtatious edgy greeting, Hannah will not allow herself a pleading apology—*I'm sorry, I was caught in traffic* . . .

Y.K. doesn't hear, isn't listening, as one would not trouble to listen to the chattering of a frightened child, pulling Hannah through the white-walled sitting room into the adjoining bedroom and to the enormous (unmade) bed in that room as Hannah tries to keep pace to keep from losing her balance and falling, how absurd to fall, humiliating, laughable for Y.K. would simply lift her, drag her to the bed, Joker Daddy shakes his head at such ignominy, such shame, for desperation in the weak is shame, how taken by surprise Hannah is this second time stepping out of a corridor and into room 6183 as if there might have been another scenario awaiting her behind a door from which the sign DO NOT DISTURB hangs with insolent intent.

By the time the gliding shadow passes over, already the prey has been extinguished: delicate bones crushed, brain reduced to pulp, fleeting shadow-memories mere soot.

Far above her *he* regards her. A conquered territory, for which the conqueror feels mingled contempt and tenderness for it is *his* territory, devastated and unresisting before him.

Her groping hands try to reach him but fall short. Her fingers are weak, her wrists are broken. He is deep inside her, she is impaled upon him as upon a hook piercing her lower body. A terrible searing flame shoots upward, in waves. His hands move upon her pliant torso, her fatty breasts, these are the hands of a blind man coolly curious to see the woman by touch, kneading and squeezing with fingers that do not hesitate to exert their strength. Like a sculptor's hands running over her, shaping her, gripping her breasts as if to test the resiliency of her flesh, its very texture. Her breasts ache with sensation like the breasts of a lactating mother, nipples as raw as if Hannah has been nursing, small hungry sucking mouths have been feeding on her, tearing at her, pitiless in appetite.

Hannah has begun to writhe, the flame rising through her body is unbearable. Darkness opening at the back of her skull like black blood. She has no name for the man, she has forgotten his name, when she cries out desperately to him he covers her mouth with the flat grammar of his hand—*No.*

Close by are twelve-foot windows, unfettered blinds pulled to the ceiling. A white-glaring sky, light ricocheting off surfaces so evenly that there are no shadows.

In such light the prey is exposed, scurrying across the ground in search of a burrow, even a shadow in which to hide. But there are no shadows.

Sixty floors below the river is so roughened by wind you could not say in which direction the current is flowing.

. . .

I have a lover. This man is my lover.

Half conscious, Hannah hears her lover moving about the room. Not daring to open her eyes from her heavy, stuporous sleep that came over her like ether.

Fearing that if he sees she is awake, he will indicate that he wants her gone.

Lying in a trance of oblivion scarcely daring to breathe. Not-moving, suspended as in a dream. Has her back been injured? Her spine fractured, broken? As if her lover dropped her from a great height like a mollusk dropped from the beak of a raptor so that its shell cracks on rocks, its moist boneless white flesh can be easily sucked out, devoured.

Yet Hannah feels a rush of joy. Wild joy, springing tears from her eyes.

I have a lover . . .

She is laughing, gloating. She is suffused with pride: astonished.

Sixteen miles from the house on Cradle Rock Road where they know her as wife, mother.

Little wifey, good Mommy.

Joker Daddy is utterly astonished, speechless for once.

Is this Joker Daddy's daughter? No more.

A phone rings, startlingly close to Hannah's head. *He* curses under his breath, goes into the adjoining room of the suite to answer it.

Hannah will not lift the receiver on the bedside table. No.

Hannah seems to know that if she lifts the receiver, if she hopes to eavesdrop on a conversation not meant for her to hear, Y.K. will storm cursing into the bedroom, knock the receiver flying from her fingers, and for good measure slap her stunned face backhandedly . . . And so, Hannah does not lift the receiver.

But Hannah has roused herself from her trance, rises from the rumpled bed. Makes her way raw-naked, barefoot, spine aching as if it has been fractured, to stand at the shut door, inclining her head to listen.

Y.K.'s voice is lowered, near-inaudible. But Hannah can hear that he is furious.

. . . fuck told you not now.

I said—not now. *And don't call back.*

I will call you.

Hannah hears Y.K. hang up the receiver. Backs away quickly from the door.

Mesmerized by the man's life, apart from her. All that in him is unknown to her.

Another call, in the adjoining room. This one, Y.K. is making himself.

Is he calling another woman?—Hannah wonders, stricken.

So petty! Sex-jealousy, a woman of her age . . .

Making plans, of course the man is making plans. You are either part of a man's *plans,* or you are not.

Hannah thinks, rebuffed: She is not wanted now, it is time for her to leave.

Better for her to leave, surprise Y.K. by leaving earlier than he'd have expected, if he offers her a drink from the minibar she will decline. *Wish I could but they are expecting me back home, the children will be just home from school.*

As if Y.K. might feel a twinge of jealousy, at the thought of Hannah's domestic life in Far Hills . . .

In a closet with paneled mirrors for doors Hannah discovers a white terry-cloth robe, of a size to fit her. A larger robe, kingly, enormous, fit for a man, hangs on a hanger beside it.

With some effort Hannah puts on the smaller robe. The terry-cloth fabric is strangely heavy, the robe weighs on her shoulders like lead. But Hannah is relieved, no longer naked, as vulnerable as a mollusk without its shell.

Avoiding the face in the mirror. Makeup gone, mascara smudged. Reddened mouth, smudged. She will lock herself in the bathroom with the Prada bag in which she carries crucial supplies in small quantities. Wash her sticky smelly battered body, try to repair the damage to her face, hair . . . Yet she moves slowly, like one awaiting instructions.

In the next room Y.K. is speaking on the phone. Hannah feels a pang of envy, whomever Y.K. has called is someone to whom he has something to say, his voice lowered, urgent. Hannah listens but cannot decipher his words.

He has never spoken to her like that, Hannah thinks.

He has never taken her *seriously* like that.

While Y.K. is on the phone Hannah dares to examine his clothes hanging in the closet—several dress shirts, two pairs of trousers, two matching coats, all of excellent quality. In the (silk-lined) coat pockets, nothing.

And there, on a stand at the foot of the bed, Y.K.'s suitcase.

The suitcase, too, Hannah dares to examine but discovers nothing exceptional inside—neatly folded undershirts, shorts, (black, silk) socks; most of the suitcase has been unpacked.

In a zippered compartment in the suitcase which might have been easy to overlook Hannah discovers a miscellany of financial statements, legal documents, computer printouts of long columns of figures, a small address book, a U.S. passport.

Hannah dares to leaf through the passport, which is thick with visas—Egypt, Israel, China, India, Thailand.

Her lover has traveled, much. This does not surprise her.

The passport is issued to *Yaakel Benjamin Keinz,* born New York City, 1935—this does surprise her.

Her lover is an American citizen, Hannah thinks. Somehow she hadn't expected this.

Is the man in the photograph her lover? Hannah isn't sure.

Yaakel Benjamin Keinz. To Hannah an exotic name, Jewish?—German?

Possibly, this is a younger Y.K. in the picture. His face leaner, the ridge of bone above his eyes less distinctive, the eyes not so heavy-lidded but clear, frank, affable.

In this face, candor. An expression that Hannah has never seen in her lover's face.

The more Hannah examines the passport photograph of *Yaakel Benjamin Keinz* the less certain she feels that this is Y.K. Though the thick-tufted hair is very like Y.K.'s hair, and the line of the jaw, there is something about the eyes, and the mouth . . .

Hannah shudders. Something is wrong here, hairs stir at the nape of her neck.

Hurriedly Hannah returns the passport to the compartment where she'd found it but in her haste she can't remember exactly where it had been, nearer the outside of the suitcase, or the inside; nor can she remember if the compartment was zipped closed, or only just partway.

All this while, Y.K. is speaking on the phone in the next room. Hannah backs away from the suitcase feeling a wave of relief.

Wanting to feel a wave of relief.

No time to take a shower here in the hotel, in the luxurious white-tiled bathroom, Hannah will shower when she returns home, in the safety and privacy of her home standing under the hot hot shower for as long as she can bear it.

Reapplying makeup on the sallow face, little dollops of liquid makeup, no time to rub expensive moisturizer deep into her skin, that, too, Hannah will do at home.

Rummages for a lipstick in the Prada bag, badly needing to enliven her face.

But her hair!—matted, disheveled like an ill-fitting wig.

Dares to smile at herself in the mirror, a flinching sort of smile, abashed, apprehensive.

Still Hannah—still you (me).

As a child she'd tormented herself with wondering if there could be a time when, when you look into a mirror, there will be no one in the mirror to look back at you.

Tormenting herself now with the most banal uncertainties: Should she seek out Y.K. in the other room to tell him that she must leave, or should she return to the bedroom, to change into her clothes?

Not wanting to interrupt his phone conversation. Not wanting to seem to be listening to it.

And will Hannah dare ask when he will see her again? When he will call her.

The protocol of lovers is foreign to Hannah, it took her years to become comfortable with the protocol of marriage. Does physical intimacy between individuals guarantee some measure of a more general intimacy, or is there no (necessary) connection at all?—will she regret it if she mis-assumes?

Always on edge with Y.K. Never feeling at ease.

Sexual excitement: essence of *unease*.

When Hannah returns to the bedroom she's startled to see that Y.K. is waiting for her there, phone call ended. His expression is curious, bemused.

He is smiling, in his way. With affection? Tenderness? *Is* he smiling?

Leaning indolently against a bureau, starkly naked, indifferent to his nakedness, arms folded across his chest in a pose of ironic stillness as if he has been waiting for a long time for Hannah to join him.

"H'lo, beautiful Han-nah!"—Y.K. seems amused.

Hannah is thinking that, if Y.K., or Yaakel Keinz, was born in 1935, he is now forty-two. (Hannah was born in 1938.) Assuming that Y.K. *is* the man in the passport photograph.

A predator male, self-delighting, exulting in his own being, unlike any man Hannah has known intimately, including Joker Daddy. For most men Hannah has known are insecure in some way, and Y.K. is not.

An attractive man, confident that women will adore him. His body is no longer the body of a young man, beginning to thicken at the waist, the muscles of shoulders, upper arms, thighs are beginning to soften, yet the man is fit, compact, probably quite strong. Probably quite quick, if quickness is required.

On his shoulders, arms, legs, and at his groin is a pelt of kinky dark hairs, grizzled-gray on his chest. Hannah knows, his muscled back is covered in thick dark hairs also, in erratic swaths.

Hannah feels a fainting sensation, recalling the patchy pelt on his back. The startling feeling, at her fingertips.

She hears herself explain that she has to leave. She hears herself laughing. She is nervous, breathless. What to say to a stranger who is her *lover*?

Almost, their relationship is like an arranged marriage. It had been determined that they would be lovers, Hannah had had no choice, as soon as she'd felt the stranger's fingers circle her wrist.

"Is something wrong, Hannah? What is it?"

Hannah sees: Y.K. seems to have posed in a way that, as she faces him, she can't avoid seeing the suitcase at the foot of the bed. In that instant she realizes—*He knows.*

That Hannah has looked through his suitcase—Y.K. knows. She has discovered the passport . . .

She knows the name he hadn't wanted her to know: *Yaakel Benjamin Keinz.*

Hannah is frightened, her mouth suddenly dry. Though Y.K. has not (yet) accused her. He is playful, flirtatious.

"You want to run away from me, eh?—can't stay for even one drink."

It is up to Hannah to determine: Does her lover sincerely regret that she is leaving, or is he being ironic?—teasing, or taunting?

Speaking with a ghost-remnant of an accent as if he were not a native American but foreign born: the spondee stress ("Han-nah") and the inflection ("eh?")—not typical of native speakers of English.

In this, Hannah thinks, beginning to panic, a circuitous reference to the suitcase: the (forbidden) passport removed from the (zippered) compartment.

An invasion of Y.K.'s privacy. Why has Hannah done such a thing!

Unless Hannah is imagining an accent. Unless Hannah is imagining much.

"Before you leave, darling. Just some minutes."

Some minutes—this, too, isn't typical American speech. Y.K. knows what she has done, and is tormenting Hannah.

"One drink—*'dlya dorogi.'*"

Hannah has no idea what this means. She has no idea what Y.K. has said. She is frightened, confused.

It seems that Y.K. has brought with him two miniature bottles of (white) wine from the minibar in the other room. But Hannah doesn't want a drink just now, not a drink just before she drives home on I-75, not a good idea, her jangled nerves, the wine she'd had at lunch, but Y.K. acknowledges none of this, remains heedless of her indecision, her anxiety; indeed, he is enjoying the small ceremony of opening the bottles, pouring the contents into two sparkling wineglasses, tapping his glass lightly against Hannah's when she has no choice but to take it from him.

"'Han-nah!' Who has come so far."

Hannah lifts the glass slowly to her lips. Takes a sip, cautiously. As if she were not tremulous, yearning for a drink.

Sweet-tart white wine, delicious wine, coursing through her blood like balm. A magical component to alcohol, Hannah thinks, a kind of shorthand, if you've been a practiced drinker you can anticipate its effect immediately, like one who, knowing her destination, feels immense relief and anticipation as she sets out.

As it's said that a drug addict feels the anticipatory thrill of the high, just assembling drug paraphernalia in her hands, these sacred tools, preparing to inject the magical solution into her veins.

Hannah takes just the cautious sip. Her hand is trembling badly.

Hears herself ask in a bright blithe way, as if nothing were wrong, when Y.K. will be leaving Detroit—and Y.K. says with a negligent shrug—"When? When my business is done."

"And your 'business' is—*business*?"

"What other kind of 'business' is there?"

Hannah laughs. Tries to think. As if amusing her lover might distract him.

"Well, not all 'business' is focused on—money . . . There is art, there is music, philanthropy . . ." Hannah's voice trails off, she can see that Y.K. isn't impressed.

" 'Philanthropy'!"—Y.K. laughs. "If you have money to toss away. If you are an 'heir.' "

Hannah laughs with her lover, uneasily. It is always like this in Y.K.'s presence: Hannah is drawn to emulate him as a torn sheet of paper is drawn into the wake of a speeding vehicle.

Does Y.K. think that Hannah has inherited money? A substantial sum of money? Joker Daddy would have found this supposition gratifying for Joker Daddy had skirted bankruptcy through much of his life and yet gave away money as well, to shrewdly selected organizations, and to select political campaigns, hoping to establish a reputation as a man of wealth and discerning generosity.

Had Joker Daddy died bankrupt? His children came to think so, for his estate hadn't included them. Pointedly, his estate had excluded them, as it had excluded their bereft mother.

Some things it's better not to know, Hannah's mother had advised, bitterly, yet in a way gratified, as if she had not anticipated the worst in vain. Determined to avoid contagion Hannah had made an effort not to learn too much about the private lives of her parents.

Wondering if Y.K. has made inquiries about her, in Detroit. Among mutual acquaintances. Inquiries about Wes Jarrett.

It isn't Hannah's family but her husband's, the Jarretts, longtime residents of Detroit, who have a history of local philanthropy.

Hannah asks when Y.K. will return to Detroit, does he know yet?

"No. Don't know."

A mild rebuff. *Of course* Y.K. doesn't like to be interrogated.

Of course Y.K. doesn't like a woman hoping to make a claim on his time.

Then, relenting: "Things happen quickly, in my business. If they are to happen at all."

Y.K. has been smiling at Hannah, as if recalling something that gives him pleasure.

"You know, Han-nah, the night we met?—all those people around us? That wasn't the first time."

"Wasn't it!"—Hannah is hoping to be enchanted.

"No. Not at all. I had a dream—dreams—of you, before that night. When I saw you, and you turned to me, and looked at me—your eyes . . . It came back to me then, the dream. And in your face I could see that you recognized me, too."

Hannah is taken by surprise, Y.K. is speaking almost humbly. He doesn't seem to be joking now.

He is saying—he loves me.

Is that what he is saying?

Hannah feels light-headed. No more wine!

Indeed Y.K. is regarding her tenderly. He takes Hannah's wineglass from her fingers, sets it down. With both hands he frames her face, he kisses her mouth.

He does not push his tongue into her mouth, he kisses her gently and almost formally, respectfully.

No kiss like this, from Y.K. Hannah is astonished.

"That was how I knew, Han-nah. That night, that we met. When I saw you. But you also—you saw me."

"Yes . . ."

"You knew me, yes?"

"I . . . I knew you."

Hannah isn't sure if this is true, yet, as she utters the words, mesmerized by her lover, the yeasty-sweaty smell of his body lifting to her nostrils, it is crucial to believe that everything she says is true.

"Will you call me, then? And not wait for so long?"—Hannah hears her voice wistful, pleading.

"Of course, dear Han-nah. You can believe that I will."

"Because I—I was worried . . ."

"No need to worry, Han-nah. Not about *me*."

"If you—could give me your number . . . Not that I would call you but if I wanted suddenly to speak to you, just to—speak with you . . . It would be good to have your number."

"Yes! Of course."

"And is there a name I can call you? 'Y.K.' isn't really a name."

"But yes, dear—'Y.K.' *is* a name. You must be content with 'Y.K.'"

Hannah hesitates, wondering if Y.K. is laughing at her. And if there is cruelty or tenderness in that laughter.

"Or, you could call me 'darling.'"

"'Darling'—!"

Hannah laughs, giddy. This is what it is—to have a lover.

The *lover* is the shadow, the eclipse. The marriage is full daylight.

The *lover* is outside the marriage, at a perpendicular angle to the marriage. The *lover* helps to define the marriage, for there is no *lover* without a marriage.

Hannah sees now, there is no true marriage without the *lover*. No wonder Hannah's marriage has been so incomplete, unsatisfying to her.

The children have made her *mother—Mommy*. Without knowing, Hannah has allowed *mother* to eclipse wife, woman. No wonder her husband has ceased to desire her, he has ceased to see her. Mommy is food, suffocating embraces, reproach, hurt at being insufficiently loved. Her lover will restore her, as a (sexual) woman.

Already, Hannah's lover has infiltrated her being, her blood. Mesmerized by him, she has not thought of Wes, she has not even thought of her children, for the past hour.

Intense sexual pleasure, annihilation of memory, conscience. The woman is left stunned, helpless.

Hannah has suspected that Wes has been involved with other women over the course of their marriage. Not in Far Hills (probably: Wes is discreet) but elsewhere, on business trips, those overnight trips when he calls her very late, or fails to call her. Fleeting relationships, she is sure. Professional escorts, possibly. These are not *lovers*, they have no role in the life of the marriage.

Hannah yearns to confide in Y.K., because he is her lover. Because she is on intimate terms with him, their sexual connection is actual, of the moment. Hannah yearns to lie in his arms, to *talk*.

To confess to him, her marriage is unsatisfying to her, ill-fitting like clothes that are the wrong size for her, too-tight shoes, she is bound tight, often she can't draw a deep breath.

Her children adore her but—do Hannah's children know *her*?

The children! Hannah realizes: She should leave the hotel. Time seems to have passed with unnatural swiftness, it has become late afternoon, beyond five o'clock. No idea how long she'd been asleep in that sodden bed, as if she'd been drugged.

Hannah needs to change into her clothes, not in Y.K.'s presence but in the bathroom, in privacy. She is desperate to be alone! But when she tries to ease out of his arms Y.K. doesn't release her.

It's simply natural, a kind of protocol, if you are being held, tight, if you make a move to detach yourself from someone's arms, the other will immediately comply—the other will release his grip, release you.

But Y.K. doesn't release his grip on Hannah, and doesn't step away. He has begun kissing Hannah's neck, in a way that makes her shiver.

Hannah laughs nervously. She should leave, and Y.K. must want her to leave, yet now, as if whimsically, Y.K.'s mood has changed, he has become amorous, impassioned. Hannah doesn't know if he is being sincere or being funny—self-mocking . . . Hannah has no choice, she thinks, except to cooperate, to kiss him in return; she cannot offend this man who is her lover, and not her husband, for expectations are very different for lovers, than for husbands. Her relationship with Y.K. is new, and precarious; the smallest misunderstanding, an unintended insult, anything to suggest sexual rejection, Y.K. may be offended and cease loving her, his desire for Hannah extinguished like a lit match that has been shaken out.

A lover is not like a husband who shares a household and cannot easily walk out of the household, has no choice but to accept an apology, or to apologize . . .

Within marriage, much is forgiven. Outside marriage, forgiveness is a matter of choice.

"Excuse me, I—I should . . . I should leave"—Hannah tries to protest, not very forcibly. Despite her anxiety, she has been made to feel, in the pit of her belly, in the pulsing fork between her legs, a stab of (abject) desire: for Y.K. is a skilled lover, his tenderness is irresistible. Yet, Hannah must leave the hotel, and return home, gently she tries to break away from him . . .

Y.K. tugs off the terry-cloth robe, lets it drop onto the floor. Running his hands over her, as one might roughly caress a captive animal, daring it to shrink away, struggle to escape. It's a gesture of supreme possession. Hannah's skin that is chafed, as with sunburn, is made to smart anew. The gesture is so deliberate, *willed*—Hannah begins to be frightened.

The *heft* of the man is fearful to her, always a factor that alarms her, for she is not his equal, he is so much stronger than she, so much taller, heavier. In their conversation, in their speech, it comes to seem to Hannah that they are equals, or nearly; but when speech ceases, this conviction fades at once.

Y.K. tugs Hannah back to the bed, a badly rumpled and smelly bed, a pig's swill of a bed Hannah realizes, mortified . . . Why hadn't she at least made a gesture of smoothing out the sheets, pulling over the coverlet, as she does routinely when she and Wes travel and stay in hotels, for now she feels a wave of shame, revulsion, in no mood for love or intimacy or tenderness, wanting only to escape. Clearly her lover is laughing at her discomfort, the rich man's wife has become squeamish, apprehensive.

Y.K. knows: Hannah has dared to open his suitcase. Intuitively, Y.K. knows. He knows that Hannah has violated his trust in her—obviously. He is furious with her but will not express his fury directly, it isn't Y.K.'s way to be direct, Hannah can only infer the man's contempt, she wonders if leaving her alone with his suitcase had been a test, a test Y.K. had known that Hannah would fail; possibly, he'd contrived a trap for her, if she unzipped the compartment something would be displaced, a hair, or a thread, a paper clip . . . (Hadn't a paper clip fallen out of the compartment, lost amid socks and underwear?)

Hannah has blundered, badly. Naïveté would not save her.

Now it's too late, Y.K. will never forgive her.

For what delight in punishing such a contemptible person, striking away her feeble defenses as he pushes away her flailing hands, ignores her pleas—*But I can't stay, really I have to leave—I—have to be home by* . . .

Hannah's punishment: Her lover will exact a primitive revenge. He will make love to her in such a way that she is excluded, she will feel nothing but pain, *he* will feel intense pleasure while *she* will feel only pain.

The predator's body is a fine-tuned machine, impersonal, annihilating, weakly Hannah tries to respond, in a desperate pretense that nothing is wrong; but Y.K. laughs, gripping her wrists, pinning her down in the rumpled bed in such a way that she can't embrace him.

She stammers that she is sorry—in a delirium begging him to forgive her . . . Grunted syllables, sounds choking in her throat like spittle.

He has spat into her mouth, he is laughing at her distress. A probing snake of a tongue, coldly curious, cruelly jamming her mouth, her throat as if to choke her.

The pig's-swill bed, where piteous pleas and cries go unheard amid grunts of laughter.

The lover's heart is the heart of the predator, hardened, shriveled. Yet, a still-beating heart, inside the fine-tuned machine that is designed to punish, not to kill but to pound into submission.

Hannah cannot resist, Hannah has no strength to free herself. She would beg his forgiveness but he pays her no heed. His lovemaking is taut, percussive, without sentiment. Without memory: no idea who she is, not the slightest interest in knowing her. Between her legs is an open wound, bleeding. She is torn, lacerated. He has raked her insides with his nails, before entering her with his hard jabbing penis. She is being punished, but no more than she deserves. Still, she feels a kind of rousing, rising crude sensation, an angry pleasure, a threat of fire, fire that rises in a spasm of pain. Her lover is forcing Hannah to feel what he feels: She is not allowed to take refuge in oblivion, even in pain. *He will force her to feel the ignominy of such pleasure, in the pig's swill of a bed.*

Hannah's eyeballs shift in their sockets, her spine is arching like a bow pulled ever tighter. A death comes over her brain.

In a delirium her eyes swim onto a small patch of the ceiling by a window where shimmering light like water is reflected from the river far below. Her breath has been shredded, torn.

No one can rescue her except the person who has brought her to this place. *He* is her (only) salvation.

This drowning, annihilation. The knowledge is crushing to one who has believed herself special, cherished. Desirable in herself, her particular being.

. . . hearing soft cries, choked sobs. Humiliation in weeping. Yet a rough scouring-cleansing, in weeping.

Her lover laughs at her, such laughter is cruel and indifferent. She has been mistaken, there is little tenderness in her lover.

Through blue-hooded eyes he observes the woman, coldly. As a fighter pilot observes the ground far below, at a distance at which all living things are in miniature, inconsequential. At such a distance there are no faces. No individuals. The most piteous cries go unheard. There is something ludicrous, laughable in such abjection. The woman cannot bear it, this distance, impersonality. The woman cannot bear annihilation. She is helpless, the predator bores into her, tendons thicken in her neck. She hears herself shout, guttural cries like gravel against her throat. She has become a sinewy snake, every sweat-slick inch of her flesh quivering, her skin a damp scaly glisten. He has yanked one of the clammy-damp pillows out of the tangle of bedclothes, there's an air of caprice in his movements, the play of a cruel child, he lowers the pillow over her face, anguished eyes and gaping mouth, pumping hard between her fattish thighs as if there is a riddle in all this, what he might do to her if he wishes, if she does not resist, if she is complicit with what he might do to her, a woman with no name in this place alit with afternoon sun. Frantically she claws at his hands, she is suffocating, drowning, his wrists are too thick for her fingers to close about, there are coarse hairs on the backs of his hands, hairs like wires at his wrists. She is blinded by the pillow, her eyes are mashed shut. Frantic to breathe but cannot breathe. She has *crossed over* to her death, there is no going back. Her body begins to fail, her soul is suffocating, dazed. Her lover holds her fixed, she is impaled upon him, a great sinewy snake helpless beneath his weight, her screams are muffled beneath the pillow, she is being extinguished. Tendons stand out in her neck, the arteries swell to bursting.

She has lost consciousness, in an instant Hannah is gone.

Starboy

When I died the lapping water by the cabin continued unchanged like whispering murmuring voices.

When I died there came a sound of owls, night birds across North Fox Lake.

When I died his arm lay heavy over me to comfort me. After the terrible struggle to breathe there was peace as he had promised.

Promise was Mister R__ would make me into a Star.

Promise was Mister R__ would never abandon me as others had abandoned me, I took hope from this.

Said, I am the one who loves you, my Starboy.

Said, Love you to pieces, Starboy.

Because my face was young for my age and my skin smooth like a girl's skin Mister R__ chose me at once, later he would say it was love at first sight and there is no going back from that.

At first I was shy of the camera. At first Mister R__ laughed at me, and pulled away my hands where I was hiding myself.

The Only One you can trust, Starboy.

The Only One who gives a damn about you.

It was a secret between us—"Starboy." For Mister R__ did not want the others to know his special name for me.

For Mister R__ did not approve of my birth name, it was an ordinary name not worthy of my "beauty."

Also secret that Mister R__ would be my (legal) father. For the other boys would be jealous and would talk and ruin everything.

Promise was Mister R__ would adopt me if that was (legally) possible.

Because there was no proof that my mother was not living, she could not give consent.

Because my mother was gone and nobody could find her and I was a ward of the state at Saint Vincent's since I was six years old.

Because that night at the lake Mister R__ said the legal difficulties had been solved. The adoption papers had been filed.

Because that was the night Mister R__ said we would never be apart again.

Said, Love you to pieces, Starboy. Would die for you.

It was our secret but Father McKenzie knew, Mister R__ said we would need consent from the director of the Mission.

It was rare a boy was adopted out of the Mission. Because we were not orphans, we were only just abandoned by our parents.

Because always it was hoped the parents would return. The mother would return. There would be that surprise one morning—Guess who's waiting out front! Your mom.

There was pride in this, Mister R__ had chosen me. Other boys he'd photographed but none as beautiful (he said) as Starboy.

That night, I would remain with Mister R__ in the cabin by the lake and not return with the others.

Woke up and my heart pounding, I heard their voices fading. Heard car doors slam, the sound of motors starting. Party's over.

Even then I could have escaped. Take me with you!*—don't leave me!—could have shouted after them returning to Detroit without me.*

Except I was high, and I was happy.

Except Mister R__'s arm heavy over me, to comfort me. Starboy!— our new life will begin soon.

When you are high you are so happy you have no fear.

When you are high you vibrate like crystal glass that has no knowledge of how it can shatter.

When you are high there is no time to come only what is now.

Except I knew, when I was left with just him.

When it was just me with him, *the other guys were headed back into the city, party's over! All gone.*

Said, Just you and me, my beautiful Starboy.

That night our blood mingled. Mister R___ "inscribed" his right forearm, and then my right forearm, with a pearl-handled knife as delicate as a surgical instrument, and then he pressed his arm against mine, I felt my eyes shutting, a strong sensation came over me like sleep.

Something he'd given me, to drink. So I would not be anxious.

The trail left by the knife was about three inches long and very thin like the line made by a pen. Thin-oozing blood from the wounds that was fascinating to see.

Said, We will be faithful to each other forever not even at death will we part.

Said, You believe me don't you, Starboy? Yes you do.

I was laughing, I said sure. *All the time I can remember I was laughing until then I was not.*

Kissing the wound in my arm, licking the slow-oozing blood and so I kissed the wound in his arm that he lifted to my face, licking the slow-oozing blood that had a thin salty taste for when you have no hope you take hope where it is offered as you take food, drink when it is offered.

As you take oxygen into your lungs throughout your life not knowing what it is to breathe *until that time when you are made to realize that* breath *can be stopped . . .*

Said, If I remove this gag you will breathe better if you promise not to scream and so I promised, there was such weakness in me by this time I could not scream and anyway I knew, at the lake in the woods at this time of year there was no one to hear for one hundred miles.

Above me, aiming his camera. Tender-eyed.

My gift to you, Starboy: Your beauty will outlive you.

Never knew his name, or any of their (actual) names.

He was Mister R___, he stood apart from the others being younger and more like one of us. It was known he had money.

Even before he drove me to his house in Bloomfield, you could tell.

Right away with me, Mister R___ was generous with tips. Fifty-dollar *bills, even a hundred-dollar bill once when he was high, his skin burned and his eyes were on fire crazy for Starboy.*

Money he gave to Father McKenzie for the Mission. A folder of photographs of Starboy, for Father McKenzie.

So Father McKenzie saw to it, Mister R___ could spend "quality time" with me.

Driving in his car along the lake in Grosse Pointe, that was "quality time." Stopping where there was no one to see.

Driving to his house in Bloomfield Hills where he said we could be alone, all the McDonald's burgers and fries I could eat, cheese and pepperoni pizzas that were my favorites, dope to smoke we'd lie in bed and watch TV on a giant screen like in a movie theater almost. Wild! His parents were in "Europe"—he said—he'd told "the help" to take the week off full pay. There was a gate ten feet high, you needed to punch in a code to open it, and such a big house you couldn't see all of it at once—some kind of stone, and brick painted white, and tall plate-glass windows and sliding doors, Mister R___ had his own entrance you could enter by his door with his own key not needing to pass through the main part of the house that was as big as a hotel.

In Mister R___'s part of the house there were "venetian blinds" on all the windows he kept drawn, for sunlight hurt his eyes he said.

In the swimming pool which was sky-blue tiles beneath there was no need for swim trunks, no one would see.

This is an Olympic-size pool, Starboy. Just for you.

But I didn't like the water. Chlorine-stinking water. Flailing like a drowning squirrel, water up my nose, fuck swimming.

Mister R___ was disappointed. Wanted to take pictures of me swimming like a "sleek little water rat" but none of these turned out.

Not such a great swimmer any longer himself (he said) but he liked to watch other people swim—boys like me.

Boys like me?—had to laugh. Mister R___ was always telling me there's no other boys anything like Starboy.

In Mister R___'s part of the house there was only one way to get to the main part of the house and Mister R___ had that blocked. Teasing me, he knew I'd like to "roam and wander"—but that was forbidden.

Smoking dope on Mister R___'s bed. Little shot glasses drinking "tequila." Laughing telling me he couldn't wait for his parents to die so he'd inherit and would sell the property (worth millions of dollars—he said), purchase a place all glass walls in the DR ("Dominican Republic," which was some island somewhere near Cuba—he said) where we would live together "openly"—after the adoption.

Laughing when he said this. Curling his long white toes, pulling at his mustache.

(Hair on Mister R__'s head was prickly and thin like he had some kind of sickness that causes bald spots but the mustache was real except for being dyed, up close you could see how it was growing out on his upper lip.)

When Mister R__ was high sometimes he was sleepy-nice and sometimes not so nice. A sign was, he'd be swallowing hard and fast like something was stuck in his throat which meant he was getting excited and might turn mean so I knew not to provoke him except once when he was talking about the "beautiful Blacks" in the DR he intended to photograph I said shit man, by then I'm gonna be a Star, I'll be in Hollywood making movies not on some fucking two-bit island and that did it—Mister R__ got nasty-mad and made me regret it.

Not right away. That wasn't his way. But when I crashed and was asleep, then.

It's okay, it was "discipline." That was lacking in my life—"discipline." Father McKenzie had said so, too.

Except wanting to murder them. Filthy pigs grunting and rutting, liked to slash their throats, saw off their filthy perve heads and toss them in the garbage.

But it's okay. All the good things they did for me, I had to admit.

For instance, never had a dog and always wanted one and Mister R__ promised me definitely, one day maybe in the DR, any breed you wish, how'd you like that, Starboy?

The guys would ask me what kind of a fuck is Mister R__ and I told them, No kind of a fuck. Best kind.

Nine times out of ten couldn't get it up, like some old skinned hot dog. Limp, cold. And he wasn't old, either—not like the other fags.

Half the time you're high your mind is floating and gone. Fuck you care about any cocksucker.

Okay it did matter, that was my weakness: pride. To know I was Mister R__'s favorite he'd taken like a thousand pictures of.

Not knowing that he'd had other "favorites" before me at the Mission. And some bad things happened to them, maybe.

(Like Michel.) (Nobody wanted to talk about.)

A boy without a family. Desperate troubled kids and most of them illiterate or what's it called—dis-lex-ic.

Father Mac did not know any of this—he would claim. He did not, he did not, he did not *know. As God is his witness, he did not know.*

Began to happen more often, Father Mac would lose his balance and fall, we'd have to help him up. Breath smelling like whiskey. Gripping our arms, hoisting himself upright.

He'd entered the seminary when he was just a little older than we were, he'd say. Shaking his head, remembering.

Fighting Irish, he said. That's what I am.

You don't give up the fight, Father Mac said wiping his red-splotched face. But sometimes, the fight is taken from you.

Before Mister R__, there was Father Mac. But then I was too old for him, after my eleventh birthday.

The other, older guys belonged to Friends of the Mission. Mister R__ did not belong. Or maybe he did belong. But Mister R__ came to the motel parties on Woodward.

The older guys were different from Mister R__ who kept apart from them. Like, Mister R__ had dignity.

Like, sad-sack losers, fat old fag cocksuckers you could see by the look on their faces like somebody took away their dentures, sad-sack mouths kind of collapsed in, still they'd be all smiling and making jokes, dumb-ass jokes, Christ! Father McKenzie told us, Be kind, my lads. You will be rewarded but be kind.

Friends of Saint Vincent Children's Mission on Woodward Avenue. Called themselves Mister Teddy, Mister Valentine, Mister Moose, Mister Mamba.

There was even a "doctor"—Dr. Dolittle.

Laughed at them all, enough to make you puke but when we were high it was just kind of funny. Just laugh and laugh.

Why Mister R__ kept apart. Wore dark glasses so you couldn't see his eyes. Mustache on his upper lip covered much of his mouth.

There was Hawkeye, also not one of the Friends. But some kind of friend of Mister R__, you could see there was some connection. And Father McKenzie, he knew them all.

Hawkeye provided the supplies—uppers, downers, meth, quaaludes, coke, hash, pot. Hawkeye handled the money.

There were no parties at the Mission. This was a place of God to be kept sacred (Father McKenzie said). Parties were at motels on Woodward south of Eight Mile.

It was understood, the old Daddy-Friends gave donations to the Mission but money never changed hands at the parties. Why they called him Hawkeye, he kept a sharp eye on that, he would not allow that and you did not want to cross Hawkeye or any guy who (it was said) reported to Hawkeye, like a spy.

There was Mikey, who'd been my friend, I thought. But later Mikey showed up, now he had a different name. He didn't live at Saint Vincent's, he'd moved away. Some way he worked for Hawkeye, we weren't sure what it was.

Sometimes there would come a look on Hawkeye's face like he'd like to slash the old fags' throats. But there was a better use for them, Hawkeye knew.

You did not want to cross Hawkeye. You did not want to wrangle a "tip" unless you were sure that Hawkeye would never know.

If you were "obstreperous"—Father McKenzie's word, we thought was a swear word in Latin—you would regret it.

. . .

When I died it was not an easy death. He'd pressed a cloth soaked in hot stinging flames to make me sleep for how long, I did not know. Yet as the wire tightened around my neck I was wakened in terror fingers clutching at the wire trying to stop it tightening. Thrashing, kicking, unable to cry out, not knowing what it was that was happening in the night in the dark not knowing where I was, not knowing who this was straddling my naked body grunting and weeping hot tears into my face.

And then afterward he lay beside me panting and sobbing in relief, in joy that the struggle had ended. For the end of all struggle is mercy and mercy is the purest love.

Snug heaviness of his arm lay over me to comfort me and he slept beside me the deepest sleep.

In the morning grieving he carried my body in his arms to the bathtub where warm soapy water awaited and in this water he lowered me and there he bathed me so tenderly, with such love no one had bathed me in my life.

Tears fell into the warm soapy water, his heart was wrung with sorrow.

Tenderly he would take pictures of these moments. For such moments did not last and must be preserved.

Why did he hurt Starboy if he had loved me so, he would explain he'd had to hurt me in order to kill me, had not wanted to hurt me but there was no other way to kill me and he'd had to kill me, love for Starboy came so strong he felt his soul tugged from him, a vise tightening around his chest so that he could not breathe.

God inside him pushing and pressing him to know of what he was capable—such courage is required, to know how far you will go, if God does not stay your hand.

But now he would take Starboy to a special place, he promised. He would display my innocence and beauty to the world that was such a crass cold place. He would lay me on the ground gently, he would place my arms across my chest, he would arrange my (naked) body so that all who gazed upon it would stare in awe and wonderment at my beauty. And my (laundered, ironed) clothing he would fold and place beside me.

And kneeling beside me, final photographs. The most beautiful.

Because no one else had loved Starboy, as he had. Because no one else deserved me, as he had.

When I died all this would become known to me.

When we die all becomes known.

Ponytail

Fuck, yes! Never say *no* to Hawkeye.

Not the first time Hawkeye has called Ponytail in an emergency, won't be the last.

Expedited, Hawkeye calls it. He's *needing something expedited.*

Now that Ponytail is staying at a place on West Warren near downtown Detroit. Three years ago at eighteen aged out of Saint Vincent's but keeps in touch with Father McKenzie and some of Father McKenzie's pals, he's available anytime almost, as needed.

His reputation is: Reliable, doesn't ask questions, and keeps his mouth shut.

"Jesus!"—Ponytail whistles seeing the woman sprawled on the unmade bed like maybe she isn't breathing?—*that's* why Hawkeye called him to the Renaissance Grand Hotel, to help dispose of the body?

No wonder there's the sign outside the door—DO NOT DISTURB.

But no, there's breath. She's breathing.

Also, her (swollen) eyes are opening. Trying to open.

A woman in her late thirties, early forties, old enough to be Ponytail's mother if his mother were alive which (probably) she isn't. Not bad-looking except she's (maybe) drunk or overdosed, breathing thinly through a mouth battered like a fish's mouth after the hook has been torn out. Blinking and squinting in Ponytail's direction as if there's a blinding light in her eyes. Face sickly pale, flushed in patches. Whiff of vomit. Soft bruised flesh beneath her eyes, disheveled and matted (blond) hair, expensive clothes that look as if they've been put on her, hurriedly, negligently, by another person.

On her limp wrist, a watch with a platinum band, tiny diamonds. On her fingers, glittery rings. Wedding band.

On the bed beside the woman, a pair of fancy stiletto heels.

One of Hawkeye's women? Ponytail has heard rumors. But he's never seen Hawkeye with a woman, in fact he's never seen Hawkeye with anyone, female, male, in a way you'd describe as intimate.

Some kind of connection with the weirdo rich guy with the mustache they called "Mister R__"—but probably not friends.

At the time, at the Mission, where he'd been "Mikey," he'd been clueless about so much. Excited to be included in Father McKenzie's special parties he'd been hearing about for years, grateful for the money, the drugs, the attention, all-night parties to which only VIP boys were invited, who also knew the value of keeping their mouths shut.

"Mikey" had been a naïve kid but he'd caught on fast.

Either you did—catch on, fast—or you did not, and you were dropped.

Ponytail has been staring at the woman sprawled on the bed. Pathetic! On her back like that and legs half spread, arms flung out like she's in the air falling, saliva at the edge of her mouth—Ponytail feels a twinge of sympathy for her, or pity. Must've been Hawkeye who half dressed her, silk shirt only partway buttoned, badly wrinkled linen trousers bunched at her hips, soiled. Ponytail tells himself probably the woman is a bitch, fuck feeling sorry for a bitch . . .

What Hawkeye has been to her, who the woman is—Ponytail doesn't intend to ask. Not his business.

Could be it's a test of Hawkeye's: See how cool Ponytail operates, minding his own business, not showing (much) surprise.

Ponytail *is* cool. All this while without hardly turning his head or even moving his eyes much he's been taking note of the setting: luxury suite, sixty-first floor of the Renaissance Grand Hotel.

Enormous bedroom, "king-sized" bed the size of the room on West Warren Ponytail is sharing with another guy, mirrored closet doors partly opened, a man's clothes hanging inside, and at the foot of the bed an expensive-looking leather suitcase—Ponytail figures the suite is Hawkeye's, not the woman's.

The woman is the visitor, and it's time to eject the visitor.

Why Ponytail has been summoned, he figures.

Wondering: Where's the camera? Hawkeye wouldn't miss the opportunity to record whatever happened on that bed.

Might be there's a camera on a high shelf in the closet, hidden beneath a stack of pillows, just the miniature lens exposed, so positioned that it can take in the entire bed when the door isn't quite closed, and that's why the door isn't closed.

Or, maybe, attached to the bedside radio clock, close to the bed.

At the all-nighters on Woodward, Ponytail helped Hawkeye with surveillance and recording. Many hours of recording. Including a few minutes of the baby-faced kid named Michel, the night he'd met his special friend *Mister R__*.

Later, Ponytail helped Hawkeye's assistant at the time, light-skinned Hispanic guy nineteen years old they knew as Tryk, before Tryk (also) disappeared no one knew where and Ponytail took his place.

Nervous joking about guys who'd disappeared. You'd hear yourself sniggering, then you'd swallow hard.

Nobody missed them, or mostly not. Father McKenzie reported them missing—"runaways." But no one was going to look for them, try to track them down.

Plenty of boys where they'd come from, and all eager. Each one thinking *Hey, I'm special.*

Ponytail had to laugh, the fat old fags—"Friends of the Mission"— never seemed to realize they were risking blackmail. Arriving already drunk or high, eyes shining like pond scum. Must've suspected but pretended not, crazy about Father McKenzie's "beautiful Mission boys."

He'd been one of the Mission boys—*Mikey Kushel*. But none of the fat old fags had put their hands on *him*.

Not one! Father McKenzie cautioned him, you can make your own way, Mikey. You are not like the others.

Then, hairs like wires started sprouting at his underarms and crotch, pimples broke out on his face, his voice changed, and he wasn't so beautiful any longer, and not so young.

Smooth hairless jaws they'd preferred, not jaws needing to be shaved. Smooth backs, asses. Not a pimple, not a glaring red bump! Boy penises like something soft, skinned, helpless, a baby bird fallen out of its nest, a baby rabbit you could crush between your fingers . . .

Hey!—Hawkeye snaps his fingers in Ponytail's face to get his attention.

Hawkeye asks him is he listening? Is he high on some shit because if he is, he'd better admit it, and Ponytail insists *no,* hell no, he is *not high* on any kind of shit, he is *stone-cold sober.*

Okay says Hawkeye, taking pains to speak slowly and carefully: "Mrs. J__" needs to be driven home and Ponytail is the designated driver.

Ponytail will drive Mrs. J__ (in her own car) to Far Hills, approximately twenty miles away, north on I-75 to her house, leave the car at the house, in the garage; leave everything pertaining to Mrs. J__, including her handbag, intact; and Hawkeye will arrange for a car to pick him up and bring him back to Detroit.

Typical of Hawkeye: no explanation, just instructions.

Hawkeye hands Ponytail the woman's address printed in block letters large enough for a slow-witted child to read: 96 CRADLE ROCK ROAD, FAR HILLS.

Plus, a ticket stub for the hotel parking garage.

Ponytail swallows hard. Ponytail is feeling—kind of edgy. He's going to do all this shit—alone?

Take a staggering-drunk-looking (white) woman down to the garage, a woman with a wristwatch edged with diamonds, get the car from the attendant—alone?

That's right, Hawkeye says. *He* isn't going to be involved.

Ponytail draws a deep breath. It's a test of his courage, he knows.

Not asking what Hawkeye intends to pay him. As if, at this moment, being paid hasn't occurred to Ponytail, it's something like masculine pride that is at stake.

Between Hawkeye and Ponytail, mutual respect. Ponytail needing to live up to Hawkeye's expectations of him, or he's fucked for the future.

It isn't driving some stranger's car that is freaking him out, it's getting a woman who isn't a hooker down in the elevator in this classy hotel, to the parking garage, to pick up her car. Like he's in a movie—the camera's on him. How in hell's he going to pull this off?

Wanting badly to ask Hawkeye to come with him to the parking garage at least, anybody happening to see them might think that Hawkeye is the woman's husband, but seeing Ponytail with her, Christ . . . But Ponytail knows better than to ask, seeing the look on Hawkeye's face like a grating pulled down over a store window.

Recalling that once Hawkeye tells you something, once his mind is made up, Hawkeye isn't going to change it. Like being in the army. You're a soldier, you take orders.

At Saint Vincent's he hadn't caught on, not right away. How serious some things could be. (Like Michel, what happened to him.) (That nobody would ever talk about.) And no way to change things back to what they'd been, before.

He'd been Mike then—"Mikey." Short for his age. Goddamned short legs, like the bones had not grown right. It was shameful to him, some of the kids thought he was retarded, but Father McKenzie knew better, it was just sadness.

If Father hadn't taken notice of him and protected him the way he protected his special boys, Mikey would surely be dead by now, over-dosed, crack cocaine, or his head broken in a fight, or pushed downstairs so a dozen vertebrae broke, and some coke-crazy old fag fucked him in the ass until his guts oozed out and he died on the street miles from Saint Vincent's discovered by the six A.M. sanitation workers and nobody would remember his Goddamned name three months later.

Kids who died at the Mission of what a medical examiner would call *natural causes*, if they didn't have relatives to take their bodies and pay for a real burial, were given a single mass in their memory in Saint Vincent's Church on Woodward then buried in plain pine coffins in the cemetery behind the residence. Old broken grave markers dating back to the 1800s. Trees that never sprouted leaves and their bark peeled off like leprosy but never actually died, weedy trash graves bordering on Railroad Avenue. Bones were scattered everywhere in the soil, it was said. Mixed together, dozens of boys, maybe hundreds, and animal bones, and chunks of concrete, plastic, Styrofoam, and nobody gave a fuck about you if you didn't have a mother or any relatives to care for you and if you did, why would you be a "homeless juvenile" at the Mission?—you wouldn't.

But all that is past. Ponytail isn't a kid now—he isn't Mikey. Ponytail has his own place, pays his own rent, hires out for the kind of work not just anybody can do. Ponytail's a Goddamned *independent entrepreneur.*

Good-looking like somebody in the movies—he's been told. A young Jack Nicholson with that weird crooked smile, the thing with the eyes—eyebrows. Carries himself like James Caan in *Rollerball*.

Built as dense and compact as a wrestler at five feet seven, weight at one hundred fifty pounds, Indian-black hair to his shoulders he ties back in a ponytail, three-day growth of beard on his jaws but a classy dresser, he thinks—torso-tight black T-shirts, black cargo pants (with deep, button-down pockets), black Nikes, dark-tinted aviator glasses that hide the shrewd glisten of his beetle eyes.

Women are attracted to Ponytail. Even as Mikey Kushel they'd been attracted to him, you could tell. Their eyes swarming on him like hungry ants, on the street. Public places (this ritzy hotel)—crossing the lobby. Eating him up with their eyes, Ponytail thinks, grinning.

Though in actual life, if he'd met them, like, face-to-face in someplace like a restaurant or a bar, women are (he guesses) a little afraid of him.

Certainly girls his own age are afraid of him. And younger.

Hell, *he'd* be afraid of Ponytail, that cool sexy assassin look he has cultivated.

Hawkeye respects him, Ponytail thinks. Mutual respect between them, Hawkeye doesn't have to spell things out, Ponytail is one to take the initiative.

You're listening, right? You're taking this in?

Yes! Yes he is.

Urgent he drives the woman home without any incidents. No reckless driving, no bullshit tactics on the interstate, showing off in her car. Let the truckers pass him, fuck them let them go, ignore them, the goal is to drive to Far Hills without getting stopped by law enforcement. Keep his speed at the limit, no more, don't take chances passing, don't use the Goddamned horn, if he's pulled over by police he might be accused of stealing the car, even kidnapping the woman if she becomes excitable, you never know how a woman will behave and especially you won't know how this woman will behave. Don't expect Hawkeye to bail him out if he gets in trouble, he will not. Also no talking to the woman. Absolutely no conversation in the car. Help the woman into the back of the car so she won't interfere with his driving and she can pass out. Make sure she isn't lying on her back, if she starts to puke she will choke. Keep an eye out. Drinking all afternoon, she's an alcoholic, something might've happened to her, there's a kind of wheezy sound in her chest, she'd been passed out for twenty minutes or more. Some kind of blackout—just maybe, if she's lucky, amnesia.

Blackout. Probably the bastard was choking her, Ponytail thinks.

Probably he'd almost killed her. That's why Ponytail was called on such short notice.

Feeling for the moment protective of the foolish woman, old enough to be his mother. Jesus!—pathetic.

Hawkeye warns Ponytail not to paw through the woman's handbag. Don't even think about taking her money or credit cards, stay out of the handbag altogether, got it?

Okay, Ponytail says. Got it.

Seeing the handbag is one of those fancy soft-leather designer bags, could be worth two thousand dollars. What's the label?—*Prada.*

One of the Friends, when Mikey had been living at the Mission. Patrician old Mr. Valentine, prissy, sniffing and snuffling, rumored to live in a big brick home in Grosse Pointe, rumpled clothes but expensive, an old worn leather briefcase (stuffed with fresh underwear, socks) but still you could see it had a fancy brand name—*Prada.*

Ponytail has "expedited" for Hawkeye in the past. Mostly drugs, pickup and delivery, short-haul drives for (exclusively male) customers too wasted to drive themselves home but in the vicinity of downtown, or possibly Grosse Pointe (the suburb nearest to downtown Detroit). Not all the way out to Far Hills where Ponytail has not actually ever been.

Beyond Ferndale, Royal Oak—the northern suburbs. Not much past Eight Mile Road is familiar territory to Ponytail.

If the woman lives out there, she's rich. Husband's rich. You wouldn't have to look at her to know she's white. Makes sense, Hawkeye has some investment in her.

"Ah! *Très bien, ma chere!*"—Hawkeye is speaking to the woman, who has managed, after much effort, and a little help from Hawkeye, to rise from the bed, and to stand beside it, unsteadily.

"Mrs. J__"—Ponytail wonders what her last name is, assumes that Hawkeye knows.

She has only just noticed Ponytail now—a quick sidelong glance, startled. A look of chagrin, fear.

Checking her clothes—silk shirt, creased linen trousers—as if to see *Am I dressed?* Fumbling to button the shirt correctly, adjust the trousers.

Ponytail guesses, she's naked inside the clothes. Hawkeye hadn't bothered with underwear. Twisted into a ball, kicked beneath the bed for the chambermaid to discover in the morning.

Ponytail sees the bleached-blond hair, bloodshot dazed eyes rapidly blinking as Mrs. J__ tries to determine where she is, what has happened. One of those dreams where you are lost, no idea where you are. Swiping at vomit on the trousers, a stricken look. Smudged mascara like somebody pushed her face into a pillow, hard.

But she has discovered the stiletto shoes, which she's going to put on her (naked) feet. Try to put on. Has to sit on the edge of the bed, sits heavily, try to maneuver the shoes on her feet.

Sexy shoes, Ponytail thinks. Pathetic.

Steeling himself waiting for Hawkeye to order him to help her—kneel on the carpet and help Mrs. J__ put on her shoes like a Goddamned shoe-store salesman—but no, after a few misses the hard-breathing woman manages to strap on one shoe, then the other.

Pitiful, rich cunt hardly able to walk in the silly, sexy shoes, wounded eyes and a face like some sick-pale meat that's been pounded.

Ponytail's gaze drops to the woman's hips, pelvis. Creased linen crotch. Probably she's all bruises inside her clothes. A woman who has been fucked, in all ways.

But maybe she's got kids. Maybe she's a *mother.* Christ!

Actually trying to smile! Insisting she can drive home by herself, she's feeling "much better" now.

Hawkeye shakes his head *no.* Just—*no.*

As if it might be a matter for discussion Mrs. J__ repeats the same words in the same pleading voice but Hawkeye shuts her up with a scowl—*I said: no.*

When Mrs. J__ reaches for her fancy handbag Hawkeye gives it to Ponytail.

For safekeeping, Hawkeye says. Not a bag you want to lose.

Mrs. J__ tries to protest. An intelligent woman, Ponytail thinks, marvels at how intimidated she is by Hawkeye, like he has a leash around her neck, all he needs to do is give it a shake, she's *his.*

Reverse of a snake charmer, where the cobra is enthralled by the flute player. Here, the woman is enthralled by the cobra.

Because she wants to be loved by him. Because she thinks there is that possibility—loved by Hawkeye.

There were guys who'd shared that delusion, at the Mission. Hawkeye was their protector, they'd wanted to think, at the motel parties, and to some extent that was true, but finally not.

If Mister R__ wanted you, you went. Sometimes you were returned, and sometimes not.

Money changed hands: from Mister R__ to Hawkeye. That, you knew. But you never saw it.

Hawkeye walks Mrs. J__ into the outer room and to the door of the suite. Wanting badly to be rid of the woman but speaking in a low soothing voice to her, hypnotic cobra voice (if a cobra could speak!) telling her she's safe, in trusted hands, she'll be home soon.

Safe, in trusted hands, home soon.

Know I love you, right?—darling.

If you knew Hawkeye you'd know this was a joke. You'd laugh in his face. But, Mrs. J__ doesn't know.

Hawkeye's fist gripping her upper arm, got to hurt the way he's keeping her upright if her weak knees buckle.

Ponytail has seen Hawkeye console others. Times of crisis. High on drugs, staggering drunk, stricken with shame, despondent and sobbing. Boys like Mikey, but also (adult) men.

Hell of a surprise, a shock, when Mikey first saw an adult man cry.

Lose all respect for them. Cocksucker fags.

But there's Hawkeye soft-speaking. *He,* Hawkeye, there to help. Everything will be all right, nothing to worry about, soon you will be home and in your own bed safe.

Though never has Ponytail heard Hawkeye tell anyone *Know I love you, right?*

Never, calling anyone *darling.*

Mrs. J__ squints up at Hawkeye. The swollen mouth tries to smile. She's grateful, he will lie to her. For Hawkeye doesn't care enough for most people, to lie.

At the door Hawkeye will kiss the bruised mouth, quick, as a cobra might kiss. Turning the woman over to Ponytail, to "expedite."

Hawkeye peels off several hundred-dollar bills from a roll carried loose in his pocket, for Ponytail. Ponytail isn't sure how many of these bills he's being given, could be five or six, isn't counting. His style is to feign disinterest. A matter of respect for Hawkeye, trust.

That's got to impress the coldhearted motherfucker, right?

Hawkeye's actual name, no one seemed to know. Ponytail had heard that a long time ago he'd been a boy at the Mission, when Father McKenzie was a young priest there, but Ponytail had also heard that Hawkeye wasn't from Detroit or (possibly) born in the United States. Hawkeye spoke in so low and rapid a voice you couldn't tell if he spoke with an accent, nor was it known how he'd come to be called "Hawkeye"—who'd been the first to note how with his heavy-lidded eyes and sharp-boned face he resembled a bird of prey.

A hungry bird of prey: Yet no one had ever seen him eat, or drink, at any of the motel all-nighters.

Definitely it was said, it might've been Father McKenzie who first said it, that Hawkeye had been some kind of bomber pilot in some war dropping bombs and vaporizing the enemy, Ponytail figured it had to be the Vietnam War he'd heard about when he was just a kid.

Cool, Ponytail thought. Fly high enough, nobody can catch you. You can't see anybody, below. Or anything that happens to them because of you.

Like, a test. Can you pull the lever, can you drop the bomb? Bombs?

Could you, feeling pissed, drop a ton of bombs, blow up the entire fucking world?

Why the fuck not, if nobody stops you. Goddamn God's fault, He doesn't stop you from doing the worst you can do.

Outside in the corridor Ponytail turns, a little panicked, has a question for Hawkeye but the door is shutting behind him. Christ!

Ma'am, c'mon. This way.

Best way is gripping her upper arm. Walking her like you'd walk a drunk.

Elevator, down. Falling-down-fast, Ponytail shuts his eyes so as not to feel nauseated.

Scared shitless walking the (drunk?) woman through the glitzy lobby. Got to know that every security cop in sight is watching him. Doormen, bellboys in monkey uniforms watching Ponytail, sneering at Ponytail's straggly hair, have to wonder who the woman is, what the fuck's *he* doing with *her*? Steels himself for some hassle but walking Mrs. J__ through the lobby isn't as difficult as he'd anticipated since the lobby is crowded with conferees, loud-talking, drinks in hand, spilling out of a pub on the first floor. Mrs. J__ unsteady on her feet doesn't merit a second glance.

Christ!—Ponytail has been worried about this, turns out it's nothing.

Whatever you are thinking Father McKenzie used to console, a warm hand on a shoulder, an arm, a thigh *think again, my child.*

Outside in fresh air! Ponytail exchanges a level look with the parking attendant, guy his own age, light-dark-skinned, thin mustache on his upper lip, what's this dude thinking, Mrs. J__ is Ponytail's woman? *His* woman?

Not likely his mother. Too classy to be Ponytail's mother.

"Okay, man, 'expedite' this"—Ponytail hands the attendant the parking ticket with a folded twenty-dollar bill.

Liking the attendant flashing a smile at him—genuine, surprised.

Hey, man. Thanks!

Liking the attendant observing the skill with which Ponytail "helps" the (blond, white) woman into the rear of the fancy car where she collapses boneless, unresisting. Eyes rolling back in her skull the way, if she was fucked, without knowing who was fucking her, the eyes would roll back, the wet mouth would fall open.

Ponytail shudders, repelled. *He* wouldn't touch a female that age, the thought is disgusting.

Prada handbag, Ponytail tosses into the rear with Mrs. J__ so she can cling to it as a small child might cling to a stuffed animal.

And yes: Makes sure she isn't on her back as Hawkeye instructed.

Yah man, you have a good ev'nin'—the light-dark-skinned dude says to Ponytail with (almost) a wink, Ponytail grins back at him, elated.

Yah man. Sure will.

Broken

*W*here am I, what time is this.

. . . desperate to return home. Hours late returning home.

Children clamoring for Mommy at home, Mommy is so, so ashamed . . .

There is a husband, too. A man whose face she can see but his name—she has forgotten his name . . .

The husband is not happy with her. The husband is staring at her in disgust.

Joker Daddy is edging close. Joker Daddy has never been impressed with the husband.

Futile to think you could replace me *with him!—Joker Daddy sputters with laughter.*

Desperate to return home to hurry upstairs, remove her soiled clothing, stagger into the shower. Shame of her odorous body, worst smells are female smells, not drunk but her legs are as weak as a drunkard's, pained feet in high-heeled open-toed shoes, only her lover's fist closed about her arm keeps her upright.

Bruises circling her upper arm.

Disgusted with her. But he has taken mercy on her, he has told her he loves her.

Calling her darling!

Though he'd made no plan or promise to see her again. And no apology, for how he has treated her.

Handing her over to the boy, couldn't get rid of her fast enough. Swaggering kid in his early twenties, three-day beard, coarse hair in a ponytail, black T-shirt, black trousers, sunglasses hiding eyes narrowed in surprise/contempt.

Where the ponytailed boy has come from, she has no idea.

(Was he in the suite all along? Was he a—witness? Hannah is sick with shame.)

(Is he someone Hannah knows? Is supposed to know? One of the uniformed staff at the hotel? Is she expected to tip him, after he drives her home?)

(Her lover has rid himself of her, she is bereft, lost.)

(She will confess everything to her husband. She is not worthy to touch their children.)

Collapsed in the backseat of her own car, hears the ponytailed driver calling her ma'am, *Goddamn she is not* ma'am! *Too tired to lift her head. Too tired to protest. Fumbling with her handbag looking for a tissue. Lipstick tube (Revlon), emery boards, rat-tail comb, wallet. Is she expected to tip the driver, must remember to tip the driver. Must stay awake and alert but sinks into a stupor-sleep as soon as the Buick enters the ramp, glides onto the Lodge Expressway north, north to her home, head lolling loose on her shoulders, smudged eyes shut and mouth agape in wonder as the mouth of a shuddering fish tossed down onto a pier.*

In the morning slow to wake. Silt has settled inside her head.

Dark, darkness. Sifting silt, muck.

It is another time! She has survived to this time.

But: Exhausted from crawling. Dragging her (useless) legs through the night. Between her legs a bleeding wound. Festering wound.

Exhausted from trying to explain where she has been, why this has happened to her, not sure to whom she is trying to explain, the stark white clown-face is blurred and shimmering, indeed there are several faces whose features she can't discern except to know that they recognize Hannah, they have always known Hannah and are passing a harsh judgment on Hannah, and a harsh sentence.

Die, why don't you die. You are female filth, you don't deserve to live.

Morning sunlight splotched against a wall of the bedroom. Shimmering reflections, amoeba-like, through half-shut eyes she watches mesmerized.

Trying now to wake up. Open her swollen eyes.

Barbiturate numbness like cotton batting is smothering her brain. She'd been desperate to sleep the night before, forget the hotel room, the hard cruel hands and pounding body of the lover. The ponytailed boy who'd been entrusted to drive her home.

He had wanted her gone, that was clear. Fear in his voice that she couldn't be made to wake up, erratic breathing and then her heart would stop . . . He'd had to slap her face, to wake her. Even then, she hadn't (fully) wakened.

Seeing through swollen eyes the expression of dread, disgust on her lover's face when he'd thought for a split second that she might be dead.

As soon as she'd arrived home taking two sleeping pills.

Staggering into the guest room, collapsing onto the bed.

As long as she's asleep she won't remember—pity in her lover's voice. *Know I love you, right?* The ponytailed boy staring at her through dark-tinted aviator glasses calling her *ma'am*.

Wordless glance of shared bemusement between the ponytailed driver and the parking attendant at the hotel—young guys (white, Black) united in contempt for the (rich) (white) (blond) woman owner of the Buick Riviera standing weak-kneed in ridiculous high-heeled shoes helpless to protest *But—this is my car! You have no right* . . .

Laughing at her, rudely. But no—they hadn't laughed *aloud*.

The ponytailed driver made a show of tipping the parking attendant. Peeling a bill out of a small roll of bills in his pocket with the swagger of one who has observed this gesture in another.

Must've been a generous tip, the parking attendant responded with the alacrity of a light switched on—*Hey, man. Thanks!*

Now they didn't trouble to disguise their laughter. Hannah knew, directed at her.

Crude young-male sexual laughter, contempt for the female no longer young, desirable. Yet not old enough to merit their sexual indifference, nor certainly their respect.

Yah man, you have a good ev'nin'—the parking attendant calls after them with derisive hilarity.

Yah man. Sure will.

How has Hannah's life come to this.

Back of the Buick like an invalid. Like a drunk. Sprawled, near-comatose. Jolting ride out of the city, blurred cityscape, overpasses, signs, flashing lights. When your total concentration is to resist nausea, vomiting.

For much of the drive convinced that she is being taken to a hospital. (Beaumont General, in Birmingham? Where they'd taken Katya?) A blinding light will be shone into her scummy eyes, her stomach will be pumped.

The bleeding wound that is her vagina, discovered by staring strangers. For Hannah will be too weak to hide her shame with her hands.

Is this an ambulance? Whistling jeering noise in her ears.

The dread is: When she wakes fully her head will be encased in a vise of pain.

That is why we never wish to wake *fully*.

Why our hands grope about on a bedside table, too exhausted to rise on our elbows, searching for the plastic pill container—desperate to sleep just another hour . . .

Hesitantly the door is being opened. Who?

Mrs. Jarrett?—ma'am? Familiar voice, familiar face leaning above her, concerned.

Ma'am? You've been sleeping for a long time, ma'am.

. . . drove them to school, told them that Mommy has a headache.

The children! Hannah has forgotten the children.

Her children. Unnatural for a mother to forget her children.

Grateful for the Filipina housekeeper. Impossible to have a *secret life* without Ismelda whom the children love also.

Yet: Hannah winces when Ismelda touches her shoulder.

For Hannah's skin has become hypersensitive as if she has been flayed. Every nerve in her body is a taut quivering wire. Her very scalp aches. Lightning flashes at the base of her brain, a migraine warning. And between her legs, the soft pale flesh of her inner thighs, a sensation of burning welts . . .

Raking her with his nails. Before forcing himself inside her.

(But had that really happened? Hannah isn't sure.)

A quick deft hand stifling her screams.

Later, weeping with gratitude that she has been brought safely *home*.

Grateful for such kindness. Helped out of the casket-cushiony rear of the Buick by a boy's hard-knuckled hands. Ponytailed driver fastidiously averting his eyes from Hannah spread-legged in awkwardness, disheveled female old enough to be his *mother*.

Not true!—Hannah thinks indignantly. She is not old enough to be the ponytailed boy's Goddamned *mother*.

Not wearing the stiletto heels at least. Abandoned these in the rear of the car where the driver, concerned for her, urged her to lie down, *shut your eyes, rest* while he drove her home to Far Hills.

Nausea quivering in her gut as in a container of water filled to the very top, the slightest jolt will cause the water to spill over.

Still wanting to know, demanding to know why this was happening, this insult, why wasn't she allowed to drive her own damned car, what right did they (men!) have to take her car key from her; to treat her like a common drunk, to treat her like a fool, a tramp, a slut; but the ponytailed driver seemed not to hear, insulting Hannah by laughing outright at her with the parking attendant but now driving the Buick Riviera north on I-75 he was sober, professional, a skillful driver undaunted by late-afternoon traffic that would have intimidated Hannah.

Giving herself up to him, whoever the hell he was. Praying she wouldn't become carsick and humiliate herself further.

So it happened, Hannah was delivered to the house at 96 Cradle Rock Road, Far Hills, in the early evening as lights were coming on.

As her lover had promised, *home.*

The ponytailed driver would ease the Buick sedan into the garage in exactly the space where it belonged beside the Ford Pinto.

Another space in the three-car garage for the Grand Safari station wagon—but Wes wasn't home yet . . .

Okay ma'am you're home now. See?

This is home—okay? Where you live, ma'am.

Just—go inside, Okay? I'm leaving now.

Entering her own house by the rear door from the garage. Holding her breath, steeling herself against a fit of vomiting.

Take care, ma'am. See ya!

Even in her dry-mouthed daze shrewd enough to avoid the kitchen and the family room, lighted rooms in which her children and their sharp-eyed nanny awaited Mommy. Taking the back stairs. Narrow, plain plank wood, stairs for servants in another era, very different from the carpeted spiral stairs at the front of the house.

And again faint with gratitude making her way shoeless, barefoot up the plain plank stairs, so weak she had to crawl the last several steps like an animal on hands and knees but grateful for even this, unseen.

Oh, to avoid them!—the needy children, the staring nanny.

Avoid gagging, vomiting. Poisoned swill of her being, exploding out.

He would be disgusted, seeing her now.

Explaining (later) to Ismelda that she had a terrible migraine. She'd taken her medication and was going to bed now. No, she can't see the children! The children are too excitable, she is in too much pain. Please explain to the children, Mommy has a bad headache.

Please explain to Mr. Jarrett that she will spend the night in the guest room so that he won't wake her when he comes home and if she's sick to her stomach in the night she won't wake him.

Please don't wake me under any circumstances.

In the morning Hannah will be herself again: She will wake before Wes does, she will prepare breakfast for him and the children, and she will drive the children to school. All will return to normal as if nothing had happened and this *as if* will become all that Hannah will recall.

Grateful for sleep, oblivion. Grateful for Ismelda to leave her, gently shutting the door of the guest room.

For Zekiel Jones, less than twenty-four hours to live.

Opening her eyes with a jolt. The lewdly dancing sun splotches on the wall beside the bed have moved and are brighter.

It must be late morning. Or later?

Wes has left the house without disturbing her deep slumber, the children have been driven to school by Ismelda—that has happened . . . Or was that yesterday?

Hannah can barely lift her head wracked with pain. She has lost the thread of time: Is this *the* day when she will meet Y.K., or a later day? The thought of returning to the Marriott for the luncheon meeting, having to hear everything a second time, uttering her own banal words a second time, is terrifying to her.

Enduring his sharp nails inside her body for a second time, the most tender part of her body, is terrifying to her.

Yet: Is there not comfort in routine? In knowing—*I did survive. I will survive.*

Yet: Wondering if, in the night, the door to the guest room had been opened, quietly.

Surely, the concerned husband stood in the darkness listening to the stricken wife breathe.

Forbidden by the wife to come closer, to stand over her. Yet concerned for her.

For which Hannah is grateful, could weep with gratitude: Wes still loves her.

She doesn't deserve his love, she knows.

Prays that, if he discovers how she has betrayed him, he will forgive her.

But now someone looms above her—"Mrs. Jarrett? Ma'am?"

Jarring to see the petite brown-skinned woman—Ismelda—standing beside Hannah's bed, concerned.

Why is Mrs. Jarrett still in bed, nearing noon? Deathly pale and sweating, bloodshot eyes.

Daring to touch Hannah's shoulder to wake her but Hannah is already awake, gives a sharp cry—"Go away! Who are you! Get away! Don't touch me!"

Death Sentence

Between *before* and *after* is an infinity.

   Before the small, seismic shift that will precipitate a mountain avalanche, *after* that shift, the catastrophic consequences.

As Ismelda lifts the phone receiver to call Wes Jarrett at his office (as Ismelda has not done in the several years she has worked for the Jarretts), the fate of thirty-one-year-old Zekiel Jones, Far Hills Marriott employee, lifetime resident of Detroit, slips into place, as rudely and abruptly fixed as a nail pounded into place by a hammer.

In the instant *before*, Zekiel's life flies before him airy and unbounded to the horizon, and beyond; in the instant *after*, Zekiel's life has been truncated to less than ten hours.

In his office Wes Jarrett takes the call guardedly, uneasily, from Ismelda, knowing that something must be wrong at home, his first panicked thought is of the children for *the children* are an exquisite burden to him, he has become an anxious father since Katya's illness, he has become a (subtly) resentful husband . . . But here is Ismelda's soft-cadenced lightly accented voice explaining to him that something seems to be wrong with Mrs. Jarrett this morning, she is still in bed, has tried to get up but is too weak, Ismelda has heard her crying, talking to herself as if she has been *hurt* . . .

Hurt, Wes hears. What does that mean—*hurt* . . .

Wes asks if he can speak with Hannah but Ismelda says quickly that Mrs. Jarrett has told her not to come into the room again, she will scream if anyone comes into the room and her skin is "very hot"— "I said, 'I will take your temperature, ma'am,' but she would not allow it."

"God!"—Wes grips the receiver tighter.

In a more forceful voice Ismelda tells her employer that if he does not come home right now, she must call 911. There is nothing further she can do alone, she will need to have professional help.

"All right, Ismelda! Of course."

Then, half pleading: "Will you watch over her? Please? Outside the room? I'll be there in half an hour, I hope."

Hurriedly leaving the office, mumbling an excuse to his assistant, on the anxious drive home recalling with a pang of guilt how, the night before, Hannah hadn't looked good, she'd gone to bed early with one of her headaches, said she wanted to sleep in the guest room so she wouldn't be wakened by him or by the children and so Wes had left early for work feeling absolved from the husbandly duty of checking in with his wife—though he'd (certainly) intended to call later in the morning to see if she was feeling better . . .

As Wes resents having become, of necessity, an anxious father, so Wes resents having become an anxious husband. He has grown to hate the mere sound of the whining word—*mi-graine*. Not *your, my*. Hard not to think that "migraine" is a stratagem empowering Hannah and disadvantaging him for "migraine" is that which cannot be questioned, the very essence of the female: a playing card that is always a winning card, irrefutable. Hannah suffers two or three "migraine" headaches a month while headaches afflict Wes so rarely, he has come to think that they might be mythical, like "hot flashes."

Fortunately, Hannah is years away from "hot flashes," Wes assumes.

At the house Wes leaves the station wagon in the driveway (for he is sure that Ismelda is watching for him at a window) and hurries inside, confers briefly with Ismelda before daring to enter the guest room, a quaintly wallpapered room, not a room in the house that Wes frequently enters, seeing in the bed beneath a ruffled floral comforter that Hannah is lying very still, face turned toward the wall and eyes tight-shut as a child might shut her eyes in a pretense of sleep, stiffening as Wes leans over her—"Hannah? *Hannah?*"

Wes is stunned, Hannah is clearly ill. Wishing not to see that a wife is *clearly ill* is the husband's prerogative, but there is the concerned presence of Ismelda in the doorway behind him, Wes dares not shrink away nor does he dare touch Hannah, the signal her tense, tight body sends is *No! Don't touch me.*

Hannah's face is all but unrecognizable to Wes, who rarely sees his wife without her face very carefully made-up, not out of vanity, or not entirely out of vanity, but out of a wish not to disappoint the husband, still less distress or disillusion him. Yet now, Hannah seems indifferent, lethargic, too weak to ask him to leave the room. Her face is mottled and flushed as if with fever. Her mouth is unevenly swollen, disfigured; her eyelids, still with a residue of silvery-blue eye shadow, are puffy and reddened. Her hair, in which Hannah takes such pride, and on which she spends so much money, is matted, as disheveled as the hair of a cheap doll. Repugnant odors lift to Wes's nostrils from his usually fastidious wife—stale sweat, sour-wine breath, vomit.

Steeling himself to keep from shrinking away as if he has discovered an unattractive stranger in his house.

Asking Hannah if she's all right?—well, clearly she isn't *all right* but *what is wrong?*—as Hannah murmurs what sounds like *nothing*, then, louder, pleadingly—*Please go away, I need to sleep.*

Wes kneels beside the bed. Dares to touch Hannah's forehead, which is hot to the touch, yet oddly dry, like parchment, even as Hannah whimpers, pushing his hand away as a child might.

Why is she not looking at him, Wes wonders. Why, her eyes averted, evasive.

Now Wes sees bruises on the underside of Hannah's jaw, which he had not noticed before. To his astonishment lurid purple, tinged with yellow, welts ringing her neck like the imprint of fingers . . .

"Hannah! What is . . ."

Wes lifts the covers from her, before Hannah can stop him. In that instant, Wes *sees*.

Inside the loose-fitting nightgown, bruises on Hannah's shoulders, upper arms, soft, slack breasts. Hannah whimpers *No no go away* but Wes pulls up the nightgown, tugs it out from beneath her hips, he sees that her stomach and thighs are covered in bruises. Red welts on the insides of her thighs like an animal's clawing.

And the smell of the naked body inside the flimsy nightgown: fever, rage, dark coagulated blood, balked, stymied, speechless, squirming beneath the husband's gaze as a great snake might squirm, not in fear but in defiance of the staring eyes.

Hannah seizes the cover, pulls it back down.

Hannah is sobbing, frantic, her secret has been discovered. Wes rocks back on his heels in stunned confusion as if an intruder, a male rival, had rushed at him out of nowhere, struck him in the face.

Thinking—*My wife has been hurt, beaten.* Not yet thinking—*My wife has been raped.*

What follows then, neither Wes nor Hannah will recall clearly.

How many times in a voice of raw male grief Wes demands to know what has happened to Hannah, who has done this to her, how many times Hannah insists *Nothing, no one.*

She is sobbing, she lies stubborn and stiff beneath the comforter. She will not allow Wes to examine her bruised body further.

Wes grips her hands, to still them. Both of her hands, in his. He is frightened, angry. "Hannah, for Christ's sake! I want to help you."

He forces her to sit up in bed, against the headboard; he pushes a pillow behind her so that he can sit beside her, of a height with her.

At last Hannah relents. Telling Wes to ask Ismelda to leave them alone, and shut the door.

And would he please bring Hannah a washcloth soaked in cold water, for her face, and her migraine pills from the bathroom . . .

In a voice so soft Wes has to lean forward to hear Hannah tells Wes that she doesn't know "entirely" what happened to her, after her Historical Society luncheon at the Marriott: She remembers leaving her friends, going to the parking garage, in the stairwell she might have missed a step, tripped and fell down a flight of concrete steps and injured herself.

A fall on steps? Concrete?

She'd struck her head, Hannah says. Her face.

Wes asks Hannah how she got home after the fall and Hannah says she isn't sure.

Hannah explains that the luncheon had been in a private room at the hotel, on the mezzanine, so after lunch she'd exited from that floor directly into the parking garage; she'd intended to get her car but she'd forgotten that she had left the key with the valet parking attendant so she'd had to go down to the ground floor after all; she'd meant to save time but had ended up losing time . . .

"Yes, and then? Then what?"—Wes asks impatiently.

"I—I'm not sure. Someone helped me."

"Who?"

Hannah is perplexed, she has lost her way. She has lost the thread of her narrative.

She'd had two glasses of wine at lunch, Hannah says guiltily. Maybe three.

Maybe it was the migraine coming on, maybe she'd been *self-medicating* without realizing, the meeting had been so excruciatingly dull, she'd stared at the other women's mouths moving, couldn't understand a word they were saying, even when she herself spoke, she couldn't understand a word!—estranged and alienated from the other women, she could sob with frustration, how lonely she was, how lonely in Far Hills, how bored, but why should she be *bored,* she is (in fact) a very happy woman, one of the happiest women of her acquaintance, far happier than her mother who'd been (also) a migraine sufferer, and something of a (secret) drinker, though Hannah *is not a secret drinker but rather a social drinker:* a crucial distinction. And unlike her mother, Hannah is happily married. And unlike her mother, Hannah is happy being a mother. Yet in her haste to escape the Marriott she'd decided to exit into the parking garage from the mezzanine floor of the hotel and so had to descend concrete steps from the second floor of the garage to the ground floor, inside the stairwell which was deserted, no one below her on the steps, no one above her, and her footsteps echoing in the hollow space, in her high-heeled pumps she must have tripped, and fallen, a wave of dizziness came over her like a sour smell lifting out of a pit, she'd been anxious to return home before the migraine came on and blinded her, the way a migraine approaches like storm clouds above the Great Lakes—by the time you see the clouds, the sky has already been eclipsed.

She'd left her migraine medication at home and so was in a hurry to get home before the pain struck, her mistake was hurrying on the steps, must've tripped, and fell—headfirst, forward and down—trying to deflect the fall with her hands, still her head struck the wall, or the steps, at the landing she opened her eyes stunned not knowing where she was sprawled on the cold dirty concrete . . .

She thinks she might have cried out for help. She thinks she recalls a sort of echo in the stairwell, a muffled scream.

Ma'am?—the door to the stairwell was pushed open, a figure stood in the doorway.

Ma'am?—whoever it was, a blurred figure, Hannah's vision had dimmed, she could barely open her eyes.

A kind man, a decent man, astonished to see Hannah fallen, whimpering in pain. Stooping to help her to her feet. He'd wanted to call 911 but Hannah insisted she was all right, she hadn't fallen far, she was sure she could walk well enough.

He'd walked with her to her car. She hadn't seen his face.

No—*she had not seen his face.*

Wanting only to return home. Desperate to drive home.

She would drive directly home, from the Marriott to the house on Cradle Rock Drive less than two miles away. She would drive slowly and carefully. For something was wrong with her eyes. And the ringing in her ears. And the headache like storm clouds blotting out the sky. She would avoid major roads, she would make her way on side streets along Cradle Rock Creek and so to Cradle Rock Road. Once home she would weep in relief. She would take her migraine medication immediately. She would explain to Ismelda that she should not be disturbed, please don't wake her, keep the children from waking her, and tell Wes not to wake her, she would spend the night in the guest room. For nothing was more precious to her than to sleep.

She hadn't noticed any bruises, yet. She'd felt pain, her right ankle, her elbows, the side of her head, but the pain of the migraine was more powerful, eclipsing other pains.

In disbelief Wes listens to this outburst from Hannah. He has never heard his wife speak in such a way, at such length; slowly and falteringly, then in a rush of words, as if she were recounting a dream whose meaning has eluded her. Almost, Wes would think that Hannah has been drinking this morning.

He has been aware that Hannah is drinking more than in the past. Where once she'd had a single glass of wine often left unfinished now she will have two glasses, finished. Not intensely aware but (merely) aware as one is aware of the clock's hand moving as in the corner of an eye so slowly, so without significance, it does not (yet) merit full attention.

Wes grips Hannah's hands, which are unnaturally cold. He sees that

Hannah is making an effort to look him in the eye as if to convince him that she is speaking sincerely.

Wes thinks—*But something is wrong. Something is not right.*

Not that Hannah is lying. Wes doesn't think so. But there is something about Hannah's way of speaking that makes Wes distrustful.

Since they'd first become lovers years ago there has been a measure of self-consciousness between them, a vestigial adolescent modesty. As, at night, they undress in farther corners of their bedroom, purposefully avoiding seeing each other, and being seen by the other, and usually dress in the morning at different times, avoiding each other altogether, so Wes and Hannah have not frequently appeared naked to each other except in bed, in lovemaking, at close, intimate quarters, and that not frequent in recent years since Katya's birth. And so it is something of a shock to both husband and wife when Wes throws the covers aside another time to expose her stricken body, pushes away Hannah's hands, ignores her cries of distress, dares to part her chafed thighs so that he can peer between her legs to see what he has dreaded to see—the vaginal area swollen, reddened, bloodied, bruises and rake-like welts in the white skin of her thighs of the hue of rotted fruit.

Wes says flatly: "You've been raped."

Hannah yanks the bedclothes from him, covering herself.

Trying to speak, to deny. Trying to draw breath.

No. No no no.

Furious and frightened Wes looms above her. In his face not love but consternation. Hannah is stunned, struck dumb.

But that is precisely true, what has been done to you: rape.

No.

"Hannah? For Christ's sake tell me—who did this to you?"

No future, she has turned her face to the wall. She has hidden her (shamed) face.

"—in the parking garage? In the stairwell? Who was it?"

Hannah takes refuge hunched upon herself beneath bedclothes, knees to her chest, arms hugging her knees. Tight as a fist. No one can pry her open.

Of course it was rape: acknowledge it.

Y.K. is the rapist. Speak his name.

The husband is breathing audibly. The husband is pacing the room.

Tight-shut eyes. She will refuse to see. She will refuse to hear the husband's anguish.

How she hates him, this man who has lifted the covers from her without her consent!—her husband.

He has dared to lay bare her battered and befouled body, her woundedness, her very nakedness. He has ignored her protests, he has denied her the privacy and sanctuary of her own body.

"Who was it who came into the stairwell? Was he the—rapist? Or did he find you after—after it happened . . ."

No no no. Not ever.

No way that Hannah can speak the truth to Wes: She has no idea what the truth is.

"—no one heard you? No one saw you? A man attacked you, beat and raped you, and—no one heard?"

Except for the quick-shallow breathing that animates her body Hannah lies very still. This, the involuntary infusion of air, greedy insucking of oxygen to maintain her battered and befouled and useless life, she cannot deny.

"Was there a parking attendant? Where was he?"

Very still. Not hearing.

Wes considers: multitiered parking garage, remote corners of the garage, a semi-deserted top floor, the stairwell. Almost, he can envision Hannah in the stairwell, heedlessly descending in high-heeled shoes . . .

"—was it one of the parking attendants? Who found you? Or—was *he* the rapist?"

Wes has begun to sound frantic, deranged. Hannah doesn't dare confront him, he would see the guilt in her eyes.

Here is another blunder: Telling Wes she'd fallen in the stairwell at the Marriott. It seemed to her crucial to establish the Marriott in Far Hills, to nullify any possibility of the Renaissance Grand in Detroit. But in inventing concrete steps to account for her bruises, Hannah has had to invent a stairwell. And in inventing a stairwell, she has had to invent being rescued from it. And in inventing a rescuer, she has unwittingly invented a (possible) rapist.

Yet Hannah insists, she hasn't been raped at all.

"—was he a Black man? Who found you in the stairwell? I seem to remember, parking attendants at the Marriott are Black . . ."

No no no.

Life in the body, terrifying. You never realize until things go wrong.

"Hannah, please look at me. We have to get medical help for you, and we have to notify the police."

Hannah wants to scream at her tormentor-husband to leave her alone, her life is over, she has destroyed her own life out of vanity, stupidity. She'd had no intention of such destruction, yet it has happened.

As the residents of Detroit's "inner city" in July 1967 had reveled in their rage, had set fire to their surroundings commensurate with their fury, only to discover when the fires subsided that they'd burned down their own neighborhoods: their homes.

Fire burns and does its duty. We must not interfere.

The fire in the body, too, we must not interfere with its burning.

Her life is over, Hannah thinks. Her life in the body. The female in the body. Where he'd raked her with his nails, penetrated her without love, jeering at her, her very hunger. Still, not rape, Hannah insists to herself it was not rape, Hannah cannot find words to explain to the anguished husband looming above her. She can only shake her head mutely *No*.

Wes persists, grieving and suspicious: What Hannah has told him—falling on the steps in the stairwell—doesn't explain the vaginal injuries. The particular bruises around her neck. Hannah is not remembering what was done to her. *She must remember.*

The raging husband, his future, too, has collapsed. At this moment, he cannot think of a future. He can only be satisfied with vengeance—an arrest of the rapist, punishment. Of the injury to Hannah he cannot (yet) think, the wound is his as well for the woman is *his wife*.

Most primitive of (male) instincts: sexual possession. *His.*

Wes has found Hannah's clothing thrown across a chair as if she'd hastily undressed the night before. Soiled, torn, smelling of her body. He lifts the rumpled white linen trousers, examines the (discolored) silken crotch and throws the trousers down in disgust.

How has it come to *this*, his life as a man! As a husband, father.

On a bureau Hannah's large leather handbag lies open. In a fury Wes turns it upside down, its jumbled contents spill out onto the bureau top—sleek black leather wallet, gold-glittering compact, tubes of lipstick, comb, small brush, wadded tissues, a silver ballpoint pen, ticket stubs . . . One of these stubs, Wes discovers, with mounting excitement, is for the Far Hills Marriott parking garage.

Wes snatches up the ticket, elated.

No idea where this will lead, but Wes will follow.

.   .   .

Insisting: Hannah must be examined by a doctor.

Not at the Beaumont Hospital ER in Birmingham where Hannah might be recognized and identified but by their primary care physician, an internist whom they know socially, who, at Wes's urgent request, is willing to see Hannah in his office on short notice.

No doubt wondering what the urgency and the secrecy are about.

"This has to be in confidence, Norman," Wes says, "you have to give me your word."

Norman Schell hesitates. He sees that usually imperturbable Wes Jarrett is agitated, and his usually well-groomed wife is looking ill, near-unrecognizable.

"I don't think that I can give you my word as a physician," Norman Schell says. "But as a friend . . ."

"Yes! Thank you." Wes clutches at Norman's hand in a desperate sort of handshake.

After Schell examines Hannah in private, he reports to Wes that yes, it does appear that Hannah has been sexually assaulted as well as beaten, but Hannah refuses to submit to a pelvic exam.

She insists that she has *not been raped.* She has no memory of rape, no memory of anyone attacking her, hitting her—all she remembers is falling down a flight of concrete steps in the parking garage, striking her head, managing to recover, and driving home with a migraine headache.

Wes listens incredulously as Hannah retells her story, now claiming not to remember anyone pushing open the door to the stairwell. She doesn't remember a "kind" man helping her to her feet, walking her to her car . . .

"Hannah! You were just telling me . . ."

"My brain aches! I'm in too much pain to think."

It's a matter of great mortification to Hannah, Wes hadn't allowed her to shower before bringing her to Schell's office. Norman Schell, seeing her in such a condition! Smelling her! Smelling *him* on her.

But of course, a victim of sexual assault cannot be allowed to shower and cleanse herself. Not ever again.

Is it a violation of medical ethics, that Norman might, or surely will, remark to his wife, Melissa, that evening that a distraught Wes Jarrett brought his wife to his office that day badly bruised, with (evident) vaginal injuries, (evidently) a victim of rape?

(The look on Melissa Schell's smug face! All the worse, Melissa is some sort of physician herself, possibly a psychiatrist. Hannah shudders.)

If only Hannah had had the strength and the foresight to have showered and bathed at home, before Wes discovered the bruises. If only she'd been shrewd enough to prevent Wes from discovering the bruises at all . . .

Areas of numbness in her body. Patches of amnesia in her brain.

"Your wife is in a state of shock, Wes. That's all that I can say with certainty."

Schell has measured Hannah's blood pressure three times and each time Hannah has winced as her upper left arm is squeezed, tight. It seems that her blood pressure is "extremely" low, she is in danger of fainting.

Schell insists: Hannah should be taken directly to the Beaumont ER for bloodwork and a thorough pelvic examination. X-rays of her skull, neck, ribs, right ankle. Vaginal swabs, in the event of rape . . .

Hannah cringes, hearing. *But she was not raped!*

It's entirely possible, Schell says, with grim satisfaction, that Hannah has a hairline skull fracture, which could be very dangerous. It's possible that she has been infected with a venereal disease—yes, instantaneously! The ER will contact the authorities. Police have to be involved if a crime has been committed, in this instance a clear case of assault and (possible) rape.

He, too, will be making a report to police. It's Michigan state law, there is no way around it.

No way around it?—Wes is dumbfounded.

"You gave me your word, Norman!"

"No. I did not, Wes."

"If this were your wife—"

"If this were my wife I would certainly take her to the ER," Schell says sharply, "since I love my wife."

Hannah protests that Schell has no right to violate her privacy, report her case to the police, she would never have consented to the examination if she'd known. Her voice rises shrilly, she would like to claw at Norman Schell's face.

Eager now to leave Schell's office. So mortified, exhausted. In the parking lot pulling away from Wes who grips her hand, as a dog might struggle against a leash tight around its neck.

No no no—Hannah can't bear the thought of the ER. Being examined, touched again.

Can't bear the thought of being *looked at*, assessed by strangers.

As if, labeled a "crime victim," Hannah no longer has dominion over her own body.

Hannah pleads with Wes to drive her home, not to the ER. She is desperate to soak in a hot bath. She will take aspirin, she will try to have a nap. One hour! He will ruin her life if he insists on the ER, she will never forgive him.

All she wants, Hannah says, is to be her normal self for the children. They will never notice anything unusual about her. In fact she wants to pick them up at school . . .

Not possible, Wes says grimly. Ismelda will pick them up, he's taking her to the ER.

Hannah weeps helplessly. She feels so filthy, she tells Wes, she can't bear herself in this state. Please, will Wes drive her home? She will be her normal self again by morning.

But Wes refuses: Not possible. Not home. Not yet. Not now.

Wes is becoming impatient with Hannah, he is losing sympathy for her. This woman, a hysteric, isn't behaving like his wife at all. *His* wife is reasonable, poised.

His wife has never taken up so much emotional space in their marriage as she has in just this brief period of time, this morning. Wes is baffled, stymied. Other men's wives are emotional, hysterical—not *his*.

He'd seen, in Norman Schell's eyes, that look of alarm, wariness—the wish not to be involved. If Hannah has indeed been raped, if a criminal case will ensue.

Wes tries to speak comfortingly to Hannah, as he might to one of the children. He squeezes her hand. Her poor, limp hand! Could crush the delicate bones in his fist.

Surely Hannah understands that she has to have X-rays, a pelvic exam. The thought that Hannah may have been infected with venereal disease is particularly repugnant to her husband who knows exactly why she wants to take a bath: To cleanse herself of the rapist's semen. To wash away all evidence.

He is suffused with rage, he can't bear to think of it.

He is certain, Hannah saw the rapist's face. In the stairwell, as the man reached for her.

Absolutely, Hannah knows the color of the rapist's skin. Wes is certain.

At the ER Hannah is taken from him. At the ER the frightened and abashed husband surrenders the wife, *probable victim of (sexual) assault.*

Behind drawn curtains Hannah is examined by a senior physician and his assistants, most of whom are disconcertingly young, and appear to be foreign-born; her "vital signs" are taken, she is wheeled away weeping to radiology. Wes is detained, Wes cannot accompany her but is obliged to explain multiple times how he'd come home at the request of their housekeeper, he'd found Hannah in bed too weak to get up, she'd seemed to be running a fever, she was distraught and not herself; in examining her, he'd discovered her bruises and injuries, including vaginal injuries; he'd taken her to their primary care physician who insisted that Wes bring her immediately to the ER.

This account Wes will tell, retell. Eventually, to plainclothes detectives.

For once the story is begun, it cannot be reclaimed. Released to the world, a matter of public record.

In this role which is new to Wes Jarrett, in which he is awkward, vehement, earnest, aggrieved, he will soon resume the entitlement of authority that is his right by birth, class, profession: the man whose word is not to be doubted.

Recalling that Hannah had described a man approaching her after she'd fallen in the stairwell: "One of the hotel employees, she said—had to be a valet parking attendant—'Black'—I think Hannah said . . . 'A Black man'—in a uniform—opening the stairwell door, finding her lying on the floor . . ."

Each time he is required to give this account Wes becomes more vehement, and more certain. The (white) detectives' attentiveness, their sympathy and respect for him, the (white) husband of the rape victim, encourage Wes to be emphatic, decisive, as if he himself had seen the door in the stairwell pushed boldly open, he'd had a glimpse of the figure in the doorway, he'd been there to see the brute face: a Black man, surely an employee at the Marriott, which means he'd have been wearing a uniform, a valet attendant who'd discovered Hannah on the floor in the stairwell where she'd fallen, unable to defend herself.

Wait, Wes is asked: Did this person find your wife *after* she'd been attacked, or *before*?

Before! Since he is the rapist.

Testing the words: *the rapist.*

It has been hours. Wes's voice is quavering, he is sick with rage. The detectives regard him somberly. The husband of the rape victim. *White* husband, *Black rapist.* The detectives' questions are repeated, Wes's account is repeated. How many times repeated, Wes will have no idea. Gradually it seems to be understood, it has been recorded and transcribed, Hannah Jarrett identified her rapist to her husband as a "Black male employee" at the Far Hills Marriott.

Without hesitation Wes makes the statement: Yes. His wife identified the rapist as a "Black male valet attendant" at the Marriott.

Since then, earlier that morning she has had some sort of relapse. She is exhausted, she is in a state of shock. Since the day before she hasn't been *herself.*

And here is definitive proof: Wes provides the detectives with the ticket stub from the Marriott, found in Hannah's handbag.

They can check at the Marriott, Wes says. See which valet attendants were on duty at the time stamped on the ticket.

(Only Hannah's arrival time at the Marriott, 11:53 A.M., is stamped on the ticket. There is no departure time.)

Interviews with Marriott hotel employees will be requested.

Not *all* hotel employees, of course. Focus will be on Black valet attendants who'd been on duty at the Marriott in the early afternoon of the previous day.

Detectives understand. Men understand. When a husband acknowledges that his wife has been raped he is acknowledging—*I have been raped.*

Hannah, too, is being questioned by Far Hills detectives.

It begins to dawn on Hannah: She has opened a door, or has she smashed a window, impossible now to shut the door or repair the window, her faltering words are being taped, transcribed.

But I am not telling you the truth! Surely you must know, why don't you stop me . . .

None of this is true! Only *the husband* believes it is true.

Badly Hannah wants to return home, she is very tired. A battery of tests performed upon her! Tries to feel relief: She does not have a hairline fracture in her skull, which (probably) means that her brain isn't bleeding, she will not collapse from a cerebral hemorrhage in a day or two, leaving her children motherless.

So exhausted! Anxious. Brain numbed by codeine.

Vaguely recalling—falling on concrete steps. Tripping.

Soon, unable to recall her lover at the hotel in Detroit, *he* is the rapist.

But no, *Y.K. is not a rapist.*

A lover cannot be a *rapist.*

She had not resisted, she'd "consented." She is sure.

Whatever happened between Y.K. and Hannah, only Y.K. and Hannah can know. But Hannah is certain: not rape.

Of course it was rape!

He might have strangled you. He is a demon.

Hannah will never see him again—of course. Y.K.'s contempt for her, his brutal behavior, crude, coarse, punitive, sadistic . . . Obviously the man is a misogynist: His hatred for women preceded his behavior toward her.

Nausea, self-loathing. Hoping to return home as soon as possible and obliterate her memory with barbiturates.

As Wes remembers ever more details of the "incident in the stairwell" for the Far Hills detectives, Hannah remembers fewer details. It's as if they are on a seesaw: As one goes up, he goes farther up; the other, down.

Hannah is just slightly panicked, her memory is fading minute by minute. Blurry, smudged, chalk marks on a blackboard partially erased by hand.

No. I didn't see anyone.

I remember falling—starting to fall. I don't remember hitting the bottom. I don't remember hitting my head.

A door opening? A man? No.

No, I don't think so. It's all blank now.

It's known that skull concussions can lead to amnesia. It's known that shock can lead to amnesia.

A childish defiance comes over Hannah: *Why* should she answer questions put to her by strangers? *Why* answer any questions, ever?

Annoying to Hannah, how Wes insists upon telling her story as if it were his own. *His* story, so much more vividly recalled than hers.

And the detectives, inclined to believe the husband, not the wife.

Hannah is being urged to describe the man in the doorway—the man's face: that is, the color of his skin.

And was he wearing a uniform? Was he a hotel employee?

Patiently Hannah repeats: She doesn't remember seeing a door open, and she doesn't remember seeing a man opening it. Certainly, she does not remember a face.

Now Hannah is being asked why, if she'd remembered seeing a man in the stairwell doorway just a few hours ago, at home, and had described him to her husband, has she ceased remembering this man now?

To this, Hannah has no reply.

Repeat, repeat, and repeat the same idiotic questions.

Hannah detaches, ceases hearing. Amnesia like a mist passing over her brain.

No one can make me remember. None of you.

And so through subsequent hours, after Hannah has pleaded to be allowed to return home, not to be kept in the hospital overnight.

So tired, Hannah is pushed in a wheelchair to the (automatic) ER doors. Wes hurries to get the car, drives around to pick her up.

The alacrity with which the *concerned husband* gets his vehicle.

Helps the wife to the car. Hannah smiles, thinking how the viewer is deceived: This *concerned husband* is temporary, on camera. Very soon the *furious husband* will reappear.

Here is a small pleasure: Hannah Jarrett shakily on her feet but able to walk to the station wagon at the curb, as strangers arriving at the hospital glance at her in amazement, a deathly-white-faced wraith rising from the wheelchair like a miracle.

Why is Mommy crying?—Mommy *is not crying*.

If Mommy is crying it's because Mommy is so happy to be home.

If Mommy is crying it's because Mommy feels as if she has been away a long, long time and so Mommy is very happy now to be *home*.

Heartbreaking, how needy the children are for Hannah—that is, for Mommy.

Her, Hannah, the children scarcely know. But of course, no children know the people who their parents are, only parents.

Hugging Mommy, kissing Mommy. Freshly showered, hair still damp, in a soft cream-colored cashmere bathrobe Mommy embraces the children.

Burying her face against them in a way frightening to them.

Still, Mommy's head hurts if their voices are loud or the TV is loud or if they bicker or scuffle with each other so they should try to be thoughtful of Mommy.

Contrite Katya presses her forefinger against her lips and then against Conor's lips but Conor hisses like a snake and slaps her hand away.

Ismelda will prepare the children's favorite supper: meatloaf with lots of ketchup, macaroni and cheese with lots of melted (Kraft's American cheddar) cheese, chocolate smoothies for dessert. Ismelda will bathe them with special tenderness since this day has been a nervous day for them and Ismelda will put them to bed and Mommy will come kiss them good night.

As if casually Wes will ask Hannah: "Why are you protecting him?—the thug who raped you."

Hannah glances up, not sure if she has heard correctly.

The man who is her husband, staring at her with a small fixed half smile like a broken wishbone. Staring.

. . .

Inner-city, high-crime area.

At 10:11 P.M. three Detroit police squad cars speeding along Brush Street! Braking in the street in front of a brownstone row house at 1181 Brush! Glaring spinning lights! Six police officers! Orders to bring Zekiel Jones, thirty-one, to headquarters for questioning.

Believed to be a witness to a reported "aggravated assault and rape" at the Marriott Hotel in suburban Far Hills the day before. Strong likelihood Jones is the perpetrator.

Detroit PD assisting Far Hills PD in what would be a "preliminary" step in the Far Hills investigation.

(Faxed) description of the suspected rapist provided by the victim: Black male, mid- or late twenties, six feet, two hundred pounds.

No warrant has been (yet) issued for Jones's arrest. No warrant (yet) to search the premises at 1181 Brush which Jones shares with nine relatives, including his eleven-month-old baby daughter and his eighty-seven-year-old grandmother.

Pounding at the front door. Loud voices, angry-sounding shouts, lights flashing against the front windows of the residence.

Police!—open up! At the hearing officers will swear under oath they'd identified themselves multiple times.

Will swear under oath they'd been given no background information on Zekiel Jones, no idea that he'd been an employee of the Far Hills Marriott for several years, no prior arrests or convictions, no police record, only wanted for questioning in a suburban rape case.

Swear under oath they have no choice but to open fire, officer safety is threatened, suspect is not complying with officers' orders, is believed to be armed and dangerous, is believed to have nearly beaten a (white) woman to death and to have raped her, is believed to be going for a weapon, is suspected to be a part-time drug dealer with weapons in the household, drug dealing everywhere in the "inner city," refuses to identify himself, shouting threats he will kill the officers, refuses to raise his hands and keep his hands where officers can see them, backs away from the door, officers break through door shattering glass, screams and shouts, pushes chair, overturns table shoved at police officers, refuses to kneel on the floor, refuses to raise his hands and keep his hands where officers can see them, refuses to provide ID, refuses to lie on his stomach on the floor spreading arms and legs, resists arrest, strikes at police officers, lunges at officer's firearm to "wrest" it away from him, high on something—crack cocaine probably; eyes flamey red like an animal or drunk, belligerent, uncooperative, flees residence by a rear door, ignores warning shots, in the alley staggers and falls, now on his knees crying Don't shoot me!—don't shoot—*even as he has been shot once, twice, three more times shot: back, shoulders, neck from distances of twelve to twenty feet, yet still considered dangerous, on his stomach in the alley writhing in pain and bleeding badly from five wounds resists arrest, makes threats, refuses to lie still, refuses to keep his hands where officers can see them, refuses to identify himself, refuses to show ID, attempts again to lunge for officer's gun, for officer safety he is handcuffed behind his back, limp arms lifted, heavy-muscled limp arms and (thick) wrists handcuffed as finally Zekiel Jones lies motionless and cooperative on his stomach scarcely breathing in the alley beside the brownstone residence at 1181 Brush Street bleeding to death from five gunshot wounds.*

Ambulance is called at 10:19 P.M., arrives in eight minutes. Sirens, flashing lights.

Lights are extinguished in neighbors' houses. No one visible at windows.

Yet officers are shouting, warning: Stay inside! Stay inside! Stay out of the street!

More squad cars arrive. Now sirens, flashing lights, megaphone.

Wrists cuffed behind his back unconscious Zekiel Jones is carried on a stretcher to the ambulance, bleeding badly he is lifted inside and the ambulance speeds away with siren deafening, red light flashing.

No weapons will be found in the alley, no weapons will be found inside Zekiel Jones's house. No "controlled substances" except prescription blood pressure pills in the possession of the grandmother.

A moderate level of alcohol, equivalent to two or three beers, but no drugs in Zekiel Jones's blood.

Taken to the ER at Detroit General Hospital where Zekiel Jones will undergo emergency surgery and be declared dead at 11:58 P.M.

Headline in the next day's Detroit News:

ARMED SUSPECT IN FAR HILLS RAPE CASE
FATALLY SHOT IN BRUSH ST. STANDOFF WITH DETROIT POLICE

Disguise

At last. After weeks. Venturing out.

Out of the house. *Out* of Far Hills.

Though her destination isn't far: Saint Jude's Children's Hospital, Franklin Hills.

Or is it, more precisely, Saint Jude's Children's Cancer Center.

In fact: Saint Jude's Memorial Children's Cancer Center.

Dark glasses hiding half her face. Silk head scarf like a chemotherapy patient, hasn't "lightened" her hair in weeks and the dark roots are showing and these dark roots glinting silver.

Not advised to operate heavy machinery but she drives very cautiously, takes a longer route to Franklin Hills avoiding serious traffic.

Often lately, can't remember names: names new to her, strangers' names, names from long ago, childhood names.

Names of persons who have died as if in dying they'd sunk into a great lightless pit pulling their names in with them.

Zekiel Jackson? Zekiel Johnson? Zekiel Jones?

Great lightless pit pulling their names in with them.

No Tears!

I am a volunteer. Yes, I have called, my name should be on the list—
'Hannah Jarrett.'"

"Yes. This is my first time at Saint Jude's."

"Yes, I am a mother. Yes, my children are still young."

"No—I mean *yes,* there was someone in my family with . . ."

"A long time ago. Treatments were different then. Radiation,
chemotherapy—I think it's all changed now."

"Thank *you.* I—I will remember: No tears!"

Often, lately: has difficulty remembering names.

Since *it* happened: a fall on concrete steps, striking her head.

"A 'concussion.' Fortunately, not a skull fracture."

Slowly, the bruises have faded. Even the welts in the soft white skin
of her thighs.

And with fading, the memory of the bruises, welts. *Him.*

Names new to her, entering her life too late in her life—these she
has had difficulty remembering.

Names of strangers: Dr. T__, therapist, smiling at Hannah thinly,
warily.

Names of long-ago. Childhood.

Susan. Susanne. Susannah?

Of course, she remembers *Susie.*

Hannah's cousin Susie, her aunt Ellen's daughter. Stricken with
bone cancer, Ewing's sarcoma, seven years old. *Seven!* Hannah had
been six at the time.

At first, pretending not to know that something terrible, unspeakable, had happened to Susie.

Nor did Hannah's mother explain, exactly. A vague nervous explanation of why they weren't seeing Susie and her parents for Christmas as usual—*A bad thing is growing in Susie's jaw, the doctors will remove it.*

What did that mean—*a bad thing growing* . . . Hannah was too frightened to inquire.

Whatever it was, Susie had "surgery" on her jaw, and later Susie had "surgery" on her left eye where the *bad thing* had spread.

Behind a closed door Hannah's mother spoke on the telephone with Aunt Ellen, her voice lowered. Sometimes, even through the closed door you could hear sobbing.

Adults did not cry, you did not hear an adult cry. You did not want to hear an adult cry, you would run away and hide.

Nor did Joker Daddy want to hear anyone crying. Not ever, not for any reason.

Tears solve nothing but make you look ugly as hell.

And so—*no tears!*

Joker Daddy did not visit with Aunt Ellen and Uncle Brian, Joker Daddy did not wish to see their maimed little daughter Susie who had once been so vivacious, *pretty.*

Adult responses tended to be incredulous, slightly reproachful.

What! Are you sure—Ewing's sarcoma? A child?

Never heard of such a thing . . .

Must be genetic.

Where voices are hushed a child does not want to listen too carefully.

After the surgeries inflicted upon Susie came "radiation"—"chemotherapy."

Hannah had no idea what these were but understood that, like "surgery," they were hurtful to her cousin, for they took place in Children's Hospital.

Children's Hospital! Words that did not belong together.

Appalling to Hannah to imagine, all of Susie's hair was said to have "fallen out." Soft fine wavy fair-brown hair very like Hannah's hair. So that, according to Hannah's mother, Susie wore little knitted caps on her bald head to keep warm.

Bald head. These words, too, made Hannah feel very sad, she wished her mother would not say such words.

One of Susie's little wool caps was knitted by Hannah's mother, in fuzzy multicolored yarn.

Fitted on Hannah's head, as Mommy was knitting it. For Mommy was not a skilled knitter and often cursed to herself, unraveling rows of yarn and knitting them again until at last she'd finished the rainbow wool cap to which she added a tassel in the shape of a white kitten.

Hannah peered at herself in the mirror, as her mother fitted it on her head. She liked the little cap very much though it was somewhat tight. It did not seem fair, Mommy had never knitted a wool cap for *her.*

There were times Mommy went to visit Susie in the hospital, and later Aunt Ellen where she was living alone now with just Susie, in an apartment in Cleveland, but Hannah was not invited to accompany Mommy, and Hannah was not encouraged to ask questions about these visits.

Strange to Hannah how once Susie had been a part of Hannah's life, the little girls had seen each other at least once a week, they'd played with dolls together, they'd spent hours playing with Susie's dollhouse which her grandfather had built for her but now Susie began to be forgotten—the name "Susie" no longer much spoken. In grade school Hannah had other friends, girls in her class—their faces, their names, began to crowd out "Susie" as a weak radio station is crowded out by stronger radio stations. Hannah was hesitant to ask her mother about Susie because of the look on her mother's face when she did.

A child learns young: You calculate what the look on the adult face will be. Most urgently, the adult male face.

What you want is a smile, approving eyes. You bask in such approval, which is love.

By the age of ten it was said that Susie had undergone eighteen surgeries. Eighteen!

Then, Susie was undergoing "reconstructive" surgery.

Rebuilding the face. The bones. A miracle . . .

But what if it comes back—again . . .

Their insurance won't begin to cover it.

Finally, one day Hannah saw Susie again. Though prepared for a surprise, warned not to register surprise, Hannah didn't recognize her cousin, now ten years old: a child with a pasty-pale face that looked as if it had partly melted, then hardened again, but unevenly; the left eyelid drooping, the eye unnaturally shiny, unfocused, like a doll's eye, scary to see. A face that might have been broken into two asymmetrical halves, then forced together again, like broken crockery.

Something mismatched about the lower jaw. And the nose, one nostril much narrower than the other, just a slit.

And on the head, which seemed unnaturally small, the rainbow knitted cap that Hannah's mother had knitted.

It seemed wrong to Hannah, Susie was not as tall as Hannah when once she'd been taller than Hannah. Bigger.

Hannah shrank from Susie, frightened.

Oh, Hannah! Come here, honey.

You remember Susie . . . Hannah!

On the verge of tears. Wanting to run away.

But then, no. Hannah steeled herself.

Susie smiled shyly, to encourage. Susie, feeling sorry for *her*.

Hannah remained tongue-tied, tremulous. Hannah was convinced, Susie *smelled funny*—like copper pennies held in the hand.

Hannah told her mother she *did not want* to sit beside Susie at dinner.

Nonetheless, Hannah was seated beside Susie at dinner.

Not able to eat much. For Susie *did smell*.

Until at last Hannah's exasperated mother excused her, sent her away from the table.

Yes, ashamed. But sickish-feeling for days afterward, provoked by any strong smell, especially smells of food.

There would be more surgeries for Susie to undergo—"reconstruction." Skin grafts, bone grafts. By seventh grade Susie had a face that might have been mistaken for a "normal" face if you didn't look too closely.

But of course children look too closely. It's in the nature of (cruel) children, particularly middle-school boys, to *look too closely*.

No matter that Susie's hair had grown back a beautiful chestnut-red, springy with curls. And Susie's mother bought her beautiful clothes, bright colors, soft textures. Still you could see that there was something wrong with Susie's face, and that look of being hunted in her face, the glisten of fear in the "good" right eye, the skin like melted/coagulated taffy.

Freak Face—the boys called her.

Laughing, jeering. Taunting. Following Susie at school, along the walkway. And if she turned to them, shrinking back in exaggerated horror.

Not all boys, only just some boys.

Not all days, only just some days.

Worse than the cancer—Susie would say bitterly. How people stared at her in the street, even adults. But always children—*always* children stared. She'd come to fear and dread children, even the "nice" ones.

Something in the human brain that fears and dreads and shrinks from deformity. Even the mildest deformity, the anxious eye seeks.

Hannah vows, she will never succumb to such ignorance.

Hannah vows, she must make penance.

Remembering the shock of the call from her mother—had to be September 1956, Hannah was a newly arrived freshman at the University of Michigan. And Susie, a dropout from UM, living by herself in a place not far from her mother, back in Cleveland, discovered by her mother comatose in a locked bathroom.

Overdose: painkillers.

But also sleeping pills in Susie's blood, alcohol. Many times fatal.

Hannah never knew: if there was a suicide note. If it had been suicide, or an accident.

Why didn't I keep in touch with her.

What is wrong with me!

Dear God, what is wrong with me.

Soon then calling to speak with her mother, burst into tears and cried, cried so hard, desperate to speak of Susie but unable to speak, wracked with sobs, her mother tried to interrupt but Hannah continued crying, finally her mother hung up—*Tears solve nothing only make you look ugly as hell.*

Which is true: Years later, Hannah looks ugly as hell.

There's the pretty lady!

Hannah has begun volunteering at Saint Jude's Memorial Children's Cancer Center in Franklin Hills two mornings a week.

Reading to children who've had cancer surgery, children undergoing radiation and chemotherapy, children with no hair, children with enormous bruised eyes, children with "melted-looking" skin, children with impossibly thin arms and legs, children in wheelchairs, children pushing walkers, children who can walk unassisted, children who've been hospitalized for weeks, children brought to the hospital as outpatients, children who stare vacant-eyed at Hannah as she reads to them in a high-pitched voice meant to be a bunny's voice, children who lapse into twitchy sleep, children who moan and mutter, children who laugh in delight at the bunny voice, children who smile happily at her—*There's the pretty lady!*

Twice a week Hannah steps through the looking glass. Leaves the house at Cradle Rock Road, drives (very carefully) to Franklin Hills, Saint Jude's where unexpected happiness awaits her.

Children have no interest in who we are, still less in what the world knows of us. Hannah *is* pretty in their eyes. Hannah in canary-yellow clothes, jangling bracelets on her wrists, red-lipstick smile. Hannah with her (now newly lightened) hair fluffed about her face. Dangling earrings, tiny green ceramic parrots.

Like inhaling helium! Hannah hasn't felt so *light* since childhood.

Hannah can be trusted by the children, for Hannah is a stranger. No anxiety in her eyes, no trembling mouth, tearful eyes.

Their own mothers cannot match Hannah, reading *Twelve Little Bunnies*.

Cardinal rule: Read slowly. S-l-o-w-l-y.

Even the older children are dulled with painkillers. Even the blank-faced may be listening, intently.

Volunteers have permission to bring colorful balloons, gifts of (small, not expensive) stuffed animals, children's books. Some of these are the books Hannah reads from, her own children's favorite books, outgrown.

When she is allowed Hannah distributes oatmeal cookies, peanut butter cookies, little fruit tarts with no added sugar. Hannah never gazes in stunned horror, never registers dismay.

No tears!—Hannah keeps her word.

Volunteers at Saint Jude's tend to burn out after a few months, so new volunteers are always welcomed.

(She has heard that Marlene Reddick was a volunteer at Saint Jude's, until just recently. But no details.)

Hannah is also a donor to the Saint Jude's Endowment Fund. Wes doesn't know yet how much she has given, Wes professes himself relieved that Hannah has left the house finally, preoccupied with this new volunteer work in Franklin Hills for such a good cause.

Six thousand dollars usually earmarked for the Detroit Institute of Arts at this time of year, contributed now to the Friends of Saint Jude's Endowment Fund.

Most contributors of such substantial sums have children or are closely related to children who'd been treated at Saint Jude's but Hannah is careful to emphasize that this is not the case with her.

"My husband and I have been very lucky so far. But we don't take our luck for granted."

"I think—I just think—that Saint Jude's does such wonderful work . . . I'm happy to help out, I have plenty of spare time."

Signal that she's the wife of a well-to-do man, Hannah has uttered this boastful remark without thinking.

Instinctive in her, she thinks. Her caste.

Also, Hannah makes it a point to hand the six-thousand-dollar check in person to the very nice woman who directs the Saint Jude Friends' volunteer program and who smiles so dazzlingly at Hannah.

"Mrs. Jarrett, thank you!"

It's clear, this very nice woman has no idea who "Hannah Jarrett" is, or was.

"And so, Hannah—you've begun volunteering at Saint Jude's, in memory of your cousin Susie?"

"I—I don't know. I've wanted to volunteer at Saint Jude's for years—but . . ."

Stammering foolishly. Taken by surprise. When had she told Dr. T__ about her cousin? *Had* she told him?

Stricken with shyness Hannah scarcely dares lift her eyes to the therapist's face for fear that the wise-old-man eyes will peer into her soul, stained as a filthy sponge.

Dr. T__ has come to Hannah highly recommended, however. A *lifesaver*, Dr. T__ has been called.

Virtually every woman friend of Hannah's acquaintance is taking prescription medication for anxiety, depression, insomnia, or some combination of all of these, as they are likely also to be seeing thera- pists; among these, Dr. T__ is said to be outstanding. *Oh that wonder- ful man!—saved my life.*

Hannah feels in Dr. T__'s office like one who has swum across a treacherous river, risking drowning, now lying exhausted on the shore, a broken figure, pitiable, not blamable.

Kindly Dr. T__, whose voice is soothing, sympathetic. If only he would not settle his girth into the black leather swivel chair so fre- quently, causing it to creak: an immense chair with levers, little wheels. Hannah has visited Dr. T__ just three times in his attractive tastefully furnished office and each time imagines that the creaky swivel chair has been made of the (amputated) foot of a large mammal—hippo, rhino, elephant.

And Dr. T__, too, reminds her of one of these creatures: massive man, pouchy eyes, sagging jowls, in his early seventies. His attention to Hannah is absolute, he could be her father.

Not Hannah's actual father who'd been Joker Daddy (who'd sneer at all this and demand to know the cost of each ridiculous session) but another kind of father—unjudging, forgiving. In a heartbeat, Hannah would trade one father for the other.

Instinctively Hannah softens her voice in Dr. T__'s office. She is pained by her shrill voice at home, scolding the children, calling up the stairs for Ismelda, querulous over the phone, not really *her* voice but the voice of a stranger who has taken her place. Here, Dr. T__ sometimes has to ask Hannah to speak just a little louder.

Carpeted office, subdued lighting: potted ferns, reproductions of Monet's *Water Lilies,* van Gogh's *Sunflowers,* comfortable chair for Hannah, the solace of the banal/familiar. After Hannah's *breakdown, collapse, relapse* following the assault in the Marriott parking garage and its complicated aftermath she has seen several therapists, in each case just one, preliminary visit; Dr. T__ is the only therapist she has trusted enough to have seen several times.

Simultaneously, once a month, Hannah sees a Far Hills psychophar- macologist, who prescribes a delicate cocktail of medications for her. Dr. T__ provides *talk therapy* which is considered equally important though Hannah is a reticent patient, often sitting mute for minutes at a time with no idea what to say that she might not, at a later time, regret: She has spoken only generally of her marriage, her family, her background, and she has provided only the most vague "memories" of the assault in the Marriott garage . . . Hannah's physical injuries have faded, or nearly.

Dr. T__ never saw these physical injuries (of course). As a therapist he doesn't examine patients, indeed his patients are "clients" and the issues between them are rarely physical, exclusively a matter of speech. It is possible (Hannah supposes) that out of curiosity Dr. T__ has looked into the (alleged) rape, the (controversial) shooting death of the Black suspect, but he would never refer to any information acquired outside his sessions with any client.

In Dr. T__'s presence Hannah presents herself as vulnerable, hesitant, seductive as a young girl might be, not sexual, or not overtly sexual, but seductive, arousing in the (male) therapist a wish to protect, to shield from harm.

It's a subtle distinction: seductive, sexual. Hannah would not want to misjudge.

For Dr. T__ Hannah doesn't dress in the bright-flowery colors she wears to Saint Jude's to cheer up child cancer patients but in more conservative colors, in more elegant clothes, never trousers but skirts, dresses; her legs are sleekly encased in nylon, her shoes are stylish pumps, but not showy; if Dr. T__ is in his seventies he has formed his notion of feminine beauty in another era, that favored dresses, stockings, pearls, soft-haired and soft-voiced women.

". . . wanted to volunteer at Saint Jude's for years, they do such good work. Nothing sadder than children with cancer. Just breaks your heart . . . I think we all want to 'give something back' to the community, the society . . . We all—we all feel . . ."

Each word Hannah utters is a sincere word, a legitimate word, yet the accumulation of words leaves her mouth numb, as with Novocain: All that she says is fraudulent, anyone can tell.

Daring to lift her eyes to Dr. T__ and sees, appalled, that the wise eyes are not kindly at all but contemptuous, cold. *He* is not deceived.

Rich man's wife, pretending to be penitent.

Claiming to have been a rape victim.

Claiming to be suicidal. What a joke!

Some bullshit about her cousin she'd avoided when she was needed, years ago.

Hannah is so stunned, for a moment she can't move, then, hurriedly, stumbles to her feet, desperate to escape this place in which she has been exposed. Her face is hot with blood. Her "soft" hair has fallen into her face. She murmurs an excuse to Dr. T__ who stares at her in surprise.

"Hannah? Mrs. Jarrett? What's wrong? Are you—leaving? So soon?"

The therapist seems to be genuinely alarmed. His contempt for Hannah, his loathing of her, he must have assumed he'd successfully disguised.

"I—I need to leave. I'm not feeling well . . ."

Hannah does feel faint. She has located her handbag, beneath her chair like a sprawled dead thing. Dr. T__ makes a gallant effort to heave himself up from the elephant-foot chair but he is too heavy, he falls back, wheezing.

Blindly Hannah flees from the therapist's office as Dr. T__ calls after her in a voice Hannah wishes to think is repentant, remorseful, but no, she will never return, she has been unmasked by the *lifesaver* himself.

In her car in the parking lot where no one can see Hannah bursts into tears, hiding her disfigured face.

Still, her happiness is Saint Jude's. Where the afflicted children adore the *pretty lady* in bright clothes, reading to them in a bright bunny voice, never betraying their trust by bursting into tears, nor even brushing tears from her eyes.

Through the looking glass, Hannah thinks. No remnant of her other life follows her here. The children see only *her*, they know nothing of Hannah Jarrett. No cause to fear Hannah as they might fear a medical worker, or their own mother stricken with hope.

"Is it—Hannah?"

On her way to the volunteers' lounge where the children await her Hannah turns, sees a (woman) physician, in a white jacket, smiling at her tentatively, as if unsure of her identity; too late now for Hannah to continue as if she hadn't heard her name called for the woman is Norman Schell's wife—Marcella, *Melissa*?—and there is no way to avoid an awkward exchange. Indeed, Melissa appears uncomfortable, as if she regrets having impulsively called to Hannah.

Not friends but social acquaintances. Tenuously linked to each other by mutual friends. It has been some time since they've seen each other, at one of the large, lavish Far Hills holiday parties the previous winter.

Hannah feels a stab of dread. Melissa Schell is Norman Schell's wife, staring at Hannah now with pitying eyes, clearly sorry she'd detained Hannah, for certainly Norman told his wife about Wes Jarrett bringing Hannah to his office for an emergency examination back in May, certainly Norman could not have resisted telling his wife that Hannah Jarrett had been (evidently) raped, badly bruised, injured, and that he'd urged Wes Jarrett to take her to the ER at Beaumont; since then, no doubt both Schells have followed the disjointed story as it made its way through local media, in which the rape victim remains unidentified though (Hannah is sure) many people know who this "victim" is by now, and everyone knows that the rapist was a Black valet attendant at the Far Hills Marriott, a violent predator involved in dealing drugs (at the Marriott?), subsequently shot and killed by Detroit police acting in conjunction with Far Hills police . . .

Suffused with shame Hannah backs away from Melissa Schell in her smart white physician's coat. Can't linger to chat, she's expected in the volunteers' lounge at this very minute, she has brought *The Cat in the Hat* to read to the children. Desperate to escape Melissa Schell's grave eyes.

But now, Saint Jude's has become contaminated. For (of course) Melissa Schell will tell others on the staff, within a day or two it will become generally known at Saint Jude's that one of the volunteers is the "unidentified" rape victim from the Marriott, and this person is Hannah Jarrett; an object of sympathy but also pity but also revulsion, Hannah *knows*.

This final session at Saint Jude's, Hannah doesn't read in so lively and entertaining a way as she'd read previously. Hannah doesn't smile as happily as she'd smiled previously. Her face is strained, stiff—not *pretty*. The children are unusually quiet, subdued. Why are they not laughing? *The Cat in the Hat* is *funny*.

But *The Cat in the Hat* is not funny. Too much happens, too much for small children to process. Too much breakage, smashing. Too much that is terrifying.

For the first time Hannah sees individual children too clearly. She glances up from *The Cat in the Hat,* distracted. Very sick children, some of them in wheelchairs. Pale, malnourished, bruised arms, stick legs, disfigured faces, eyes fixed upon Hannah in unspeakable yearning. Why on earth had she ever imagined, in her vanity, that she was bringing happiness, any kind of *cheering up,* to these children . . .

Hannah's eyes fill with tears, tears spill over onto her cheeks, exactly as forbidden.

"Suspect"

There comes the (dreaded) day Wes will ask Hannah how her volunteer work at the children's hospital is going and Hannah will say quietly *It isn't.*

Holding her breath as Wes seems about to reply except a headline in the newspaper rivets his attention. It is breakfast time, for Wes, but it is also newspaper time, the two times overlapping, conflicting, for as he peruses columns of newsprint Wes is also consuming food on a plate Hannah has placed before him, scarcely glancing at the plate, scarcely aware of the food, for something in the columns of newsprint absorbs him utterly, causes his shoulders to stiffen like a soldier's.

Silent as a wraith Hannah passes behind the husband to place a mug of steaming-hot coffee before him. Her vision which has been underwater since dawn seems to further occlude so that even if her eyes move involuntarily onto the front page of the *Detroit Free Press* she is unable to make out headlines, photographs.

Hannah has arrived at that stage in life: soothing underwater. Floating beneath the surface of a stagnant lake nonetheless dazzled with sunspots as alive as algae. The drug cocktail promises to blur harsh headlines, ugly photographs.

Steeling herself for the husband's reply to her abashed murmured words but clearly Wes hasn't heard a syllable.

It isn't. Is not.

It is not.

Much else in Hannah's life *is not.* She isn't sure what Wes knows, wishes to know, does not know, does not wish to know. A murky area of underwater, unexplored.

No reason for Wes to know what Hannah does/does not do in his absence. Since *it*—(unnamed by Wes: *the rape*)—he avoids her as discreetly as a husband who shares a (king-sized) bed with a wife can avoid the wife, rising early, going to bed (calculatedly) later than the wife, away from the house approximately twelve hours each (week)day but sometimes also gone overnight, over the weekend, "on business."

Avoiding Hannah, which means avoiding touch. Avoiding close quarters, intimacy. Eyes lifting to eyes, smiling in the old way—*no*.

Her touch is poison to him, Hannah thinks: He is the husband of a woman who (he believes) has been *raped*.

More shameful yet, to Wes: *raped by a Black man*.

That is the shame, the mortification. What Wes knows, or believes he knows. What he believes, when he is most unhappy, that a substantial number of people in Far Hills know.

(Though the alleged "rape victim" has never been identified in the media and the alleged "rapist," shot dead by Detroit police officers, has never been linked definitively to the rape and had not even been arrested at the time of his death, not a "suspect" but only a "person of interest" in another police department's investigation.)

Wes never, but never discusses *it*. Those events of the previous spring he'd endured stoically. Enough!

After Hannah's *breakdown, collapse, relapse* when Wes was obliged to be sympathetic, husbandly. And somewhere around that time, he'd still loved her. Or felt as if he loved her. Or could recall *having loved her*.

Still, husband and wife share the spacious bed, and husband and wife share the spacious house. Most mornings, if she is downstairs in time, and if her hands don't shake too badly, the wife prepares the husband's breakfast, reasoning that this is something she can do, a simple task, a task that suggests loving attentiveness while requiring a minimum of neither, even underwater and with the wife's vision occluded.

Hannah also prepares the children's breakfasts. This, too, she reasons, is something she can do, though the children are pickier than their father, which cereals they will eat, which fruits, which flavors of yogurt, changing their tastes frequently as if to stymie her.

If the kitchen at breakfast time is too much for the wife/mother, Ismelda will take over. Profound relief for the wife/mother, knowing that Ismelda is close at hand: as a tightrope walker is grateful for a net to break her fall.

Somehow, Wes has managed to finish breakfast but for a yolky scum and smear on his plate, amid toast crumbs the size of tiny ants. Swiftly and efficiently if without tasting anything, scarcely glancing at it, the husband has eaten. He has finished with the *Free Press*, its pages shuffled dismissively together, set aside. Rising now hurriedly from the table—(for the children are clambering downstairs, accompanied by Ismelda, Daddy just doesn't have time for the children at this hour)—on his way to work, half-hour commute if he leaves early enough, which he intends to do this morning.

Wistfully Hannah recalls the (young) husband kissing her cheek before leaving for the day but that has been years, years ago, possibly romantic-minded Hannah isn't even remembering clearly, confusing a breakfast-husband-goodbye scene from the movies with a scene out of her own (younger) life, probably yes, this is so, for the scene in Hannah's memory is in black-and-white, the wife was wearing a ruffled apron, the husband a fedora, might've been Claudette Colbert, James Stewart.

With a vague distracted-husband smile, not quite meeting her eyes, Wes is assuring Hannah how good it is for her, volunteer work that's important, worthwhile, helping out those poor children and what an excellent opportunity, too, for Hannah to meet new friends—which reminds him: He will be late coming home tonight, don't wait dinner for him, no need to keep his dinner in the oven, he'll probably eat out with __, __ (Hannah never remembers the names of Wes's associates).

Hurrying now to escape the house, to drive away in the station wagon, before the children burst into the kitchen crying *Where's Daddy? Is Daddy gone?*

Only after the children have had breakfast, and Ismelda has driven them to school, and Hannah is alone in the eerie silence of the house as in a mausoleum from which even echoes have faded, does Hannah realize that something is wrong: She'd seen Wes set the newspaper aside as he usually does for someone else to discard but the paper isn't in its usual place on a counter, isn't anywhere in the kitchen, which means that Wes made a conscious decision to take it away himself, without Hannah noticing; which means, Hannah thinks, that there is something in the newspaper that Wes prefers Hannah doesn't see though Wes must know that Hannah has more or less ceased reading local papers even as she has ceased watching local newscasts, in fact Hannah avoids "news" whatever the source. And so, Hannah thinks, whatever is in the *Free Press* this morning that Wes doesn't want her to see must be serious, indeed.

Hannah hurries to the garage, to retrieve the slovenly slew of newspaper pages from the trash where Wes tossed them, seeing nothing of interest on the front page but then, in the lower right-hand corner, an article headlined *Police Shooting of Rape Suspect Ruled "Justified."*

Hannah begins to tremble so badly, she can barely hold the newspaper steady enough to read the article.

Hannah learns: There has been a five-week investigation by a Wayne County civilian review board, determining that Detroit police officers have been cleared of charges of "excessive force" in the fatal shooting of Zekiel Jones back in May.

Hannah turns to the continuation of the article, on an inner page, but not much more information is provided.

It is stated that several police officers fired shots into the back of the thirty-one-year-old "rape suspect" Jones as he was fleeing them from his residence on Brush Street, Detroit; officers claimed that Jones was believed to have a weapon and to be threatening them, though no weapon was subsequently found in the alley, or in the vicinity. It was believed that Jones was involved in drugs and illegal firearms though neither were found in the house, or in the vicinity. Nonetheless, the review board ruled "mitigating circumstances" and found the shooting "justified."

At the end of the article it is noted that the shooting of Zekiel Jones has become a "controversial local issue" and that demonstrations have been held in front of Detroit police headquarters resulting in the arrests of several activists. A "midnight candle vigil" was held following the decision of the review board but after several hours was "peacefully dispelled" by Detroit riot police.

Hannah is relieved, little is said of the "Far Hills rape victim" whose identity has not been revealed. Nor is there a photograph of the deceased Jones.

Hannah tries to recall—was Zekiel Jones an official *suspect*?

Hannah tries to recall—had she ever accused anyone of *rape*?

She is confused, she is trembling badly. Despondency has clouded her mind.

Wes has said *Stop thinking about it.*

Wes has advised *There's nothing you can do about it now, so stop thinking about it. You have the children to think of, you are their mother.*

Wes is practical, pragmatic. Wes has had enough of Hannah's stricken conscience as Wes has had enough of Hannah's migraine-prone femaleness.

He stiffens if she touches him, so she has ceased touching him.

She stiffens if he touches *her,* so he has ceased touching her.

Hannah has overheard Wes on the phone speaking with an unknown party: *She's been like this since—you know. She's been—what's the term—"self-medicating."*

It is true, Hannah has been *self-medicating*. For Hannah is a convalescent. From what precisely, Hannah doesn't know.

Certainly, Hannah is *unwell*. She could not begin to sleep at night without medication. Her thoughts are obsessive and as clotted as meat mangled in a grinder, often she finds herself standing very still, thinking, or trying to think, as time passes by her in a drifting stream.

Initially Hannah tried to confront Wes, insisting to him that she'd never identified a Black man as the rapist, she'd never acknowledged that she had, in fact, been raped; it is Wes who has made the accusation. But Wes denies this vehemently, Wes tells Hannah that it is she who remembers wrongly, she has been ill, she has been *not herself,* confused, her brain has been affected, she'd fallen and injured her brain, she is amnesiac, she takes too many drugs, she drinks too much, just stop, for Christ's sake—*stop.*

And so, Hannah *stops*. Hannah *will stop*.

Desperate at the prospect of losing her husband. For it can happen, it has been happening ever more frequently in Far Hills—*losing the husband.*

Begging to be forgiven for what she recalls, what she believes, what she knows to be true. No one raped her, certainly not Zekiel Jones, why will none of them believe her.

He has not called her, since. Her lover.

Unless it is her husband whom Hannah loathes, and hopes he will leave her: for if *he* leaves *her,* she will retain the house and the children, she will not lose her place in Far Hills.

Don't be ridiculous, what are you saying. You can't live without him. Can't live without a husband. Not in Far Hills.

You adore him, you are lost without him. He is the only man who has ever loved you and even if, now, he no longer loves you, still he is the only man who has loved you.

Also, you won't retain the house. Alimony and child-support payments will make of you a genteel beggar in a rented row house in Franklin and your Far Hills friends will never see you again.

Almost, Hannah has come to believe that Zekiel Jones was someone she'd known. Not a friend exactly but someone in her life. Despite the difference in their ages, a classmate of hers in Cleveland. One of those Black students she'd observed at a distance in high school, attracted to them, the girls as well as the boys, in a way envious of them, believing that they were together in ways their white classmates were not but with no way to bridge the distance, or no way that Hannah knew.

Now, trying to summon the face of the parking attendant at the Marriott smiling at her as if indeed he knew her, and she knew him—*You have a good day, ma'am!*

But Hannah can't recall, the smiling face has vanished.

"No Help"

He was not the one. Not him.
    I never identified him. Never named him.

Not sure why, why she is here, or what exactly this place is.

Something has urged Hannah *here*. Ascending the concrete steps to the Far Hills police station in the single-story municipal building it shares with the post office.

Except, two steps from the top, Hannah hesitates, considering.

In an instant, struck still. A paralysis has slid over her body as invisible as a second skin.

In dark glasses, a wide-rimmed straw hat obscuring half her face. A Guatemalan bag of woven hemp slung over her shoulder.

Strangers pass by Hannah entering the police station, exiting the police station, taking little notice of the woman in linen trousers, linen jacket, silk shirt, and high-heeled sandals.

He should not have died.

I don't understand: Why did you kill him.

If one of the figures passes brazenly through her Hannah will understand that this is the zone she has come to call *underwater*. Here, sounds are muted, imprecise. It is not possible to distinguish clearly between the harmless chittering of birds and the staccato cries of sirens in the distance. If there are human cries, or babies' cries—these, too, are obscured in *underwater*.

Sometimes in this fugue state Hannah is distracted by an agitation of the air at her elbow. She turns, but no one is there.

Turns again, and no one. But the *possibility* of someone whom now she sees at a distance as if, in an instant, this person (usually male) has the power to veer rapidly away from her, silently.

In this way she has seen, or imagines she has seen, Y.K. at a distance, in the act of turning away from her. She has glimpsed the ponytailed boy whose name she doesn't know, unshaven and swaggering on a Far Hills street where his kind doesn't belong.

How far the Far Hills police station is!—at the very end of Main Street, a longer walk than Hannah has anticipated in her high-heeled shoes.

Hannah has patronized the post office countless times but she has never once entered the police station. *That other* dimension of life, like a hospital, or a mortuary, with which, she has liked to think, she has nothing to do.

A weekday morning of tasks, errands. For months in her trance of shame, mortification, soul-fatigue, Hannah has not often left the house, but today boldly—bravely—she has stopped at Village Pharmacy, Village Stationer's, Village Cobbler where she has taken a pair of Wes's (heavy, leather) Florsheim shoes to be reheeled.

Tasks, errands. Proof of domestic life. There is solace in these as in the bracketed spaces of a calendar or the precisely measured bars of a window.

Hannah is feeling blurred, dreamy. It is possible that, indeed, Hannah is dreaming and this is all underwater.

Yet, Hannah is *here*. Something has drawn Hannah *here*.

Except, Hannah cannot seem to decide: to enter the police station, or to retreat.

"Ma'am? Can I help you?"

A police officer leaving the station has noticed the blond-haired woman in her late thirties standing very still on the steps, like a mannequin. Grateful for dark glasses, so dark her dilated eyes are not visible to the officer.

The man is brisk, courteous. He is not unfriendly but he is not smiling. Hannah isn't accustomed to uniformed public-service persons not smiling at her, this is subtly wrong, ominous.

Her smile is stiff, involuntary. It fails to meet her frightened eyes.

"Thank you, officer. No one can help me."

Abduction

*F*ear *a ringing phone.*

Rare for Wes to call Hannah at home during the day, from his office, a signal that this is (surely) bad news.

Bad news Hannah dreads to hear. *More* bad news.

Already she has begun trembling.

Already since the police station the other day, paralysis on the steps, Hannah is susceptible to bursting into tears.

Why why did you. Why did I.

Calmly Wes asks if the children are home, if the children are in the house, Hannah says yes of course, the children are home, not in the house but in the backyard, Ismelda is watching them as they play in the wading pool. At least *Hannah thinks* that is where the children are . . .

. . . faint-headed stumbling to the rear of the house carrying the phone anxious to see if indeed Conor and Katya are in the wading pool, hearing their uplifted happy voices, a vast wave of relief as Hannah assures Wes that yes, the children are safe, of course the children are safe at home, never allowed out of the sight of a protective adult.

Is this a rebuke of her as a mother, Hannah will wonder. As if the children would be otherwise than *safe.*

Not so calm now, his voice quavering with disgust, fury, helplessness Wes tells Hannah that there has been another child abduction, this time in Far Hills—*The first time, in Far Hills.*

According to a news bulletin he has just heard, the abduction took place that morning on Ashtree Common, less than a mile from the Jarretts' home, a private road that intersects with Cradle Rock Road.

Wes is incensed, indignant. That that pervert-murderer would dare to strike *here.*

Hannah opens the sliding glass door, steps out onto the redwood deck, sunshine strikes her between the eyes as a steer is struck by a sledgehammer yet in the same instant recovering, frantic to see that yes the children are safe, of course. Splashing noisily in the wading pool oblivious of Mommy staring at them faint with relief that they are *safe.*

Remaining out of sight. Doesn't want to alarm the children should they happen to glance up at her and see something in Mommy's face of which Mommy isn't aware.

Difficult for Hannah to follow the thread of what Wes is telling her, often lately she has difficulty hearing what others say to her, the more vehemently they speak, the more difficulty, as something willful and stubborn in Hannah resists the vehement emotions of others, as a weak swimmer resists forceful waves, out of a wish for self-preservation. *Why, why are you telling me these things. Leave me alone, I do not want to know.*

But yes, terrible news, Hannah is responding as one does—*Oh! Oh, no . . .*

Sickened to hear, as a mother, as a neighbor, that a ten-year-old boy has been abducted from Ashtree Common just a few hours ago, name not yet released to the media, though the boy has been identified as a student at Far Hills Day School and so it's possible (Wes is saying, excitedly) that Wes and Hannah know the parents, it's possible that Wes and Hannah have even met the boy who'd been walking the family dog in a wooded area frequented by joggers and bird-watchers only a few minutes from his house, sighted by a neighbor shortly before he "disappeared into thin air . . ."

Soon afterward the dog turned up whimpering and abashed, trailing its leash.

Babysitter, drawing closer.

Hannah watches the children in the little pool constructed just for them in mimicry of the larger pool for adults with its elegant

Mediterranean-blue ceramic tiles. Weak with love and the anxiety of love for such small bodies, small perfect bodies, as vulnerable to predators as fledgling birds to hawks swooping out of the sky. As she'd stood frozen on the steps to the police station, so Hannah stands frozen now in a paralysis of terror that might be mistaken for resignation as one might stare at a great volcano erupting that had been smoking and smoldering for centuries, flaming lava now spilling from its crater, rushing down the volcano's sides to annihilate everything and everyone in its path: the innocent as well as the guilty.

"But *was* it Babysitter?"—Hannah asks, as if Wes might be able to answer such a question, and Wes says, "Christ, Hannah!—d'you want two of them?"

Hannah bites her lip, rebuked. Like a child who has said the perfectly obvious, yet forbidden thing.

Wes tells Hannah that yes, the modus operandi of the new abduction appears to be similar to the previous abductions to which Babysitter has laid claim, as if there could be any doubt—(for what are the odds against a second pervert, behaving so like the first!)—except this abduction is bolder, more daring than the others: The abductor had driven on a private road, a cul-de-sac, risking being seen by witnesses; he'd parked his vehicle in a small parking lot with only a few other vehicles; he'd risked abducting a child in the late morning, in full daylight, in a sparsely populated area in which his presence might have been noticed; and he'd risked abducting a child with a dog.

Most of all taking a chance in a neighborhood with so many small winding roads, where you can get lost even if you know the area.

"But maybe he knows the area," Hannah says, "maybe he's from Far Hills."

Wes laughs dismissively. As if Hannah has meant to say something witty and not something very stupid.

"Nobody in Far Hills would do such things! Whoever it is he's from the city—the police are sure."

Hannah remains silent. Wes continues: "It's revenge. It isn't even about the children, it's about *us*. He wants to terrorize *us*." In a lowered voice adding, "*White people*. It's what police think but it's kept out of the papers and TV."

Hannah has not heard this. Hannah has not read anything hinting at this. Yet there has come to be a kind of consensus among suburban residents, that Babysitter must be a resident of Detroit.

Implied, Babysitter must be non-white.

But a Black man would be easily noticed in Far Hills. Turning onto Ashtree Common, of all roads. Hannah doesn't point this out.

"—they're thinking, he's *light-skinned*. Or could be *Hispanic*, working for a lawn crew, or construction, and coming back some other time, knowing exactly where to go."

Far Hills is serviced primarily by individuals who are *non-white*. And it's certainly true, many of the workers know the area well, in some cases better than the residents.

"It's like we're held hostage in our lives. In our *white skins*."

Hannah murmurs *yes*. A vision comes to her of Zekiel Jones, in his Marriott uniform, calling after her—*You have a good day, ma'am.*

"Just keep the children safe," Wes says, in the jovial voice with which he ends most conversations, "that's all we can do. We'll go away in August for three weeks, we'll be safe there—northern Michigan."

With a promise to call back when he has more news Wes hangs up. By this time Hannah has returned to the house, unseen by the children in the wading pool.

Sickened, dismayed. Another child! So close.

Hannah considers turning on the TV, or the radio. Yes? No?

A rush of her blood like lust, a sudden yearning to know the worst.

Vigil

And now, the vigil.

A day, a night, another day and another night, no further news of the missing child.

Each of the seven previous abductions attributed to Babysitter has ended in death. Limp child bodies, naked, on their backs displayed in public places in a way to evoke nineteenth-century photographs of dead children in their beauty and serenity.

The shortest interim between the abduction and the discovery of the body has been three days. The longest, eleven.

Hannah tries not to be aware. Hannah tries not to think.

On the brink of sleep, Hannah tries not to dream.

What would it be, to be the mother of the missing child.

What would it be, to be the missing child.

Another morning, another interminable day. So long as the body is not discovered the missing child is still alive.

What would it be, to have hope.

Hannah can think only of her children: She must shield them from knowing. Since it's summer and school isn't in session it isn't difficult to keep the children in quarantine, make excuses for not driving them to see their friends, or allowing their friends to visit them; not so difficult since other parents are keeping their children in quarantine as well.

Hannah dreads their knowing: Something terrible has happened to a child who lives not far away from them, a child like them, who attends their school.

Yes but he's older. Fifth grade in September.

As soon as Wes comes home in the early evening he turns on local

TV news, then again at eleven more news, Hannah keeps away, out of earshot in another room or in bed early steeling herself for a profane outcry of Wes's from downstairs which would signal that the body of the missing boy has been found.

Waking from a gnarled sleep to hear muted voices, discovering Wes gone from the bed, downstairs in his office listening to a radio, volume low.

Outside the windows, darkness. Not the dark that precedes dawn but a pitch-dark. Hannah is astonished, it's three-forty.

Not like Wes, to care so much for "news." To care so much for the lives of strangers.

He is afraid, too. Babysitter, so close.

And—*For the first time, Babysitter has taken one of ours.*

Upstairs in their bedroom before returning to bed Wes lifts a hand to claim Hannah's attention: "Hannah."

"Yes?"

"See here."

Gravely Wes removes a key from the drawer of his bedside table, lifting the key so that Hannah can see it clearly, leading her then to the mahogany cabinet against a wall of the bedroom where he unlocks one of the cabinet doors and removes the gun, which Hannah hasn't seen since Wes purchased it some months ago.

This time Hannah is more attentive to what Wes has to show her: a Smith & Wesson revolver, .44 Magnum. Blue-black finish, short barrel. Always kept loaded, safety lock on. Wes demonstrates how the gun is held in the hand, how the safety lock is switched *off*.

"Y'see? Ready to fire."

Hannah feels a shiver of dread, light-headedness, seeming to see, in her own shaky hand, the weapon *ready to fire*.

"I would only—*we* would only—use this if someone broke into the house, if our family were in danger. And if I'm away, you must be prepared to take my place." Wes speaks in a lowered voice though they are alone in the master bedroom, door shut, at four A.M.

"Hannah? Do you understand? You would call out to him that you're armed, if he's downstairs, for instance—chances are he'll get out of the house immediately. Though you might have to fire a warning shot . . ."

Hannah laughs nervously. Who is *him*? What if it's *them*?

Hannah knows nothing about guns, but she does know that before using a gun you should be trained to use a gun. Wes claims to have had a lesson or two, at the gun store, but Hannah suspects he knows little more than she does.

"Like this."

Wes holds out the revolver, aiming the barrel toward the door. His finger is very loosely on the trigger, Hannah sees, uneasily.

(Is the safety *on* or *off*? Hannah can't recall.)

Steadying his right hand with his left hand, clasping his right wrist as he has seen in movies and on TV, partially shutting one eye, creasing his forehead in a frown.

"Fire."

Hannah steels herself for the earsplitting shot. But there is none.

Wes insists that Hannah do the same. Gun in her right hand, gun lifted, barrel aimed toward the door, finger loosely on the trigger . . . Certainly this isn't a plastic gun, there is nothing toylike about it. Hannah thinks—*Death in my hand.*

Wes lifts and steadies Hannah's wrist, sinking beneath the weight of the gun, for of course Hannah is doing this incorrectly, her heart isn't in it, or her concentration.

In an alternate world, the gun goes off, a bullet penetrates the door, behind the door is the couple's seven-year-old son who screams and falls down dead . . .

Hannah shuts her eyes, cringing. When Hannah opens her eyes nothing has changed.

We are all still here.

Wes in his usual nighttime attire—shorts, T-shirt. Hannah in an attractive apricot-colored silk nightgown, beneath a sashless chenille robe. How bizarre, they are awake at four, whispering, focusing on a "revolver."

Wes, who'd been drinking earlier in the evening, seems stony-sober now, exuding an air of subtle reproach as if, for a long time, he has resented his wife's indifference to the urgent need to defend the household, but is coming to forgive her now.

"The cardinal rule of self-defense is—d'you know, Hannah?"

"The—rule?"

"'You don't owe your adversary the first shot.'"

Wes laughs with grim satisfaction, in an expansive mood now, swiping the gun against his T-shirt and locking it away with a flourish, replacing the key in the drawer of the bedside table and shutting that drawer, too, with a flourish, as if he were being observed.

"That wasn't so bad, was it? Think Annie Oakley."

Hannah laughs, this is so absurd a remark. She, too, is feeling elated, or rather relieved, the gun is locked safely away, the marital crisis has passed.

Each day a marital crisis, for months. Since *it*.

For never will Wes forgive his wife, for having succumbed to *it*.

But for now Wes turns to Hannah, his face warm, enlivened. He is a handsome man, Hannah sees. When the muscles in his face relax and he doesn't look so angry.

Wes kisses Hannah roughly, a mock sort of kiss, mocking its very sentimentality. He squeezes her breast inside the nightgown, dares to press the palm of his hand between her legs. Hannah steps back astonished, laughing nervously.

The first defense, laugh.

Lovemaking for the first time in memory. Many months, Hannah thinks. She has forgotten how even to mime the act, wincing with pain, but not an unbearable pain, certainly she has felt worse pain. *He* is laughing at them, fumbling and drowning amid rumpled bedclothes.

Self-defense. You don't owe your adversary the first shot.

On the second day of the vigil the name of the missing boy is released to the public: *Robbie Hayden*.

The names of the parents are released: *Jill and Brian Hayden*.

Relief!—these names are not familiar to Hannah.

No one Hannah knows. She is sure.

Though the Hayden family lives less than a mile away at 16 Ashtree Circle.

Though Wes insists that they have indeed met the Haydens who are close friends of the Cavanaughs and the Mears, in fact (Wes is certain) he and Hannah went to a Boxing Day gathering at the Haydens' two years ago.

Hannah repeats *no*. She is sure.

Also, Wes points out, the Haydens belong to the Far Hills Country Club where (certainly) Wes has met Brian Hayden on the golf course, more than once. Wes expresses doubt that Hannah hasn't encountered Jill Hayden at the club or at their children's school since Hannah attends Far Hills Day parent-teacher evenings and it would be surprising if Jill Hayden didn't, also.

Nervously Hannah insists *no,* she doesn't think so. Trying to recall "Jill Hayden" and her mind goes blank.

Attractive woman in her late thirties, stylishly dressed, scissor-cut "lightened" hair, cochair of the membership committee at the Friends of the Detroit Institute of Arts.

No!—Hannah has never met Jill Hayden. Hannah has never glimpsed Jill Hayden at Far Hills Day picking up a child—or two—at the rear of the school in a Cadillac Fleetwood station wagon in a long line of vehicles.

They have come to arrest me for the murder of Zekiel Jones.

By chance Hannah is standing at an upstairs window in her house when a Michigan state police vehicle turns into the driveway and approaches the house. Her heart beats calmly, unalarmed.

But no, the plainclothes officers only want to ask questions about *unusual or suspicious persons or activity in the neighborhood, anything out of the ordinary* on the morning of the abduction of Robbie Hayden, or on the preceding day.

Neighborhood. Hannah considers this word. As if Cradle Rock Road residents in their large stately homes on never less than three acres of land are attuned to the street side of life and not rather to the domestic, fortified life within those houses.

There are no sidewalks on Cradle Rock Road as there are no sidewalks on Ashtree Common. There are no children "playing in the street"—there are no "streets" only roads, drives, lanes, passes. Rarely are children visible from the roadway. Rarely are adult residents visible. Daytime traffic is almost exclusively service-oriented—delivery trucks, repairmen, lawn crews, contractor crews, pool maintenance, sanitation truck, UPS.

Nonetheless, Hannah replies to the officers' questions with care. She speaks so softly, the officers ask her to repeat what she has said.

Hannah feels a fleeting excitement for the thought comes to her— *I have the power to confess. That is in my power.*

But Hannah tells the officers apologetically that she has seen nothing, she has heard nothing, nothing unusual, nothing suspicious, not on the morning of the abduction of Robbie Hayden, not the previous day, not ever. Not *here*.

Asked if she is acquainted with the Hayden family, Hannah says *no*.

Asked if her husband is acquainted with the Hayden family, Hannah says *no*.

Asked if her children know Robbie Hayden, Hannah says *no*.

(Adding: Robbie Hayden is much older than her children, who are only seven and four.)

Asked if she is aware of sex offenders residing in the neighborhood, Hannah says with a look of disdain *no*.

Asked if she is aware of "formerly incarcerated" individuals residing in the neighborhood, Hannah says sharply *no*.

Asked if she is aware of sex offenders or formerly incarcerated individuals living anywhere in Far Hills, Hannah shakes her head irritably *no*.

Hannah knows that these are formulaic questions, no insult is intended. Still, Hannah feels subtly insulted, as if one of the police officers has wiped the sole of his shoe on her carpet.

Hannah is surprised that, instead of leaving, the officers ask to speak with Ismelda, too. As if the housekeeper were a resident of Far Hills on a standing with her employers.

"I don't see how Ismelda could help you, but of course," Hannah says stiffly.

As it turns out, Hannah is impressed that Ismelda can provide the officers with much more information than Hannah could: which delivery trucks she'd happened to see on the morning in question, at which house she'd recently seen a plumber's van, which lawn crew services are on Cradle Rock Road on which days, which mornings the Oakland County sanitation truck is in the neighborhood . . . To

Hannah's astonishment, Ismelda knows the names of the Jarretts' lawn crew and their pool-maintenance service, which Hannah herself doesn't know, or would never remember if asked; Ismelda knows that, in recent weeks, there have been two or three new lawn-crew workers at the house, Hispanic she thinks, maybe Guatemalan, who don't speak much English—"But none of them would be *him,* who you call 'Babysitter.'"

"And why do you say that, miss?"

"Because the man who takes children, he could not be one of them. He could not work so hard as they do. They would be too tired to take away children. They would have to have the time. He has a van, to put the children in. He has some place to keep them that was not a crowded place, that nobody would know. He has to be 'white' to go anywhere he wants to go, and not be seen and asked questions like they would be."

Hannah listens in astonishment. Shocking to her, that Ismelda speaks so astutely in her soft humble voice. That Ismelda should utter the word "white" in a way both matter-of-fact and condemning.

After the police officers leave the house Hannah turns away without a word to Ismelda. Hurriedly she goes upstairs, she is too upset to speak with Ismelda just now.

She doesn't help Ismelda prepare the children's evening meal as she usually does when she is home. Her heart flutters with dislike, or fear, of the Filipina housekeeper, the unerring soft voice, the resolve. The betrayal!

As sharp as a steak knife when it's the bland dullness of a bread knife you have depended upon.

Fourth day of the vigil, still no news.

In the matter of a child abduction, no news is *not good news.*

"Mommy, what's *wrong*? Why can't we go *anywhere*?"

Conor is petulant, peevish. Tugging at Mommy's arm, appealing to Mommy in his whiny voice.

Hannah assures Conor that nothing is wrong. Hannah assures Conor that he and his little sister are safe, nothing bad will ever happen to them. And they will be going away soon to northern Michigan to stay in a beautiful quiet place on a lake.

"Is he coming back—the little boy? Where is *he*?"

"What do you mean? What—'little boy'?"

Hannah is mystified, how Conor knows as much as he knows. He has approached his questions in a roundabout way twitching, and squirming, and squinching up his face like an anxious little monkey.

Hannah acknowledges that there is a "lost" little boy—but he is much older than Conor, and his parents had not watched over him carefully enough, the way Mommy and Daddy look after him and his little sister. But everybody thinks that the "lost little boy" will be found and brought home soon so Conor shouldn't worry about it, and above all Conor shouldn't tell his little sister about it, and worry her.

Conor says with a smirk: "They don't take *girls*."

"What do you mean, 'they don't take girls'?"—Hannah is astonished by this remark, and the scornful certainty with which Conor utters it. "But—who told you that?"

Conor shrugs. No idea how he knows, but he *knows*.

In fact, Babysitter has abducted girls, though most of the recent victims have been boys. Hannah isn't about to explain this to Conor.

The children haven't left the house since the Hayden boy was abducted, they haven't been allowed to see newspapers or TV news. Hannah wonders if Conor has overheard Wes on the phone, or another adult speaking carelessly.

Not Ismelda, surely. Hannah knows that she can trust Ismelda never to upset the children.

Wes, Hannah can trust less certainly. Even if he doesn't say anything about the abduction his moods have been extreme, the children sense that something is wrong. But Hannah has no intention of confronting Wes.

Later that day Katya runs to Mommy tearful because Conor has told her that a "big dog" is waiting outside to bite her. A "big dog that bites and bites and bites."

The Haydens' dog, Hannah thinks. Whatever Conor has heard about the "lost" boy involves a dog in some way.

Hannah assures Katya that there is no dog. Conor has made it up just to scare her.

Hannah asks Conor where he has gotten such a silly idea and Conor again shrugs, with a smirk.

Hannah doesn't scold Conor but hugs him and Katya assuring them that there is no dog, certainly no dog waiting outside to bite them. Hiding her face against the children as she hugs them, hugs them tight until they fidget, recalling the Saint Jude warning: *no tears.*

At last! Hannah dares to drive to Ashtree Common.

These several days she has been in a fever of curiosity. Not for "news"—she does not want to confront "news." She wants just *to see* where the Haydens live.

Taking a detour off Cradle Rock Road, impulsively turning left instead of right, winding her way into the upscale subdivision as if this were the most natural route to the Mayhews' house on Dupont Drive, where Conor and Katya have been invited to swim with the Mayhew children.

Hannah is surprised to see at 16 Ashtree Circle a fieldstone Colonial that resembles, to an unnerving degree, the Jarretts' fieldstone Colonial at 96 Cradle Rock Road.

What a shock! The houses have been built to the same architectural plan, it appears. Though the Haydens' house looks slightly older, perhaps a little larger. Four chimneys instead of three.

Red-painted shutters and front door at the Haydens' house, dark-green-painted shutters and front door at the Jarretts'.

In the driveway are several vehicles, Hannah wonders if one of them is law enforcement. She feels uneasy, she would not want to attract attention and be discovered.

The house looks empty, or deserted. Drawn blinds at all the windows and outdoor lights burning at midday.

Because a catastrophe has happened to the residents of the house. They have lost all track of time. They are clinging to their lives for the unspeakable has happened, a child has been taken from them.

Babysitter takes only children not loved & not deserved.

So unfair, Hannah thinks. Surely this is not true, such an accusation.

She feels a sensation of vertigo, unease. As if the unfairness, the injustice, of the accusation might spill over onto her.

"Mommy, come *on.*"

Conor squirms with impatience, Mommy is parked in the road staring at a stranger's house.

Hannah wonders how Jill Hayden is bearing this vigil. If Jill Hayden knows something about the fate of her son that has not (yet) been released to the public.

Hannah had seen the sick-stricken parents interviewed on local TV the other day. Pressing her hands against her mouth, scarcely breathing. A man's slow pleading voice—*Please if anyone is listening if you know anything about where Robbie is, who has taken Robbie, please call this number, there will be a reward* . . .

On Ashtree Common Hannah drives past what she assumes must be the "wooded area" from which Robbie Hayden was taken. A three-acre lot that has been allowed to grow wild, a short walk from the Haydens' house. No one should blame parents for allowing a ten-year-old to walk the dog in such a place, so close to home.

Yes but they should have known. In the summer of Babysitter.

The "wooded area" is very attractive. Not a park, a natural woodland, mostly deciduous trees, a field of tall grasses and thistles, wildflowers. Wood-chip trails, a single bench. No parking lot, vehicles park on the shoulder of the road.

Strange, the *crime scene* isn't restricted. Surely it was, days ago. But now someone is nonchalantly walking a dog on one of the trails. A couple is sitting on the bench. As if nothing terrible has happened here recently.

Strange, too, that Babysitter would come here. Risking being detected so easily.

He has to be white to go anywhere he wants to go, and not be seen and asked questions.

Hannah stands in the hall, listening. *Is* that someone knocking?
 The children will be at the Mayhews' until five-thirty, Ismelda
has the afternoon off and will pick them up as she is returning home,
Wes is at work, Hannah is alone in the house in the kitchen when she
hears a curious sound from the rear of the house—a kind of knocking,
not loud but persistent, coming not from the front door, nor from the
side door that leads into the kitchen, but from the back hall that leads
to the garage.

Why is someone knocking at the door to the garage instead of at the
front door?—Hannah is alarmed.

Who could this be, Hannah wonders. Not a friend or an acquaintance. Not a delivery person though (possibly) the man who delivers
oil at the rear of the house and leaves the receipt attached to the door
in the garage.

Fortunately, the door is locked. Hannah is faint with relief, she'd
remembered to lock the door when she'd returned from driving the
children to their friends' house.

Before Babysitter, Hannah rarely locked doors during the day. Such
a practice was commonplace in Far Hills, where crime has been a rare
occurrence.

There might be wind, inside the garage. Might be a raccoon. Rac-
coons, burrowing in the green trash container.

Frequently in the morning Hannah discovers the green container
overturned, trash scattered on the floor, food-stained paper napkins
torn to shreds.

Possibly, Wes has returned home early and has misplaced his house key. Knocking now for someone to let him inside except (of course) Wes wouldn't be knocking so quietly, he'd be shouting to be let in.

The knock returns—quick, deft, somehow playful, a light rapping of knuckles.

Hannah dares to approach the door. Surely there is no danger, a burglar or an intruder would not be *knocking*.

And no danger from Babysitter, he'd have no interest in an adult woman.

"Wes, is that you? Or—"

Hannah stares in appalled fascination as the doorknob is being turned.

"Who is it? Go away."

Could it be *Conor*? Playing one of his jokes on Mommy?

But not possible, Conor is miles away. And Conor would be giggling by now, Hannah would have heard.

Boldly the doorknob is turned again, this way, that way, with an air of childish impatience, Hannah cries, "Stop! I'm going to call the police."

Whoever is on the other side of the door knows her, she thinks. She is certain.

He knows that the door is locked against him. Yet, he's taunting Hannah as a child might do but with an air of menace.

What Hannah should do: barricade herself in the interior of the house, in a locked bathroom, and call 911. Instead, Hannah impulsively opens the door, sees to her astonishment the ponytailed boy standing before her, not three feet away, baring his teeth in a sneering wet smile.

Y.K.'s driver! *Him.*

In a grungy black T-shirt that fits his tight-muscled torso like a glove, in low-slung army-camouflage pants, in ankle-high black running shoes. Smelling of his body, excitement. His hair is coarse, dull-dark, pulled back into a straggling ponytail, his dark-tinctured skin is flushed and oily, eyes gleaming like hot coins as if he's drunk or high, immensely pleased with himself.

"Hey Mrs. J__, know what? You fucking forgot to tip me."

Beautiful Boy

When I was taken it was within an instant.

When I was taken it was between one breath and the next.

When I was taken it was on the trail as Lupa trotted ahead.

Swiftly he came up behind me, his arm clamped around my neck strong enough to snap my neck and I could make no sound, Lupa trotted ahead unknowing when he took me.

Against my nose and mouth a cloth like flames, in that instant I could not breathe.

Could not draw breathe to scream when I was taken, my knees buckled and I could not stand upright when I was taken, my brain was fainting, failing like a light switched off to blackness.

When I was taken no one knew, no one saw.

Grunting laughter as he half lifted me, dragged what remained of me out of the woods moving with such speed, such strength in his arms, his legs bearing me away and Lupa now whining, at a distance flattened against the earth ears laid back teeth bared yet quivering in fear not daring to come nearer when I was taken between one breath and the next.

Beautiful boy no one will hurt you, no one has loved you the way I will love you beautiful boy this is the best thing that will ever happen to you in your life.

Never Say No

Fuck, yes! Never say *no* to Hawkeye.

Steeling himself to learn what it is Hawkeye wants done this time—*expedited.*

Drive to Bloomfield Hills, emergency situation, R__ is in bad need of help, a kid he'd picked up on Cass he brought to the house has had a heroin overdose (*not* R__'s fault, the kid brought the drugs with him).

R__ can't handle the situation himself, isn't in great shape himself, can't drive a vehicle himself, in no condition to leave the premises, calling an ambulance isn't an option.

Just get out there, fast as you can, *expedite.*

What *expedite* means is: Clear up shit. R__ will pay up front in cash.

And take the "little camera" with him. Of course.

(The "little camera" is a Leitz Leica small enough to fit in a pocket of Ponytail's cargo pants. Given to him by Hawkeye who says *Nobody can take too many pictures of a good thing.*)

Ponytail wonders how much R__ has paid Hawkeye, up to now. How much more he can expect.

Weird shit Ponytail has heard about R__, known as Mister R__ at the Mission.

Living with his parents, in Bloomfield Hills. His father's a "top executive" at General Motors.

At his age, has to be almost forty. *That* is weird.

The parents, Hawkeye says, are gone on a trip. Just R__ in the house by himself, and the overdosed kid.

Rumor was R__ had been arrested for "sex abuse of a minor" more than once but charges are always dropped with sons of bitch perverts like Mister R__ living in Bloomfield Hills.

When Mikey was still in residence at the Mission was the time Mister R__ began to show up at the motels. Younger than the old asshole fags and didn't want to mingle with them like he was some kind of aristocrat and not a sick fucking fag himself.

Hanging out at the edges of things. Little rat eyes behind dark glasses, dyed-looking mustache, camera slung over his shoulder. Called himself a *photojournalist*.

In a good mood Mister R__ was okay. Generous! He'd pay you for just being photographed, all you had to do was strip, roll around on a bed, get high. His special boys he'd inject with heroin, he'd pay extra for that.

Ponytail had felt Mister R__'s rat eyes moving on him when he was clueless Mikey Kushel but nothing ever happened between them, maybe Mikey hadn't been sexy enough.

There'd been an accident, Mister R__ and one of the boys, no one knew exactly what happened, but (it was said) Father McKenzie gave testimony to police the boy had a "severe asthmatic condition," plus he'd taken drugs, his breathing just stopped. Not *smothering*, not *involuntary manslaughter*, but *death ruled accidental*.

R__ has no idea, Hawkeye has plenty of "evidence"—photos, videotapes of him at the all-nighters. Ponytail has some curiosity how it will play out and how *he* might be involved.

Don't overthink it. Stay cool.

Hawkeye is instructing Ponytail: If the kid is still alive when you get to the house, get him off the premises, fast. Bottom line is, he can't die *there*.

Transport him in the trunk. Not the backseat of the car. Got it?

Got it. (Ponytail scowls, he's no asshole.)

Anywhere is okay to dump him, like a mall parking lot, at the edge. Somebody will see him there and call an ambulance.

Don't take him to an ER, don't let anybody see you or see your license plate. If you do, you're fucked.

Ponytail asks uneasily what if the kid's dead? Before he gets to the house?

Hawkeye says irritably what d'you think, if he's dead? Especially then, you have to remove him from the premises. Dump with discretion.

Ponytail says okay, cool. But getting a bad vibe from this.

Worst case, Ponytail might know the kid. He has acquaintances hustling in the gay bars on Cass. Kids who'd aged out of the Mission.

Weird to be talking so casually about *dead*. Like Ponytail is familiar with *dead*.

Hawkeye gives him the address, Ponytail writes it down: *11 Balmoral Drive, Bloomfield Hills*.

Hawkeye warns Ponytail: Get *in* and get *out*. R__ invites you to come back after you've dealt with the kid, get high with him, have some drinks, swim in his pool—don't. Got it?

Ponytail nods: He's got it.

Don't take anything from the premises. You do, you will regret it.

Ponytail protests: He isn't a thief!

Hawkeye says: R__ will pay you. We've negotiated. Don't talk to him more than you need to. Take what he gives you. Don't take time to count it—it's all there. And wear gloves.

Gloves?

What's called surgical—"latex." Get them in a drugstore. You're not going to leave prints.

Ponytail considers this. Distinctly feeling bad vibes.

Ponytail asks can he use the camera wearing gloves and Hawkeye says *try*.

No need to warn Ponytail not to let R__ see the camera. (You never let anyone see the camera, and if it looks like they're unconscious, eyes closed, even then don't take a chance.) However Ponytail fucks up, he'd better not fuck up in that regard.

Hawkeye tells him: Maple Road is "Fifteen Mile." Exit west.

Ponytail remembers that exit. Cool!

Rare for Ponytail to journey out of the city. Rarer, into the rich white suburbs north of Royal Oak. Last time/first time he'd exited at Maple Road was when Hawkeye had trusted him to bring Mrs. J__ home in her fancy car.

Thoughts of her come to him, often. In the night.

How she'd trusted Ponytail, kind of. Didn't fight him. Like he'd saved her life. Drove her home in the (classy) car it was a thrill to drive like in a dream where you can't hear the powerful engine, can't gauge how fast you might be driving, nothing like an ordinary car. For people who lived in Far Hills were nothing like ordinary people.

How he'd found the house, drove around to the back and parked the car in the garage as he'd been instructed by Hawkeye, point by point. Helped the weepy drunk woman out of the car and into the house, smart enough to use her house key on the chain with the ignition key to unlock the door.

Christ! Has to smile now thinking how when so many things could've gone wrong he hadn't fucked up once.

Remembered to hand her the Prada bag. And not to take anything from her. Might've emptied her wallet or at least taken a few bills but he had not.

Ponytail could find the house again, he thinks. Far Hills, a smaller version of Bloomfield Hills. Not so rich, but rich. Weird road name—*Rock Cradle.* Or was it *Cradle Rock.*

A natural instinct for geography like he can shut his eyes right now and make his way through every room in the house on Wyandotte where he'd lived as a young kid with his mother until she disappeared.

Christ!—twenty years. Mikey's old, lost life.

Hawkeye is giving Ponytail his phone number, tells him to call only if something serious goes wrong, and even then don't call from R__'s house but from a pay phone.

Ponytail knows now this is serious. Never heard of Hawkeye giving anyone his telephone number.

Ponytail gives a nervous laugh—okay, cool.

He's in some kind of weird state lately, not sure what, might be what's called an "allergic reaction" making his heart beat funny, tingling sensation in tips of fingers, toes. He'd taken some steroids, plus smoked some weird dope called *kif* picked up at the Eastern Market.

So half the time he's feeling *high* and half the time he's feeling *wasted.* *High as a kite, wasted like shit.*

Doesn't tell Hawkeye that. Crucial to keep that to himself.

Ponytail hangs up the phone. Grabs the Leitz Leica, trots out to his car parked on West Warren. Always relief he feels, the motor turns over, car *starts,* which wasn't true of previous cars he'd owned.

This car, a 1973 Pontiac Firebird sedan, royal blue, buff interior Hawkeye has given Ponytail on "permanent lease."

Meaning that Ponytail is on "permanent lease" to Hawkeye.

. . .

Good*damn*. Ponytail arrives at the address on Balmoral Drive, Bloomfield Hills, thinking for sure he's fucked, there's a wrought-iron gate blocking the driveway, ten-foot stone wall stretching out of sight, no way for him to get inside to ring the doorbell, and the house is barely visible from the road, but good luck!—turns out the gate isn't locked, all Ponytail needs to do is get out of his car, push the gate open, he can drive through.

The kind of fancy gate that operates electronically, he supposes. Somebody up in the house buzzes to open it. Nobody in sight.

Ponytail makes sure that the gate remains open, doesn't swing shut and lock him inside. He intends to leave swiftly as Hawkeye advised: *in, out.*

Already wearing the "latex" gloves. So tight-fitting, his hands feel like they're being strangled.

It's a long drive, uphill. No vehicles in the driveway. Nobody in sight. Ponytail parks the Firebird in front of the portico of the house with its several white columns. Wondering if, if he's going to be carrying somebody out to the car, he should be parked at the rear.

Up close now Ponytail can't see where the house ends, it's so big. Washed-looking pale brick, tall windows, white-painted stucco. By midsummer every yard in Detroit is burned out, but here in Bloomfield Hills the grass is weird emerald green and moist-looking, like a golf course.

Ringing the doorbell, and no answer.

Worried that R   will recognize him and wonder what the fuck Mikey Kushel is doing here.

Mikey Kushel who's packed on weight, sheer muscle in his upper body, his hair has coarsened and sprouted from his forehead, his jaws are hard-clenched like the jaws of a pit bull, fuck Mister R__ recognizing *him*, he's not going to obsess over it.

Mikey who'd never looked like this, Hawkeye's first lieutenant in black T-shirt, cargo pants, black running shoes as heavy as boots.

After what seems like a long time the door is opened. At first Ponytail doesn't recognize R__—this middle-aged guy so wasted he can hardly stand. Leaning against the door, panting. Squinting at Ponytail with bloodshot pinwheel eyes.

Sobbing what sounds like *Thank God you're here.*

Clutching at Ponytail, to pull him inside. Shut the door!

Ponytail is astonished to see Mister R__ in such a state, he's a guy who tries to appear *cool*. Now looking much older than Ponytail remembers, and shorter. Face as sickly white as a fish's belly, dyed-looking drooping mustache needs trimming and is wet with mucus. Bloated belly. Spindly legs. Wearing just (soiled) boxer shorts and a T-shirt stiff with smeared blood, dried puke. And barefoot, ugly white toes and toenails caked with grime.

Ponytail's sensitive nostrils pinch. *Gross.*

Problem is, R__ can hardly stand upright. Drunk, or drugged, or (maybe) he's had a stroke. Trying to explain something to Ponytail but he's sobbing, his words are slurred, incoherent.

Christ!—an adult man, crying. Ponytail is repelled.

The most that Ponytail can comprehend is that R__ needs help desperately because he can't drive in his present condition. He'd intended to deal with the emergency himself but discovered that he can't. His eyesight is blurred like he's underwater and he can't walk straight, can't use his car.

Ponytail asks if R__ has something to give him. R__ hands over a medium-sized paper bag to Ponytail who takes it and only just glances inside—cash.

How much cash, Ponytail won't know until he counts it.

Could be a thousand dollars? More?

All for Ponytail. Though he guesses that Hawkeye will be paid, too, as the *chief expediter.*

R__ instructs Ponytail to follow him. He's got to lead Ponytail through the house. This is his parents' house, R__ lives at the back, has his own entrance, that's where *the boy* is.

Explaining that his parents are away in Europe, he's by himself in the house, told the staff to take two weeks off. He'd planned some photo shoots, just got started and things got fucked.

Ponytail can smell alcohol on R__'s breath. Probably he's high, too, on coke, sniffing and wiping at his nose.

Leading Ponytail through the enormous house. Like through the lobby floor of the Renaissance Grand. Ponytail has an impression of spacious rooms, elegant furnishings, glittering things. A long polished dining-room table, gleaming candlestick holders, chandelier. God-damned fucking joke, Ponytail thinks, how some people live.

Yet: If his mother could see Mikey *now.* She'd be impressed!

Along a corridor, into some open space like an atrium, plate-glass windows on all sides. Outside is a swimming pool so large Ponytail can't see either end of it.

From somewhere ahead, what sounds like cries, muted screams. Thumping rhythmic bass like music.

So much effort leading Ponytail through the house, R__ has become short of breath. Asshole is sweating, shivering. Has to lean on Pony-tail, too weak to walk by himself. Stumbling together like some stupid dance. Ponytail's heart is beating hard in revulsion for the reeking breath, filthy T-shirt and shorts. Ponytail tries to ignore the naked white legs covered in hairs. And R__'s feet, grimy-webbed between the toes.

So this is the rich "auto executive's" pervert son: pitiful.

In the past Ponytail had only seen Mister R__ kind of stiff-backed, superior. Dressing like some cool dude but always wore a baseball cap, probably going bald. Boasting he's a *photojournalist.*

Looking down on you even if (in fact) you are taller than he is.

One good thing, R__ is so wrecked he doesn't recognize Mikey Kushel. Hasn't noticed the latex gloves that'd love to strangle his scrawny neck.

As the music is getting louder, the thumping bass more emphatic, R__ is becoming more agitated, talking faster. Not his fault he's saying, what happened. *Not his.*

Ponytail averts his eyes from the sweaty face. Pleading eyes.

Not his fault. His *fault.*

Ponytail doesn't know what to make of this babbling. He has a sick feeling in the gut, it isn't an "overdose" he's been summoned to deal with but something worse.

In all his life Ponytail has never actually seen a dead person. A *body.*

He's seen pretty sick people who would later turn up dead. Cocaine junkies. Jaundice-yellow hookers, hepatitis C. Male hustlers, collar-bones and ribs jutting like skeletons. Christ!—broken out in running sores.

He's smelled *dead.* But not up close. Not to touch and not his responsibility.

Thinking now, maybe that's what R_ has—some kind of rotting

sickness like syphilis. Why he's falling apart so young. Why his breath smells. Sick-white skin. Runny nose. Can't catch his breath. Having to lean on Ponytail, panting and wheezing.

Steering Ponytail into a newer part of the house. There are fewer items of furniture here—low-slung leather sofas and chairs, scuffed hardwood floor. Walls are dark blue and at every window venetian blinds have been shut tight against the sun. Dirtied glasses and plates, cutlery scattered on tables and on the floor, plastic takeout containers. Stale pizza crusts, crumpled napkins. A smell of something rancid, rotted. Empty wine bottles. Scuttling beneath a sofa, a hard-shelled beetle. Clothes scattered about, towels, wadded tissues. Camera equipment. On a worktable, glossy photos amid more dirtied dishes. Music from stereo speakers is deafening. A female voice so high-pitched it hurts Ponytail's eardrums.

Ponytail locates the stereo, shuts off the Goddamned screaming. Sees the album cover—Verdi, *La Traviata*.

Weakly R__ objects. *That's beautiful music, man.*

Christ! Ponytail is relieved, the noise is ended.

With a groan like some asshole on TV, R__ collapses onto a sofa. White toad-face glistening with tears. Bawling he has a hard time with *silence.*

Too much inside my head like it's gonna explode.

Fucking self-pity, Ponytail thinks. What kind of a man! Disgusting.

At the farther end of the room there's a (shut) door. R__ is gesturing toward it mutely with a sick-pained expression, meaning that Ponytail should head in that direction.

Sniveling R__ trying to explain that none of this is *his fault,* it's *the boy's fault.*

So now, *the boy* has to be taken away, R__ says. Just anywhere—*away.*

Ponytail assures the motherfucker—okay.

Takes a deep breath steeling himself for what he's going to find in the next room which is a bedroom dim-lit with fluted paper lanterns casting a faint orange glow, as in a child's room. Bad smells here—Ponytail doesn't want to think.

Nothing on the unmade king-sized bed except stained bedclothes, looks like bloodstains, but something on the floor beyond the bed, Ponytail approaches cautiously expecting to see the body of a young man in his late teens, or Ponytail's own age, a Detroit street hustler, instead Ponytail is staring at a very young child, ten years old, or younger, lying on the floor on his stomach, on a terry-cloth bath towel, arms tied behind his back with wire, ankles tied, a blindfold tied over his eyes, and a gag tight over his mouth.

Jesus!—a little kid. Not an overdose, something else.

The boy is lying very still, but he is breathing. It's his breathing that Ponytail has been hearing—rapid, shallow. The boy is wearing just underwear, elasticized white shorts, badly bloodstained, like the bath towel. His feet are bare. The soles of his feet seem very small to Ponytail.

The boy has been bound elaborately with wire, not just his wrists and ankles, there's a length of wire looped around his neck. A coil of wire lies on the floor beside him. Close by, a large black plastic trash bag as if R__ had thought of wrapping him in it but had changed his mind.

Positioned above the boy, (unlit) lights on rollers. On a table, camera equipment. A photo shoot?

Jesus!— R__ has been torturing the boy. There's a smell of vomit, excrement. Ponytail can see, the boy's underwear has been soiled, blood and shit. So utterly disgusted, Ponytail wants to murder R__.

He doesn't follow news, rarely glances at a newspaper or watches TV, still Ponytail is aware there's a missing ten-year-old boy from one of the Detroit suburbs, this has got to be the boy.

Sick motherfucker the newspapers call *Babysitter.*

Father McKenzie always insisted there was nothing to the stories told of Mister R__, Mikey had been naïve enough to believe him. But not surprised now that R__ might be Babysitter himself.

Needing to remind himself: Get *in* and get *out.*

Making sure that R__ isn't watching him from the doorway, Ponytail removes the Leitz Leica from a pocket, takes pictures rapidly: the bound boy, the setting, a wide angle, evidence where the picture has been taken.

Close-up of the boy's head. Wire cutting into his neck. An angle that includes R__'s messy bed, framed artwork on the wall above the bed, other walls, a window with a blind lowered to the windowsill.

Nobody ever took too many pictures of a good thing.

Leans over the little boy saying in a low voice *Hey! You hear me? You're gonna be all right.*

Ponytail loosens the wire around the boy's neck. Christ! So tight, he's having trouble. Feels the imprint of the wire in the boy's flesh, you'd think the boy would be strangled by now.

R__ must be skilled at this, Ponytail thinks. Cutting off full breathing but leaving enough breath so the victim doesn't die.

Pitying Ponytail touches the boy's shoulder. Touches the back of the boy's head. Nape of the neck, which is clammy-cold.

No response from the boy but at least he's breathing.

Ponytail is calculating how to proceed, has to act fast, like a pilot flying a plane into uncharted territory, not so sure of how a plane is actually flown but knowing he can't hesitate, and he certainly can't turn back.

He's guessing that Hawkeye hadn't known it was a child R__ had brought home, not a junkie-hustler, though maybe Hawkeye had known and hadn't wanted to share the information with Ponytail because Ponytail might've freaked out. He'd given Ponytail precise instructions to follow in either case.

All Ponytail has to do is *expedite.* Follow those instructions. *Don't overthink.*

Ponytail yanks a comforter off the bed, wraps the boy's limp body in the comforter, lifts the boy in his arms. The boy's head falls back, all Ponytail can see is eggshell-pale skin at the forehead, cheeks—the boy's eyes are hidden by the blindfold, the gag hides the lower part of his face.

Ponytail tugs the gag down, a little. Make sure the boy can breathe through his nose at least.

Is he breathing? Ponytail leans an ear close, he thinks so.

Jesus!—adrenaline rush to the heart. Goddamned lucky he'd self-medicated with steroids, the boy is heavy in his arms but Ponytail is fucking *strong.*

Thinking Olympic-class athlete, wrestler, weight lifter. Fucking fantastic upper-body strength, hard tight muscles, not an ounce of flab.

Hawkeye would be impressed. Maybe he'll call Hawkeye, after the emergency has been expedited.

Man!—wait'll you see the pictures I took out here.

And wait for Hawkeye to ask *What kind of pictures?*—but fuck Hawkeye, coldhearted bastard would never ask.

Ponytail has noted there's no door to the outside from this room so he'll have to carry the boy into the other room, bring the car around to the door there, fuck he's going to carry the boy through the fucking house to the front where the Firebird is parked.

Thinking fast. Why Hawkeye hired Ponytail and not somebody else.

When Ponytail carries the boy in his arms into the other room R__ sits up straight on the sofa staring as if this is a sight utterly unexpected. A sight having to do with Ponytail, not him. In fact, a sight he can't comprehend. Like the sick motherfucker has *no idea* what this could possibly be, some child-sized object carried wrapped in the bloody comforter from R__'s bed.

Stammering *Get him out! I said—get him out!*

Ponytail ignores R__, lays the boy on one end of the sofa. Hopes to hell there'll be bloodstains on the sofa. Bloodstains on the rug, floor. Some cleaning woman will discover.

Ponytail adjusts the comforter so that the boy's head is entirely hidden. This way, he figures he can carry the boy out to the car without the boy's head falling back limp.

Jesus, man, I told you—get him out . . .

Voice rising like a girl's. His fish belly face is oily with sweat. Dilated eyes, he's high, but it's a bad high. Thinning hair across his head like seaweed. You never see a rich person with stained teeth except this rich man's motherfucker son is a junkie, teeth rotting in his jaws.

Making no effort to hide his disgust, Ponytail informs the pervert motherfucker he's going now to get his car, bring it around to the back of the house, what R__ can do for him is open the door for him, so Ponytail can carry the boy out.

When that's expedited, R__ can shut the door. That's it.

That's *it?*—R__ is relieved already.

That's it. Deal done, I'm out of here.

Addressing R__ without looking at him. Hasn't looked at R__ since he'd carried the boy to the sofa. It kills Ponytail he didn't have an opportunity to take even one picture of R__ in the same frame with the boy but unfortunately that wasn't possible.

Missed the money shot, Hawkeye might say. But there's plenty of good shots you got, kid. *Good work.*

Not that the coldhearted bastard would praise him, Ponytail thinks. But he might *think it.*

On his way out, not a backward glance. Doesn't trust himself to look at R__ for fear he will want to murder the pervert, beat him with his fists until the fish-belly face is pulpy and bleeding, kick him, on the floor kicking his ribs until they crack and his gut until the intestines are torn and leaking shit, kicking the ugly face, the head, cracking the fucking skull until brains spill out, think Ponytail can't do it?— Ponytail fucking *can.*

But now's not the time. Some other time.

Hawkeye's voice sounding clear and calm in Ponytail's ear: *Get in, get out.*

Wild! His heart so happy.

So thrilled, Ponytail has forgotten the paper bag stuffed with cash carelessly tossed onto the floor by the passenger seat of the Pontiac, fuck Ponytail has more crucial things to think about than is it a thousand? more than a thousand? looks like more than a thousand but how much?

Driving east on Maple Road. Figuring he'll see a sign for a hospital, ER—has to be a hospital close by.

In Detroit, he'd know where a hospital is. Detroit General on St. Antoine a few blocks from his place on West Warren. Fucking sirens waking him through the night.

Like gunshots, Detroit at night. Every night.

Too far to drive, fifteen miles to Detroit General. For all Ponytail knows the boy is dying.

Breaking into a cold sweat. Minutes are passing, he isn't seeing a hospital sign.

Should've asked R__ how long the boy had been tied like that, wire around his neck. Gag over his mouth. What the fuck R__ was doing to him? And taking pictures? Christ!

The boy might be in shock. Ponytail has seen people in shock. A wound like a gunshot, lots of bleeding, blood pressure goes down, you go into shock and can die of that.

Ponytail had driven the car to the rear of the house where R__ was standing with the door open. Sniveling, wringing his hands. Like this child he'd kidnapped and tortured was causing him trouble, *he's* the one who's pissed.

No! Put him in the trunk!—R__ is all but screaming as Ponytail ignores him laying the boy in the backseat wrapped in the comforter so nothing showed: not the bare toes, not the top of the head.

Taking a risk. Hawkeye wouldn't approve. If a cop pulls Ponytail over. If there's an accident. But hell, Ponytail couldn't put the boy in the trunk.

After all the boy has gone through. Might smother there. Or be poisoned by carbon monoxide.

Another mile east on Maple Road. Rivulets of sweat running down Ponytail's face, underarms.

Where's a fucking hospital? Jesus Christ.

Feeling the adrenaline rush begin to subside. Something like sobriety returning.

Turns off the radio listening for some sound of life in the back. Breathing?—just barely.

He'd loosened the wires binding the boy's wrists and ankles so they didn't cut in so tight. But he hadn't loosened them so much the boy could get free.

Hadn't removed the blindfold or the gag. Reasoning that would be a mistake he'd regret. The boy hadn't seen R__'s face probably and had no idea where he'd been, no awareness of his surroundings, and Ponytail has no intention of being the face the boy would recall, if he survives.

Ponytail decides to turn into the strip mall near the ramp for I-75, where he'd stopped at a drugstore to purchase the latex gloves. (Which he's still wearing.) This time Ponytail doesn't park in the front but drives around to the rear, along a bumpy dirt alley, past a dumpster.

Back of the strip mall, no one's in sight. Ponytail parks behind the dumpster.

A scrawny young cat runs by, teats dangling. Another cat, ears laid back, stares at Ponytail. Colony of wild cats living out here, scavenging from the dumpster.

Ponytail feels a thrill of apprehension, maybe this is the one mistake of his life he will long regret.

He pulls the small body wrapped in the comforter out of the car, positions him on the ground behind the dumpster. At a little distance, several scrawny cats are staring at him as he checks the pulse in the boy's neck again: Barely beating. But beating.

"Just hang on, okay? You'll be okay."

Ponytail feels the boy quivering. Alive!

Squatting, sweating, Ponytail dares to peer inside the comforter but can't determine if the boy is conscious, can't see the eyes, can't see the mouth. All he can see is the eggshell skin, forehead, cheeks, underside of the chin. His heart is pierced with pity, the boy is so *small*.

"Y'hear me? I promise."

For the record, so Hawkeye will see, he takes a few pictures with the little camera.

Returning then to the Firebird. Good: Can't see the boy from here, you'd have to look behind the dumpster deliberately.

Ponytail drives to the front of the strip mall and parks. Considers whether he should buy a soda in the drugstore and bring the kid something to drink, must be thirsty, dehydrated, but decides no, better not. He'd have to undo the gag, couldn't trust the boy not to scream if he became conscious.

Next, Ponytail calls 911 from an outdoor pay phone. Speaks through his fingers into the receiver, tells the dispatcher that there's a "lost boy" behind the strip mall at 2933 West Maple, behind a dumpster where somebody left him.

Quickly repeats this information, hangs up the receiver.

Jesus!—he's covered in clammy-cold sweat. Adrenaline rushing again, heart beating so hard he feels faint.

His heart lifts, soars. Feeling so good!

"See, I saved the kid's life. *Me*."

He'd like to double back to see when an ambulance arrives at the strip mall, he's listening for a siren, wonders how soon they will arrive but decides, hell no, he's not going to turn up anywhere in the vicinity, the task has been *expedited*.

Too soon to return to Detroit. Fuck Detroit.

Laughing to himself. Driving east on Maple. There's the ramp to I-75 south but Ponytail is hovering above the highway like a helicopter observing the Pontiac gaining speed, passing the entrance.

That's funny. Can't stop laughing.

Fuck Detroit. Fuck fucking West Warren.

He's *here*, and he's *high*.

Thought comes to him like it's blown through the partly lowered window: The rich bitch never tipped him.

The Intruder

You forgot, Mrs. J__. *I* didn't."

Pushing the door to the garage open, stepping inside the house.

Is this real?—Hannah stands paralyzed just a few feet away, disbelieving.

So many times Hannah has glimpsed the ponytailed boy in Far Hills, in the corner of her eye, at a distance, his insolent figure not quite in focus, the threat of his being registering as a rush of alarm, yet each time Hannah has been mistaken, and greatly relieved to be mistaken—now Hannah stares at the nightmare figure that has entered her house thinking that it has happened, at last: *He has come for her.*

Y.K. has sent an emissary, he has not troubled to come himself. He has sent the swaggering boy in his place, to fetch Hannah.

Not a *boy,* a man. Coarse-skinned, unshaven with bright jeering eyes just visible through dark-tinted glasses.

His face is flushed, his teeth are bared in a lewd wet canine grin. Hannah sees that he is drunk, or high on drugs. Reckless, dangerous.

She'd opened the door out of curiosity!—she thinks.

Repenting now. Realizing her mistake now.

Must stand her ground, must not retreat or he will rush at her, a wolf on the attack.

Hannah orders the ponytailed boy to leave her house even as he interrupts to ask insolently does she remember him?—calling her "Mrs. J__" in a familiar way, chilling her blood, so that Hannah quickly retorts *no,* she does not remember him, but he must leave now, please he must turn around and leave, leave now, *now before she calls the police.*

At this the ponytailed boy laughs as if he has never heard anything so comical. "Ma'am, *you*?—calling the police?"

Hannah feels her face heat with blood. Panic, shame. Guilt.

"I—I will call the police if—if you don't . . ."

"What're you going to tell them, you forgot to give me a *tip*? So I had to come back in person to *get it*?"

His eyes drop insolently to her bare feet in sandals.

Lifting slowly: the woman's bare legs in shorts, sleeveless summer top with the first two buttons, tiny white mother-of-pearl, unbuttoned.

Advancing upon her, laughing. Teeth glistening.

Without knowing what she's doing Hannah takes a step backward: this, her first mistake.

Hannah's nostrils pinch against the heat of the ponytailed boy's body—a rank animal smell, not altogether unpleasant, of unwashed hair, underarms, crotch. The very odor of male arrogance, male arousal, alarming to Hannah whose thoughts fly to the safety of the children—but Conor and Katya aren't home, they are at the Mayhews'.

Hannah stammers that her children are in the house, upstairs with their nanny, her husband is expected home within a few minutes, *he must leave now.*

These desperate words don't seem to register with the ponytailed boy who is excited, aroused, thrilled. On his face a strange fixed smile as if in his eyes Hannah is as astonishing a sight as he is in hers: as if he has been seeing Mrs. J__'s elusive figure in the corner of his vision as she has been seeing his, how many times in the past several months.

Hannah pleads: "Leave. Leave *now*. If you leave now I won't call the police . . ."

The ponytailed boy is amused by these words. Laughing, teeth glistening, advancing upon Hannah even as Hannah steps back, retreating in the hallway that leads to the kitchen.

Hannah has never exactly seen the ponytailed boy before, not as she is seeing him now. The shock of him is, how *forceful* he is: only slightly taller than Hannah but densely built, as of a substance other than flesh, a tight-muscled torso like hard rubber, neck nearly as wide as the span of his jaws. His hair, too, is dense, as coarse as a horse's mane, matte-black and without luster, tied back in a ponytail so straggling and unkempt that Hannah cannot help but think that he has no one, no woman, no mother, to see after him, to groom him.

Something soft in Hannah's face, in that instant, the ponytailed boy registers. Stops him in his tracks as if Hannah has reached out to touch, calm him.

"Last time I was here, you were a lot friendlier, Mrs. J__."

"I—I don't remember that . . ."

"Sure you do. How'd you get home, without me?"

Hannah is trembling badly. All she can do is repeat that if he leaves she won't call the police or tell anyone. If he leaves *now*.

The ponytailed boy laughs at this threat for Hannah's voice is weak, wavering.

He brushes past Hannah into the large, light-filled kitchen. Glances about, assessing. The tile floor is a rich russet Mexican tile, sunlight reflects on copper pans displayed like art against a white brick wall.

The ponytailed boy whistles thinly through his teeth—"Jesus!"

He laughs, he's impressed. But he's also laughing at the fact that he is impressed. Hannah understands that such laughter is meant to be *placating*.

Signaling to her: No danger! Mrs. J__ is in no danger.

"Thought I'd drop by, I'm in the vicinity on business. He sent me here—you know, *him*."

Hannah swallows hard. No need to inquire who *him* is.

"I'm, like, his 'lieutenant.' He trusts me. Like he trusted me driving you home."

Hannah is standing very still. Hannah's thoughts flutter and flail about like moths stymied by light.

Hannah thinks—*I will not ask. I have no reason to ask.*

"He doesn't know I'm here, though. This is 'solo.'"

Swaggering farther into the kitchen. Hannah has no choice but to follow. On the wall beside the refrigerator six feet away from her is the beige plastic telephone.

. . . *get the receiver into her hand, dial 911 before he can stop her* . . .

But no: The ponytailed boy would slap the receiver out of her hand, Hannah can foresee.

Any sudden gesture of hers, to protect herself, to defend herself against him, will trigger him to lay his hands on her, Hannah knows. Cannot risk.

Yet—*must* risk.

The ponytailed boy has removed his dark glasses. His skin is heated, his eyes unnaturally alert, alive. He turns to look pointedly at Hannah, seeing in her face a sick-guilty look, something like shame.

Hannah is wearing very little makeup. Her hair hasn't been "lightened" in weeks. Without mascara her eyes are naked, raw—disconcerting for the ponytailed boy to see, up close.

Like any woman, any-age woman, her frightened eyes, just—staring into his. Christ!

He, the intruder, has seen Hannah disheveled, near-naked sprawled in filthy bedclothes. He has seen her utterly vulnerable, exposed in a way no one else, including her husband, has seen her. She has not (therefore) the privilege to refuse him.

She has surrendered her right to resist. She has been broken, defiled—haphazardly mended, a delicate vase whose broken pieces have been inexpertly glued back together.

Hannah tells the intruder that he must leave. Must leave her house *now*.

Her children will be returning home soon, their nanny will be returning them. Her husband—

"Fuck 'husband.' He isn't coming anytime soon. I did some surveillance and nobody's here." The ponytailed boy's voice rises in derision.

It's true, the large Colonial house is silent, empty. The intruder hasn't been deceived by the woman's feeble lie.

Only just Mrs. J__ alone drifting undefined as a wraith through the rooms.

"Like I said, Mrs. J__, I'm out here on business—'Bloomfield Hills.' So, came to see you."

Sounding jovial, yet wistful. Pushy and boastful, but uneasy.

Doesn't Mrs. J__ *like* him? In those eggshell-thin dreams behind his eyelids Mikey Kushel has thought so, he has imagined.

In *Rollerball*, he'd have risked his life for her. No greater glory than to be a warrior for the sake of a beautiful woman . . .

Hannah is confused by the ponytailed boy's tone, uncertain. Whether to be terrified, or—to feel tenderness? The intruder is *so young*.

Hannah hears herself saying she will get her handbag, her wallet, she will give him a "tip." She'd meant to give him a "tip"—but she'd forgotten. That night.

Barely, Hannah can remember *that night*. But she does remember the ponytailed boy.

But now, the ponytailed boy is looking hurt, crestfallen. It isn't money he wants, he has plenty of money he tells Hannah boastfully, he'd just dropped by to see her.

"That's all—just to, like, say *hello*." Adding, "This business I expedited today—it's gonna be 'news' soon."

"It is!"—Hannah laughs nervously.

No idea what the ponytailed boy is talking about in such an elated voice but she feels some relief, he seems less hostile to her now.

"You watch TV news? Maybe gonna be on TV tonight."

Hannah has been moving slowly in the direction of the wall phone. Like a sleepwalker determined not to misstep, stumble. As it happens her hemp-woven shoulder bag is on a chair near the phone, and inside the bag is Hannah's wallet . . .

Hannah concentrates on approaching the telephone as unobtrusively as possible, yet openly, so that the ponytailed boy has no reason to be suspicious of her; there is a kind of spell or trance between them which Hannah doesn't want to break. The ponytailed boy does not fully trust her, she supposes, neither does he *distrust* her.

Except: Hannah wouldn't dare touch the phone in these circumstances. Akin to an excruciating close-up in a movie, heightened slow motion, suspense that leaves the actors short of breath in the exigency of the scene.

Don't dare touch, nor even appear to be aware of the phone (now) within her reach. Hannah is keenly aware even as the ponytailed boy doesn't appear to be aware at all.

Hannah is fascinated by the possibility the phone represents: the temptation to risk all, to seize it.

Though the possibility the phone represents is identical to its impossibility, practically speaking.

As Hannah's performance in the kitchen precludes a violent sexual act perpetrated upon her, unless it precedes such an act.

In each, there is a casual connection which, once triggered, will appear to have been inevitable, irrevocable; yet, at this moment, is entirely improvisational, a matter of choosing.

As turning the steering wheel of her car leaving the Far Hills Marriott, whether to the left (downtown Detroit) or to the right (Cradle Rock Road) was likewise an act of free will even as, as it was happening, the astonished driver seemed to be observing her own hands belatedly, in the act of *turning*.

Each (involuntary) (voluntary) action of ours leads to (a) death, inevitably. The only variant is *when*.

In a lifetime contiguous with this lifetime, parallel with it, separated from it by the sheerest membrane, the impossibility has been overcome and Hannah has managed with groping fingers to lift the phone (unnoticed by the ponytailed boy) from the wall, to press the magic numerals 911 . . .

But no: It's her wallet that Hannah is holding out to the ponytailed boy like a talisman, with a brave smile Hannah has unsnapped the beige kidskin wallet displaying the interior, credit cards, large-denomination bills, her hand trembles with chagrin as the ponytailed boy stares at her, his young face darkening with indignation.

"Lady, I said I didn't want your fucking money. That's not what a 'tip' is."

Still smiling bravely, blindly Hannah has removed a bill, two bills, to offer to the indignant young man, no idea what the denominations are, indeed Hannah would hand over the entire wallet to the intruder if he demands it, she is abject in apology, humbled in shame and guilt, but instead he slaps the wallet out of her hand, cursing.

"Fuck it! I fucking *told you*."

Hannah is shaken, for a moment thinking that the intruder has struck her, she feels faint, head swirling, but wills herself to recover, she will be *all right*.

How fast it has happened, this eruption of violence. Provoking the male she has brought disaster upon herself for now it is his prerogative to punish.

"I want a Goddamned *drink*. That's what I want, lady."

Adding, as Hannah shrinks from him: "Also I'm hungry, too. Haven't eaten all day."

The ponytailed boy is speaking with an air of reproach. His face is sullen, his red-rimmed eyes accusing. He has been genuinely wounded by her insensitivity, *she* is to blame.

She, the woman. The mother.

A slut, slut-woman, purely a cunt yet: the mother.

What he wants from the mother is nourishment: drink, food. Hannah is astonished, she should have realized.

That tone of male reproach, Hannah recognizes. No woman has not heard it, the deep thrill of it, the threat, cringing as you await the next blow, the blow (you know) you deserve and when the blow does not come, oxygen flows into your lungs, veins, arteries like joy.

Realizing now, even as perspiration breaks crudely in her armpits and between her thighs, that the intruder is, like Hannah, improvising desperately, inventing.

Like hers, his heart is beating rapidly. All of his senses are alert. Edging out onto thin ice, aware that the ice may begin to crack at any moment, frightened of the danger, thrilled by the danger.

"Sit here. Of course—you must be hungry . . ."

Not a hostage in the house, a *hostess*. Hannah is determined.

Hannah pulls out a chair, invites the aggrieved young man to sit at the kitchen table, she will bring him something to drink, something to eat.

If she feeds him, he will not hurt her. If she serves him, humbles herself before him. If he *pities her*.

Trying to think: When will Ismelda return with the children? In an hour? Within an hour?

Or, no: not until after four. Closer to five.

If Ismelda returns, the ponytailed boy will be defeated. He will certainly flee, Hannah will be safe from him.

But the possibility that Ismelda will see the ponytailed boy is terrifying to Hannah who has not the words to explain the stranger's presence in her house.

No words!—no words with which Hannah might explain the deep shame of the ponytailed boy.

Recalling a favorite joke of Joker Daddy at which no one ever laughed—*If I tell you this secret I will have to kill you.*

From a cupboard Hannah fetches a bottle of Italian red wine, opened by Wes the other evening for just himself and Hannah. She tugs at the cork, pours half a glass of wine for the ponytailed boy, sees her shaky hand set the glass before him like an offering. He's suspicious (perhaps), unfamiliar with wine (perhaps), but lifts the glass to taste, makes a face, as a child might, as Conor might, but decides it's okay, empties the glass in a single swallow.

Beer might have been more appropriate, Hannah supposes. Indeed, there is some of Wes's beer in the refrigerator.

"You, too. *You* have a drink, too, Mrs. J__."

Hannah laughs, startled. Now the hostess is being invited to drink with the intruder . . .

Rapist! The rape victim, sharing a bottle of Italian wine with her rapist.

It will be held against her, a judgment. All that happens between them, as soon as Hannah opened the door of her own free will, a door otherwise locked, and allowed the intruder into her house, a judgment against *her*.

Hannah pours wine into the ponytailed boy's glass and into a glass for herself. These are beautiful wineglasses, ultra-thin glass, sparkling clean for Ismelda washes them by hand with much care. With a hostess's innocent vanity Hannah hopes that the ponytailed boy is impressed.

Not accustomed to drinking from a *wineglass*, Hannah thinks.

Will that spare her? How the thug intruder is impressed by the suburban hostess!

Saying, with a lopsided grin, now wine-warmed, not so belligerent— "Sit down, Mrs. J__. Keep me company."

"I—I will . . . I will."

It's a movie scene, Hannah thinks. The terrified woman becomes an automaton, to save herself.

Rape victim desperate to save herself, serving the rapist.

Through a roaring of blood in her ears Hannah brings a loaf of multigrain bread to the kitchen table, several pieces of cheese. Brie, cheddar, Jarlsberg. Leftover chicken thighs, wrapped in tinfoil. An opened jar of Mott's applesauce with cinnamon, a favorite of the children. The ponytailed boy is indeed hungry. He chews rapidly, wipes at his mouth as he eats. Hannah gives him a paper napkin imprinted with bunnies, the children's napkins. (Wes detests paper napkins and will only accept cloth napkins.) The ponytailed boy isn't offended by paper napkins, and does not hesitate to eat with his hands. Hannah provides him with a spoon for the applesauce, which he eats from the jar. He finishes his second glass of wine, indicates with a grunt he'd like more. He eats, he is very happily eating. Certainly high on some drug and now beginning to be drunk, festive. Perspiration beads on his forehead, his mouth twitches into a smile. His eyes seem to Hannah unnaturally bright. Raw like her own, naked.

Hannah should be grateful, her rapist is not a mean drunk.

"You don't know my name, do you. It's Mike."

"Mike." Hannah utters the name tentatively, as if it were foreign, wondrous.

"Mikey—used to be. When I was a kid."

"Mikey."

Boastfully he confides in Hannah that before he'd come to Cradle Rock Road to see her, he'd been in Bloomfield Hills. "A really big house—bigger than this one. Behind a high fence."

Hannah has begun to listen. Bloomfield Hills?

". . . 'Bal-moral Drive.' You have to know a secret code to open the gate but when I got there the gate was open." Adding: "Because I was expected."

Hannah has to wonder who it is living on Balmoral Drive who would be expecting Mikey. She can't recall any one of her acquaintance who lives in that most prestigious area of Bloomfield Hills, an enclave of GM executives . . .

The ponytailed boy is sucking at his lower lip, defiant yet wistful. Like Conor when he'd hoped for more attention, praise. Hannah ponders how to flatter this volatile person without arousing his suspicion, she is skilled at flattering people yet she's cautious of blundering in her very flattery, saying the wrong thing: doesn't want the ponytailed boy to strike at her again, as quick and vengeful as a snake.

She wonders, could he kill her? *Would* he?

She doesn't want to think so, there's a bond between them.

"Know what, Mrs. J__? We could watch TV news."

Suddenly, the ponytailed boy is excited. As if this suggestion makes sense. Hannah has no choice but to lead him to the TV room.

There, Mikey whistles thinly through his teeth at the sight of the TV set, presumably its size: set in a solid mahogany cabinet with double doors, a screen measuring twenty-seven inches (diagonally). He squats before it, turns it on, switches impatiently through the channels encountering no news, only talk shows, cartoons, advertisements.

"Fuck! Where's the fucking *news*."

Hannah tells the indignant Mikey it's the wrong time. This time of day there are no news broadcasts on TV, you have to wait for six o'clock.

Feeling a chill wash over her, having said this. How heedless, stupid, to have suggested that ponytailed Mikey should wait in her house more than two hours, until six . . .

"Fuck fuck *fuck*. There's big news coming, where the fuck *is it!*"

Rising to his feet with a grunt, stumbling to sit on a leather sofa, heavily. His words have become slurred, he has become drunk within a few short minutes. Hannah guesses that he has rarely drunk wine. Glaring at Hannah he shakes his head as if to clear it.

"All I can say—*fuck*."

Seven-year-old Conor could not be more disappointed. The ponytailed boy's elation has vanished within seconds, like air escaping from a balloon.

Hannah holds her breath hoping he won't think of asking her to turn on a radio.

Holds her breath hoping he will suddenly decide to leave . . .

She dares not suggest it. She dares not beg him. Dares not speak to him at all.

Unnerving, that Mikey didn't want her money. He'd said he wanted a tip but no, he hadn't wanted a tip. Hannah doesn't want to think what he might want.

"Fuck 'news.' Know what?—we can finish that wine."

With the alacrity of an obedient wife Hannah goes to the kitchen for the remains of the wine, both wineglasses, glancing covertly at the wall phone six feet away.

How strange of the ponytailed boy, how (naïvely) trusting, he'd let Hannah out of his sight. Let her walk away.

No. You can't.

Can't risk it, he could kill you.

The way he'd slapped the wallet out of her hand. How swift his reflexes, like a young athlete. Hannah hadn't seen his hand flying at her until it had struck hers.

Yet: She could run outside screaming for help. Out the driveway, into the road?

No neighbors would hear her of course. Shut up in their air-conditioned houses set back from the road, or away on vacation. But there are surely workmen in the area, a lawn crew, roofers . . .

But no, dare not.

Drunk and crazy enough to run after you and drag you back.

Beat you with his fists, in a bawling rage like a momma's baby, rape you on the tile floor until he tore up your insides . . .

Almost, Hannah can recall the violent rape on the (concrete, filthy) floor of the stairwell at the Marriott. The faceless assailant, squeezing the (white) woman's slender throat in both his hands until she loses consciousness.

No, no! Cannot risk.

Must show your captor that you are eager to obey him.

And so Hannah's bare legs in chic Bermuda shorts move numbly returning her to the wood-paneled TV room transformed by the insolent figure sprawled on the leather sofa in the very place where Wes sits in the evening with his shoes kicked off, drink in hand, staring at the screen in his stiff attentive way to indicate to anyone who has stepped into the room *Don't interrupt!*

The children have their own, smaller TV to watch, and so don't often interrupt Daddy. But if Hannah joins him, Wes will acknowledge her with a minimal nod of his head without breaking his attention: He will be very annoyed if Hannah speaks to him before there's a break for an advertisement.

Astonishing to Hannah, Wes has vanished, a coarse-skinned stranger in army fatigue pants and black T-shirt, hair in a slovenly ponytail, has taken his place on the sofa.

Squinting up at Hannah sleepy-eyed, baring his teeth in a grimace of a smile—"Thanks, Mrs. J__!" Taking the bottle from Hannah and drinking from it, wipes his mouth on his T-shirt.

Hannah in an open-eyed trance with no idea why she has returned to this room, to her captor. Why she hasn't fled screaming. Or locked herself in the guest bathroom, phone in hand.

Why simply standing there irresolute, blinking and smiling inanely and her knees quivering like water.

Frowning Mikey reaches up, seizes Hannah's wrist, and pulls her roughly down beside him. The delicate wineglasses fall from her hand to the carpet, where they will be discovered hours later, miraculously intact.

Grunting, grimly tugging at her light summer clothing: white poplin top, beige cord Bermuda shorts. As Hannah weakly protests *No, don't—please* . . . Tries to kiss her mouth, mauls and pummels her, panting now, instantaneously aroused as Hannah pushes at his chest, not hard, not hard enough (she thinks) to seriously offend him, antagonize him for in the confusion of the moment Hannah wants to think that this is a playful interlude merely, not so serious, for isn't this person waiting to try the TV again, isn't he intensely interested in TV news, also he is so young, Hannah is so much older, in terror of provoking a temper tantrum in one so young, a rage for which she, the mature and responsible woman, will pay; the surprise is, the pony-tailed boy is unexpectedly strong, close to breaking her wrist when he'd grabbed her and yanked her down beside him.

Mouth fixed in a pathetic smile Hannah hopes to placate her assailant by not resisting him exactly, stiff-bodied and uncooperating yet not openly fighting him, a weak creature displaying its throat in denial of the predator's teeth. So long as the ponytailed boy is laughing, Hannah reasons that she is not in (serious) danger, but the laughter is coarse, a kind of grunting, possibly not laughter but grunting; and then Hannah's head is gripped as in a wrestling hold, neck straining, the assailant forces his mouth on hers, hot, damp, smelling of wine, forces his tongue into her mouth, Hannah begins to gag, choke and gag as her dazed brain tries to explain that she is (probably) misunderstanding, this is not what it appears to be, not an assault, will not end in rape, her lower body is tightening, shrinking in terror of being forced open, her muscles clench, hadn't she and the ponytailed boy reached a sort of understanding?—in the kitchen?—that he wouldn't hurt her, not if she fed him properly, which Hannah has done, which Hannah is happy to have done, exulting in her power to provide such nourishment; and so, isn't he grateful, isn't he indebted to her, she must not resist him but remain calm, must not scream or seriously fight him, he is so much stronger than Hannah, only the greatest restraint keeps him from breaking her neck in the headlock or closing his fingers around her neck to strangle her.

Take him upstairs. Your only hope.

In the bedroom, in the bedside table: the key.

Key to the cabinet, and in the cabinet: the gun.

He is drunk, he can be beguiled. He will stagger into the bedroom, he will express naïve amazement at the size of the king-sized bed, he will sprawl on the white quilt coverlet which in his coarseness he will hope to soil, Hannah can lean over him like Delilah leaning over the prostrate Samson tugging off his shoes, she can begin to undress him, soothe him with her hands, he will be foolishly mesmerized by her, it is not too late to secure the revolver, she will lead him to believe that she is undressing but in fact she will turn from him to unlock the cabinet, she will remove the (loaded) gun from the drawer into which Wes had so pointedly placed it and she will hold the gun in both hands aiming the barrel at the target as Wes had taught her, or tried to teach her, pulling the trigger blindly as she sucks in her breath, stunned by the deafening sound of the shot, the near-naked boy with the build of a wrestler convulsing as bullets tear into his chest, blood bubbles out of his anguished mouth . . .

No. Cannot.

Not possible.

Never could Hannah pull the trigger, never could Hannah shoot another person, it is not possible to extinguish another's life, even the life of one who wishes to hurt her; and it is *not possible* for Hannah to shoot someone in her bed, a stranger, whose (bloodied, limp) body would have to be explained to others . . . So Hannah understands sobbing helplessly, hopelessly for she is utterly trapped as one trapped in a glass cubicle rising in deathly silence into the sky as into oblivion as if what is happening to her and around her is happening beyond her volition as in a dream in which Hannah is not the dreamer but a participant: Who is this stranger ranting furious and aggrieved (she has no idea why!), tearing at her clothing, the chic white "classic" poplin top from Saks, the "classic" Bermuda shorts from Neiman Marcus, accusing her, calling her *bitch, cunt* as if he is angry at her but why, why angry at *her,* Hannah has not opposed him, in fear of her life Hannah has not dared to oppose him, she has tried to flatter him, the maleness in him that is so needy of flattery, has she not made herself abject that she might survive, has she not emptied herself of all will, the instinctive female strategy, the desperate female strategy, how can it possibly fail her now?

Young stallion-eyes rolling white above the rim of the dilated black iris, quick percussive panting, flaring nostrils—no words now but guttural moans as the ponytailed boy has bared Hannah's breasts, torn away her clothing, the tight-strapped brassiere, white striated skin exposed, once beautiful and now flaccid, fattish, deflated for Hannah has lost weight, her skin is too loose to hold the tender flesh tight; yet still the roseate nipples shimmer with beauty, a girlish beauty, or the memory of such beauty, the size of copper pennies, oversensitive, unbearable sensation like a raw nerve. In a delirium her assailant has begun to bite and suck at the nipple of Hannah's right breast, he has gripped Hannah so tight she dare not struggle for fear of her ribs cracking. This is nothing like the sweet-sensuous nursing of Hannah's babies, the elation, euphoria of that nursing, a mild pain at first, discomfort, chafed and raw-aching nipples, bruised breasts at the time firm and hard with milk, and a great pride in that milk, the young nursing mother praised, flattered and praised, how well she is doing, how well the baby is nursing, even Hannah's mother (famously stinting with her praise) had been impressed. Nursing, an *aria*! For one scarcely able to sing, what a triumph! But now struggling on the leather sofa in the TV room with the flung-open doors of the mahogany cabinet exposing the large scum-colored screen in which reflections are dully mimicked there is no milk in the mother's breasts, there is no *mother* remaining in the luckless woman, there can be no elation or euphoria nor even relief, only the hard hungry sucking of a mouth, a disembodied mouth sucking sullenly at a stone, furious with the stone for being but a stone, yielding no milk. Rocking against Hannah as he sucks the life out of her, bites and sucks, giant furious infant hunched at the breast, faceless, eyeless, shameless all mouth, moaning uncontrollably as in excruciating pain, anguish sucking at the tender roseate nipple until the nipple becomes a hard little pit retreating into the breast raw and bleeding and even then the ravenous infant will not release the wounded breast, in a convulsion of desire he will not release it, to save herself Hannah clutches at him, her arms gripping the stranger's head, as a drowning swimmer might grip another swimmer in the delusion that he may save her, no longer conscious of who the assailant might be, or who she is expected to be, or where the two of them are, what is happening to them. Her jaws are clenched against the terrible urge to cry *I love you*—no idea to whom she is speaking, only the brute physical necessity—*Don't stop, don't leave me, I love you.*

Pressing her face against the coarse hair smelling of the assailant's scalp, his body, the tight-muscled boy body rocking against her, shuddering and expiring against her, very close to being suffocated Hannah strains to turn her head, lifting her head at an angle, neck craning, tendons in her neck straining for the hope is simply to breathe, one breath indrawn and then another, and another as Hannah's chest is tight-compressed in the viselike arms, her lungs compressed, a shadow eclipsing a lung as shuddering ripples course at last through the assailant's body and through Hannah like waves washing over both, extinguishing them, rendering them helpless, obliterated like bodies left on the littered shore as the tide retreats.

Love love you.

Don't leave me.

Evidence

Ma'am—is this yours?"

Where usually Ismelda addresses her employer with a neutral expression not wishing to incur her employer's (unpredictable) wrath, on this occasion Ismelda is looking frankly perplexed.

Within ten minutes of returning to the house with the children, in the kitchen beginning to prepare their evening meal Ismelda has discovered, in a corner of the room, looking as if it has been flung there, Hannah's wallet.

"Oh. Yes. I think—*yes.*"

Hannah betrays no surprise. No shock, or embarrassment. Calmly takes the wallet from Ismelda, thanking her.

Fragrant from the luxury of a late-afternoon bath, hair damp, in a white terry-cloth robe, bare legs, bare feet in sandals. Nerves soothed, humming: five milligrams of Valium. The wife of the house, unalarmed. The wife of the house, restored. Preparatory to dressing for a late dinner with Wes, after the children have eaten and are in bed.

No attempt to explain to the nanny why, how her wallet had come to be flung into a corner of the kitchen, but politely thanking Ismelda for finding it, no fuss, no exclamations of surprise, gratitude. Matter-of-factly Hannah checks credit cards, cash (intact), and returns the wallet to the hemp shoulder bag on a chair, leaves the kitchen to take the shoulder bag upstairs to her bedroom where it belongs not allowing herself to think—*She knows. Knows something.*

Nor even to think—*She can't know. How could she!*

The smell of him? Ismelda's sharp nostrils? No.

He'd left forty minutes before Ismelda returned. He'd left abruptly, taciturn and abashed and sober. (Possibly) alarmed at his own behavior. Leaving no trace.

Suffused with euphoria filling her lungs like helium—*No trace! No trace.*

The smell of him gone, soon the memory gone. Briny odor of semen, oily hair, wine-stained teeth. His belching breath, dirt-edged nails. In loathing of him she'd flung open the French door to the deck, she'd turned the ceiling fan on *high*. The befouled leather sofa she'd wiped clean with Windex, wads of paper towels carried to the trash bin in the garage so that no one (that is, Ismelda) might notice them, the perplexing quantity of them, in a wastebasket. The empty wine bottle, even the wineglasses that had not cracked when dropped—all thrown away in a fit of loathing.

So happy!—Hannah has been spared.

Again, another time—spared.

If the ponytailed boy had refused to leave. If the ponytailed boy had been too drunk to leave. If Ismelda had returned home earlier, and seen him sprawled there on the sofa slack mouth agape. If the children had seen him. If Wes had seen him.

No words to explain him. No possible words.

And she had not killed him with the gun upstairs on the bed. That, she has been spared.

The adulterous wife dazed with gratitude for her own good luck that might have been, so easily, unspeakably bad luck.

Imposter Mommy, basking in such luck.

On her knees hugging, kissing the children, laughing in delight as they chatter excitedly about all the fun they'd had that afternoon, Mommy is moved to tears by their beauty and has to be helped to her feet by the alert brown-skinned nanny—*Ma'am? Are you all right?*

For a confused moment thinking that Conor and Katya have been at the Haydens' house on Ashtree Circle and not the Mayhews' house on Dupont Drive.

Since they'd been chattering about a dog named Ziggy. *Mommy can we have a dog! Mom-my!*

Something about a dog? Is this the dog that fled from Ashtree Common and left little Robbie Hayden behind to be murdered?

In a trance of relief and happiness soaking in a hot bath. Bruised breasts, bleeding nipples soothed by the hot bath. To calm her racing heart, her favorite medication in dark green plastic five-milligram capsules. Half hour, forty minutes as the bath water cools planning the surprise for Wes: a candlelit dinner, Hannah in a white summer dress with a pleated skirt, freshly bathed, hair brushed and shining.

Love me. We can try. It isn't too late. I will make up everything to you. I love you.

A bottle of Tuscany wine near-identical to the wine Wes opened the other evening, Wes will have no way of knowing that this isn't the very bottle he'd opened.

Alive!

The Hayden boy has been found—*alive*.

The first of Babysitter's eight victims to be found *alive*.

On TV news, footage of a littered area behind a strip mall on Maple Road, Bloomfield Hills, where the abducted boy, missing since Monday, was discovered that afternoon *bound and gagged and wrapped in a blanket, severely dehydrated*.

Cut to the facade of Beaumont Hospital, Birmingham, where *the ten-year-old was brought by ambulance, is in critical condition*.

Cut to the WXYZ van outside the hospital, swarm of reporters pursuing the Haydens as they enter the hospital accompanied by uniformed Far Hills police officers—*parents of the abducted boy ten-year-old Robbie Hayden, Jill and Brian Hayden of Far Hills, Michigan, arrive at the Beaumont Hospital in Birmingham.*

Cut to the facade of a stately Colonial house set some distance back from the road—*Hayden residence, Ashtree Circle, Far Hills, Michigan.*

Hannah feels a moment's vertigo, confusing the Haydens' house with her own.

Cut to parkland, a hiking trail amid tall trees—*Ashtree Common believed to be the site of the abduction of Robbie Hayden this past Monday.*

Cut to a photo of an abashed-looking moist-eyed sand-colored spaniel—*nine-year-old Lupa left behind when Robbie Hayden was abducted from Ashtree Common.*

Cut to photos of attractive couple Jill Hayden and Brian Hayden. Photo of Robbie Hayden looking younger than ten.

Family photo of Jill Hayden and Brian Hayden on a beach with two children (Esme, Robbie) and spaniel Lupa, in a happier time.

Cut to recent TV footage, the elder Haydens interviewed by a popular WXYZ broadcaster by the name of Trim Bangor, a Detroit personality usually associated with sports events. Hannah had not seen this hastily arranged and painful interview in which the parents of the missing boy desperately appeal to the phantom abductor to *please release Robbie unharmed,* and to anyone *who might have information about the abduction,* and to Robbie himself—*We love you, honey! Please come home if you can, we are praying for you.*

Reward money of ten thousand dollars for *information leading to the return of Robbie Hayden.*

Ghastly smile of Jill Hayden, clenched jaws of Brian Hayden trying to answer Trim Bangor's questions as relentless as ping-pong.

Cut to previous TV footage: trails in the woods at Ashtree Common, rescue workers and volunteers making their way through woods, fields, vacant lots.

Cut to a WXYZ interviewer asking brisk pert questions of a grave-voiced Far Hills police captain.

No, the 911 call can't be traced—the caller hung up too quickly.

Yes, there is a recording of the conversation but no, the caller's voice isn't clear.

No, no indication where Robbie was confined for four and a half days.

No, we have no "suspects" at the present time.

Yes, we have been following all leads. Hundreds, thousands of "tips"—we take each one seriously.

Yes, we are questioning "persons of interest."

No, we are not prepared to release any names yet.

No, no other child of the eight abducted since February 1976 by the person or persons designated "Babysitter" has been found alive.

No, we have no idea why Robbie Hayden was an exception.

No, it is not believed that "race" is involved in any way.

Not while the investigation is underway, those details will not be released to the media.

Cut (again) to the littered area behind the strip mall. Close-up, behind a dumpster where the missing boy was found *bound and gagged and wrapped in a blanket, severely dehydrated.*

Cut to store clerks, shoppers at the strip mall interviewed near the site—*No, we didn't see anything! Not a thing.*

Jarring cut to happily smiling faces, bicyclists, an advertisement for Coca-Cola.

Wes switches to WJBK News where the sheriff of Oakland County is explaining to a very blond young woman interviewer that "details" of Robbie Hayden's abduction and medical condition will not be released to the media for the foreseeable future.

Yes, we will interview Robbie when we can of course. When he is able to speak to us.

No, we have no idea why he was allowed to live. No idea where he was confined for four and a half days.

Yes, such information may be released at a later date. But not while the investigation is underway.

Jarring cut to happily smiling faces, beautiful tanned bodies in scanty swimwear running into the surf, advertisement for Camels.

Wes mutes the volume and switches to another channel—another advertisement.

Wes tells Hannah that the police always hold back information from the media. Details about the abductions, the killings. The condition of the children's bodies. So that when they question a suspect they can check what the suspect seems to know against what they know. And if some crazy person tries to confess, for instance.

"When they find Babysitter," Wes says, "he will be the only person who knows certain facts. So police will know that they have the killer."

Hannah hesitates to question Wes who speaks with such authority but wonders: Is this true?

The abductor could share his secrets with someone else, surely. A trusted friend. An accomplice.

"There's the privacy factor, too. Whatever was done to that poor kid. You wouldn't want the public to know. Things I've heard, I wouldn't tell you, Hannah. About the other kids he'd murdered—their bodies . . . We have a sick sick monster here, it's all of us in the 'suburbs' he's targeting. Don't tell *me*."

Wes is alluding to the *race thing*, Hannah thinks. Hannah has no wish to pursue the subject for it is unpleasant to see Wes become excitable and impatient with her.

"There hasn't been a single Black child taken," Wes says, as if reading Hannah's mind, "has there? Eight white children."

Because Babysitter lives outside Detroit, Hannah thinks. One of us.

TV news resumes, Wes unmutes the volume. Familiar film footage, Hannah is sure she has seen before. Stricken parents, photographs of young children, mostly boys, a girl, another girl—*previous victims of the serial killer known as Babysitter*. Hannah thinks how tragic it is, the parents of previous victims can have no rest, always the history of Babysitter is exhumed, seven small beautiful faces identified onscreen.

As Wes stares frowning at the screen, Hannah glances at the sofa he's sitting on, and at the carpet.

She'd been careful. Working swiftly. Fastidious. Windex, paper towels. All stains removed. No trace.

In the kitchen frantically scrubbing surfaces the ponytailed boy hadn't even touched.

This business I expedited today, it's gonna be news . . .

Excitement in the ponytailed boy's face. Flushed coarse skin, hot to the touch.

And now, TV news a few hours later. Coincidence?

Balmoral Drive comes to mind like flashing neon—then fades, vanishes.

Impossible to comprehend. No.

As a moth struggling in a spiderweb has no idea how it has come to be trapped in the spiderweb. Scarcely a memory of its life before the spiderweb. No idea of a life apart from the spiderweb.

Hannah knows: She should contact Far Hills police, as residents of the area have been urged to do if they have encountered anyone or anything "suspicious."

But what would she say to police?—how to find the words . . .

She doesn't know Mikey's last name nor even if Mikey—Mike—is really his name. She doesn't know where he lives or how to contact him. No idea how to contact Y.K. No idea how she could explain Y.K. or Mikey in her life if police questioned her. When police questioned her. For of course she would be *questioned*.

Thinking how no one understands what it is to be *questioned* until you are confronted by *questioners* empowered by the state to demand the truth of you.

A life that's a tissue of lies loosely strung together, serviceable as a life until one day it isn't.

Hannah would rather kill herself than revive her association with the Far Hills police department. Where she is known, though her name has never been publicly released, as the (white) suburban woman (allegedly) raped by a Black man employed by the Far Hills Marriott.

They'd never believed her, Hannah thinks. Not surprising, she'd never believed herself.

And what shame—Y.K. The passport issued in New York City identified the man as Yaakel Benjamin Keinz yet the photograph in the passport didn't appear to be the man Hannah knows, or knew, as Y.K.

In a lurid slew of dreams, Hannah has dreamed of Y.K. Sloughing off such memories as a snake would slough off its old skin yet (surely) bits of skin, scales, stick to the tender flesh beneath.

Numbly smiling to think—*No access. No trace.*

She has passed through walls, she has eluded discovery like a time traveler. Wes knows nothing of her truest self.

Her children, who adore Mommy. No idea who Mommy is, so they can adore her absolutely.

Katya might have been taken from Hannah, as punishment. Yet was not. So much Hannah has risked, yet Hannah remains (brazenly) untouched.

There is only one question: Of what am I capable?

If ponytailed Mikey is in any way linked to Babysitter, the fact that Mikey appears to be in the hire of Y.K. suggests that Y.K. is linked to Babysitter, too.

Impossible to comprehend. No.

After the children are in bed Hannah returns to Wes downstairs in the TV room.

Still watching WXYZ news but now the subject has shifted to *rising tensions in the Middle East* which doesn't interest him nearly as much as local Babysitter news.

Hannah had been disappointed this evening when Wes arrived home forty minutes late having had an "early dinner" with business associates at the Grosse Pointe Yacht Club, insisting he'd told Hannah about the engagement beforehand; he'd seemed to have totally forgotten that Hannah had planned their dinner together—romantic, candlelit, Tuscany wine, white summer dress with tight bodice and pleated skirt, amber beads around her neck, flowery scent of Chanel No. 5.

He is repelled by me. The Black man, he imagines.

Often, Wes speaks to Hannah without looking at her.

Or, if looking at her, not meeting Hannah's eyes.

Wes has switched to another local news station. If he doesn't hurry, the news hour will be over and late-night programming will begin.

". . . no one has satisfactorily explained why Babysitter released his eighth victim but not the other seven . . . One theory is that the abduction from Far Hills might not have been by Babysitter but by another person, a *copycat* . . . It is not uncommon, in such lurid crimes, that *copycats* begin to appear, attracted by the publicity."

A criminologist at the University of Michigan in Ann Arbor is speaking earnestly to an interviewer.

". . . another story is: Babysitter may be repenting. He'd tortured the poor boy it seems but decided not to kill him. That is . . . despite the tragedy . . . some cause for *hope*."

When an advertisement comes on, Wes mutes the TV.

Saying, in disgust, "Christ! A sick pervert like that could never *repent*."

Hannah wishes that Wes would lose interest in this subject which has obsessed him for months. Not wanting to think that, for Wes, the humiliated husband of the humiliated wife, an obsession with Babysitter is preferable to an obsession with the humiliation.

Still, it's rare for Wes to *care* so deeply about anything beyond himself and his family.

Wes is complaining that the police haven't been searching hard enough in the right places to find Babysitter. Now they're pinning everything on interviewing the Hayden boy—"But what *I* think is, if the abductor released him, it's because the boy can't identify him. He was blindfolded and gagged. Chances are he never saw who did it. Maybe he never even heard his voice . . ."

Not intending to be contrary, really just to allow Wes to know that she is listening, she is engaged with what he has been saying, Hannah says carefully, "Maybe someone else released him. Maybe there are two people involved in the abductions."

Wes snorts in derision. "Well, I doubt *that*. It's known that serial sex abusers are solitary people, they operate alone. Especially, a pervert like Babysitter would operate alone."

Pervert is a word Wes has uttered often recently, Hannah notes, with a particular relish.

"If the Hayden boy is interviewed, he probably wouldn't remember much, he'd be in a state of shock. He might even be mute. The brain's way of dealing with trauma—shut down."

There is a pause. Hannah wonders if Wes is thinking—*Like you. My wife. State of shock. Brain shut down.*

Hannah suggests that, since they are almost neighbors with the Haydens, she might contact Jill Hayden: "Just a note to say that we're thinking of them, and are so sorry that such a thing has happened to their son, and if there's anything we can do to help . . ."

This notion, this comforting fantasy has drifted into Hannah's head like a bit of silkweed fluff borne by the wind. The sort of neighborhood gesture you would expect in a movie of the 1940s: Claudette Colbert, Greer Garson, Jeanne Crain, the good-neighbor woman, wife of the good-neighbor husband Dana Andrews, Joel McCrea, James Stewart . . .

But Wes isn't so sure. Telling Hannah *no*, not a good idea.

"Not much we can do. Better not to get involved."

"But—just to show support. Because I am a mother, like Jill Hayden. Because she might like to know that—someone is thinking of her . . ."

Hannah's voice trails off. No doubt, Wes is correct. So little that anyone else can *do*.

"She isn't a friend of yours, you've said. You'd never met her, you've said."

Wes speaks dismissively. Hannah sits silenced, rebuked.

"Of course people are *thinking of them*. They've been in the news for days, it's gone national. What good will it do them to be told that?"

Wes has worked himself up to being exasperated with Hannah when she'd meant only well.

He has never forgiven me. The rape.

He is repelled by me. That is his secret.

Impatiently Wes switches TV channels. But no—nothing.

Saying, as if relenting, "I suppose it wouldn't hurt to write to her—to *them*. Both Haydens."

Hannah is relieved. Wes will dismiss an idea of hers, then reconsider and rephrase it in such a way that it will seem that he is being generous to her, to see her point of view; if possible, he will improve upon it.

"And sign my name, too. It will mean a little more, with both our signatures."

As in a romantic comedy Hannah laughs in delight. No acrimonious scene, in a Hollywood romance, is likely to end without a reconciliation: grumpy husband, relieved and forgiving wife.

"Thank you, darling!"—making use of the occasion to kiss her furrowed-brow husband lightly on the lips as if there'd never been any doubt that the disagreement, like this turbulent day, would end with a kiss.

That night in the dark, in their bed Hannah touches Wes, shyly. Flat of her hand against his back in a thin T-shirt yet still Wes shivers, Hannah's hand is (evidently) chilly.

He'd come upstairs an hour after Hannah, almost exactly. Having had enough of TV for the night.

Hannah has had a sleeping pill—just one! hoping that it will not fail to take effect, as a single pill sometimes does. So that, in the middle of the night, desperate for a few hours' sleep Hannah will take a second pill which will knock her out as if with a mallet to the head and in the morning she will be groggy, underwater, scarcely aware of Wes rising, leaving the room, departing for the day.

Wes is lying very still. If TV news of Babysitter has set his thoughts to a boil he gives no sign now.

He'd undressed quietly, in his bathroom. To not disturb Hannah. Whether because he truly doesn't want to disturb Hannah's sleep or because he doesn't want to speak with her, Hannah could not have said.

Don't hate me, try to love me. Desire me.

Hannah tells Wes that she has missed him, that day. Disappointed about dinner but she must have misunderstood. She will plan for another time.

(She hadn't eaten the elaborate dinner she'd prepared for Wes, of course it remains in the refrigerator in a heavy casserole dish. No appetite for dining alone. Marriage is the promise—no more dining alone! Hannah wonders if the meal should be frozen promptly in the morning, for economy's sake. For food proffered with love is the female body.)

Daringly, as if impulsively Hannah slips an arm over her husband's side. Presses against his impassive back, her breasts in a thin nylon nightgown, fatty-bunched, warm. Exquisite soft skin of her breasts, a woman's breasts, so much softer and more vulnerable than skin elsewhere. Hannah shivers at the thought.

How you know that you are alive. At least.

Wes murmurs something inaudible. He is relieved, perhaps, that Hannah seems to have forgiven him. But he has not turned to her, as Hannah has hoped he would.

She reaches for Wes's hand, brings it to her breast. Belatedly he stirs to life, turns to her, she presses herself into his arms, kisses him, again shyly, light moth kisses, in apprehension of being rebuffed. And indeed, just perceptibly Wes is stiffening, like one who has just thought of something. Failing to kiss Hannah in turn, only just lightly, as in a greeting between friends.

Another time Hannah says, "I missed you today." Hearing her voice, the reproach in the voice, female hurt, disappointment. She does not intend this tone, that comes unbidden. "The children were at a playdate, Ismelda was out, I was alone and I—I thought of you . . ."

"Did you!"—Wes murmurs, embarrassed.

How flat, how trite. Indeed, embarrassing.

Hannah wonders if it is true, what she has feared—her (white) husband loathes her, for having been "violated" by a (Black) man.

Convinced that his (male) friends pity him, and talk of him behind his back. His fellow partners, his associates, and (even) his employees.

Of course, Wes would deny this strenuously. Ridiculous!

Hannah has taken Wes's hand again, more assertively, and now Wes throws off her hand, irritated: "Don't, Hannah! Please just *don't*."

IV

*R*un, run! When you die it will be running.

 Feet sinking into sand soft-seeming but not soft.

 Bare feet sinking run run for your life.

 Looming behind you, to catch you around the ribs with his big-bear hands.

 Never any progress. Quicksand. Yet, always running.

 No choice but to run. Run for your life!

 Thick-piled carpet, high-heeled shoes sink into it like (quick)sand.

Nape of your neck bare resting in the shallow groove, a very cold stainless steel utilitarian table.

 Bare skin the hue of snow at dusk, faint-blue-tinted.

 Are you aware of the drain beneath the table?—you do not (actually) see the drain.

 Are you aware of the glaring fluorescent tubing overhead?—you do not (actually) see the tubing in the vinyl-tiled drop ceiling.

 Dimly aware of the white-coated figure looming over you. Latex gloves gripping the sharp utilitarian instrument.

 Dimly aware of arterial-red color—(berries?)—above the double doors opening inward where someone has placed, perhaps prankishly, a sprig of mistletoe.

 It's that season—mere weeks before Christmas.

 Somehow, time has accelerated. It is a riddle, how.

 So long you'd taken for granted that time is an infinite supply to be used as you wish, dipped into, measured by the calendar, the clock, and the watch, now you realize that time is the river rushing you along heedless of your wishes.

When you die, such pranks will continue. Such jokes.

Mistletoe in such a place! Pucker your mouth to be kissed.

Joker Daddy in his stained white coat stoops for a kiss. Pike-mouth Joker Daddy whose kiss is a sting.

Run running here.

Refrigerated air, sharp odor of disinfectant.

Fingers brushing your wrist. Closing about your wrist.

Because your heart is broken, wanting only to heal your heart.

Not wanting to end, only to heal.

No way to solve the riddle except to pursue to the end.

Which one of them was she?—*on the cold stainless steel table.*

"I Am So Sorry"

No words! She has tried.

On embossed cream-colored stationery, deep-dark-blue ink, schoolgirl penmanship.

I am so sorry about what happened to your son . . .

I am so sorry about the terrible thing that happened . . .

As your neighbor who would like to be your friend, I . . .

I am so sorry that what happened to your family happened . . .

It was a terrible . . .

. . . thank God a happy ending.

If there is anything I can do . . .

We have not met but our children attend the same school . . .

Picking up my children I believe I have seen your Robbie . . .

(My son, Conor, will be in second grade; my daughter, Katya, is in preschool . . .)

I think that I am just trying to say . . .

. . . praying that your son is recovered.

. . . praying that your son is recovering.

. . . your family.

Those terrible days and nights when your son was missing I could not sleep for thinking of you, hoping that you were brave as I could not be in such circumstances . . .

Those days and nights praying for you though (I should confess!) I am not what you would call a *believer* . . .

Oh I am sorry: I know you are (probably) trying to forget . . .

Your son is *so lucky to be alive*! But you know that . . .

Forgive me, am I making things worse?

Forgive me, is this an intrusion?

. . . we have friends in common, I think.

Our husbands know each other, I think.

If there is anything I can do please call me, my number is . . .

Several times Hannah tries, each time Hannah fails.
Cannot find the right words, magical words with which to address Jill Hayden.
(Hannah addresses her pleas only to Jill Hayden. No intention of writing to both of the Haydens, nor of signing Wes's name to her letter.)

I am writing to ask if there is . . .

. . . wishing that we had met before this terrible . . .

. . . not sure what I am trying to say to you.

. . . "there but for the grace of God go I."

Hannah tears up the many sheets of stationery. Furious at herself for wasting expensive stationery. Not only are the words inadequate, they are also insincere: Hannah didn't pray for Robbie Hayden's return, Hannah didn't lie awake thinking of the Haydens except that, having difficulty sleeping, waking intermittently through the night, she might have thought of the Haydens less than a mile away sleepless in their vigil.

Weeks later Wes will remember and ask if Hannah has written to Jill Hayden, and did she sign the letter with his name, too?—and Hannah assures him yes of course.

"Well. Have you heard back yet?"

Not yet, Hannah says. But she is sure that she will.

Dry Heat, September

He calls, he says he must see her.

Quickly she tells him *no*.

She is adamant, her heart is a brave clanging bell. All that is over—she is a different person now.

Indeed she has forgotten him. Approaching a ringing phone, lifting the receiver without a stab of dread.

For what is *dread* but the fear of *hope*.

For what is the loss of *dread* but the loss of *hope*.

He lets her speak. A rattling kite, set to soar but trapped in the lowest branches.

Quietly he asks when can he see her.

She says she can't. No more.

But when can he see her?—he asks.

Kiss Mommy

Terror of waking too late: The children have been fed breakfast and driven to school, the husband has been fed breakfast and has driven to his office at the Fisher Center at West Grand Boulevard, no one has required Mommy or even noticed her absence since the live-in nanny is so competent.

Terror of waking too early: When the sleeping pill wears off waking with a jolt before objects are defined in the visual field inducing panic of blindness, paralysis. In that unmeasured hell before dawn.

He has been with her, she knows. In the night.

As an infection slips into the bloodstream. Undetected, until a fever erupts.

A sensation in the lower belly, in the soft moist folds of flesh between her thighs that are the portal to the interior, where nerve endings are highly sensitive, as uncontrollable as firing neurons . . .

He enters her body at will, in unmeasured time there are no defenses.

Her cries are muffled, inaudible. She wakes, her knuckles hard and wet against her mouth. Beside her and facing outward in the enormous bed the husband continues sleeping, oblivious.

Yet, there is no memory. No words, and so no memory.

And at last there's dawn, where objects are clearly defined and the persons with whom we live have names.

By the time the children are ready to leave for school she has been awake for hours. Very tired, her head aches.

Ma'am?—Ismelda offers to drive Conor and Katya to school.

But no, Hannah insists. *She* will drive them.

Driving the children to school is the focus of the early-morning hours. Driving the children to school is the meaning of the early-morning hours.

Preparing breakfast for the husband, that is also a focus of Hannah's morning.

"Thanks!"—lifting his head in affable acknowledgment even as his eyes continue to rapidly scan the newsprint before him.

Clean-shaven jaws, slight thickening of jowls, tiny tucks and puckers in ruddy flesh. Fresh-laundered and ironed white cotton dress shirt, necktie, coat, slow thickening of the body, opacity of being. A man accustomed to giving orders quietly and not needing to repeat himself.

And when Hannah brings his coffee to place before him, again he will lift his head, nodding affably, reluctant to break his concentration on the column of newsprint, not impolite, certainly not rude, only just oblivious, a kind of mercy.

See?—I don't loathe you, your touch. Your smell. I do not even see you, how could I loathe you, my dear wife? No.

The children are finicky eaters who will eat only their favorite (cold) cereals (Honey Nut Cheerios, Frosted Flakes, Cinnamon Alpha-Bits, Rice Krispies), they are not interested in Mommy's (hot) prepared breakfasts which are too much like real meals and take too much time and are not sweet enough.

Ismelda will clear the table, rinse the dishes, and place them in the dishwasher.

Precision timing: leaving the house with the children promptly at seven-forty before the husband leaves for his office at eight, returning after the husband has left thus minimizing time spent with the husband, or rather with the impenetrable affability of the husband. This, too, gives focus to the morning.

Of course Mommy intends to drive the children to school!—annoyed with Ismelda asking this question for the second time in fifteen minutes.

Both children in the backseat of the Buick for safety's sake. Though Hannah drives cautiously, taking back roads at a slow speed knowing how easily, irrevocably an accident can happen.

Rumor is, Robbie Hayden will not be returning to Far Hills Day. At least not at the present time.

Rumor is, the Haydens are considering selling their house, leaving Far Hills.

Still, turning into the school grounds Hannah glances about looking for Jill Hayden.

The other one—Hannah has come to think of Jill Hayden.

At the school, a slow procession of cars at the rear of the school, letting children out to run inside.

Kiss Mommy goodbye at the rear of the school. Wet smacking kisses, lingering hugs from which fretful Conor shrugs before Mommy can release him; Katya, still fragile after the meningitis scare, allows Mommy to hug much, much longer.

"Oh! I love you so. *So* much . . ."

In hot September gusts of warm air lifting grit, dust, desiccated leaves in swirls.

So soon, fallen leaves? In early September? Parched-brown, papery-thin shaken from the branches of the weaker trees.

". . . will pick you up this afternoon, honey. Bye!"

Climbing back into the Buick startled by the sight of the strained face in the rearview mirror: she'd left the house unaccountably without brushing her hair, no lipstick on her mouth that appears lipless, and her eyes lashless, realizing belatedly why Ismelda had spoken to her as she had and dared to regard her employer with perplexed eyes.

Who is it in the Jarrett household who *sees* Hannah? not Wes, not the children. Only Ismelda.

Mortified at appearing so disheveled in public. Being seen, possibly recognized, at the children's school.

The other one of us, that is me.

The Lover: The Call

At first, she doesn't recognize the (male) voice.

Only belatedly realizing, *his* voice.

Must see her, he says urgently.

Something he must tell her. Which he has just realized.

In his own life, much has happened since they'd last been together. *I am free now, I was not free before.*

"If you won't come to me I will come to you, Hannah."

That lightly inflected name—*Han-nah.*

Quickly Hannah says no!—that isn't possible.

"But I love you, Hannah. You have come to dwell in my heart."

And these words, too, mysteriously inflected as if translated from another language, uncertain in English, yearning, vulnerable: Hannah has never heard her lover speak in such a way.

It is *him*. Yet—something has altered.

Hannah is feeling exhilarated, light-headed. Barely can she hear Y.K.'s voice through the beating of blood in her ears.

"Hannah? Darling? You will let me, won't you?"

They could meet in Far Hills, he is saying.

Hannah doesn't think so. No.

Astonished, galvanized with fear. Yet with excitement, hope—the impossible has happened, her lover is begging *her*.

Now that she no longer loves him. Now, emotionally detached from him.

Not possible to be seen in public with Y.K. Not in Far Hills.

And she is wary of him, the power he'd had over her, that she'd been so heedless, reckless, risking her marriage, losing her children in a custody battle . . . She considers herself a survivor, one who has narrowly escaped a deadly disease.

And so, she should hang up the receiver. Quietly.

For if she allows him to speak she will weaken, she will give in.

She has ceased loving him, that part of her life is finished. In a week she will be forty years old.

Barely remembers him. No.

Sending her home with the ponytailed boy. Getting her drunk, rendering her helpless, she has tried to forget, *she has forgotten.*

And then, he hadn't called her for months. Obviously no thought of her, she'd meant nothing to him. Regardless of what he is claiming now.

Yet: stepping into the house just now hearing the phone ring. Plaintive sound as of pleading, begging, the ringing of a phone in an empty house.

She'd hurried to the kitchen to pick up the receiver.

"Yes? Hello? Who is this? What do you want?"

Only your heart, I want to eat your heart.
Of what use is your heart, otherwise? Than to be eaten?

The Lover: The Assignation

On the sixty-first floor of the hotel tower he awaits her.

A final time, they have agreed.

Gliding upward silent, weightless in the sleek glass cubicle in which Hannah is the sole passenger.

Such silence, a kind of deafness. Scarcely daring to breathe in such suspension.

Cannot hear her own clamorous thoughts.

Mistake! Mistake, mistake.

Below, the crowded lobby floor of the hotel sinks away in a vertiginous drop like a stage set.

At eye level, open floors and railings sink away as in an accelerated film.

Above, the atrium ceiling is clear glass dissolving into the mottled-blue sky like the top of the skull sawed off.

Since she is no longer in love with the man who calls himself Y.K.

Since she is no longer vulnerable to Y.K. as one who has survived an infectious disease is no longer vulnerable to reinfection.

Since (she tells herself) this will be the final time . . .

Since, admittedly, Hannah has been flattered: *he* begging *her*!

His words echoing in her ears—*You have come to dwell in my heart.*

It has been decided, they will see each other one more time. Most practically, at the Renaissance Grand Hotel.

Impossible to continue, they have agreed.

Her marriage, her children. Impossible!

Since all that has happened between them, has happened most intimately in the suite sixty floors above the river.

Wide Detroit River gliding like liquid lava.

Fact is, not a river but an estuary, linking two lakes . . .

Intending (this time) to be utterly frank, truthful in her relationship with her lover yet Hannah hesitated to ask on the phone why he hadn't called her in months.

Or why, so suddenly, he has decided to call her now.

Welcome to the Renaissance Grand, ma'am!

Handing the ignition key to the attendant brightly smiling at her—*Thank you, ma'am!*

Hannah's heart clutches, for a moment she thinks the dark-skinned young man is—

(Has Hannah forgotten the name?)

—Zekiel Smith.

—Zekiel *Jones*.

For if this is so, if the smiling young parking attendant is Zekiel Jones, Hannah has the opportunity to relive and to redeem . . .

Except: This is September 1977. Time has jolted forward, there is no going back.

He is dead. You are alive. You are the murderer.

Always present tense in the silently ascending glass cubicle in which numerals flash in succession above the door: 26, 38, 49, 53 . . . Stare transfixed: Never will you reach your destination.

Sleepless through the night. White-water rapids splashing amid rocks, boulders. Foam, froth, broken things in eddies swirling, too swiftly passing to be *seen*.

At dawn, numbed, exhausted. But now, Hannah's brain has become a thrumming hive.

The lethargy of weeks, months has melted away. Melancholy of sharing a bed with one who does not love you, melted away.

In the hot stinging shower that morning a grimy patina of old, dead cells, skin cells, washed away in a delirium of joy.

You have come to dwell in my heart.

Preparing herself with care. Hair brushed to a glossy sheen, makeup flawless, poreless. Beautiful understated clothes, autumnal colors.

Saint Laurent stiletto heels not worn for months as tight on the feet as foot-binding.

That thrill of such pain. Stirred memory like muck rising in water.

Too soon, the glass cubicle stops with a small jolt at the sixty-first floor.

Not prepared. Never are you prepared for the sixty-first floor.

Blindly Hannah steps out of the elevator. *He* is awaiting her.

"Darling! You came."

Y.K., sooner than Hannah has expected him.

For never has Y.K. waited for Hannah by the elevators, always Y.K. has waited for her in his suite halfway down the corridor.

Taken by surprise, weak-kneed as her lover kisses her, covers her stunned face with kisses. In her stiletto heels Hannah clutches at Y.K. to hold herself erect.

His lips feel cold against her heated skin, like the wings of moths.

Overcome with emotion. Helpless, as disoriented as a compass whose needle has begun to spin.

"You came, darling! I wasn't sure if you would."

Almost, Y.K. is sounding surprised, himself.

"Yes, I—of course, I . . ."

"I've been waiting out here, watching the elevators. The rising numbers. All those people in elevators, none of them *you*. Until now."

Is this Y.K.?—speaking so lightly, lyrically? There is nothing reproachful in his voice, only just pleasure, relief.

Behind Y.K. is a wall of floor-to-ceiling glass panels overlooking the sprawling city. When Hannah leans back to see her lover more clearly, his face is obscured from her by blinding light.

Awkwardly, stooping, his arm around her waist, Y.K. walks Hannah down the corridor to his room. He has left the door open, hanging from the doorknob is the sign DO NOT DISTURB.

Hannah is aware that Y.K. is walking stiffly, with a near-imperceptible limp, as one walks to mitigate pain, trying not to wince.

Embarrassed, Y.K. explains that it's an old injury from wartime—shrapnel in his thigh that acts up if he strains the muscles.

Shrapnel!—Hannah is moved to sympathy.

"Yes, but it's nothing. I didn't want to use a cane just now—out of vanity."

And this, too—affable self-mockery. Not like Y.K. as Hannah recalls him.

Hannah wonders at this change in her lover. As if he has been ill and is now convalescent. He seems to her less aggressive, gentler in his manner.

With a flourish Y.K. shuts the door behind them, and secures the safety lock.

"Hannah, you're so beautiful! As I remember you."

Hannah feels her face smart with blood. In Y.K.'s presence, Hannah *is* beautiful: She'd caught a glimpse of her reflection in the elevator mirror, impressed by the flawless cosmetic mask she herself had composed that morning.

Shyly Hannah laughs. She tells Y.K. that he, too, is looking very good—very *well.*

"I am. I am *well.* At least now that you're here."

Framing Hannah's face in his hands. It has been a very long time since anyone has gazed into Hannah's eyes with such adoration.

This new sobriety in her lover, and this new gaiety! Hannah feels a wave of vertigo, too much is happening too soon.

Gravely he kisses her mouth another time. He leads her into a sitting room which is bathed with light, blinding autumnal light from windows whose heavy drapes have been pulled open; Hannah notes, there is something wrong about the drapes, some small snag in the mechanism, that have opened asymmetrically like a drooping eyelid.

On a marble-topped table, a pear-shaped vase filled with creamy-white roses surpassingly beautiful.

"For you, darling. As soft and white as your skin."

Hannah stoops to smell the roses, though thinking that roses have no scent, do they?—indeed, she can smell nothing.

"Beautiful . . ."

Glancing about the room, which is a room she has seen before but which does not look familiar to her at all.

As beautifully furnished as a stage set. Sofas, chairs, tables meant to suggest antiques of a bygone era—Edwardian? Framed sepia illustrations on the walls, the City of Detroit in the 1890s.

History of Detroit: trains, lake freighters, Model-T, Ford Motor Company, Ford Tri-Motor Airplane (1925).

Incongruity of "antique" furnishings with sleek modern white walls, recessed lighting fixtures, tall windows.

Incongruity of luxury hotel, superficial glamor, pounding of Hannah's heart and that sensation of wheezing in her lung, childish hope, adult female dread.

There appears to be nothing of Y.K.'s in sight. Not an article of clothing, not a briefcase or anything to suggest his work. (What *is* Y.K's work?) Except, on a chair, a cane of polished dark wood startling to Hannah, as an unattached prosthetic limb would be.

Wanting her to see this, Hannah thinks. As in a stage set.

Through a doorway would be the bedroom. With the enormous king-sized bed.

A medium-sized roller suitcase had lain on a stand at the foot of the bed, looking newly purchased, dark blue fabric, unlocked.

She had dared to open the suitcase. Dared to slip her hand into an unzipped pocket.

Why had she done such a thing? Hannah is astonished at the recklessness of her behavior, recalling.

"This time, dear Hannah, we must tell each other only the truth. Yes?"

"Y-yes."

Hannah laughs nervously. Not sure to what she is agreeing. Has she admitted that, previously, she hadn't been truthful with Y.K?

Can't recall telling this man anything of a personal or a private nature, there hadn't been the opportunity.

" 'The truth will set us free.' So it's said."

Y.K. is smiling but Hannah can see in his face an expression of obscure hurt, woundedness. *I have suffered for you, you are not the only one who has suffered.*

Indeed there has been a considerable change in Y.K.: the lighter tincture of his skin, his height, the width of his shoulders, his eyes—the heavy, bluish-tinged lids Hannah remembers, suffused now with a look of tenderness.

A tall man, at least six feet, yet not so tall as Hannah remembers, nor so solid-bodied. Where once Y.K.'s manner had been ironic, playful, (subtly) mocking, now he appears to be intense, sympathetic. Hannah is acutely conscious of him looking at her—at *her*.

His jaws are clean-shaven, smelling of something astringent. Tiny welling of blood on his cheek for he has shaved within the hour.

He is wearing a blue-striped cotton shirt with a miniature, near-invisible monogram on the pocket, his trousers are khaki-colored but of a much finer fabric than khaki, fitting his hips loosely as if he has lost weight. His cheekbones are more sharply defined than Hannah recalls.

He is an actor, skilled in more than one role. Hannah regards him with amazement. She may as well concede, she is faint with love.

"Are you hungry, Hannah? I thought—since it's midday . . ."

Hungry! Hannah is ravenous, Hannah has not eaten yet that day.

With gentlemanly courtesy Y.K. leads Hannah to a small sofa he has positioned beside a window overlooking the Detroit River sixty floors below; on a low glass-topped table are a lavish cheese-and-fruit plate, a bottle of chilled white wine, two long-stemmed wineglasses, and a slender vase containing just one white rose.

"How beautiful!—all this—the view of the river . . ."

Hannah is overcome with emotion. Y.K. squeezes her shoulder, stoops to kiss the nape of her neck.

Together on the sofa, side by side. Hannah, closer to the window.

Y.K. opens the bottle, pours wine into their glasses.

"My darling! I'm so grateful that you've forgiven me."

Forgiven him? Hannah tries to think what Y.K. means.

He lifts his glass to tap hers. Hannah laughs, drinking.

She'd been too excited to have eaten anything that morning. Now, the wine rushes to her head—a delicious faint-flamey sensation in her mouth, in her throat, expanding warmly in her chest.

"You have, haven't you? Darling?"

Hannah smiles at Y.K., uncertainly.

"You've forgiven me?"

Hannah laughs, yes. Blood rises into her face. Impossible to utter the somber word *forgive,* this would mean that her lover had wronged her in some way that she can't truly remember.

"My mistake was trying to live without you, Hannah. These months—my life became complicated, my 'family life'—I couldn't stop thinking of you."

And I couldn't stop thinking of you. Hannah smiles confusedly into a blaze of light.

Astonishing to Hannah, that Y.K. is saying such things to her, not ironically, nor even playfully, but with genuine feeling. He has never spoken of "family" before—it's a jolt to her, to realize that yes, even Y.K. must have a family.

"You must know, Hannah. I love you. That was my mistake, too—not having told you. Not realizing."

I love you. Hannah listens, in disbelief.

Moved by her lover's words yet uncertain how to reply. He has always had this effect upon her—this man.

Not other men, not most men—*this man.*

Like an actor who has drifted off script and can't find her way back. Not daring to improvise for fear of making a fatal blunder. In a mild panic Hannah stares out the window at the river far below. In the pale autumn light the river is dull-luminous, like liquid lead; dispiriting smells emanate from this river if one comes too near. But sixty floors up is not *near.*

How odd, Hannah thinks, a river is *named.* A river is *mapped.*

As if anything in nature were in any way connected with its *name,* its placement on a *map.*

Sensuous, luminous. Beauty in polluted waters, seen from a safe distance.

"... first saw you, Hannah, that night at the fundraiser, it was as if I'd 'recognized' you. As if we'd met before. As if we were 'fated.'"

Hannah laughs nervously. She tells Y.K. that she, too, felt—a connection ...

Trying to recall: a stranger's fingers brushing her wrist. Her instinct was to remain turned away, to ignore, assume it was an accidental encounter like many in that crowded gathering.

"... it's thought that the feeling is a sort of déjà vu—a neurological tic of some kind. But I think that's just a rationalization. People need to diminish profound emotional experiences by categorizing them, giving names to them. 'Infatuation'—'love at first sight' ..."

Hannah listens with a sort of pleasurable discomfort. Is this her lover?—*is* this Y.K.? Her face is very warm.

"I think—I'm fairly sure—I've had a recurring dream. You are at the center of my dream, Hannah."

Hannah tries to laugh, nervously. She is flattered, but she is unable to believe; she is unable to believe, but she is flattered.

"Have you ever dreamed of me, Hannah? I have wondered."

Y.K. speaks thoughtfully, wistfully. Hannah thinks—*Is he the man in the passport? Is that how I know him?*

And this thought, too, brings with it a pleasurable discomfort, like intoxication.

Hoping to deflect the intensity of the man's attention Hannah asks Y.K. about the injury to his leg. Perhaps this is ill-advised, a flicker of displeasure in his face, he shrugs dismissively. Vietnam, south of Chu Lai, his plane had crash-landed in the jungle, he'd been lucky to crawl out of the wreckage alive.

Does Hannah know what "shrapnel" is?—fragments, tiny filaments, working their way through the meat of his thigh.

Meat, thigh. Hannah is struck by these words, which seem so clinical and so cold.

Awkwardly Hannah asks, does he have medals?—and Y.K. laughs saying of course, *medals.*

"We all came home with 'medals.' That's the easy part."

He might need more surgery, Y.K. concedes. He might need to use a cane more often than he uses it now.

"But there's nothing wrong with using a cane!"—Hannah means to console.

The wild thought comes to her—*He will need someone to take care of him. I will be that person.*

A fleet memory of Joker Daddy intervenes: near the end of his life, when he'd walked awkwardly with a cane. Lifting his eyes to his daughter Hannah abashed, resentful . . . stiffening as she'd helped him with the steps, but allowing her to help.

Scarcely aware, Hannah wipes tears from her eyes.

Meat, thigh. A profound truth in these words that seem almost to rhyme but do not.

Very gently Y.K. leans forward to kiss Hannah's right eye, on the eyelid; then, her left eye. No one has ever kissed Hannah in such a way, with such gentleness, precision.

A shudder runs through Hannah, like an electric current. Her eyelids are alight with flame.

Suddenly they are laughing together like children. They begin to speak at the same time, interrupting each other. They have veered yet more wonderfully off script. Their speech is breathless, clumsy. Yet it is quite all right, to be clumsy. Hannah understands that she is beautiful again, she is desired, there is a blindness in desire, as if a flame were illuminating both her face and her lover's face. Y.K. kisses her eyelids another time, this time touching his tongue to her. He kisses her throat.

An artery beating in Hannah's throat, her lover kisses with sudden feeling, force.

Something falls startled to the floor, a white linen napkin. A knife, from the cheese-and-fruit plate.

He will slash my throat. He will use a dull blade, to prolong the ordeal.

Hannah has begun to shiver, sitting very still, straight-backed, as Y.K. continues to kiss her throat, gripping her slender shoulders with his (strong) fingers.

Hannah seems to have forgotten, this was to be their final meeting. This is not the outcome she has been led to expect.

Y.K. lifts Hannah in his arms, half carries her toward the other room. Like a drowning woman Hannah clutches at him blindly.

A flicker of panic, yet a warm suffusion of lethargy, weakening her limbs. Impossible for Hannah to deflect her lover's attention, his desire for her; impossible for Hannah to object—*No, please—this isn't what we'd planned* . . .

As soon as the thought comes to her, it is belated—too late.

Hannah sees that the king-sized bed has been opened, the brocade coverlet drawn back exposing white sheets; half a dozen pillows neatly arranged along the headboard like decorative grave markers. Bedside tables frame each side of the enormous bed, twin lamps with lampshades designed to mute, not amplify light. In a heavy zinc urn with fractal ornamentation, a bouquet of copper flowers, branches.

Again the dark-blue suitcase on the stand, unlocked but not opened, again the mirrored closet door a few feet away slightly ajar . . .

This time, Hannah will not make the mistake of searching through her lover's suitcase, daring to examine his passport.

Hannah will not make the mistake of displeasing him. She has learned.

Yaakel. What if she were to call him by this name, and not by his initials?

With nothing of his previous impatience Y.K. undresses Hannah as if reverentially. He kisses her mouth, she clasps his head against her breasts. Wishing that one of them had thought to pull the drapes together for the whitish autumnal light pouring through the tall windows is as bright-blinding as a hallucination.

The nakedness of another person!—Hannah feels faint, she is made to see too clearly.

Rarely does Hannah glimpse Wes's naked body. She is familiar only with the naked—perfect—bodies of her children. Because so small, so young, their perfection is of no distinction, it is utterly natural.

Hannah steels herself for the weight upon her. Steels herself for the discomfort, the abrasive of his skin against hers, the sensation of near-suffocation, but Y.K.'s lovemaking is gentle, as if tentative. As if there is no history between them—no memory.

As if they are newly lovers, uncertain of each other, each wanting only to please the other.

"Oh—I love you . . ."

"I love *you.*"

Hannah hears a raw, brutal sound—a sob escaping her throat.

Her lover's face is no longer visible to her, buried in the hot curve of her neck. Her hands on his back discover whorls of flesh, old scars. His breath is harsh, hot. He is straining over her, grunting. She seems to see herself at a little distance, the fleeting white body, naked as if skinless.

Trembling with desire for him, for this. Lying in the man's arms, no turning back.

Clenched tight against him in a frantic muscular anguish, the breath knocked out of her as with a powerful blow.

And afterward, a voice out of a dream, oddly formal as if reciting a vow: "My darling, you have come to dwell in my heart where no other woman has dwelled."

. . .

Above the sepia sprawl of Detroit, a thin sickle moon.

Hidden by gusty clouds like rags, then again visible, if faintly.

By the time Hannah returns to the house on Cradle Rock Road, at dusk.

Soon then, in secret calling the number Y.K. has given her.

Just to hear your voice. My dear one.

And again then, later that night as Hannah has promised, calling her lover before she joins her husband upstairs in bed, in a lowered voice on the phone she has brought into the downstairs bathroom after Wes has (finally) turned off the TV news and gone upstairs.

Will she think of him that night? His love for her?

Yes, Hannah assures him. She will.

And will she call him in the morning, when she is free?

Yes, Hannah assures him. She will.

And they will make a plan, when to meet again?

Yes, Hannah assures him.

And does she love him, as he loves her?

Yes, Hannah assures him.

And she will be with him, one day soon? When she is free?

Yes. She vows, she will.

Only after they have hung up does Hannah dare whisper *Yaakel* into the receiver.

Armor

Wears her love, her lover like armor.

    He is always with her, she has become invulnerable, invincible.

No harm can come to Hannah that does not come from him.

On the escalator at Saks, ascending. Never alone for she is with *him*.

    In the Food Mart, unassailable. For she is one who is *loved, desired.*

    On the street, the eyes of younger men glance at her, through her. She pays no heed, scarcely notices. Her heart lifts: Don't need *you.*

    Even the children can't hurt her, Conor's sudden tears—*Mom*-my!

    In Wes's presence she is quiet, subdued. Her silence unnerves him, it has long provided a cover for him, his unfettered mind. A lustful dog nosing about in curbside debris. Now, she sees him glancing at her quizzically. Perhaps he will love her more, he will find her more beautiful, desirable, as she needs him less. The children press themselves against her legs, needy and clinging. Mommy love *me.*

    Hannah laughs, she has become almost gay, giddy. Like one who tosses gold coins from her pockets believing that she has an infinite supply.

    For always, she is living for *him.*

    When not likely to see him, she speaks with him on the phone. He is elsewhere, in another city, but he has not abandoned her as he had in the past. This new phase of Hannah's life.

    Darling what can do we, how can we be together . . .

    So badly yearning to be with you . . .

    One day, soon . . .

    Her heart has a fine crack, *he* has entered it like a breath.

. . .

"Have you ever been to Bali? No? I will take you there."

Hannah laughs nervously saying that would be wonderful—someday.

"Bali is the most beautiful place I've ever seen. The people are the most 'spiritual' I've ever seen. Nothing like this country—where *things* are worshipped."

Hannah listens gravely. Hannah says yes, but she is married, she has young children.

"Of course you're married *now*. But relationships change, circumstances change."

Later, as Hannah is preparing to leave: "You will always be the mother of your children, Hannah—that can't change. But remaining the wife of that husband—that's a different proposition."

He accompanies her to the elevator. Waits with her. In this interregnum of the present tense Hannah is baffled into silence as her lover continues to speak to her as if hypnotizing her.

". . . what's to come. *That* is the proposition."

Descending in the elevator, in a state of trance as the interior of the hotel atrium rushes upward, out of sight.

A succession of floors, too swift-ascending to be comprehended, rushing upward and beyond Hannah's range of vision, to oblivion.

And in the car, driving home. Face shining with tears, a radiant hurt smarting her skin.

You will always be the mother of your children.

Like armor, his love. More crucially, the secret of his love.

For Wes can't hurt her now. She has become immune to him now.

The husband who'd so long been the dominant one in their marriage. His sexuality—waxing, waning to an algorithm exclusively Wes's own—determining Hannah's self-worth.

But now, no.

At the Beaumont Hospital fundraiser in late October where Wes abandons Hannah soon after their arrival. Though she has made herself beautiful. Though to her lover she is beautiful. How quickened, Wes's interest in the company of others. The sound of his laughter tears at Hannah's nerves. The way in which women friends, greeting him, lean forward to kiss him on the cheek, which inspires Wes to kiss them in turn, more robustly.

I hate you. I will never forgive you.

I will have my revenge on you.

In the open lobby of the hospital, a festive crowd. Familiar faces that turn out to be strangers, strangers that turn out to be old friends. Sleek marble floor, banks of flowers, jazz quartet aggressively loud, uniformed waiters holding trays aloft as they make their way through the crowd like knife blades cutting through uncooked dough: dull-resistant, but parting for the knives.

Champagne frothing in flute-shaped glasses.

Seeing how eyes drift onto her, staring. Hannah ignores.

Hannah's women friends whom she rarely sees now. The Schell woman—Melissa. (So often seeing this woman in Far Hills, or some-one who closely resembles her. Sometimes Melissa lifts her hand in a friendly greeting, smiles at Hannah even as Hannah turns away as Hannah is turning away now.) Heavyset pouch-eyed Dr. T__ is here as well, regarding his former patient more with pity than contempt. Perceiving the filthy gnarled sponge that is Hannah's soul, that Y.K. (it seems) has never seen.

For *he* loves her. *His* love protects her from insults, harm.

How badly Hannah misses her lover! She could weep, missing his arms tight around her, the warm eager weight upon her holding her down, a kind of ballast to prevent her soul from flying out of her body, to annihilation.

He wants to marry her, Hannah thinks. A frightened smile twitches at her mouth. For that is *her* secret.

He wants her to leave her husband, to marry him. To take her chil-dren with her, and marry him. She thinks so. Yes.

Soothed by champagne, feeling hopeful. Always hopeful.

Joker Daddy has said *We make our own luck, kids. Excelsior!*

At a little distance Hannah sees the Haydens. Surprised that Jill Hayden would appear at such a public gathering . . . Hannah intends to speak with Jill but as she approaches the woman she sees that this is not Jill Hayden after all.

Another time, Christina Rusch. Hannah is sure that she sees Christina Rusch, heavier than Hannah recalls, aloof in matronly navy blue, on the farther side of the lobby beside her stout husband. This friend, too, Hannah is determined to speak with but never manages to find her amid the crowded gathering.

Later, stout red-faced Harold Rusch turns out to be a stranger who resembles Harold Rusch only to the degree that high-echelon automobile executives who live in Bloomfield Hills resemble one another. With a rakish smile staring at Hannah: "H'lo! Which one are *you*?"

Of course, Hannah thinks. The Rusches, local royalty, would never turn up at so plebeian a gathering.

As the evening winds down Hannah has no choice but to seek out Wes in a corner of the lobby where the laughter is loud and raucous. She is careful to smile before she is within the range of his vision. Always smiling, in public, never melancholy, sad-sulking, always gay-giddy, assured of a man's love, *his* love. Not daring to touch Wes's arm in this public place for fear that he will throw off her hand, and everyone will see, wide-eyed, scandalized, thrilled.

Poor Hannah Jarrett! Since that rape, or what she'd claimed was rape, the woman has not been the same.

Poor Hannah? Poor Wes! He's the one to feel sorry for.

Raped by a Black man, a parking attendant . . . Was that it?

What she'd claimed.

God! Poor Wes, so humiliated.

None of this can wound Hannah. No longer.

Out of mercy one of the others indicates to Wes that his wife is behind him. In tall stiletto heels, teetering.

"Ah! Hannah."

With exaggerated husband courtesy turning to the wife as if startled, gentlemanly in tight black tie, slightly puff-faced for Wes Jarrett has been drinking for two hours and twenty minutes. Claiming to detest these fundraiser evenings he has no choice (evidently) but to seek out companions who share his convictions. His eyes crinkle in irony. Out of the slant of his mouth joking, the others laugh loudly.

The wife, though not quite hearing the joke, understands that it is playful, meant to be harmless, funny and not cruel, she laughs, too, for the others to register.

Wes sets down his (empty) glass on a table, as sharp as a retort.

Abruptly now they are leaving. Wes has had enough, he is leaving. Headed for the nearest exit scarcely checking to see if Hannah is behind him.

Driving home, in silence. Except Wes is humming to himself, a guttural sound that conveys satisfaction, or a defiant pretense of satisfaction, a new habit of his. Hearing him, often in his bathroom in the morning, Hannah wonders uneasily if these are secret thoughts of Wes's own, emerging without his awareness.

"You never used to like those people," Hannah can't resist saying though probably (she knows) she should remain silent for there is dignity in silence but rarely dignity in words even if those words are resolutely unaccusing, unreproachful. "You'd told me, how many times."

"Well, then. I'm a hypocrite, am I?"

"*Are* you? I didn't say that."

"Didn't you!"

"No. I did not. I said—"

"I know what you said: 'You never used to like those people.'"

Wes laughs, and shrugs. He is drunk, which is why he feels good about himself.

The kind of selfish good feeling, Hannah thinks, that deliberately excludes another.

"But that was then, this is now, Hannah. Even a rat in a corner has to 'like' someone."

This, too, is meant to be funny, Hannah knows. Out of the slant husband mouth, much that is meant to be funny, not hurtful.

In any case Hannah isn't hurt. Hannah is too beautiful and poised to be hurt. Hannah laughs, she, too, is in a good mood. You would think that Hannah is amused by her witty husband but in fact Hannah is armored against him as if encased in steel.

And that night calling her lover after her husband has collapsed in bed. Speaking in a low quavering voice on the phone in the guest room where she will spend the night.

Missing you so badly, what can we do.

. . . will have to make some decision. Soon.

Oh God. I love you.

Think of me tonight?—with you? All night.

All night! Yes.

. . .

Except: With the children, no armor protects her.

Feeling now a new tenderness toward the children, who know nothing of Mommy's truest self. How, in her lover's arms, in a delirium of sensation, reduced to harsh helpless sobbing, Hannah forgets them entirely as if a part of her brain had been scooped out, obliterated.

This wonder that has touched her, through the years. That her own mother could look upon her children with detachment, in her eyes a curious flatness of affect, as if something had been extinguished inside.

Don't ask me to be "mother" any longer. I am worn out, I am finished with "mother."

But not Hannah! Hannah feels panic, that she might ever be so detached from Katya, and from Conor.

As soon as she sees them, whatever thoughts have been preoccupying her vanish in an instant. She is *theirs,* utterly.

As, she recalls, her breasts had leaked milk at the sound of their cries, as babies; a few times, astonishingly, at the mere thought of them. The thrill of the mother who is *needed.*

For no one else in Hannah's life needs her. If Wes ever did, as a young husband eager to make love with his wife each night in their bed, in response to his own intense need, it isn't that way any longer, and has not been in years.

Being needed, a kind of addiction. But a sweet, pleasurable addiction in the service of others.

Reading to the children not just at bedtime but at other times. Nap time, that happy time when both the children were younger; for now, Conor is likely to be restless, fretful. Katya is still little but Conor insists he is *not little.*

Soon, they will have separate rooms. Conor will want a room of his own away from his little sister . . .

Still, Conor likes Mommy to read to him, most nights. Katya falls asleep almost immediately, Conor actually listens to Mommy. Nothing more pleasurable, Hannah thinks.

Leaning over to kiss a sleeping child's cheek. The warmth of the cheek, the miraculous softness against Mommy's lips.

Yet, there is more pleasure now, Hannah basking in the (imagined) vision of her lover.

Beautiful Hannah! It's no surprise your children are beautiful, too.
One day, he will meet them. But—how soon?

Hannah trembles with excitement, apprehension. It will—must—happen within a few weeks, surely.

But how does one introduce small children to a lover? A (potential) stepfather? Surely this is commonplace for divorce has become commonplace.

Fifty percent of American marriages end in divorce!—this statistic seems unbelievable to Hannah, who knows very few couples who have been divorced, in fact.

In the days of her own childhood, in the 1940s, divorce was a rarity, a scandal. Very wealthy people divorced one another, you read of their scandals in the newspapers; but wealthy people did not count.

Conor? Katya? I'd like you to meet . . .

. . . my friend, a new friend, his name is . . .

Hannah's hands have turned icy, the children's book nearly falls from her chilled fingers. A sensation of weakness wells up in her, a kind of nausea.

Then, the book does slip through Hannah's fingers, falls to the floor with a thud, waking Conor who has just fallen asleep.

"Mom-*my*?"—Conor is startled, frightened.

Fortunately, Katya isn't wakened. Hannah soothes Conor, shows him that it was just the book, nothing to be frightened of, don't be silly. Leaning over him, another kiss, a hug, Mommy, too, has been frightened, but Mommy has recovered, switching off the bedside lamp that is the figure of a long-necked white goose.

Hannah lingers in the half-light until Conor has fallen asleep. A voice quiet in her ears, as stealthy as a caress.

You will always be the mother of your children, dear Hannah.

God help me. I am *so happy*."

The eye sees the pearls, not the (plain sturdy) string that binds them together. Each pearl perfect, exquisite. And the string that binds them invisible, undetectable.

He has become the string, binding Hannah's days together. Miniature islands of happiness, a sequence of hours. And all secret.

Without the string, the pearls would fall loose, scatter in a dozen directions.

Without the string, chaos.

"Hannah! You're looking quite radiant lately."

Wes smiles his tucked-in smile, a slant sort of smile, even as his eyes move upon her quizzically.

Hannah feels blood rush into her face. She laughs uneasily, she has been trying to fasten a strand of pearls around her neck.

It is rare that Wes has looked at her in recent weeks. Rarer still, he has addressed her in a way that might be interpreted as intimate, almost teasing.

Unless, just slightly reproachful.

Why are you happy, when I am not? What is your secret, that we are not sharing?

Upstairs in their bedroom preparing to go out for (another) evening. In this room in which they are so often silent, brooding. In this room in which, standing at her mirror, Hannah has so often observed her husband across the room, his back to her, oblivious of her.

Only a few weeks ago Hannah's eyes had filled with tears of wonderment, hurt in this very room. That this man with whom she shared a bedroom, and a bed; this man with whom she'd had two children, beloved by both parents; this man who'd been the first man she had loved, seemed no longer to love her. No longer *cared for her.*

He is unfailingly polite to her, however. Or usually.

Only just so often absent. In his being, and in his thoughts.

Except now, Hannah is protected from hurt. Y.K. has come into her life newly *in love* with Hannah, her life has been transformed.

His eyes observe her in all of the mirrors of the house. In reflective surfaces like aluminum, glass. Fleeting glimpses of Hannah's beauty that passed unnoticed for so long.

Fleeting glimpses of the face she'd long shrunk from seeing, now indeed *radiant.*

Wes has returned home from work earlier than usual, he has shaved for the second time that day. Hannah smells his shaving lotion, as familiar to her as the scent of her shampoo, her hand lotion. The faint scent of Chanel No. 5, which she dabs behind her ears and at her left wrist.

Hannah sees that Wes has changed his clothes for the evening. He is wearing a necktie that doesn't look familiar to Hannah, soft-silver stripes, a silk tie, surely a designer tie; his skin is ruddy from the shower, his hair parted cleanly and severely right-of-center of his head.

Hannah chooses to take her husband's remark as a compliment and not a veiled accusation. Always wisest to take a husband's words literally, and ignore his tone.

Yes, Hannah says, she has been feeling good lately. Now that the children are back in school she has resumed yoga classes three mornings a week . . .

"Yoga! I hadn't realized that you'd quit."

Can't be true, of course this is absurd. The husband knows well how the wife had quit most of her activities in town, had scarcely left the house for months.

The single strand of pearls Hannah is fastening around her neck once belonged to her mother's mother and was passed on to Hannah at the time of her wedding. Pink-tinctured pearls, luminous, beautiful in Hannah's eyes though (she is sure) they are only cultured pearls, far less expensive than genuine pearls would be.

Family legend has it that the pearls are from the South Sea. (Wherever that is: Hannah has no idea.) The clasp appears to be genuine gold, rimmed with tiny diamonds.

Hannah rarely wears these pearls, they are oddly shaped, old-fashioned, not *chic*. Indeed, Hannah hasn't worn them in years.

Made self-conscious by Wes regarding her in the mirror Hannah fumbles with the clasp.

"Shall I help you, Hannah?"

Hannah smiles, shakes her head *no,* but Wes insists. These odd unpredictable occasions when Wes seems to rouse himself to a husbandly task though usually Hannah would rather he did not.

Still, Hannah is grateful for the offer. A gesture of kindness.

"These are beautiful pearls. You should wear them more often."

But Wes's fingers are clumsy, as Hannah could have predicted. As the necklace begins to slip from Hannah's neck Wes grabs at it too roughly, the string breaks, pearls tumble away in a dozen directions.

"Damn! I'm sorry."

Quickly Hannah kneels, to gather up the pearls. She doesn't dare look at Wes, her face smarts with annoyance.

Dismay, anger, guilt. But now, everything is guilt.

Wes apologizes profusely. His lightly veiled sarcasm has vanished. Awkwardly he stoops, searching for pearls on the carpet, one has rolled beneath a chair, he grunts as he retrieves it, Hannah sees that he is genuinely contrite.

Hannah assures Wes that the string was old and must have become weak, the necklace is very old, she should have had it restrung years ago, it's all right, not to mind. So quickly Hannah reassures her husband, she risks offending him by seeming to placate him, revealing that she is frightened of him, his moods, his temper, his rage at her, none of which he ever displays for he is Wes Jarrett, he is above such petty behavior.

"Put the pearls in an envelope, and I'll take them to be restrung myself. I'll do it! I'm so sorry, Hannah."

"Oh, Wes! Really. It's all right."

"No, I want to. It's the least I can do."

Hannah is touched, Wes is being so gracious. There is no time now, they must leave for their dinner party, Hannah will search on her hands and knees for the rest of the pearls in the morning.

Of course, Hannah has no intention of entrusting her grandmother's South Sea pearls to Wes, she will take them to be restrung herself. By morning Wes will have forgotten the necklace entirely, she can depend upon it.

A Door Closes. A Door Opens.

Almost casually it is suggested: *travel together, a new life.*

Almost casually: *a child of our own.*

In his ropey-muscled arms unclothed, vulnerable as if the outermost layer of her skin has been peeled away. As if lovemaking has been the way *in.* And once the lover is *in,* love will course giddily through her veins, love will inhabit every part of her as an invasive microspecies inhabits its (unwitting) host nurtured by the moist warmth of the host. In his arms after lovemaking and floating, too, in a wine-sweetened haze, happiness of a kind unfathomable in Hannah's life until now. Confiding in her as (he has claimed) he has never confided in anyone before. Not any woman, not ever. For though he has known many women he has never loved any woman until Hannah.

Never wanted to have a child with any woman until Hannah.

How flattered Hannah is!—not yet awash with unease, panic at the prospect of a pregnancy at her age but rather dreamy-lulled, suffused with joy for in the euphoria of love all is possible.

Beginning again, anew. After coming close to losing each other. And now, certain of each other.

In his family, among older relatives who'd emigrated to America in the early 1930s it was said often—*A door closes. A door opens.*

He owes his life to her. It is that simple, and that profound.

Disjointedly now he begins to speak. Voice quavering, eyes spilling tears. Hannah is deeply moved, she has rarely seen any man cry, indeed she has never seen her husband cry.

Years ago she'd seen hot tears shimmering in Joker Daddy's eyes like molten glass. But those had been tears of rage, not sorrow.

So deeply unhappy with his life he'd been determined to take his life. After their father's death a struggle with his older brothers over his father's estate, for (it was revealed) the brothers had falsified a section of the will with the (apparent) connivance of their father's attorney; worse, it came to light that (evidently) the brothers had embezzled from the family business during the last years of their father's illness. And his mother dependent upon him to shield her, keep from her the devastating truth of her older sons' betrayal. For he was the youngest and most loved by his mother—always resented by his brothers. Truly he'd thought they might kill him when they were boys. It was a shock and an outrage but not a surprise that his brothers had stolen from their father; what was surprising to him was that certain relatives in the family sided with the brothers, for what reason he could not know. But he'd wanted to avoid litigation. He'd wanted to avoid bringing charges against his brothers, for their mother's sake. Months they were negotiating, trying to work out a settlement, at which time Y.K. had frequent business in Detroit and had to be here. Then the brothers fired their lawyers and defied Y.K. to take them to court. Knowing he would be reluctant to tell their mother, who was emotionally unstable after their father's death. It would be a tragedy for her if the family was split, she would be denied access to her grandchildren. In just a few months she'd become broken, frail, once so beautiful, already in her early seventies beginning to suffer from dementia yet Y.K. had been determined to claim what was his mother's and what was his . . .

Hannah comes to learn that Y.K. is the youngest son of a large immigrant family. His parents were not educated, had to quit school to work during the Depression, yet his father managed to start his own business, eventually he became a (relatively) rich man but he was never content, never satisfied, always insecure, combative, buying new properties, buying and selling, quarreling with his own brothers, pitting his sons against one another. As a teenager Y.K. was lonely, friendless. He had higher grades than most of his classmates, especially in math. He avoided sports, he disliked physical contact. It was his fate to be singled out by teachers in a way that made others resent him, hate him; he surprised everyone by dropping out of school before graduation, to go to work (initially for his father, but that didn't turn out well); at eighteen he enlisted in the army, qualified for flight school in Colorado then was sent to Vietnam where he'd almost died and where he'd been disgusted by the war, the drugs, the corruption, in Saigon he'd seen for the first time in his life child prostitutes, as young as ten, taught the coarsest obscenities to mouth at American soldiers. For he'd been naïve, inexperienced. For there had been many like him. Contrary to what is generally believed, the average American soldier in Vietnam was very young, religious, even pious, many Catholics, hadn't had sexual experiences, had to be trained to be insensitive killers, brutes; and among these, many who could not be so trained, who were just destroyed. But he'd survived, some part of him. Like a husk. Hit by shrapnel, almost killed. Developed a drug habit—heroin. Took years to get clean, back in the States. His father had wanted him to join up with the family business but he'd been wary. He began to have some good luck, accepted into a business-school program for returning veterans. He began to do well. In the sixties when things were booming especially here in Detroit: Motor City USA.

But the family business, the family situation, worsened. He'd hoped to keep clear of it but could not, he couldn't abandon his mother. And there were other family ties, obligations. IRS demanded a costly audit of the business. There were accountants, attorneys. He was angry much of the time, and then he was depressed. He started to drink heavily. He got involved with some people it was (maybe) a mistake to be involved with, some of them here in Detroit. But this anger—it had always been part of him, even as a boy—along with bouts of depression, despair. *Wanting to die*—he couldn't remember a time in his life when that wasn't in his thoughts, in some way. And finally one night this past summer—a hot July night—he was in a city (not Detroit: five hundred miles away) and driving along a riverfront area where there were taverns, a certain sort of street life, prostitutes on the streets, he saw a woman with a young girl no more than ten or eleven who seemed to be her daughter, a very young girl, angel-faced, like the child prostitutes in Saigon, and he'd been upset, agitated, he'd brought the woman and the little girl back to his hotel room, so that they would have a place to stay; he gave the woman money, extracted a promise from her that she would take the daughter off the street but just a few nights later he saw them again in the same part of the city . . . He'd gotten drunk, parked his car by a bridge at about two A.M., walked out onto the bridge trying to summon the strength to throw himself into the river, could not think of a single reason to keep on living except he remembered someone who'd jumped from a bridge but struck an abutment on the way down, it was said that his bones had jutted up through his thighs, part of his skeleton had been thrown out of his body . . . And then, too, he was remembering Hannah: how they'd met, how he'd known as soon as he saw her that she was unique in his life, he'd known but had not wanted to accept it, he'd been frightened of loving her, throughout his life he'd been frightened of loving anyone, and of being loved; his mother's love had kept him alive, yet he had not been able to keep her alive; he'd failed her, he feared that he would fail anyone who loved him, he was just not strong enough. But the memory of Hannah returned to him, her face. Her beautiful face. Her love for *him*.

He'd fled from her, last spring. He knew. But now, he had to return to her. She has saved his life, she has come to dwell in his heart.

In astonishment Hannah listens to this flood of words. With a part of her mind she is disbelieving—incredulous. Yet with another part of her mind she is totally convinced. For never has anyone spoken so openly to Hannah, never has a man wept in her arms. The emotion, the shuddering tears—Hannah is sure that they are genuine.

She feels exalted, empowered. Comforting her distressed lover.

Of course she can become pregnant again, forty is *not old*.

Asking her lover if he could love Conor and Katya? As if they were his own?

That's to say—another man's children. As if they were his own.

Asking in a wistful voice. For she has shown Y.K. pictures of Conor and Katya, he'd been struck by their beauty.

But of course, if Hannah is their mother, it isn't surprising that the children are beautiful, Y.K. told her. The little girl especially resembles Hannah.

"Yes, darling. Of course. I've already begun to love them—just see-ing their pictures."

Most of his adult life, Y.K. says, he'd despaired of having children. Bringing children into this despoiled world. But now, his feelings have altered. *She* has entered his life.

He has lost his mother but Hannah has come to him. *A door closes. A door opens.*

When will Y.K. meet Conor and Katya?—the lovers must make a plan. He will come to Far Hills, they will meet in a park, perhaps. The first meeting should be casual, brief. They can walk together, the children can have ice cream.

Hannah shivers with excitement, dread. How calmly she is discussing introducing her lover to her children! Perhaps it's all unreal, beyond comprehension.

This is strange: Of the children's father Hannah scarcely thinks at all. As if Wes has ceased to exist, and would register no objection to another man taking his place with the children.

None of this is remotely possible. You must know that.

In the light-filled room on the sixty-first floor of the Renaissance Grand Hotel. In the enormous bed, in the lover's arms. Her toes curl in the very ecstasy, Hannah has entered a realm of being beyond probability.

Basking in the lover's arms. Becalmed, at peace.

After a moment Y.K. says—quietly: he isn't a boastful person—that Hannah should know, he has made a fair amount of money in his business dealings, apart from his family business. Particularly real estate.

For instance, one of the companies with which he is associated has been a sizable investor in the Renaissance Plaza.

Ah!—Hannah understands now, she thinks. This is the link between Y.K. and Detroit businessmen.

"Like the Jarretts," Y.K. says. "Your husband's family."

How does he know this?—Hannah wonders. She feels flattered if slightly uneasy.

"Though my investment isn't as large as theirs, I think."

Y.K. seems to be waiting for Hannah to respond. But Hannah has no idea how to respond. She has never discussed her husband's business dealings with Y.K. in the past, she has very little knowledge of them.

Instead she brings up a subject that is awkward for her to speak of even in this intimate setting: "Do you think—should I—should I be thinking of telling Wes about us? About—maybe . . ." Hannah's voice falters, she cannot utter the word *divorce*.

But what am I saying!—Hannah thinks. She could never leave Wes, he would refuse to allow it. The humiliation for him would be ruinous. Out of revenge he would win custody of the children, he would crush her.

Still, Hannah is hopeful that her lover will say *yes.*

But Y.K. doesn't reply, for some time. Even as he is kissing Hannah's neck, caressing her shoulders.

Finally telling her *no.* Not just yet.

Hannah says that it's becoming increasingly difficult to live with Wes, to share a bed with him. To see him.

All the while thinking of *him*—her lover.

But Y.K. says it's too soon to be thinking of divorce. Too soon to be telling her husband anything.

"There's a considerable loss of money," Y.K. says. "On both sides if there's a divorce, but particularly the wife's side."

Their estate would be halved, at best. It's possible that Wes has money in accounts she knows nothing about, in the Cayman Islands for instance. In the event of a divorce, her income would plummet.

Hannah has stiffened in her lover's arms, hearing this. Quickly Y.K. adds that an angry husband, a husband who feels that he has been "wronged," can be a vengeful adversary.

"Believe me, Hannah. You don't want to provoke him."

"But if we want to be together . . ."

"We will be together. Soon."

Hannah supposes, Y.K. is simply being honest. She hasn't wanted to think that Wes might be hiding money from her as (she knows) other husbands of her acquaintance have hidden money from their wives prior to divorce. But she would have no way of knowing.

What had Marlene Reddick said—*We have no idea what they* really *do. Our husbands.*

She thinks of Wes's laughter at the hospital fundraiser. Women teetering on high heels to kiss his cheek, hug him in greeting. Pressing too pointedly their breasts against him.

She thinks of Wes in their bed that night pushing away her poor groping hand, that had wanted only the warmth of touch. As a lonely creature, a dog perhaps, might hope for a kindly if fleeting touch from its master but is rudely pushed off.

She hates Wes, he has so wounded her. He has so insulted her without troubling to realize it.

Her only happiness is with her lover. Only when they can be together.

Hannah wipes at her eyes. Hannah is determined not to cry, she recalls Joker Daddy forbidding tears. Much better results, Joker Daddy has said, from laughing.

As long as she is married to Wes, Hannah tells Y.K., she can't be with him. She can't live with him. She can't take the children to live with him. It isn't possible, not in the world she inhabits.

Y.K agrees, gently he caresses the nape of Hannah's neck, pleasantly warm beneath her hair, pressing against Y.K.'s shoulder.

"But not divorce, darling. Not just yet. Sometimes marriages end when it's time for an ending."

Hannah has no idea what this means. Hannah waits for Y.K. to tell her.

"Things happen to people," Y.K. says matter-of-factly. "Within marriages there are illnesses, accidents. There are deaths, inheritances. How much is Wes insured for?—I'm just curious."

Insured? Hannah isn't sure she is hearing what (it seems) she is hearing.

In fact, Hannah doesn't know how much Wes's life insurance is. She may have been told but she has forgotten, as she tends to forget such matters. Five hundred thousand dollars? One million dollars? Surely less than that? Wes's finances are so complicated, he has so many investments, Hannah has no idea what his estate might be worth.

He's a young husband, not yet forty-five. They are a young couple. No reason to be thinking about wills, estates, inheritances at this time in their lives.

Though in fact, both Wes and Hannah have made out wills, soon after Katya was born. Just to be cautious.

He means, Wes might die. Is that what he means?

We could marry, then.

Hannah has begun shivering almost convulsively. Y.K. gathers her in his arms, to warm her.

"Darling, don't be upset. Don't think of it now. Our love will endure secrecy—it has blossomed in secrecy. No one has to know yet.

Your children can meet me in secret, we'll do that soon. But your husband—no. When it's the right time for me to meet your husband, that will be arranged."

Soon then they begin (again) to make love. Gently at first, like lovers in a shared dream not wanting to dispel the dream.

By degrees, Y.K. is more forceful. Hannah feels herself overwhelmed, confused. All that she can do is grip the man in her arms—try to grip him in her arms. She is not so strong as she has imagined, the man could snap her wrists if he wishes. His weight upon her is massive. His weight upon her is a god's weight pressing upon a mortal being.

Hannah's rib cage feels crushed, she is having difficulty breathing. Yet still she is suffused with joy, hope. It is just ahead, not far ahead, she can glimpse it—all that she yearns for. The high-ceilinged white-walled room is saturated with light, she must narrow her eyes against such light. She wonders if it is the light shone into the eye of the afflicted to determine if the brain is alert and alive, the field of vision alert and alive.

Love love love love you.

Her brain is awash with dreams. Her brain is deprived of oxygen, she cannot draw air fully into her lungs. Her life seems to be flashing before her, inside her like a bright tattered ribbon, a Möbius strip of a ribbon, endless. The helpless writhing begins. Muscular writhing like a snake, excruciating sensation in the pit of her belly near-unbearable as if she is trying to squeeze out of her very skin as a snake might do. Impaled upon the man, the rapid compulsive motions of the man, his name unknown to her, forgotten, she is unable even to scream. Pitch-blackness rises suddenly to envelop her. He has scooped out her brains with his jubilant claw hands, all that is *Hannah* is annihilated.

Fairy Tale

When it's the right time for me to meet your husband, that will be arranged.

These words, disembodied, like the lyrics of a song whose music has faded, echo in Hannah's mind.

Reminding her of the old fairy tales, told to her when she'd been a child and unable yet to read or to think for herself. A comfort, a solace. *Once upon a time. Happily ever after.*

Seemingly, no human agency is involved. Hannah is not involved. Whatever will be, will be arranged.

Home Invasion

Like a wildfire in a season of drought the news spreads rapidly among Bloomfield Hills, Far Hills, Birmingham.

Hannah is stunned, speechless. Through the pounding of blood in her ears she has not fully heard what her friend has been telling her, calling in the late morning of a weekday near the end of October.

Terrible, tragic news: Christina and Harold Rusch have been found murdered in their house on Balmoral Drive in what police are calling a home invasion.

Hannah clutches the receiver against her ear listening in disbelief as her friend continues breathlessly: The bodies were discovered early that morning when a contractor arrived at the house for an appointment with Harold Rusch and no one answered the door, the news is just breaking on radio and TV, nothing more seems to be known, no idea who murdered them but it's presumed to be a robbery, there's a police alert advising residents in the vicinity to lock their doors and windows, report anyone or anything unusual . . .

Hannah feels weak, light-headed. She has heard only a fraction of Miriam's story but does not want to hear more.

Quickly interrupting Miriam, thanking her, and hanging up.

Murdered? Home invasion?

Hannah's friend, Christina Rusch?

It's a windy autumn day. Cold blue sky, clouds like blown froth. The noise of the wind in the tall trees surrounding the house is confused with the sound of blood pounding in Hannah's ears, a threat of vertigo.

Hannah has just returned from driving the children to school.

First thing she hears, stepping into the house from the garage, a ringing phone, Ismelda's voice uplifted—*Mrs. Jarrett, ma'am? Phone for you.*

Icy-palmed, in that instant. Steeling herself for Y.K.'s deep-chested voice (for which she isn't prepared at this hour: their plan was for Hannah to call her lover at a later time) and determined not to betray any emotion that the sharp-eyed little nanny might detect.

As Ismelda is regarding her employer now with concerned eyes.

"Ma'am? Is something wrong?"

Hannah shakes her head *no.* Can't talk, not right now.

Retreating, out of the kitchen. Could not have said if her rapid heartbeat is in response to the (terrible, unfathomable) news or to the blunt fact of the phone ringing, the possibility that her lover was calling her at this hour.

Within a few minutes the phone rings again, and again Ismelda summons Hannah to the phone, no choice since it's Wes calling from his office, excited, vehement, Wes is certain that this is a deliberate murder of a top GM executive, a "high-profile" white man, meant to send a message, could be Black Panthers, Nation of Islam, Marxist anarchists, whatever they call themselves, no accident they targeted Harold Rusch for a *home invasion.*

Weakly Hannah murmurs *yes, yes of course* as Wes instructs her to lock all the doors and windows, double-check the door to the garage, make sure the garage door is down, don't answer the door if someone rings and don't let Ismelda answer, don't let anyone in, don't leave the house.

It's an "emergency situation" in the northern suburbs of Detroit, Wes isn't the only person who believes this.

Could be the start of the *race war* that's been threatened.

Both sides, *theirs* and *ours.* First Babysitter killing white children, now Black Panthers, or whoever, killing auto executives . . .

Wes has decided to take the rest of the day off. It's being said that there might be other, coordinated attacks on residential homes and businesses in the suburbs. Martial law may be declared by the governor, soon. There may be police barricades in the streets, the National Guard may be called as it was in 1967. He will pick up the children at school on his way home.

Hannah protests: That will be upsetting to the children. They will see Daddy, they will be frightened. Since Daddy never picks them up they will know that something is wrong.

But Wes insists. By the time they arrive home, God knows what might have happened. In 1967 there were fires in the inner city, gunshots in the streets, snipers on top of buildings, looting, squad cars overturned and set afire, pandemonium but at least not beyond the Detroit city limits, confined to *their territory*. But now they are invading the suburbs, into *our territory*.

"What did I tell you, Hannah! It's a damned good thing that we are *armed*."

Weak-kneed Hannah finds herself on the sofa in the TV room. Can't bring herself to turn on the TV. A pulse has begun to beat dangerously in her head.

Trying to comprehend: Christina Rusch *murdered*.

Both the Rusches, *murdered*.

There has never been a *home invasion* in Far Hills, Hannah is sure. She has never heard of such a thing. *Invasion* is a word incompatible with *home*.

Soon after, the phone rings again. But Hannah instructs Ismelda to say that she isn't home, she will call back.

I can't, I'm so sorry. Can't talk about it to anyone. Christina was a friend of mine—a new friend . . . It's unbelievable that I will never see her again.

Recalling how by chance they'd met in Neiman Marcus, and Hannah helped Christina with her packages, placing them in the back of the car. And the son behind the wheel she'd mistaken at first for a chauffeur, what was his name: *Bernard*.

Hannah shudders, recalling. How rude Bernard had been to his own mother, as well as to Hannah. Steely eyes, sallow acne-scarred skin, shellacked-looking mustache, weak but defiant chin. She'd mistaken the baseball cap pulled low over his forehead for a chauffeur's cap at first.

An obscene name, he'd called her. Looked at her with loathing. Can't recall how this could have happened, in Christina's presence. Yet . . .

Hannah remembers: It hadn't been in Christina's presence. She'd seen this man in the hotel corridor outside Y.K.'s room. Closely he'd passed behind her, she had not noticed him as she'd stepped back and collided with him, he'd recoiled from her as if in loathing and called her *cunt*.

That particular sort of visceral loathing in the male, for the female. Hannah had felt it, leaving her defenseless.

At the time she'd forgotten the incident immediately. Just an accident. Sheer chance. No meaning. The man with the ice-pick eyes, ridiculous mustache, baseball cap—no one Hannah knew, then.

"Hannah! I have to speak with you."

Hoping to ward off the clamorous pain of a migraine Hannah has taken her medication, is lying in the darkened bedroom with a cloth soaked in cold water over her eyes when Wes bursts into the room. He is agitated, excited. Telling of rumors of planned attacks on "high-profile, white" businessmen, a rumor of martial law, National Guard forming a buffer between the suburbs and the city of Detroit, stationed for miles along Eight Mile Road. Rumors of a *race war*.

Hannah has removed the cloth from her eyes. Hannah dares to ask why would Black people want a "race war" when they are a minority of the population and would surely lose?—and Wes says cuttingly, "Don't ask me, Hannah. Ask *them*."

Wes is looking grim but enlivened, alert. A youthful flush has risen in his face. Hannah recognizes her husband's combative mode, hopeless to reason with him at such a time.

Wes removes the key from the bedside table drawer, unlocks the mahogany cabinet, removes the revolver from the shelf and weighs it in his hand. The flush in his face deepens. Hannah sees there a kind of *awe*.

As if she has glimpsed by chance her husband's naked body, cruelly exposed.

So little in Wes's life has prepared him for this. All the more reason then, Wes is thrilled and enlivened by this.

Warrior male, protecting his family. Protecting his race: white.

Hannah dreads an accident with the gun. So many guns in Detroit in the past fifteen years, Motor City USA has become Murder City USA, a designation of which many locals are perversely proud. Each day's news brings with it more shootings, more deaths, some of these designated "gun accidents."

Hannah is sure that Wes has never gotten around to taking a single lesson at a gun range, nor has he cleaned the gun once since bringing it home.

Doesn't a gun have to be *oiled*? So far as Hannah knows, Wes doesn't even have the equipment to clean his gun.

She'd imagined leading the ponytailed boy into this room. A promise of lovemaking in her bed, upstairs in the fancy Colonial, how thrilled Mikey would have been, utterly astonished when Hannah used the gun against him.

What a thought! Sheer fantasy. Hannah could not lift a gun, aim a gun at another person even to save her life. She could not.

". . . keep the gun in the drawer beside the bed from now on, where it's accessible in an emergency."

Wes is addressing her, sternly. He has shut the cabinet, the gun will now be kept in the bedside table at close hand.

Hannah tries to absorb this new information. Weakly she objects: What about the children? Guns are supposed to be locked away . . .

"The children never come into this room. They have no interest in this room. Keep the damned door closed. Make sure Ismelda keeps it closed. These are not normal circumstances, Hannah. Our friends were brutally murdered just last night in their house a few miles away."

Our friends. So Wes, too, has come to think of the older couple as *friends.*

Almost, Hannah has forgotten why Wes is so agitated, in such a state of panic, why she has been lying with a cold compress against her eyes, why the phone has been ringing.

Wes takes care placing the revolver in the drawer of the bedside table. The weapon so large, bulky, he has to reposition it in order to shut the drawer.

"And you were opposed to having a gun in the house at all! Imagine, if our house was 'invaded' and we didn't have a weapon to defend ourselves, and couldn't get to it quickly, what happened to the Rusches last night might have happened to *us.*"

. . . .

In stealth, while Wes is watching TV news downstairs, Hannah calls her lover in the hotel. But the phone rings unanswered.

Hannah tries several times, out of nervousness earlier than they'd planned but later, at the designated time, Y.K. doesn't answer, either.

Listening to the futile ringing, trying not to become further upset.

Trying not to think—*But you love me! You have promised.*

.   .   .

By morning much more is known of the *home invasion* in Bloomfield Hills.

Lurid banner headline on the front page of the *Detroit Free Press,* articles related to the murders comprising most of the page, photographs of the victims at which Hannah can't bring herself to look.

The surprise is, there is a third victim: the Rusches' housekeeper of twenty-six years, overlooked in the first reports as if mere collateral damage.

Wes insists upon reading from the newspaper to Hannah before he leaves for work in the morning. A drumming in Hannah's head, a residue of the migraine of the previous day can't entirely block Wes's words uttered in appalled indignation describing the murder scene on Balmoral Drive: the housekeeper discovered downstairs bludgeoned to death, the Rusches discovered in their upstairs bedroom bludgeoned and stabbed to death by an intruder who'd forced his way through a rear entrance of the house sometime, it is estimated, between ten and midnight.

In a hallway outside the kitchen the housekeeper was struck down as she was fleeing her assailant, and killed with multiple blows to the head; the Rusches, preparing for bed upstairs, were struck numerous times with the hammer and stabbed as well, dozens of times, with a steak knife taken from the kitchen. The bedroom was said to resemble a "slaughterhouse" but each of the Rusches, lying on the floor, though badly disfigured, was covered with a sheet pulled from the bed.

The hammer was removed from the scene and hasn't been found, the knife was left at the scene, dropped on the floor beside the bodies.

Christina Rusch, sixty-one. Harold Rusch, sixty-three.

Housekeeper Elizabeth Derry, forty-nine.

A "third resident" of the household is Bernard Rusch, thirty-two, son of the murdered couple, who, according to his attorney, had not been in Bloomfield Hills that night, or indeed since Labor Day; instead, Bernard Rusch had been staying at a family property at North Fox Lake, in northern Michigan, two hundred fifty miles away.

Like other properties on Balmoral Drive the Rusches' house is surrounded by a six-foot fieldstone wall with a gated entrance, discovered unlocked when a contractor arrived in the early morning to meet with Harold Rusch.

The gate was usually locked at night though routinely kept unlocked, and open, during the day to let workmen, tradesmen, and deliverymen in and out.

When the contractor knocked at the front door of the house at about seven-fifteen no one came to answer. Usually, he said, Mr. Rusch was waiting for him, or the housekeeper might open the door, but that morning there was no one, he called *Hello?* a few times and peered through downstairs windows, saw, or thought he saw, a body lying on the floor inside, and called the police.

The motive appeared to be robbery, Bloomfield police are saying: several rooms were ransacked, drawers containing Christina Rusch's jewelry were yanked open and partly emptied, Harold Rusch's wallet was found on the floor empty of cash and credit cards . . .

All this, a torrent of words, Hannah has been hearing discontinuously as Wes paces about the bedroom reading to her in an excited voice. She has slept fitfully the night before and is feeling exhausted already: Wes woke early to hurry downstairs and bring in the newspaper as soon as it was delivered at six-twenty.

"There's never been anything like this!—not where we live. Detroit is 'Murder City'—but not *here*."

Reluctantly Hannah takes the newspaper from Wes and stares at the front page in dread of what she will see.

"First, the serial sex pervert—Babysitter—abducting and murdering our children; now, a *home invasion*."

At first Hannah doesn't recognize Christina in this photograph taken years ago: an attractive woman in her forties resembling the mature Joan Crawford, something tense about her mouth, dark lipstick. Her hair is incongruously bouffant, lifting from her head like an explosion of confetti. The eyes are steely, ironic.

Harold Rusch, too, looks different than Hannah recalls, certainly younger, jowls less prominent. A somber face, a self-important face, crease between his eyes, eyes fixed on the camera. A shrewd executive, it has been said of Harold Rusch. *Did Harold Rusch have enemies? How possible, a man of his stature in a very competitive business would not have enemies?*

Hannah reads briefly of Christina Rusch: active in local charitable organizations, philanthropy. There is much more in the paper about Harold Rusch, of course. Very little, a mere sentence or two, about Elizabeth Derry who'd emigrated to the United States from Cork, Ireland, in 1949 and had worked for the Rusches since 1951.

A touching photograph of Christina and Harold on their wedding day in 1937: each so young, Christina a mere girl, smiling happily, untouched by irony; and her tall smiling bridegroom in a marine dress uniform . . .

On page sixteen of the newspaper Hannah finds what she has been looking for—a photograph of *Bernard Rusch, 32.*

The only child of Christina and Harold Rusch. Photojournalist, freelance.

Adjunct instructor at the Cranberry School of Art, Detroit Artists League, Wayne State University Continuing Education.

Residences in Bloomfield Hills and North Fox Lake, Michigan.

Another time it is stated—clearly: by his lawyer—that Bernard Rusch had not been living at 11 Balmoral Drive since Labor Day.

Hadn't been in contact with his parents for several weeks. Not a working phone at the lodge at North Fox Lake. Had known nothing of the murders until police officers came to inform him in the late morning of the day following the murders . . .

In the photograph, taken in 1973 for a formal occasion, Bernard Rusch is well-dressed: natty sport coat, stylishly narrow necktie, Oxford shirt. His hair is thicker, and has been neatly trimmed and combed. No mustache, his chin is clean-shaven. The acne-pitted skin isn't evident, nor are there visible lines and dents in his forehead. But: those ice-pick eyes. A coy curve of a smile, a wish to deceive.

Cunt he'd called her. Certainly, this is the man.

Hannah sits heavily at the edge of the unmade bed. She is feeling nauseated suddenly. She is feeling like a compass whose needle spins dizzily.

Wes is in the shower, he will leave soon for the Fisher Center. Ismelda is with the children, dressing them for school—Hannah can hear their uplifted voices, and feels relief. She is still in her nightgown which feels slatternly to her, smelling of her body. Too lethargic, too headachy, to take a shower, to dress herself and come downstairs; too sick at heart to play *Mommy* this morning.

For you do need energy, to play *Mommy*.

Children plucking at Mommy's heart, tearing out handfuls of Mommy's flesh. Mommy's love for these small antic creatures is a soft warm taffy, stopping up her throat. Can't chew, can't swallow, can't spit out.

Ismelda can drive the children to school this morning. If she's feeling stronger by the afternoon Hannah will pick them up.

Christina Rusch, too, had been a mommy. But long ago.

You could see in her face, that warning *Don't touch me!*—it had been a very long time ago.

Strange, a mother might come to be repelled by her own child. By the physical being she has given birth to.

When a child is no longer a child but has grown into something else.

How he'd sneered at her, and at her companion Hannah, seated behind the wheel of the silver-gray Cadillac. *Why* was he his mother's chauffeur on that occasion, to what purpose was the son pressed into such servitude, clearly against his wishes?

Strange, and terrible, to think of self-possessed Christina Rusch murdered in the beautiful house on Balmoral Drive. Six point five million dollars the magnificent house had cost, Hannah has heard; and that had been years ago in the mid-1950s.

Bludgeoned, stabbed.

Slaughterhouse.

What will police make of it, that the housekeeper had been struck with the murder weapon just a few times while the Rusches had been struck multiple times, and then stabbed. And then, their mutilated bodies covered with bedclothes.

Hannah thinks uneasily of Y.K., who hadn't answered her call the night before. After he'd extracted from her a promise that she would call him at the precise hour of midnight.

I love you so much, Hannah. We need to be together.

She will call him this morning, she thinks. If he doesn't call her.

As soon as Wes is gone. Ismelda, the children gone from the house—she will call the number she has memorized.

His voice, his comforting voice, the solace of his voice—*Darling Hannah, you have come to dwell in my heart.*

She will not speak of the *home invasion.* She will not ask him if he'd known the Rusches.

The subject is too upsetting, too awful. How frail romantic love, whispers of love between lovers, set beside *bludgeoning, stabbing.*

No. She won't ask.

It's rare that they speak of anything beyond themselves, or beyond the hotel room in which they meet. No reason for Hannah to speak of a terrible triple murder just a few miles from her home.

If Y.K. detects that Hannah is upset about something she will tell him it's only because she misses him. Because she has to live a false life, apart from him.

Yet with a part of her mind trying to determine: what possible connection between the son of the murdered Rusches and her lover Yaakel Keinz. If that is his name.

For, hadn't the ponytailed boy drunkenly boasted of visiting a house on Balmoral Drive, a large house behind a gate; and wasn't the ponytailed boy in the hire of Y.K.? And in the corridor outside Y.K.'s suite at the Renaissance Grand Hotel Hannah had seen Bernard Rusch, she is sure.

Like pushing together the pieces of a shattered vase, nothing to make the pieces adhere. Yet, you can see that they fit together.

When Wes goes downstairs Hannah remains in the bedroom to make the surreptitious call. With mounting desperation she hears the ringing phone, unanswered.

Perhaps it's too early for Y.K. to answer the phone. He hadn't answered at midnight when Hannah called, he may have been out late the night before.

"Please answer! I am so lonely."

Hannah hangs up the phone. She will wait a while, she will try again.

Wes has left the drawer of the bedside table open an inch or so, Hannah pushes it shut. The gun! So close beside their bed, loaded, ready to be fired. Hannah is filled with dismay, repugnance.

It may be true, the children would never come into this bedroom. They have never evinced the slightest curiosity in the room, only in Mommy and Daddy in the room.

But Hannah resents it, that Wes should put them all at risk on a whim of his.

Ignorant, racist. If only a whim.

Yet: Hannah cannot defy Wes, she would only antagonize and madden him.

Recalling with a shiver the matter-of-fact way her lover had assured her—*When it's the right time for me to meet your husband, that will be arranged.*

A Loaded Gun

And another time, Hannah calls the number at the Renaissance Grand. With mounting anxiety that her lover is not returning her calls, very conspicuously not returning her calls.

He has left Detroit. Gone away without me.

But no! Not possible.

Hannah is dismayed, distracted. Hadn't Y.K. asked her to call him at a specific time, to make a plan for meeting again, and for bringing Conor and Katya to meet him?—yet now he isn't answering her calls, though Hannah has left messages each time.

Such love for Hannah, such tenderness, he'd professed when they were last together! He'd bared his heart to Hannah as no one had, she'd been deeply moved, suffused with hope.

Certainly Y.K. is sincere. His eyes welling with tears. Hannah knows, cannot believe otherwise.

"Mommy?"—Katya is frowning at her, as Hannah seems to have lost her place in *The Littlest Hedgehog*.

So distracted! Half listening for the phone to ring elsewhere in the house though knowing (of course) that Y.K. would never call her at such a time, when Wes is home.

Katya has been regarding Mommy with concern lately. Leaning forward to touch the bridge of Mommy's nose, to smooth away the (evident) frown line between Mommy's eyebrows.

Hannah laughs sharply, this *was* funny . . .

Well, no. Not so funny.

Is it showing in my face?

Can everyone see?

She wonders if Wes suspects. If Wes knows.

But Wes avoids thinking of her at all, Hannah guesses. That a woman would wish to protect a rapist, a (white) woman, a (Black) rapist . . .

Often, in weak moments, self-pitying, self-loathing, Hannah has come to believe that a dark-skinned parking attendant had indeed assaulted her, in the concrete stairwell at the Far Hills Marriott.

Not that she'd seen his face, she had not. Possibly he hadn't been dark-skinned, exactly.

Hannah resumes her reading of *The Littlest Hedgehog* with renewed vigor. She is resolved to keep her voice light, animated. This is something Mommy can do for the children: reading them to sleep at night, as her own mother rarely did, and her father, never.

They will remember me as a good mother. Reading to them at bedtime. Before—we moved away . . .

But Hannah cannot imagine how that will happen: *move away.*

How she can possibly leave Wes to live with another man, or marry another man.

How she can possibly bring the children with her.

Hannah has made some vague, discreet inquiries. A call to a divorce lawyer of her acquaintance, explaining that she was calling for a friend, to ask about finances, how one would find out if a spouse had secret bank accounts offshore . . . The divorce lawyer advised Hannah to tell her friend that that might be difficult (if not high-risk), for if the spouse suspects that divorce is even being contemplated he could retaliate immediately by withdrawing all their money from joint accounts and engaging a lawyer of his own.

Assume that a husband shrewd enough, and ruthless enough, to maintain stealth bank accounts offshore is also a husband likely to be alert to a wife's suspicions; like a chess grandmaster, he will be roused to killer mode by the first naïve move of his far less experienced opponent.

Once the war is *on*, there's no stopping it. So Hannah has been advised.

And Y.K. has cautioned her not to speak of separation or divorce to Wes. To keep their relationship secret for the time being.

Marriages end. When it's time for an ending.

Hannah has been realizing, she has no idea where Y.K. lives

when he isn't in Detroit. No idea where his family lives. Where he was born, what the family business is, or was. His parents emigrated from—where? So intimately, so openly, Y.K. has spoken of himself, his brothers, his mother, his near-suicide in an unnamed city—Hannah can't believe that he would cease loving her, and so abruptly.

Though (of course) Hannah knows, everything he has told her is probably a lie, haphazardly and cynically invented on the spur of the moment, yet at the same time she cannot believe that it is, or might be, a lie. No.

. . . come to dwell in my heart.

At last, Mommy has finished reading *The Littlest Hedgehog*. Both the children are asleep.

Such a solace, children's stories! You can count on them to always end happily, often children are pictured snug in bed asleep on the final page.

Hannah switches off the bedside lamp, slips from the children's room.

Resolved not to call Y.K. at midnight. No more.

Wes wants to tell Hannah the latest news—"not pretty"—of the Rusch murders but Hannah presses her hands over her ears.

"No! Please."

Trying not to think of the murders. Trying not to think of poor Christina Rusch struck down in her own bedroom, stabbed to death only a few miles away.

While Hannah was adrift in an erotic daze thinking of her lover. While neighbors of the Rusches in Bloomfield Hills were oblivious of the nightmare taking place behind the six-foot fieldstone wall next door.

But Wes wants to talk; he has just come upstairs from watching the eleven o'clock news and is excited, agitated.

In fact, Wes has been following the investigation into the Rusch murders closely. He has made calls to friends and acquaintances who might have some connection to Harold Rusch, even to relatives in his own family.

Though Wes still seems to believe that the murders of the Rusches and their housekeeper, like the child abductions, are preliminary assaults in an imminent "race war," he has had to concede, based on new developments in the case and rumors racing like wildfire through Bloomfield Hills and adjacent suburbs, that Harold Rusch might have been the targeted victim, and the wife and housekeeper collateral victims, of "organized crime."

Hannah has no idea what this could mean. *Mafia?*

Nothing has been stated outright, everything is speculative. News broadcasters only know what has been released to the media and have to be circumspect in their commentary but it does seem, Wes says, that Harold Rusch might have had investments in questionable real estate deals as well as in a possible shell company in Wyandotte.

Hannah believes that she knows what a "shell company" is, in theory. Money laundering? A business that deals in cash?

"Of course, everyone is denying it. Everyone associated with Harold. It seems to be a total surprise. My uncle Edmund, who knew Harold since college, says it's a ridiculous charge. The poor man is no sooner dead, murdered in such a terrible way, than his reputation is under attack. All the detectives are saying is that they 'have to follow all leads.'"

If Harold Rusch had been involved in illegal business practices, Hannah thinks, Christina wouldn't have known about it. A suburban wife, like Hannah herself is on a smaller scale, ignorant of her husband's complicated financial ties.

"What kind of 'shell company' is it, in Wyandotte?"—Hannah tries to sound knowledgeable, she can't help trying to impress her husband even now.

"Something related to cars. Maybe a car wash. Body shop."

Wes speaks with an air of regret, as of one who has missed an opportunity.

Hannah has overheard Wes on the phone: shocked that the Rusches have been murdered, grieving, he and Harold Rusch were getting to be friends, Harold was a kind of mentor to Wes, and his wife, Christina, was "very fond" of Hannah . . .

Hannah says in defense of the murdered man: "He probably just owns properties. Owned properties. Like your father, and my father. You know—'investments.'"

Wes turns a blank face to Hannah, as if one of the children had spoken. The novelty being not what has been said but that anything at all has been said, from such an unlikely source.

Humoring her: "Yes. That's right." Then, adding: "The surprise seems to be, Harold's estate is something like forty million dollars. If you count GM stock, properties in northern Michigan and in Sarasota."

Hannah feels a moment's vertigo. The smirking pinpoint eyes, the spiteful mouth, the murmured *cunt*.

He will inherit. The only child.

At last Hannah is ready for bed. Yet reluctant to be the first to actually slip into the bed, to lie horizontal beneath bedclothes while the other remains vertical, on his feet, moving about the room. Is Wes reluctant, too, to slip into bed beside Hannah?

Bizarre *nakedness* of sleeping in the same bed with another, inside flimsy nighttime clothes.

An awkward shyness, discomfort between them as in the earliest days of their marriage when neither quite trusted the other not to see too clearly, to *judge*.

Hannah hopes that Wes will lose interest in the one-sided conversation. She feels an ache in the region of her heart, the loss of Christina Rusch, the (possible, dreaded) loss of Y.K.

In her bathroom before bed, taking a twenty-five-milligram barbiturate to assuage heartache, to assure sleep.

As Wes, downstairs watching TV news for much of the evening, has had a succession of beers, after two glasses of red wine with dinner. His breath is beery, boozy. He has been belching, hiccupping. Hannah will feign early sleep, to avoid even the simulacrum of a good-night kiss.

Sitting heavily on the edge of the bed, on his side of the bed. Wes in nighttime attire, T-shirt and pajama bottoms.

Hannah hates it, that Wes can't resist, every night, easing open the drawer in the bedside table to determine that yes, the short-barreled Smith & Wesson Magnum is inside, exactly as he'd left it. No one has touched it. No one has dared. Yes, and it is loaded. Wes has seen to that.

"Suicide"

A Glock .45-caliber revolver equipped with a "silencer," Hawkeye is providing Ponytail.

Instructing how Ponytail will use the heavy gun: Just a single shot. But a very particular shot.

Then, contrary to what you'd expect, leave the gun at the scene *where it falls*.

Because it's untraceable, no history. And even if the (scraped) serial number can be recovered, still no history except as a "stolen" weapon.

No connection with the suicide victim, no way to establish that he'd purchased it, but also no way to establish that he *had not* purchased it.

No way to establish that the fucker didn't blow out his own brains with his own gun at point-blank range.

Fuck yes! Never say *no* to Hawkeye.

Can't say *no* to Hawkeye.

Can't say *Jesus!—what the fuck* or *Let me think about it, man.*

Can't say *I guess I don't want to . . .*

Trying not to panic. Mouth so dry he can't swallow. Instead of speaking words he's moving his mouth just to shape words. Like his tongue has lost all sensation.

Summoned to meet with Hawkeye on neutral territory: parking lot at the corner of Cass and Howard, desolate at this time of night.

Wishing to hell he hadn't answered the phone ringing on a chair beside his bed, not a good hour for a call. Not good when wakened from a deep sleep and his brains are scrambled. And before this, high on coke he hadn't slept for like a night and a day. Goddamn!

But he'd answered the phone, half hoping it was Hawkeye—(Ponytail is in serious need of cash)—and half dreading because . . . Hawkeye.

Hissing in Ponytail's dazed ear *Get up, get dressed, get in the Firebird and get your ass over to Cass and Howard. Something has come up that needs to be expedited, fast.*

Jesus! Last time Hawkeye was needing something expedited fast was that drive out to Bloomfield, rescuing the boy from Mister R__. Ponytail is still having bad dreams about that.

Knows better than to ask what this is. Hawkeye provides information on his own terms.

And how much he's paying, you don't ask, either.

Trying not to show shock in his face when he learns what the instruction is, Hawkeye wants to send him back to Bloomfield. Again!

Mister R__, now needing to be expedited himself.

Never mind saving some kid tied up with wire. Never mind trying to come to an understanding with the cokehead fucker pervert.

This mission is: Blow out the fucker's brains and make it look like suicide.

Hawkeye will provide Ponytail with the gun, gloves, oversized nylon jacket with deep pockets, a pair of oversized rubber boots he can get rid of afterward. And a "suicide note" to leave someplace where it will be seen.

And no camera this time!—he can leave the Leitz Leica at home.

Ponytail grimaces, as if this is a joke.

The "suicide note" is a sheet of plain white paper folded in half, block letters in pencil that look as if they've been executed with a ruler by an earnest child:

GOD FORGIVE ME ALL THERE BLOOD IS ON MY HANDS

Ponytail reads this two, three times before he understands—*their blood.*

A confession to murder, as well as a suicide note. Could be the parents but also Babysitter's victims.

He'd wanted to murder Mister R__, last time he'd seen him. Badly wanted to crack the skull of the pedophile-pervert for the terrible things he'd done to the Hayden boy and to the other children, but now, not so much.

Cold blood. Premeditation. He isn't so sure.

Ponytail is rattled, has to ask Hawkeye to repeat the instructions. Too much to absorb.

You repeat it, Hawkeye says. You're the one going to expedite it.

Seeing the sick look on Ponytail's face, Hawkeye has to laugh. Mean mirthless laugh like breaking glass. The kid is always good for a laugh, eager and earnest and aspiring to more than just a punk kid, a street hustler, what's special about Mikey Kushel is Hawkeye knows he will follow instructions and he can trust him.

Problem is, Hawkeye isn't himself tonight, Ponytail is noting. Usually cold-cobra-calm but tonight his voice betrays indignation, rage. There's a tic in his left eyelid, his jaws are stubbled. Something has upset him plenty.

All these years Hawkeye has been extracting money from the rich man's pervert son out in Bloomfield. Some kind of sniveling dependency on Hawkeye, needing help from him when he's been in trouble, like other pervert friends of Father McKenzie, Hawkeye has come to their rescue, they are damned grateful, desperate to be kept out of the newspapers. Cops paid off, social workers. Judges? Wouldn't be surprised. All Ponytail knows for sure, they keep one another's secrets. And how they're connected with Father McKenzie and the Mission, that isn't clear.

What Ponytail guesses is that Rusch has had enough. No more blackmail.

Rusch's parents have been murdered, that's the signal. Crazy fuck-all Rusch is out of control.

Showing Hawkeye what he's capable of doing, is that it? Or—he's a cokehead, crazy?

He's in line to inherit the estate unless he's arrested for murder. Even then, unless he's convicted, he will inherit. Some of this "estimated forty million dollars" Hawkeye might reasonably expect to come to him in normal times. But Rusch has indicated, these are not normal times.

You don't cross Hawkeye. You don't make Hawkeye think you're threatening *him*.

All this Ponytail is speculating. Sick, slipping-down sensation in his guts. *You don't say* no *to Hawkeye.*

Also by this point, Ponytail knows too much. Hawkeye has told him too much. That Glock in Hawkeye's (gloved) hand, with the silencer. Hawkeye could shoot Ponytail in the head, leave his body in the Firebird in the parking lot, no one would give a damn.

No going back, Ponytail thinks, swallowing hard. Only himself to blame, Mikey Kushel had so badly wanted this, or something like this, in the employ of someone like Hawkeye who'd acknowledge that he *exists*.

Someone, something that would impress his mother. If she could know, and (maybe) she could. Maybe someone would tell her. Maybe she makes inquiries.

You can't know God's design for you, Father McKenzie said. He'd held out his hands to the sniveling boy, palms up to signal openness, frankness.

Whatever you think now, my son. Think again.

So, tomorrow morning: Hawkeye is explaining that he'd had a talk with Rusch, and he's arranged a (final) meeting with Rusch. So far as Rusch knows Hawkeye has agreed to Rusch's demands.

Rusch is making a "final payment" of what he owes Hawkeye this month. And not a full payment, just a fraction. This payment Hawkeye's emissary will receive in exchange for a packet of photograph negatives and two tapes to be handed over to Rusch.

After this, the deal is: Payments to Hawkeye end, and these are the last of the negatives and tapes.

Deal is: No more connection between the men. *Nada.*

Hawkeye instructs Ponytail: When you hand Rusch the manila envelope, let it slip through your fingers like it's an accident, let Rusch stoop to pick it up like he will be eager to do, you have the Glock out of your pocket, place the barrel against Rusch's head at his right temple, repeat: right temple, pull the trigger immediately and let the gun fall.

Just—let the gun fall. However it falls, don't move it.

Retrieve the manila envelope (containing negatives and tapes, but not negatives and tapes in which Bernard Rusch appears), take the envelope with the payment, place the "suicide note" on some surface near the body like a table.

Walk away, get in the car, drive, and don't look back.

It will happen fast. Don't think, just act. *Expedite.*

(No one will see. It's a private place Hawkeye has rented back from the street, with which Rusch is familiar because he's been there before, he's kept children there probably, for purposes of his own. His lawyers had been told by Rusch he's got a dentist appointment he can't postpone.)

(Later, they plan to take Rusch to Bloomfield police headquarters to continue being questioned. But that's later.)

Ponytail is listening. Ponytail is very quiet.

Where's this happening?—Ponytail asks finally.

In Bloomfield, but not the house. You're not returning to the house, it's a crime scene. There's this place a few miles away, I told you it's been arranged, it's "neutral" territory.

Still Ponytail is very quiet. Peering at the slip of paper, the address means nothing to him, 1182 Lasher Road.

Is this clear?—Hawkeye asks.

Ponytail nods *yes*. Absolutely clear.

Okay, repeat it.

Ponytail repeats it. His tongue isn't so numb now, he's okay.

Just like, when he'd been Mikey Kushel, on his knees in the sacristy, or in Father McKenzie's quarters at the Mission, kneeling on the thick-piled carpet beside Father McKenzie's bed he'd repeated the prayers with Father McKenzie leading him tenderly but firmly—*Our Father Who art in Heaven, Hallowed be thy Name.*

At last, after five days of no calls, no contact, no sleep (except the dry-mouthed headachy barbiturate sleep that Hannah hates), he calls her.

He calls *her.*

Hearing his voice, Hannah feels as if she might faint. Awash with relief, yet the ignominy of such relief.

Of course, he has an explanation. Not an apology exactly, for Y.K. isn't the kind to apologize, but an explanation hurried and vague, a family crisis, financial, legal, no choice but for Y.K. to return, involve himself in matters he'd vowed he would not be involved in, ever again.

Hannah stifles tears, she is so relieved to hear her lover's voice.

Hannah stifles outrage, she suspects that her lover is lying to her, she is too cowardly to confront him.

They must see each other soon, he says. Too much time is passing.

He speaks rapidly, yet distractedly. Hannah has the idea that someone else is in the room with him, listening. Smirking?

But no, her lover is sincere. He clears his throat, he sounds as if he is half sobbing. His visit with his family has exhausted him, Hannah is made to realize.

My darling. I have missed you so.

Hannah? Did you miss me?

He has returned to Detroit, he tells her. He's at the hotel. Tomorrow morning is business meetings but in the afternoon, after three . . .

"But I thought you wanted to meet Conor and Katya," Hannah says. "Weren't we planning that?" Trying not to sound reproachful, hurt, that Y.K. seems to have forgotten what has meant so much to her. "If we want to plan for our future together . . ."

Y.K. hesitates a moment, then agrees: "Yes. Of course."

"You don't want me to tell Wes. You've said."

"No, not—not yet."

Something is wrong, Hannah thinks, dismayed. He is distracted, his mind is elsewhere.

Wistfully Hannah says, "You do want—you've said—for us to be together . . ."

"Yes! Of course, dear Hannah. But—not immediately. From what I know of your husband, he could make things very difficult for you."

"What do you mean?"

"The Jarretts—the family. What I've heard of them."

Hannah's heartbeat quickens. Does Y.K. mean, Wes might win complete custody of the children? Or—Wes might punish her some-how, for betraying him?

"I don't understand. How do you know Wes's family?"

"How do you *not* know his family if you do business in Detroit?"

Hannah hesitates. She is uneasy discussing her husband or his fam-ily with her lover; she has seen in her lover's face, when the subject is raised, something covert, sidelong.

"I—I know them as my in-laws . . . I don't know much about them in the business community. Is that what you mean?"

In truth, Hannah doesn't know the Jarrett family well. Her in-laws (who live in Grosse Pointe) have been friendly enough but at a little distance. As a young wife and mother Hannah hadn't flattered Wes's mother as much as the older woman had wished to be flattered, perhaps—Hannah had been too preoccupied with her own life, and her small children, and had missed that opportunity.

She has only a vague idea of the Jarrett family's reputation in the business community. One of Wes's father's brothers had been the Detroit city planner during the 1950s when interstate highways were constructed in a complex network gouging through urban (Black) neighborhoods, leaving behind a ravaged cityscape subsequently re-arranged in brute symmetry to prevail through decades well into the next century. Property owners, major investors in the post-riot Detroit "renaissance" of the late 1960s, the Jarretts and their close relatives.

Much in that world is puzzling to Hannah: that multimillionaire bankrupts are not *bankrupt*, as in the commonplace sense of the word.

Obviously the Jarretts are a rich family but far from the wealthiest of Detroit families. Wes has a carefully calibrated relationship with his father from whom he is financially independent yet with whom he feels obliged to act with deference. He jokes that his father, like all the Jarretts, is "litigious"—continuously involved in lawsuits, as plaintiff and as defendant.

"Do you mean that they are 'litigious'—vindictive? That Wes might be vindictive, too?"

"We'll discuss it another time. You're becoming emotional, Hannah. I don't want to upset you."

"Well—I am upset, I think. You didn't call me—you didn't answer my calls—for so long, I thought that something had happened to you . . ."

There, Hannah has said it. Exactly what she hadn't wished to say, and in this plaintive reproachful voice, shameful to hear, afterward mortifying to recall.

Quickly Y.K. assures her that he is very sorry, he will never neglect her again.

And yes, he wants to meet Conor and Katya. Very badly. As soon as Hannah can arrange it, he will be there.

How warm, how sincere he sounds! Hannah is moved to tears.

Rapidly Hannah calculates: next day, afternoon, after the children's school. The weather has been unseasonably warm for early November, they can meet outdoors. She will pick Conor and Katya up at school and bring them to meet her lover, at a county park a few miles from Far Hills where no one will recognize her.

Yes, I have missed you.

Yes, I will love you forever.

"Today, a decision will be made."

Hannah wears the (restrung) pearls, to meet her lover in Lone Lake Park.

To introduce her children to her lover, in Lone Lake Park, Hannah wears the (restrung) pearls that were a gift from her grandmother.

"If he notices. If he says something."

For the pearls are a good-luck omen. A gift to Hannah from her grandmother who'd seemed to favor Hannah over the other grandchildren.

For this occasion Hannah wears tailored black trousers in an exquisite light-wool fabric, a dove-gray suede jacket (newly purchased, Neiman Marcus) open at the throat to display the pearls with their subtle pink cast. On her feet black leather Ferragamos, medium heel.

Her mouth, that wound of yearning, is pale-glossy-pink, as luminous as the pearls.

In the (restrung) pearls, in her beautiful understated clothes Hannah has brought the children directly from Far Hills Day to Lone Lake Park at the edge of West Bloomfield Township, miles west on Hickory Grove Road where they have never been before. Though taken frequently to small boutique parks in Far Hills, usually by Ismelda, they have never been to this large park in a semirural area.

"This will be our secret. No one else will know."

Promised to them as a "special outing"—"a surprise"—just Conor and Katya and Mommy, who has been mysterious about the visit. The children sense Mommy's excitement, perhaps they are beginning to be baffled *why*.

Lone Lake Park is large, sprawling, undistinguished. The lake (if there is a lake) isn't visible from the road. Hiking trails into a deciduous woods seems to be the main attraction. There is a small perfunctory playground—a single set of swings, a battered-looking slide, a children's wading pool dry and littered with leaves. A sinister-looking concrete shed—faded signs MEN and WOMEN at opposite ends. An asphalt parking lot in which less than half a dozen vehicles are parked and in the near distance a weedy baseball field and a café with a red neon sign rawly lit in daylight.

The sky is a bright chill eye-aching blue. An autumnal wind is blowing, leaves scuttle across the ground like the husks of beetles.

"Looks like we have the park to ourselves!"—Hannah speaks brightly, nervously, sensing that the children are disappointed to see no other children.

A park this size, a county park for hikers, for adults primarily, not a park designed for Far Hills children.

Like all Far Hills children, Hannah thinks, her children have grown up with certain expectations. They are not "spoiled"—not exactly. But a single glance at this county park and you know that something is missing.

Observing the smaller, lower-income houses on Hickory Grove west of Bloomfield Hills, strip malls, gas stations, and fast-food restaurants, you can see that something is missing.

The small café is nothing like restaurants to which Conor and Katya are usually taken. Neon signs in the windows advertising Molson, Budweiser—clearly a tavern. But if food is served they must have ice cream, too, Hannah thinks. That will be the reward: a short hike through the woods with Mommy and Mommy's friend, looping back to the café, ice cream before supper, an unexpected treat.

Mommy means: bargaining with children who must never sense that you are bargaining with them.

Hannah glances about for a male figure. For *him*.

But there are few other visitors in sight. Teenagers smoking cigarettes at a picnic table, a lone hiker at a trailhead entering the woods. A burly man just emerging from the men's lavatory but then, for some reason, disappearing again inside. No one who resembles Y.K.

But Hannah and the children are early; she has brought them directly from school.

He has said he couldn't get away from Detroit until three. But he will come directly to the park on I-75, he has checked the location on a map.

"You don't want me to meet you in Far Hills?"—Y.K. asked not accusingly but teasingly, as Hannah stammered, "I—I think—it might be better if . . ."

Y.K. laughed, pleasantly. Of course—he understood!

He doesn't want anyone to know about them yet, either.

Hannah is trying not to be (visibly) nervous. The children will sense Mommy's mood. Especially Conor who seems to be suspicious of her. She steels herself for the maddening whine *Mom-my, why are we here!*

Katya, at least, is never suspicious of Mommy. Utterly trusting of Mommy.

Why Mommy loves Katya best.

(This is a secret!)

She'd been too restless to remain at home staring at the clock. Thinking—*Today, a decision will be made.*

When Wes returns home in the evening, Hannah may inform him—*Today, a decision was made.*

In the house Ismelda was vacuuming, cleaning rooms that are already clean, the roar of the vacuum abrasive to the nerves but if Hannah were to tell her please never mind, don't bother, you just vacuumed yesterday, Ismelda will blink at her employer in surprise, alarm; too much effort to try to explain and then, subsequently, Ismelda will neglect parts of the house that need daily cleaning like the kitchen floor and Wes will notice, for Wes invariably does notice such neglect.

Hannah, what the hell? Why is the floor sticky?

Or, *Hannah? These shirts are poorly ironed.*

Choosing her clothes with care, trying not to be overwhelmed by the plenitude of her closet(s). Almost easier, Hannah thinks, to purchase new clothes than to try to sort through the old like sorting through tried-out, failed dreams drooping from cushioned hangers, too painfully reminding her of past efforts, failures.

Will no one ever love me? . . . Enough?

I have tried so hard. I have worn out my heart in trying . . .

A black silk-and-wool sweater beneath the chic suede jacket and the crisp-creased black trousers. Sensibly, the Ferragamo shoes in which she might walk without wincing in pain (for a short distance at least) in the autumn woods with her children and the man who will be their stepfather.

Hannah laughs, frightened. None of this is remotely real, is it!

Nonetheless, fastening the little clasp, adjusting the pink-toned pearls around her neck. Her perfect face powdered, the pale-glossy mouth primed to smile.

Try as she did to locate every pearl that slipped from the broken string to roll about the bedroom floor Hannah must have missed several, for the restrung necklace seems to her shorter than the original.

At the children's school Hannah arrived twenty minutes early. Parked at the rear as usual, the gleaming white Buick Riviera first in line though soon another vehicle pulled up behind her, another early-eager parent, also a mother, attractive made-up face blurred through a tinted windshield except for the mommy anxiety which leached through.

Losing the children. That will be the punishment.

"Litigious"—know what that means?

Go for the jugular. The husband's strategy.

Hannah peers through the rearview mirror but cannot make out the face of the woman/mother in the vehicle behind her.

Hoping that they might lock eyes. Exchange smiles, mouth greetings.

Be very careful, Hannah. Don't make my mistake.

On her way out of the house Hannah brought with her the morning paper, left by Wes in an untidy heap on a kitchen chair. No longer does Wes try to shield Hannah from upsetting news, there is too much of it now, spilling over, uncontainable.

In his usual hurry to depart for the Fisher Center. Unfailingly courteous to Hannah without quite looking at her. When she'd called after him in a friendly/unreproachful voice did he know if he'd be home for dinner and if so, approximately when?—Wes called back over his shoulder *Don't know, will let you know.*

If there's a call, it will likely be from Wes's assistant. Girl with the squeaky voice, whom Hannah has never met.

Mrs. Jarrett? Mr. Jarrett says he is sorry, he has a dinner appointment this evening . . .

"Fuck 'Mr. Jarrett.'"

Hannah's mouth in a (silent) spasm.

Opening the *Free Press,* seeing the shocking front-page headline— *Son of Murdered GM Executive Rusch and Wife, Probable Suicide.*

Hannah reads in disbelief, astonishment: Christina's son has killed himself?

Yes, there is the identical photograph Hannah saw a week ago in the *Free Press.* Frowning *Bernard Rusch, 32*—ice-pick eyes, spoiled petulant mouth.

Evidently Bernard had shot himself the previous day. Death is believed to have been "instantaneous," a single shot to the head fired from a weapon discovered at the scene. A "suicide note" was discovered also but its contents have not (yet) been released to the media.

The body of the deceased was found not at the Rusch house, where Bernard Rusch lived and where his parents had been found dead the previous week, but elsewhere in Bloomfield, in a private rental property.

Bernard Rusch's attorneys reported him missing when he failed to turn up at Bloomfield police headquarters where he was scheduled to be interviewed the previous day.

Hannah is shaken. There can be only one reason Bernard Rusch killed himself shortly after his parents' deaths: He was their murderer. The middle-aged son killed his parents, and now he has killed himself.

Hannah wonders why Wes hadn't told her this shocking news. Why he'd hurried out of the house without showing her the newspaper. Too much, too much terrible news too close to home, spilling over, an oil slick, uncontainable, a rebuff of Wes's conviction that the Rusch murders, like the Babysitter murders, have been racially motivated: opening skirmishes of the *race war* in which, eventually, the "white race" will triumph . . .

But Hannah has never believed that. Far more likely, Bernard Rusch murdered his parents for their money, and out of personal animosity.

"Christina! I am so, so sorry."

Her lips move numbly, she has no one to whom she can speak.

The shame of it, along with the heartbreak! Hannah cannot even imagine her friend's last minutes, realizing that her son wanted her to die.

No woman ever imagines that a child of hers might grow up and one day slaughter her, Hannah thinks with a shudder.

"Mom-*my*! Why are we *here*!"

Pettishly Conor calls to Mommy, he has investigated the derelict playground, he has found nothing that interests him.

The swings appear to be for older children, even the lowest is too high for Conor, if he tries to sit on the seat his feet can't reach the ground. Brashly he climbs to the top of the rusted slide then thinks better of sliding down it.

"Mom-*my*! When can we go home?"

"Conor, we've just *arrived*. We're going to walk in the woods . . ."

Conor mutters something inaudible. Hannah is dreading to hear, one day, all too soon, her irritable son cursing.

Fortunately, Katya is much easier to please. The four-year-old is excited just to be in a new place. A murmuration of black-feathered birds exploding out of a marsh enthralls her, a sudden galloping of white-tailed deer into the forest. Discovering a rotted rubber ball in the weeds is enchanting to Katya as if the ball were a special gift for her.

Bored with the playground Conor comes to play ball with Katya, bouncing the ball against the concrete wall of a public lavatory. Hannah is grateful that the children seem oblivious of ugly graffiti scrawled on the wall.

Mommy means: hoping the children won't be bored, restless, unhappy, clamor to go home early.

Mommy means: hoping to please the children's father. Somehow.

Oh but where is *he*? Hannah's lover?

Nervously Hannah has been watching the parking lot, the road that leads to the parking lot, one or two vehicles have turned in since her arrival, neither belonging to Y.K.

He has borrowed a car from a friend, he'd said. He has no car of his own in Detroit.

Calmly Hannah thinks—*I am waiting for my lover in this place, at this time. I will introduce my children to him.*

Thinking how soon she will be leaving her familiar life in Far Hills and living in places new to her. And in those places Hannah will discover a self new to her, not her own, a transmogrified being.

I am still young. I have scarcely lived half my life.

Until now, I have been waiting.

(But how realistic is it, that Hannah can bring Conor and Katya with her? Wherever Y.K. takes her? He has spoken of living in Europe, of traveling. Hannah has no clear idea how others manage divorce.)

(*He* will help her, of course. He seems to have a plan . . .)

The children's laughter is distracting. Mostly it is Conor's laughter, laced with cruelty. Since Katya's illness Conor has not been so protective of her as Hannah would wish, he seems eager to mock her relative weakness, frailty. He has made Katya scramble for the ball rolling along the cracked and weedy walkway into a pile of debris.

Conor's mocking laughter reminds Hannah of the headlines in the *Free Press*. She'd been unprepared to see Bernard Rusch's photograph on the front page, the astonishing headlines. *Son of, heir to, "person of interest" not yet a "suspect."*

So a suicide note was discovered. Hannah wonders what the note said.

Someone will know, word will get out. The attorneys will know. Spreading like wildfire in Bloomfield, surely.

Forced to think again of Christina. Sick-sinking horror of Christina Rusch's death at the hands of her own brute son.

Though Bernard Rusch had (evidently) killed his father, and the Irish housekeeper, a woman obviously well-known to him for years, it is Christina's death that most obsesses Hannah as unspeakable.

Wes had wished to think a Black man, or Black men, had committed the murders. But Hannah had known immediately: the (white) son.

Is it possible that Bernard Rusch is Babysitter, too? Perhaps his parents had suspected him, that is why he killed them . . .

Hannah has speculated what connection the ponytailed boy—Mike—Mikey—could have had with Bernard Rusch. For Hannah is certain, he'd been at Rusch's house the day he'd come to hers.

He'd seemed to know that the Hayden boy was going to be discovered by police. He'd boasted of TV news.

And through the ponytailed boy, what connection Y.K. might have had with Bernard Rusch . . .

She will ask him, Hannah thinks. If she dares.

Glancing at her watch: Y.K. is twelve minutes late. Once a person is *late, later* follows swiftly.

Bright chill autumn air. Wind high in the trees, a flurry of falling leaves. Smell of wet earth, leaves. The sky above Lake Michigan is layered with clouds like wetted tissues. Another time, nervously, Hannah glances at her watch: only a minute has passed.

"Mom-*my*! Conor threw the ball into the *mud*."

Katya cries plaintively, Conor giggles. Hannah calls to the children to just leave the ball where it is, they have plenty of balls at home.

Katya cries, "It was *my ball*, I *found it*."

Mommy means: refereeing children. Nonstop.

Mommy means: trying to love your children equally.

At last, when Hannah is about to give up, gather the children, and trek back disconsolately to the car in the parking lot, return to Far Hills chastened and nursing a secret wound, a gleaming red sports car rends the dun-colored scene like a sudden flash of Technicolor in a black-and-white film: turning into the parking lot, capturing Conor's attention at once.

Like a sleek rocket, slung low to the ground, as out of place among the other ordinary vehicles as an exotic vulpine predator among dumb-grazing sheep.

Y.K.!—Hannah stares transfixed as her lover climbs out of the sleek red car, long-legged, not (evidently) limping, tall, lithe, handsome in a casual corduroy jacket, trousers, on his head a khaki-colored cap that gives him a military look. Hannah stares as if she has never seen this man before, a wave of utter weakness, helplessness passes over her. She laughs with delight, how well Y.K. has chosen a car to arouse the admiration of a seven-year-old boy!

Seemingly oblivious of Hannah, Y.K. makes his somber way toward the trailhead as if intent upon hiking. His stride is purposeful, he is wearing hiking shoes. He has sighted Hannah but doesn't wave to her, their meeting must seem to be accidental.

Hannah has taken Katya's hand, without haste she is walking with Katya on the walkway perpendicular to the path Y.K. is taking. Eagerly her eyes leap to the man, but he has not looked at her, what anguish if he doesn't acknowledge Hannah, if this is all a fiction, a fantasy; clearly this person is a stranger, in this unfamiliar setting Hannah wouldn't readily recognize him, nor would he recognize her.

Approaching each other, fifteen feet apart, Hannah and Y.K. greet each other with surprised smiles.

"Hello! Is it—Hannah?"

"Hello!—Y.K.—"

"What are you doing here?"

"What are *you* doing here?"

Laughing together, this meeting so delights them. Hannah's children are alert, intrigued.

Conor joins Hannah and Katya, to be introduced to Mommy's tall smiling sharp-eyed friend. Conor will never remember the name *Keinz*—"Mr. Keinz"—children never remember adult names but he is impressed with Y.K., Hannah can see.

Squatting on his heels to greet the children at eye level, smiling to put them at ease, repeating their names, "Con-or," "Kat-ya"—as if these names are special to him—Y.K. has charmed Hannah's children as she has never seen them charmed by any stranger, indeed any adult. Ordinarily they would be shy, wary in the presence of an adult stranger but Y.K. has won them over within seconds.

Awestruck Conor asks what kind of car is it.

"A Ferrari Testarossa." An Italian sports car, Y.K. says. Very easily, with its high-powered engine it can travel at one hundred eighty miles an hour.

One hundred eighty!—Hannah is shocked to hear this.

"But I've never driven it that fast," Y.K. tells Conor. "Once, one hundred twenty, on the Interstate, late at night."

Hannah wonders: Y.K. has borrowed this remarkable car? From whom?

He has friends in Detroit, it seems. Wealthy friends. Of course. Of course! Predating Hannah.

A blazon of a smile Hannah has never (quite) seen before as Y.K. rises to his full height, taller than she recalls, now clasping Hannah's hand—warmly, yet respectfully; the children are accustomed to seeing men and women shaking hands, this would seem to be no different though (secretly) the man draws his thumb roughly, bluntly across the palm of the woman's hand leaving her weak-kneed.

"Beautiful children, Mrs. Jarrett! But not surprising. Considering."

Daring to lean to Hannah, brushing her cheek with his lips. As if this, too, were the most natural of gestures, nothing to arouse a child's suspicion.

Between the couple there is a hesitancy, a cinematic freeze, as if they are about to kiss more forcefully, but Y.K. draws back. The heavy-lidded eyes, just slightly threaded with blood, suffused with emotion, desire, for *her*.

Hannah is overwhelmed. Whatever in the comforting fantasies of her bedtime dreaming she has imagined of this very meeting, what *is* spills over, uncontainable.

"It's—a very nice surprise, meeting you here . . . Y.K."

Y.K. laughs, Hannah is so awkward uttering this name, if it is a name. But he doesn't provide her with another.

"And a very nice surprise meeting Conor, and Katya, and Mrs. Jarrett, here." Adding, as Hannah blushes: "A beautiful necklace, Hannah! Is it an heirloom?"

"Yes—an heirloom."

So, he has noticed!

A sign.

"You are looking particularly beautiful. But then, you must know." Whispering into her ear, "My gorgeous *shiksa*."

Shiksa? Hannah has no idea what this means, has never heard it before. Or, she has misheard.

Is this a movie scene? Hannah has no script and must improvise. Even if she has lived this before she cannot remember how. What she has wished for has come to pass—yet she has no idea where it will lead.

For here they are, strolling together in a park. Hannah and Y.K. *In broad daylight.*

The walkway is in poor repair, strewn with leaves, storm debris. There is a fresh raw smell to the air. Their voices are uplifted, elated. Exactly as acquaintances might do, having encountered each other accidentally, in a random place. *And how have you been? And how have* you *been?*

Hannah is flooded with relief, gratitude, that her lover has not disappointed her, he is here in the presence of her children. She has never seen him outdoors before, in any natural setting. Always before, in the Renaissance Grand Hotel.

The adults chatter, the excited children run ahead, and run back to them, following a half-mile trail looping around a marshy area of cattails and rushes, fallen trees. The children hope to be noticed by the tall man who drives a gleaming red sports car—mysterious "Mr. Keinz" whose attentiveness to Mommy has (Hannah thinks wryly) elevated Mommy in their eyes.

It has worried her that Wes's indifference to her has registered with the children. She supposes yes, inevitably. Certainly with Conor who seems less respectful to his mother than he'd been.

Still, Hannah is proud of her children! The beautiful little boy, the beautiful little girl. And how anxious she is, that her lover will want to be their stepfather.

A child is the mother's best self. A child is the mother's soul.

Has this man actually said to Hannah, they will have a child of their own? Has he seemed to *promise* this, once he and Hannah are together?

In the throes of their lovemaking Hannah has thought *yes*. She will have another baby, forty is not too old.

Hears herself laughing, as gay as a drunken woman. Tempted to slip her arm through Y.K.'s arm. The man's nearness invites this gesture of casual intimacy.

As if he has had the identical thought Y.K. stops Hannah on the path, as the children run ahead. He grips her head in outspread fingers, he kisses her hard, hard enough to hurt, pushing his tongue into her mouth, for a dazed moment Hannah cannot breathe.

He releases her, Hannah nearly loses her balance. A wave of sexual desire washes over her, a sense of weakness, helplessness.

"I've been missing you. Missing *that*."

"Yes, I—I also . . . I've missed you."

The wind blows strands of hair into Hannah's eyes, mouth. Black-feathered birds erupt out of the marsh just a few feet away, like shouts of joy.

Hannah's heart is pounding erratically. The sidelong glance of the man, his teeth bared in an intimate smile, has the force of a hard caress.

How long half a mile is! Hannah's feet ache in the beautiful absurd pumps and (she sees, flinching) the flawless black leather is wetted, sure to stain.

After their hike around the marsh Y.K. invites them to the café. Of course, the children clamor *yes!*

Hannah, too, is overjoyed. How grateful for a drink to calm her nerves.

And in the near-empty café, in a booth with sticky vinyl seats (Mommy and Katya on one side, Y.K. and Conor on the other), the adults order drinks, the children are served ice cream, double scoops in paper cups, a treat usually forbidden at such a time of day, just a few hours before their dinner. And now they are thrilled to learn that Mommy's tall handsome friend, though encountered in the park seemingly by chance, has "gifts" for them in the deep pockets of his jacket: a small white fluffy-furred stuffed bunny with shiny black button eyes, for Katya—"Her name is Snowball"; a six-inch replica of a bomber plane, the Vought F-8 Crusader, which, Y.K. says, he'd flown in Vietnam, for Conor.

Both children are delighted with their gifts. Katya's eyes shine with tears. Conor marvels at the intricately constructed airplane, he has toys at home, including airplanes, but made of plastic, nothing like this model made of metal with a cockpit that opens to reveal a single, solitary pilot complete with miniature goggles. Conor plies Mommy's astonishing friend whom he has never seen before with questions: How fast does the plane fly? How do you get to be a pilot? Did he really *drop bombs*? How many?

Hannah listens in fascination. She would never have guessed that her lover had flown a plane at a thousand miles an hour—indeed, that any planes reached such a speed. Or that he'd gone on a hundred and twelve missions, in his two-year deployment.

She feels an ache of disapproval, that her lover participated in the unpopular war, that he'd dropped bombs on the Vietnamese. Yet, at the same time she feels immensely proud of him, he has totally won over the children.

Y.K. shows Conor how several miniature torpedo-shaped bombs are released on the underside of the plane. Conor asks Y.K. what kind of bombs did he drop and Y.K. hesitates before saying—"Bombs designed to explode."

Hannah thinks—*Napalm. He doesn't want to say.*

Hannah feels a shuddering sensation. The heavy-lidded eyes glide over her, a look of sexual appropriation, possession as palpable as a caress between her legs.

"But war is a terrible thing," Hannah says, nervously. "Even for the 'winners'—there is so much loss."

"Really!"—Y.K. smiles at Hannah, bemused. "And what do you know of loss, Mrs. Jarrett? I mean at first hand."

"I—I don't know of—actual 'loss'—I suppose. But I know that war is hell."

Y.K. laughs. There is something particularly funny, touchingly funny to him, in Hannah Jarrett declaring *war is hell*.

Y.K. summons the waitress to their booth, a slouch-shouldered woman of about forty who has been staring openly at him, and at Hannah, as if assessing them, trying to establish if they are married, if the children belong to both of them. The woman is impressed by Y.K., she is resentful of Hannah, glancing at Hannah's ring finger, otherwise ignoring Hannah.

Without asking Hannah, Y.K. orders two more glasses of wine. Overly sweet, heavy, the café's drinks menu is limited. Hannah shakes her head *no* but Y.K. ignores her.

Of course (Hannah thinks) Ismelda will note at a distance of five, six feet her employer's wine-sweetened breath. Unavoidably.

Terrible wine, but Hannah feels festive. Wine-warmed! The pale-glossy mouth keeps smiling.

Grateful that Y.K. addresses Conor so seriously. Rarely, virtually never does Wes speak to his son like this except (and this, too, rarely) to scold.

Gravely Y.K. says, "There is nothing like flying, Conor. Nothing can compare. I felt it immediately the first time I was taken up by an instructor, as a student, just nineteen. You would feel it, too. You know that people on the ground are looking up at you but they are the size of ants. If you pass over them at a low altitude they will run like hell, they will throw themselves down as if that would save them." Y.K. laughs, baring damp teeth. "You have the power of life and death over them. They have no power at all."

Conor laughs. Something feral in the child's laughter, in the grimace of the small white damp teeth.

Between the man and the boy, a feral look, of understanding. Hannah sees and is excited by it, this intimate connection between the two that excludes her, the mother.

Conor will adore him. Conor will not miss his father.

And Katya, too. Both children gaze in awe at the tall striking man who smiles at them with such *complicity*. This man is very different from Daddy, it is a puzzle why. His eyebrows are dark, heavy. There is a ridge of bone above his eyes, his features are sharp-chiseled. Not all of his words are spoken aloud, it seems—he means more than he says. The khaki cap, tilted on his head, which he hasn't removed in the restaurant, gives him an impersonal, military look. His hair has been shaved severely short at the nape of his neck but is longer at the sides of his head. Hannah is thrilled, edgy, that Y.K speaks so frankly to the children.

She realizes what is different: Y.K. doesn't banter with the children, as adults invariably do; he does not address them as children, as Wes does. As Hannah herself does, knowing no other way.

Conor asks Y.K. if he owns an airplane and Y.K. tells him *no*.

Conor asks Y.K. if he still flies an airplane and Y.K. says of course *yes*.

"Not often, but when I have time. And I take passengers."

A look of intense satisfaction comes into Conor's face, at the same time a look of wariness, even fear.

Y.K. leans forward, elbows on the Formica-topped table. He is feeling expansive, robust. The children's awe is a tonic to him, like the woman's rapt attention. He touches her fingertips with his own. The children do not notice: Hannah feels something like an electric current course through her.

And then, reaching his hand beneath table, pressing the palm of his hand between Hannah's (trousered) legs, in a swift gesture, retreating at once, leaving Hannah stunned, a hot flush rising in her face.

In his face, frank brute desire. *I want to fuck you, you know.*

Hannah looks away, dazed. Her mind has gone blank, she tries to focus on something that Katya is asking: Can they have fizzy water?

Yes! "Fizzy water"—two bottles—Y.K. signals the waitress.

As the children are preoccupied with their gifts Hannah speaks to Y.K. in a lowered voice of the "terrible things" that have been happening recently in Bloomfield Hills, only a few miles from her home.

"Really!"—Y.K. nods in sympathy, but vaguely.

"In this morning's paper—you must have seen it—it's reported that Bernard Rusch committed suicide yesterday. He's the son of a Bloomfield Hills couple who were murdered in their home twelve days ago."

Y.K. frowns, yes he has heard about this. But he avoids local Detroit news as much as possible.

"You don't know the name—Rusch?"

"Maybe from the papers, TV. He was a GM executive, I know that."

"The father, yes. Harold Rusch was a friend of Wes's, actually . . ."

"Really!" Y.K.'s manner is flat, unimpressed.

"You have never heard of Bernard Rusch—I suppose."

"Why would I?"—Y.K. asks smilingly, as if Hannah's question is naïve.

During the exchange Y.K. glances at the little boy beside him, peering so intently at the toy airplane.

"People who know the family are shocked," Hannah says, "first by the murders of the parents, now by Bernard's suicide. It has all seemed unbelievable. The son, Bernard—he'd lived with his parents. I'd met him just once, I didn't know him at all." Hannah speaks rapidly, nervously. Why is she telling her lover these things, in which he can have no interest? "You've never met him, you said?"

"Well, I've met many people in Detroit over the years," Y.K. says, with the air of one replying politely to a silly question, "but most people I encounter are of no lasting significance to me, I don't make any effort to remember their names."

"I can understand that," Hannah says quickly. "Of course. It's just that—for us—some of us—it was a shock to read this in the paper this morning. Evidently there was a suicide note."

"Is there!"—Y.K. seems minimally interested.

Hannah persists: "Are you sure that you didn't know him—meet him?—Bernard Rusch? . . . I thought I'd seen him in your hotel once, when I met you there."

Y.K. stares at Hannah for a beat, then smiles at her. "You're joking, darling? You think you saw this person in the hotel? Once? How many thousands of people pass through the Renaissance Grand Hotel?"

But in the corridor outside your room! Hannah hesitates, not sure she should proceed. Despite his smile of polite incredulity Y.K. is looking at her somewhat hostilely.

"I told you, dear Hannah—I don't follow local news. In any of the cities I visit on business. There is nothing more boring than local news especially local news that is 'scandalous.' Anyway, this person 'Rush'—'Rusck'—apparently confessed to murdering his parents, yes? So that should be a relief to everyone."

When Hannah looks blankly at him Y.K. says, "So you—they—can all stop worrying? About being murdered in your beds?" Y.K. laughs, amused.

Hannah stammers, "He—confessed? He did?"

"You just said so. A suicide note."

"The suicide note was a confession? Also?"

"What else would it be?"

"But it hasn't been released to the public, the contents of the suicide note," Hannah says slowly. "At least that's what I read . . ."

Y.K. says irritably, "What would a suicide note likely say? If there was a crime, this person wrote the note to confess to it, and to acknowledge that he was killing himself for that reason. Why else would he kill himself, just now? You have only to wait, police will link him to Babysitter, too."

Hannah is feeling overwhelmed. Y.K. speaks so indifferently, and yet is saying extraordinary things.

Hannah tries to recall what she'd read in the *Free Press*. *Is* there a confession, as well as a suicide note? Had Bernard actually confessed to murdering his parents and the housekeeper? She remembers none of that from the news. And—what of the serial child killer? It would make a sick sort of logic, it would not even be so very surprising, if Bernard Rusch turned out to be Babysitter as well.

Bored with the subject, Y.K. has turned his attention to the children, who bask in his attention. Hannah is relieved, she has sensed her lover's annoyance with her naïve questions.

Y.K. means to entertain the children, it seems, by asking if they know where their daddy is at the moment?

Katya seems puzzled but Conor says brightly: "In a sky-building."

The adults laugh affectionately at him: "Sky*scraper*."

Yes, and no, Hannah points out. Daddy's office is in a relatively high building in the Fisher Center in midtown Detroit but it is not *sky-high*.

And where do Daddy's parents, their grandparents, live?—Y.K. asks the children.

Again, Katya isn't sure how to reply but Conor knows: "Grosse Pointe."

Do they live in a "big house"?—Y.K. asks, with the air of one who knows that the answer is *yes*.

Proudly Conor says that the grandparents' house is "real big" and that it is on the lake—and they have a dock, and a boat.

Y.K. asks what kind of a boat?—and Conor says a "big white boat" with a "downstairs" to it, with little rooms—"cabins."

"A yacht?"—Y.K. is amused, smiling at Hannah. "*You* must enjoy that, Hannah. Cruises on the Detroit River."

Hannah laughs ruefully, shaking her head to indicate *no*, not really.

She doesn't tell Y.K. that there aren't that many invitations that involve her.

Y.K. turns the conversation to Hannah: How many grandchildren do the elder Jarretts have, apart from Katya and Conor?—and what are their ages? Where do the older grandchildren go to college? How many "siblings" does Wes have, and are any of them involved in the family business? And what of Wes, is *he* involved? Is Wes close to his father?

Vaguely and evasively Hannah answers. Some of these questions Y.K. has asked her before, when they were lying in bed together, in the hotel. Hannah says that she doesn't know much about her father-in-law's business, though she does know that he owns "properties" in Detroit and elsewhere in Michigan.

Between her legs in the most vulnerable, the softest fork of her body, the sudden assault, a caress as hard as a blow, a frantic pulse, frail as a bird's heartbeat, now weakly beating. The exchange between them, Y.K.'s veiled hostility, has excited Hannah even as it has discomforted her.

Wanting to be alone with him, the man. Away from this place, the vulgarity of the café, the sticky cracked-vinyl seat on which she is sitting with Katya and the sticky Formica-topped table before them, cheap wine in cheap wineglasses, the rudely staring waitress, the maddening chatter of children like flies buzzing.

Crazily calculating, even here, in Lone Lake Park, how they might find a way to be alone together, to make love . . . In one of the lavatories? He might take her into the men's lavatory and (somehow) barricade the door.

Swiftly, expediently. No need to remove their clothes.

But no: The men's lavatory is filthy. What a thought! Hannah feels a wave of sickness, nausea.

What is Y.K. asking Hannah?—with an effort she tries to concentrate, no she has no idea, or she has forgotten, she'd meant to check with Wes but forgot, what his life insurance is. And their joint accounts, investments.

She rarely discusses these matters with Wes, Hannah says.

"Really! And you say this as if you're proud of your own ignorance."

Ignorance. Hannah laughs, stung.

Is that her identity to Y.K, a man's wife, *ignorant*?

"Women think that ignorance is a kind of femininity," Y.K. says, with scorn, "and that may be true. But not the smartest kind."

Then, seeing that he has offended Hannah, Y.K. says, "My mother discovered too late, you pay for what you don't know in any relationship with a legal standing."

And: "You could look into the accounts, Hannah—assuming they are joint accounts. And accessible at home."

He wants to know how much money Wes has. That is the attraction. How much I will have if Wes dies.

Hannah drains her second glass of wine. Terrible-tasting, irresistible. Pulses beat hotly in her head, she feels a moment's vertigo.

Though taking perverse pleasure seeing how the few patrons in the café glance at her and at Y.K., and at the children in the booth, with curiosity. Because they are attractive? Because they appear to be affluent? The tall man in the military-looking hat, the blond woman in the chic suede jacket, pink-luminescent pearls around her neck, scissor-cut hair. Possibly a couple, but are they and the children a *family*?

Not possible. This man is not likely to be the blond woman's husband. Not likely to be the father of these fair-skinned children. Not likely to be anyone's *husband, father, or (even) stepfather.*

A fleeting expression of scorn on Y.K.'s face. His contempt for Hannah, yes, and for her children, unmistakable. She has seen.

Staring at the small oval face of her watch without seeing the time. Is it late? It is late.

Is Hannah mildly drunk, or rawly sober?

As if he has sensed Hannah's dismay before Hannah herself has fully absorbed it, Y.K. again compliments Hannah on her pearls. Something about the pink-pearlescent pearls around Mrs. Jarrett's slender neck has engaged Y.K.'s interest.

He is being gracious, gentlemanly. He is loving to Hannah, effusively attentive. As if he understands that he may have offended her, he may have gone too far. Seizing her hand in a playful manner as if in farewell—but no, he is just going to pay the check at the counter.

In that instant a wave of weakness sweeps over Hannah. Thinking that Y.K. was going to walk out of this place and abandon her.

Oblivious to their mother the children chatter excitedly about their gifts. Hannah wonders how she can explain the gifts to Wes.

Without wishing to be looking in his direction Hannah sees how Y.K. is joking with the slouch-shouldered waitress at the cash register. So quickly, so bizarre an intimacy, between strangers! She is dismayed, she is oddly aroused. *He* is no one she knows, really: not even his name.

She sees how between Y.K. and the waitress a slow lewd smile passes, a look of frank sexual complicity, recognition. Y.K. glances back at Hannah smiling his easy smile, with kingly composure assuring her *But it's you I want to fuck, darling. Only you. I promise.*

Hannah looks quickly away, not seeing.

She is shaken, her face burns as if she has been slapped. She *does not* look back at Y.K. and the laughing waitress.

Hurriedly she leaves the café, with the children. He will wonder if she has left him, Hannah thinks.

It appears to be much later in the afternoon, the November sky has roughened like coarse fabric. Gusts of wind send scuttling leaves underfoot. Hannah stares, those *are* beetles.

She might have left. She might have walked away with the children. Driven away in her car without a backward glance but no: She is waiting when Y.K. leaves the café, she will remember this.

Hannah is quiet, distracted, walking with Y.K. beside her and the children trailing close behind in the direction of the parking lot. The cheap wine has gone to her head, she walks with care in the tight-fitting Ferragamo pumps. She wonders if Y.K. has laughed at those pumps, without her knowing. And if he forgives her, for her foolish vanity. And halfway to Hannah's car Conor suddenly decides he needs to use a restroom!—how like Conor this is, having just left a place where there was a restroom, and because Mommy didn't think to ask if either of the children wanted to use a restroom of course they hadn't given it a thought, and now Conor is insisting in a plaintive voice that he needs to use a bathroom *right now,* which means that Hannah will have to take him into the derelict concrete lavatory close by, walls covered in ugly Day-Glo graffiti, a stench to make her nauseated, Hannah dreads.

She has been a sweetly devoted mommy to the children, until now. Certainly she has impressed her lover. But now crying, vexed: "Oh Conor! Why couldn't you have said something in the restaurant . . ."

"Because I didn't need to go then," Conor says defiantly, "I need to go *now.*"

Y.K. offers to take Conor into the men's restroom, it isn't far away. Hannah can take Katya to the car and meet them at the exit.

Of course: This is only sensible. *He* will take the boy.

But Hannah laughs nervously, *she* will take Conor . . . as she always does in public places, into the women's lavatory.

"But you take the boy into the women's restroom, Hannah, not the men's. You said he was seven years old. It's appropriate for him to use the men's room, not the women's."

That Y.K. should lecture her, so sternly, in front of the children! Hannah feels a thrill of excitement and dismay. She grips Conor's hand to hold him fast.

"No, really," Hannah protests, laughing, trying to laugh, as if Y.K. is offering her a gift so generous that she cannot possibly accept, "of course I will take him."

Conor slips out of Mommy's grasp and bats at Mommy's hand.

"I want to go with *him*."

Taken so by surprise, unprepared for this betrayal, Hannah stares speechless as Y.K. takes Conor's hand as if the gesture were altogether natural, and familiar: gripping her son's small pale hand in his large-knuckled hand. Conor melts at once, doesn't shrink from Y.K. or bat his hand away rudely as he'd done with Hannah.

Before Hannah can react, Y.K. leads Conor across a grassy stretch to the cement-block restroom a short distance away. Staring after them, Hannah feels a twinge of unease, dread.

Hannah has been noticing men entering the men's restroom since she'd arrived at the park. Though there are few visitors to the park there appear to be frequent visitors to the men's restroom. A burly man in a wool cap pulled low on his head, a spillage of carroty curls at the nape of his neck. A thin acne-faced teenaged boy in an army surplus jacket . . .

Weakly Hannah calls after Y.K. and Conor—"*Wait . . .*"

Neither Y.K. nor Conor pays Hannah the slightest heed. The tall broad-shouldered man in the khaki cap, the little boy clutching the model bomber plane. What is the connection between them, confirmed by their grasped hands? Are they talking together?—what on earth are they saying to each other?

Hannah stares blankly after them, beginning to panic.

Licks of panic like flames. Suddenly she is terrified.

Running after Y.K. and Conor, calling to them, begging: "No! Wait! Conor, come back . . ."

In an instant desperate, running clumsily in the tight-pinching shoes even as Y.K. and her son disappear into the entrance to the men's restroom.

"Come back! Come back! Stop!"

A middle-aged man with white frizzy hair in a pouf around his face, and his face rubefacient, puffy as if with medication, emerges from the entrance adjusting his trousers and staring at Hannah in astonishment.

Hannah pushes past the pouf-haired man but hesitates at the threshold to the lavatory, which she has begun to smell. "Conor! Come back! Come here!"—her voice is a wail, scarcely human.

Y.K. reappears, with Conor, each staring at Hannah in disbelief, she is behaving so strangely. But panic has overcome Hannah, she acts instinctively, blindly plucking at her young son's hand, seizing the recalcitrant boy in her arms and dragging him forcibly away from the entrance.

"I—I don't want him taken into this place . . . I'm taking him home. Conor, come with Mommy . . ."

Hannah has closed her arms around Conor, viselike. The child struggles with her but she overcomes him as Y.K. looks on in surprise and contempt.

Hannah reaches for Katya's hand as well, pulls the children with her half running, half stumbling to the parking lot fifty feet away where her car is parked. Both children are crying and appear to be frightened of their distraught mother.

Cannot look back at her lover whom she has humiliated, insulted. On the walkway Y.K. stands silent and unmoving, too furious to call after her.

Hannah manages to get the children into the backseat of the Buick. "Stop! Stop! Stop crying!"—screaming at them. Mommy has lost all composure, control. Jamming the key into the ignition, unable to look back at Y.K. Frantic to escape Lone Lake Park and return home.

In the backseat of the car the children continue to cry as Hannah exits the park. She is roused, veins pulse wildly in her head. Not sure if she should turn left—yes, left—on Hickory Grove Road. Directly behind Hannah in the driver's seat Conor is kicking the back of the seat shouting that he hates hates *hates* Mommy.

Pale-faced Katya is shrieking in terror, too, never has she seen an adult in such a state of raw emotion as Mommy.

"Stop! Just stop! You are *my children*—not his. You will do *as I say*."

In fear of her, the children grow quiet. Hannah cannot bear to seek out their stricken faces in the rearview mirror. By the time her panic attack has subsided Hannah is in familiar surroundings—Hickory Grove Road intersecting with Lasher Road entering Bloomfield Hills, twenty minutes from the house on Cradle Rock Road—and she has regained her composure again, or nearly.

You fool! You have lost him now.

What have you done!—he will never love you again.

The Stone

Yet: next morning the phone rings.

At a strategic time: when Wes is certain not to be home, and the children are certain to be in school.

In dread that Ismelda will answer the phone downstairs and take a message for her Hannah hurries to pick up the receiver.

"Yes? Hello?"—her voice is feathery-light, hesitant.

And for a moment he is silent. She hears the measured breathing, she knows that it is *him*.

Seeing again the expression of incredulity on the man's face, and fury as quick as leaping flames.

His contempt as she'd pulled Conor away from him at the entrance to the malodorous men's room.

Through the interminable night reliving the scene. Unable to sleep for a single sleeping pill wasn't enough and she feared taking a second so soon after the first as Wes slept beside her on the other side of the bed oblivious of her misery.

Trying to calm herself. Trying to reason—*What was the harm? There could have been no harm, he would never have hurt Conor.*

"Hannah?"—the voice, deep-chested, not angry as she'd expected but tentative, questioning.

Hannah replies, faint, weak: "Yes . . ."

Relieved that her lover isn't angry with her. Doesn't appear to be angry with her. She has tried to comprehend her panic but cannot.

No harm could possibly have come to Conor. Y.K. was only taking him into the lavatory, Hannah was waiting outside in full view of the entrance . . .

Had Hannah thought that Y.K. might be *Babysitter*? Is that why she'd panicked?

Y.K. is speaking to Hannah in a genial, measured voice. He is certainly not angry with her though he acknowledges that he has been "shaken"—"baffled"—by her behavior the day before. Her (evident) distrust of him, in front of the children, the children she'd so badly wanted him to meet, he doesn't understand.

"We need to talk, Hannah. Today."

Not Babysitter. This man is not Babysitter. What is wrong with you!

Hannah is trembling badly. Had the thought actually come to her, if but for a split second, that Y.K. was *Babysitter*? How was that possible!

"Our future depends on straightening up this terrible misunderstanding—this insult. Our love for each other . . ."

Hannah thinks: It is Bernard Rusch who might have been Babysitter. Not her lover.

Too much for Hannah to absorb. Her life has been a narrow creek bed, now suddenly rushing with water, overflowing its banks.

Recalling when her life had been so peaceful a life, so orderly and predictable a life. She'd confused the calendar on her desk for the flow of life itself: each day a rectangle on white space, emptiness waiting to be filled.

A matter of appointments: day following day in a calm progression.

She had been in control. Filling in the blanks in the smug warm hive of suburban life.

And family life: hive within a hive keeping wife, mother safe, nourished.

She has lost that now, Hannah thinks. That calm, and that control.

Her lover has entered the calendar life, he has demolished the dull order of her hive days. He is threatening to destroy her family, she must escape him.

Even so, badly frightened, Hannah has been conditioned to be courteous, polite.

"Today?—I wish I could but I can't . . . I have two appointments this afternoon."

How guilty the placating voice. And how strange this is: Where once Hannah would have been weak with excitement at the prospect of meeting her lover in their private place, now she dreads seeing the man again.

He will be angry with her, she thinks. Once they are alone together.

He will punish her. He will hurt her, badly. A memory of her bruised neck, shoulders in the mirror . . .

But Y.K. is saying that he misses her. He'd had a "bad night." What happened in the park is "baffling" to him. He can only think, he says, that Hannah was upset about something before they'd met, that had nothing to do with him.

"What you'd been reading in the newspaper, I think. That was it. People that you know, neighbors of yours, that have nothing to do with me." A pause. "And that second drink—I shouldn't have ordered it for you, it had a noticeable effect upon you."

Y.K. is being enormously reasonable, generous. Offering to blame himself, for Hannah's rude behavior.

He pauses to give Hannah time to respond. Reluctantly Hannah murmurs *Yes*.

Thinking—*Must never see him again. Never let the children near him.*

Of course, Hannah doesn't believe that Y.K. would harm her children. She doesn't (seriously) believe that Y.K. is Babysitter.

Yet, there exists the *possibility* that Y.K. is Babysitter. As quicksilver as the flicking of a card on a table the *possibility that Y.K. is Babysitter*. Seeing how Y.K. gripped Conor's hand and tugged him along the walkway in the direction of the filthy lavatory: the inclination of Y.K.'s head, the trusting upward tilt of the child's head, the two (adult male, male child) close as conspirators, exchanging words which the mother of the child can't quite hear.

The mother, excluded, unable even to guess what Y.K. and Conor might say to each other. In that moment forced to realize how perilous it is, her possession of her children: how easily they might be taken from her, and how (possibly) willingly they might wish to be taken from her.

It has not occurred to her until now, the children taken by Babysitter might have been enticed by him, to go with him. Maybe force wasn't needed.

"Hannah, dear?—are you still there?"

"Yes—of course. I—I'm—I'm here."

"Where, exactly is that?"

"In the kitchen. But I'm not really alone, Ismelda is—is nearby . . ."

In fact Hannah is still upstairs in her bedroom. Eleven-fifteen and she isn't yet dressed, hasn't yet showered. Lying awake through most of the night has left her both lethargic and anxious. She has been awaiting this call from Y.K. for hours—or, no call from Y.K.

In the park she'd insulted him irrevocably. Clearly he would never forgive her. He is not the kind of man to forgive, she is sure.

Not knowing if she would be devastated, if he failed to call her. Or profoundly relieved.

Y.K. is sounding uncertain, even just perceptibly plaintive, like a man stumbling along a path he'd believed to be familiar, that has turned out to be surprising him: "You haven't been sounding like yourself, Hannah. Something must be wrong."

Quickly Hannah protests: "Nothing is wrong. No."

"The way you behaved yesterday, in a panic over nothing . . ."

Y.K. is waiting for her to apologize, Hannah realizes. But she cannot summon the words.

I am sorry.

I am not sorry.

I could not help myself, I would do it again.

I must protect my children from you.

Y.K. is saying he wants to see her, he has missed her. He has begun to repeat himself, he is sounding distracted. Very angry with Hannah but determined not to betray his anger.

Telling her again that he'd had a "bad night." Expecting her to apologize for the "bad night."

Hannah says yes, she'd had a "bad night," too.

He loves her, he insists. He doesn't want to lose her.

Why had she behaved as she had, pulling Conor from him?—he demands to know.

Hannah cannot answer. Seeing the fury in her lover's eyes. Heavy-lidded predator eyes, livid with appetite.

"You know I love you, Hannah. You have entered my heart, you have saved my life . . ."

These words! Hypnotic. Hannah wipes tears from her eyes, she cannot but believe.

If he touches her . . . No.

He persists, they must see each other soon. If not today, tomorrow. If she can't come to the hotel in Detroit he will come to Far Hills.

Or they might meet somewhere in between, a private place. He can arrange.

No!—Hannah is panicked. Cannot.

Not today, not tomorrow. Not possible.

Her mouth is so dry, her voice is barely audible. Feeling his fingers tighten around her throat.

"Hannah? What are you saying?"—Y.K. is baffled, balked.

"I—I—I think that I can't . . . This week."

"But why not?" Then: "Didn't the children like their presents? I thought they did."

"They did," Hannah admits. "Yes. Thank you."

"Such beautiful children." Y.K. pauses, then says, as Hannah expects: "But that isn't surprising, considering that their mother is a beautiful woman."

Beautiful woman. Hannah imagines Y.K.'s mouth twisting in derision.

But thanking him, weakly. How like coercion flattery is, always demanding a meek *thank you*.

Y.K. repeats, he's at the hotel. A business lunch soon but after three he could see her.

"I told you, I can't!"—Hannah pleads. "I have appointments through the afternoon."

Y.K. is beginning to be stymied, a master chess player outmatched by an amateur. He is uncertain how to proceed, he must be very careful. Keeping his voice pleasant, in no way reproachful or accusatory. Quietly he says, "Well. Call me, Hannah. When you are feeling more like yourself."

Hannah murmurs *yes*.

"Because I love you, you know that. And I want to make love to you."

Hannah murmurs *yes*. She is feeling faint, uncertain.

Then, suddenly vehement: "If you loved me you would want me to tell Wes about us. You would want our relationship to be open, honest."

Suddenly, these trite words which Hannah has no intention of saying. Her voice is wounded, childlike. *He* has harmed *her*, the blame is *his*.

"I thought I'd explained that, darling. We can't—yet."

"Yes, you've said. But you didn't really explain."

"Hannah, I *did*."

Like a stone placed in the palm of Hannah's hand, something tangible, something to grip, with which to blame *him*.

"No. I can't do this any longer. It's dishonest, it's exhausting. Goodbye!"

Hannah hangs up the phone.

Unbelievably, Hannah has hung up on *him*.

Close to fainting with her own audacity. But she is elated. She has broken the connection, she will not speak with him again.

Thinking—*He's too proud to call me. This will end it.*

The Lover. The Stalker.

But he does call. The phone will ring, ring. And each ring an accusation.

You don't want to do this, Hannah.

This is a mistake, Hannah.

You know I love you, Hannah.

You know you love me, Hannah.

We need to talk, Hannah.

We need to save you from a very bad mistake, Hannah.

. . .

Instructing Ismelda not to answer the phone, just let it ring. And leave the voicemail *off*.

Chagrined that Ismelda so readily assents—"Yes, Mrs. Jarrett." The (discreet) way in which the employee does not ask her employer what is wrong.

Nor does Hannah offer any explanation.

She knows! Of course, how could she not know.

She has cleaned up after me. She has smelled him on me.

But has Ismelda overheard Hannah calling her lover late at night, not so long ago?—this is a possibility Hannah doesn't wish to consider.

She'd always been so careful. Wes asleep, all of the house asleep. She was sure.

What madness! Hannah is mesmerized by her own recklessness, she cannot comprehend how she'd behaved as she had.

In desperation staying away from the house during those hours of the day when *he* is likely to call. She would arrange to have the telephone number changed but how to explain to Wes? She cannot.

No words. No words she can imagine.

In a haze of self-recrimination. Self-loathing. Unable to concentrate during the day and unable to sleep at night composing messages, pleas, she might leave for Y.K. at the Renaissance Grand Hotel for she is too cowardly to speak to him, frightened to hear his voice in her ears.

Please forgive me! I am sorry . . .

I made a mistake. I am begging you to leave me alone.

No words will placate an offended lover, Hannah thinks. She cannot tell him that yes, she is still *in love* with him but no, she can't see him again.

She scarcely comprehends, why she can't see him again.

Seeming to know that Y.K. will not be a gentle lover from now on. Seeing again his aggrieved face, heavy-lidded eyes brimming with the fury of one betrayed when she'd dared to pull Conor from him.

Even his limp had vanished, in Lone Lake Park. The shrapnel in his leg—had that ever been real?

She'd imagined taking care of him as he recovered from knee surgery. How he would need *her*, what pleasure this would give her.

How helpless she'd felt in his presence. A compass with a spinning needle. At a loss, unmoored. His hand on hers, his touch. His mouth on hers sucking oxygen from her lungs.

I don't love you, I am terrified of you.

Let me go! Please.

Driving into town in a haze of anxiety seeing, or thinking she sees, a vehicle following hers by approximately half a block.

Not (of course) the gleaming red Ferrari but a less striking American car, dark gray sedan with tinted windows so that the driver's face is obscured.

If Hannah accelerates, this vehicle accelerates; if Hannah slows her speed, the vehicle drops back. If Hannah impulsively turns a corner, without signaling, the vehicle may continue through the intersection but rejoin Hannah in another block or two.

Driving the children to school, picking the children up after school. Hannah is determined to be remembered as a *good mother*.

"Mom-*my*?"—Conor is annoyed, Hannah doesn't seem to be paying attention to him.

No idea what Conor has been asking her. Or what Katya has been chattering about.

For in the rearview mirror Hannah has been observing the phantom sedan following behind; though, when she peers into the side mirror, she can't see it.

Her heart beats calmly, she reasons that if she is with the children, if she is not alone, *he* will not approach her to cut her off, force her out of the car. He will keep his distance.

When Hannah turns into the school grounds the sedan does not follow. But when Hannah returns to the road the sedan is waiting not far away to follow her back home as slow and unerring as a great sleek predator fish.

Know you love me, Hannah.

Need to talk.

Need to save you from a bad mistake, darling.

And so if Hannah says *I want to report that a man is following me, he has called the house many times and he follows me in my car* they will ask *Do you know the identity of this man, Mrs. Jarrett?*

No words. She cannot.

If she says, pleads *I am afraid of him, I want him to stop and leave me alone, I am afraid that he will hurt my children or me,* they will say *But has he threatened you, Mrs. Jarrett? How exactly has he threatened you?*

A gag shoved into Hannah's mouth, it will suffocate her.

Didn't the children like their presents? I thought they did.

These plaintive words Hannah hears, rehears. Almost, she'd weakened.

Katya adores her soft white-furred bunny Snowball who sleeps with her every night, cuddles close beside her as Mommy reads her to sleep from a favorite book; Conor plays with his miniature Vought F-8 Crusader, making dive-bomber and demolition noises with his mouth, which Hannah can hear rooms away.

Her solace is: Katya has many stuffed animals, Conor has many expensive toys—automotive, aerial, interplanetary.

Her fear is that the children will call their daddy's attention to their new gifts, or, less likely, that Daddy will notice the gifts . . . But no, Wes has no more than a polite feigned interest in the children's toys, even those he is supposed to have helped Hannah select for birthdays or Christmas.

Only once, Katya asks if "that nice man who gave me Snowball" is going to visit them, and Hannah says *no,* probably not, he lives in another city.

Careful not to speak of Y.K. by any name for the children have no doubt forgotten his name.

Hannah has steeled herself for queries from Conor but oddly there are none.

To recall Y.K. would be, for Conor, to recall the shameful way his mother had behaved at the entrance to the men's room at Lone Lake Park. She'd frightened him, she'd hurt him dragging him away as she had in both arms.

Mom-my! I hate you.

Though it's clear that of all his expensive toys Conor particularly prizes the miniature bomber, which (possibly) he doesn't consider a mere *toy,* exactly.

A talisman, perhaps? A promise?

"Mikhail"

Fuck, yes! Never say *no* to Hawkeye.

He calls you, you go. Whatever it is to be *expedited,* you don't say *no.*

Putting a bullet into a man's brain, he's wishing he had said *no.*

Like *crossing over* to some new place but you can never go back to where you were.

But: kind of proud of himself, he'd been scared shitless but he hadn't fucked up.

What's it feel like to kill somebody?

Is it—like, weird?

Like your jaw is numbed at the dentist, that sensation—some kind of *nothing.*

You know there's pain inside but you can't feel it.

Okay it's sexy-cool. Rock-star cool like Sid Vicious.

Why his new street name is Mikhail. Speaks with an accent like there's pebbles in his mouth. In a coke haze hacked off most of his hair so he couldn't be identified.

High on coke twelve days/nights after the *expediting.* Alert and bloodshot-eyed trying to "sleep" sitting up in a chair in a barricaded room on West Warren. No more he'd lie on his back like a turtle on its back out of its shell. Or shut his eyes.

Waiting for cops to bang on his door. Or, fire through the door.

Paid a friend to bleach his hair platinum-blond like a hooker. Inch-high stiff spikes sprouting from his head like little horns.

Whatever he'd looked like before with the (shit-brown) ponytail straggling down his back, that look is gone.

He's cool with punk rock. Sex Pistols punk rock. Anyone who knew Ponytail wouldn't recognize Mikhail, he's thinking. Hoping.

Though punk music is mostly heroin, he's always been afraid of.

But a cool way to die: heroin. Just—shut your eyes, nod off, never wake up: OD.

Coke won't let you sleep. Coke is a buzz saw in a glaring white-walled room and you're ricocheting from wall to wall.

Coke might burst your brain, your heart, but you're flying high like an eagle not crawling like a broke-back snake.

Jesus!—Hawkeye whistled through his teeth at the sight.

(And the bastard is *never* surprised.)

And changing his street name to "Mikhail"—what the fuck, Mikey Kushel has been dead a long time.

Mikey Kushel? Wasn't he the kid who died?

Babysitter's first victim?

. . . his eyelids start to close, can't sleep but can't stay awake either, not fully awake. Twelve days/nights after Hawkeye sent him out to Bloomfield for the second time, *expediting* a task involving Hawkeye's old buddy they'd known as Mister R__. And the heavy Glock revolver is back in his hand, finger at the trigger.

Don't do it. You can stop now.

Like time has stopped, like you'd stop with your finger the second hand on a clock. That kind of *numb*.

But Ponytail has nothing to do with the decision. In fact there is no decision but the finger on the trigger twitches, the Glock is discharged. Only a second while Rusch stoops to pick up the envelope that has fallen to the floor, grunting a little, breathy, smelling of whiskey but also of something talcumy overlaid on the stink of unwashed armpits, obviously trusting Ponytail, in fact relieved to see Ponytail at the

door and not a stranger, he's in this fragile emotional state, *orphaned*—
(a "mob hit" the deaths of the elder Rusches is beginning to be called)—
trusting Ponytail he'd used to know as Mikey Kushel he'd never gotten
around to fucking because there were always better-looking boys at
the Mission, boys with smoother skin, smoother asses, who wouldn't
cause trouble like coarse-skinned Mikey Kushel might've done.

So as Rusch stoops to retrieve the hefty manila envelope he believes
to contain the final installment of negatives and prints linking him to
certain underaged boys, including one or two no longer living, the gun
discharges, a single bullet slams into his head, splintering the bone
at his right temple; in spite of the silencer affixed to the weapon the
sound is deafening and Ponytail feels a kick, a nudge, recoils with a
whimper like a frightened girl (but no one to witness) remembering
to release the heavy gun which drops, Goddamn, onto Ponytail's right
foot protected by a clumsy rubber boot but still hurting like hell.

Falling to the floor more swiftly than the (dead) man falls.

*Dead because no way he wasn't dying. But not instantaneously as
you'd think from a bullet point-blank in the brain and the sharp smell
of gunpowder.*

. . .

This time Hawkeye calls him it's *expediting* a simple task that needs to
be done exactly right.

Delivering a "floral display" to "Mrs. Jarrett" out in Far Hills.

Mikhail listens not sure what he's hearing. Hawkeye who, last time,
sent him out to the suburbs to put a bullet in a man's brain, and before
that to bear away a child bound, blindfolded, and gagged from that
same pervert, is sending him out now to *deliver flowers*?

When stunned Mikhail doesn't reply at once Hawkeye says sharply,
Remember her?—the blond woman you had to drive, she was too
wasted to drive herself home.

Her. Mikhail is feeling panic.

Heart quickening like a key is being jammed into an ignition, the
motor alert and aroused but going nowhere, not yet.

High on coke he's been losing track of time. Mixing up time(s).
Weird anguish dreams of his mother lost long ago but then Mrs. J__

holding him in her arms, why were the two of them sobbing together, Christ knows.

Carrying the poor kid tied in wire, blindfolded, gagged, in some kind of blanket—*Christ!*

But that finger on the trigger, weird to think it is *his finger.*

Of all of the universe—*his!*

Day/night/day distinguishable if you listen to traffic out on West Warren beyond the solitary window over which he'd nailed a strip of tarpaulin. Mornings and late afternoons the rush of traffic is like a waterfall, nights it's as subdued as a pounding of blood in the ears. So he'd realized what time *is:* a stream of water passing over you as you lie motionless on your back in a creek bed, sometimes a swift current, sometimes much slower, trickling over stones, passing over you on the way to somewhere else.

This somewhere else you can't see, have no idea of any more than you know where the stream began.

Feeling a hand—light, but with a promise of firmness, force—on his shoulder, sliding to the nape of his neck. *Son? Open your eyes.*

Eyes snap open. Father McKenzie? *Here?*

You listening?—Hawkeye is sounding impatient.

Yeh!—sure.

Pressing the receiver against his ear as Hawkeye continues. Like bits of information might be spilling out between the receiver and his ear, he's getting panicked he'll lose.

Hawkeye's instructions: In the morning at nine-thirty drive the Firebird to the parking-garage entrance to the Renaissance Grand Hotel, Hawkeye will be waiting at the curb to give him a message, a note in a sealed envelope, he is not to open the envelope, he is to drive north on Woodward to Shamrock Florist at Six Mile Road, pick up a "floral display" (which Hawkeye has purchased) he will load in the trunk of the Firebird making sure it doesn't tip over (there will be water in the vase), he will insert the envelope inside the cellophane wrapper, then drive to Far Hills on the Lodge Expressway, exit at Far Hills, and drive to 96 Cradle Rock Road where he will ring the doorbell and wait for the door to be answered.

If a housekeeper answers the door tell her it's a special delivery, "Mrs. Jarrett" has to sign for it.

If the housekeeper tries to say that "Mrs. Jarrett" isn't home just insist that you can't leave the flowers without the signature.

Mikhail listens, doubtful. This is *all*?

Half expecting Hawkeye to tell him to *expedite* the woman. But no, evidently not: just deliver flowers.

Mikhail wonders if Hawkeye knows he'd gone to the woman's house on that day he'd sent him out to Rusch. He doubts that the woman would have confessed to Hawkeye what happened between them but if she had, Jesus!—Ponytail might've been killed . . .

Well, maybe not *killed*. Hawkeye has a fondness for him, he is sure.

Like a son? Some kind of younger relative. Mikhail thinks so.

(Maybe Hawkeye is Russian? Mikhail is thinking they have some traits in common.)

Hawkeye cautions Mikhail to wear clothes like a delivery boy would wear. Not a uniform but nothing to attract attention. Definitely a baseball cap to hide the punk-style blond hair that's noticeable half a block away.

Mikhail mutters *yeh*. Though hurt, the contempt with which Hawkeye speaks of his fantastic new hair.

Does he think I'm a fag? Punk is anti-fag.

Hawkeye asks Mikhail to repeat the instructions, which he does more or less exactly for (even in his wasted state) Mikhail is one you can rely upon. No asshole like every other street kid aged out from Saint Vincent's. Knowing to falter when it comes to the address on Cradle Rock Road not wanting Hawkeye to become suspicious.

Hawkeye tells him to write it down for Christ's sake: *96 Cradle Rock Road*.

Hawkeye warns him: deliver the flowers, no conversation, walk away, *gone*.

Feeling like a released balloon, when Hawkeye hangs up. Mikhail soaring up to bob against the ceiling.

Not shaving for twelve days and scarcely washed himself in that time, smelling of his body and itching all over but particularly crotch and armpits (possibly lice?) (he's had lice before, Jesus!), still he's feeling fucking good, crash for a long night with a handful of quaaludes then get his ass up early enough to take a shower, shave off the stubble covering half his face, he's liking his new look, sexy-cool "Mikhail" with platinum-blond hair in spiky tufts shaved at the nape of the neck and sides and with dark roots like the fashionable hookers at the Renaissance Plaza, almost classy-looking enough to confuse with a truly classy rich woman like *her*.

Dreamy bobbing against the ceiling thinking of the woman: *her*.

The Emissary

You have come to dwell in my heart.

Yet her lover has ceased calling, Hannah realizes. Exactly which morning (in mid-November) she could not have said.

Evidently Y.K.'s pride has outweighed his rage at her. He is resigned that Hannah will not answer the phone if she believes he is calling her; and he will not call at any time when Wes might be home.

Hannah is grateful to Y.K. for that. He'd never wanted Wes to know about Hannah and himself, she has Y.K to thank that her marriage hadn't been destroyed by her own recklessness.

"He does love me, then. He doesn't want to hurt me."

And: "He understands that I am weak, frightened. I am not strong enough for a divorce. I am a *mother.*"

(Though wondering what will become of her, the flimsy husk of Hannah, when Mommy has departed: when the children no longer need her.)

Nor has Hannah noticed recently the dark gray sedan following her when she drives into town or to the children's school: as sleek and silent as a predator fish, this vehicle. And the dark-tinted windshield through which no face has ever emerged. Pausing at intersections peering anxiously into the side mirror where there appears to be no vehicle behind her and into the rearview mirror where at last, one day, finally, there appears to be no vehicle.

"Is it over, then? It's over."

She is relieved! She is not disappointed but relieved, relieved.

Her life returned to her unscathed.

. . .

(*Her* life returned to her unscathed but Marlene Reddick has not been so fortunate.)

(Hannah hasn't wanted to ask. *Of course Hannah has wanted to ask!*)

(Learning from mutual friends whom she'd quizzed casually that after behaving very strangely for months Marlene has—simply—disappeared . . .)

(Having withdrawn six hundred thousand dollars from her and her husband's joint savings account in cash, *disappeared.*)

"Katya! Is your pretty bunny new?"

In the way of a daddy almost entirely lacking in curiosity about his children's lives who nonetheless, on the average of once a week, feels obliged to mimic genuine daddy concern, Wes asks Katya this question seeing her cuddling and fussing over her fluffy white rabbit one evening.

Hannah listens. Not daring to breathe as the child replies *yes*.

"And what's the bunny's name?"

"Snowball."

"And who gave you Snowball, Katya?"

A near-inaudible murmur—*Don't know.*

Listening close by, Hannah allows herself to feel relief.

Of course Katya has forgotten Y.K.'s name, if she has ever known it. And she is as embarrassed at having forgotten the adult name as she would be at having a potty accident at her age, which is four years, eleven months.

Conor has so many similar toys, Wes never notices the replica of the Vought F-8 Crusader.

That morning when the doorbell rings.

Half listening as Ismelda goes to answer the door. A delivery, probably. In the Jarrett household there is a new calm, a distinct diminishing of morning anxiety since telephone calls are being answered now, as before. The threat of unwanted calls seems to have passed.

Relief! Hannah hadn't had to explain anything embarrassing or awkward to Ismelda, nor appeal to Wes to have their phone number changed.

And today, resuming some semblance of normal life: a Friends of Literacy fundraiser at the Bloomfield Hills Country Club which Hannah will attend with two women friends whom she has not seen in quite a while and who (she'd feared) had dropped her since the Zekiel Jones fallout . . .

Do you think she really was—raped? By a Black man?

If she was, she's been very brave about it.

Very—something!

Downstairs at the front door, a raw male voice, and Ismelda's near-inaudible reply, and again the male voice—unmistakably, what sounds like *Mrs. Jarrett.*

Ismelda calls up the stairs to Hannah, it's a delivery, her signature is required.

When Hannah descends the stairs she sees, on the floor of the foyer, a large floral display in a wicker basket; wrapped in cellophane, as many as two dozen gorgeous roses—crimson, pink, cream, yellow. For *her*?

It has been a very long time since Hannah has been surprised in such a way.

Thinking—*But is it my birthday? What is it?*

Thinking—*Because he loves me. He is releasing me.*

Oddly, the delivery man has stepped into the foyer instead of remaining out on the stoop. And instead of asking Hannah to sign a receipt he hands her an envelope with *MRS. JARRETT* block-printed on it.

Not a delivery *man*, more a gangling arrogant *boy.* In a black leather jacket, jeans and silver-buckled belt, he's removed a baseball cap as if to display a bleached-blond punk-style haircut, brutally shaved at the sides of his head.

Hannah feels a kick to the heart, she recognizes this person: the ponytailed boy whose name is Mikey.

An emissary of Y.K.'s, in her house.

His face is flushed with excitement, audacity. Behind tinted aviator glasses his eyes are as dark as coals. He is breathing audibly, his hands tremble. Heat wafts from his skin, he is high on a drug, likely cocaine:

brazenly smiling at Hannah, a nervous twitch of a smile, fading as he loses his composure.

"For you, ma'am—Mis-sus Jar-rett . . ."

He laughs, awkwardly. He has handed the envelope to Hannah but her stunned fingers fumble it, the envelope falls to the foyer floor, quickly the delivery boy turns away eager to escape.

"Ismelda! Shut the door."

The door is shut. If Ismelda is astonished by Hannah's agitation, and the odd behavior of the platinum-blond delivery boy, she takes care to give no sign. Like any employee she has learned not to see, not to infer, not to hint at either seeing or inferring, anything that might interfere with her employment.

Blood is beating in Hannah's ears. For a long moment she can't seem to think—the ponytailed boy Mikey, returned to this house. *In* this house.

She has all but forgotten him. These many weeks she has given him *no thought.* Except sometimes passing by the TV room, seeing the leather sofa. Appalled, yet fascinated. For the sofa, the entire room, looks—*normal.* Attractive furniture, beautiful pale green carpet. No (visible) stains anywhere. Not possible that what had happened between Hannah and a stranger, many years younger than Hannah, on that sofa, weeks, months ago had actually happened . . .

And something about Babysitter. Some connection with Babysitter. In this house! *Him.*

Hannah shudders. Not possible.

Through a foyer window seeing the vehicle in the driveway—*not* a delivery van—being driven away, jerkily, too fast. In the exigency of the moment clear-minded enough to register that this isn't the dark gray sedan she'd seen, or imagined she'd seen, in the rearview mirror of the Buick following her . . .

"Ma'am? I'll take these."

With some effort Ismelda lifts the wicker basket brimming with roses, hauls it out to the kitchen. Hannah would certainly help her but is too distracted regarding the envelope in her hand: return address Renaissance Grand Hotel, Renaissance Plaza, Detroit Michigan.

In no haste, even calmly, as one might open a medical report that might likely contain a death sentence, Hannah opens the envelope, pulls out and unfolds a sheet of elegant Renaissance Grand Hotel stationery upon which, in stilted block letters, is the cryptic message:

DARLING—
YOU REALLY DON'T WANT TO MAKE THIS MISTAKE DO YOU.
                                                    Y.K.

Delivery Boy

*R*ich spoiled bitch, what the fuck do you care about her!
  Fuck her. Fuck both of them.
Expedite. Get in and out, delivery boy.
Don't look back.

Negative

Something very strange Wes would call it.

At his office that day he'd received, via certified mail, a manila envelope containing just a single item: an eight-by-eleven photograph negative.

"No return address. No explanation. And whatever it's a picture of, it's too dark to make out."

Hannah laughs, uneasily. Not curious to see what this is, that Wes is removing from the manila envelope.

A sensation of dread, like black bile, rising at the back of her mouth.

"It's an utter mystery! I showed it to people in the office, and at the Athletic Club, at lunch, nobody could make anything of it. Yet it isn't a mistake, it was addressed to 'W. Jarrett.' I had to sign for it."

Hannah has no choice but to examine the very dark negative Wes is showing her.

At first he'd thought it was an X-ray, Wes is saying, there's this faint cloudy shape that could be a lung . . . The negative is almost totally black, like an explosion of squid ink. Or, a dark painting that has been purposefully smudged.

Hannah holds the negative to the light, staring.

At first, Hannah sees nothing. Then, by degrees her brain, if not her eyes, decodes the scene: a vague horizontal space beneath a tangle of dark shapes is likely a platform, or a bed; if a bed, one with bedclothes so rumpled their creases resemble fissures in the earth; on this bed is a figure, prone, likely a human body, possibly a mannequin, possibly female, unclothed, limbs spread; its face is (mercifully) obliterated in darkness yet there is a glimmer, scarcely discernible, of an open, gaping mouth . . .

You, Hannah. Naked in his hotel bed.

Hannah is stunned. Just barely, Hannah manages to maintain her composure.

The figure on the bed, the grotesquely spread limbs, the face—these seem clear to Hannah, unmistakable; yet, to another person, like Wes, with no expectation of what the confused image might be, the negative appears to be just a swirl of dark shapes laced with lighter shapes like ectoplasm, a botched photo.

What it represents, Hannah supposes, with a sinking sensation, is one of a sequence of photographs taken at the same time, from a distance of about ten feet. A darkened room, a badly disheveled bed, a naked woman, unconscious . . .

Just a degree lighter, these figures would be clear. The terribly exposed female body. The face.

"Hannah, you're holding it upside down," Wes says, amused, for Wes is often amused by his literal-minded wife; taking the negative from her and deftly reversing it, "see, if you hold it this way it's more like an X-ray, but one of the men at lunch thought it could be a marine photo, taken on the ocean floor, fathoms deep it's said to be pitch-black there except for bioluminescent creatures . . ."

Hannah makes an effort to look where Wes is pointing. She can barely see, her eyes are welling with tears.

The thinnest sort of salvation, that Wes can't (evidently) see what is so obvious to Hannah. He'd shown it to others, none of them had seen.

". . . certain kinds of deep-sea fish, octopus . . . the strange thing is, I think that some of these fish are blind, yet . . ."

The female figure sprawled on the bed so obliviously: Hannah. The legs have been spread in mockery, the fleshy thighs, naked, flaccid, stomach, pubic hair, vaginal area shadowy, smudged.

The female body, stark-white, slovenly. At its core a hungry mouth that can never sate its hunger.

Other photographs of the scene, Hannah knows, will not be such puzzles.

Had he drugged her? How many times has he photographed her? Was someone else in the suite with them? The ponytailed boy?

Hannah is stricken to the heart, mortified. *But what did you expect, that he loved you?*

He'd placed a pillow over her face, he'd played at suffocating her. She has not remembered that humiliation in a very long time. Amnesia has shielded her.

Of course, Y.K. has always been contemptuous of her.

She has known, Hannah has certainly known. Telling her he adored her, contempt shining in the heavy-lidded eyes.

She'd commanded Ismelda to take away the flowers he'd sent. The other day, soon after the delivery, even as Ismelda was dividing the roses into three bouquets, in three vases, for there were too many gorgeous roses for a single display in the unwieldy wicker basket, Hannah approached Ismelda in the kitchen and told her in a quavering voice get rid of them! Throw them in the trash!—eyes dilated as if she were drugged, a ghastly pallor in her face at which Ismelda stared, so taken by surprise.

But of course, Ismelda understood. In the moment, no need for her distraught employer to repeat the request.

Never question the employer's request. However unexpected.

Though afterward Hannah would wonder: Had Ismelda thrown out the beautiful roses, or had she carried them upstairs in secret, to keep in her room?

If so, Hannah is annoyed. But in no way is Hannah going to inquire.

Wanting to run away now to hide, hide her eyes, her eyes that have seen too much. Crouch in a corner in a safe part of the house, a room Wes isn't likely to enter. Lie on the floor in a fetal position like a worm that has been kicked, curling to protect its contemptible life.

But you can't! Can't even shut your eyes.

Play out the scene, get through it.

So much of her marriage, indeed most of her adult life: *Play out the scene, get through it.*

Shaking her head as if baffled, intrigued but equal to the puzzle that looks, to her, for she is a resident of Far Hills who often attends gallery and museum openings, like a work of art—"Abstract expressionist. Is it—Rothko? Pollock . . ."

Hannah turns the negative sideways: now it is more likely a work of art. The female figure sprawled on the bed has disappeared, even Hannah no longer sees it. Wes examines the negative and agrees yes, it could be an abstract painting, but why would anyone send it to *him*?

"Maybe it's from one of the galleries in the Fisher Building. The one that exhibits avant-garde art, like Andy Warhol, Ad Reinhardt . . ."

But it more resembles de Kooning, Hannah should be thinking. Big-toothed female ghouls grinning through layers of pasty paint.

"Yes, I thought of that, too"—Wes appropriates Hannah's interpretation with the ease of a catcher lifting his gloved hand to capture a baseball that might have spun past his head otherwise—"except there's no return address. The negative came in a plain manila envelope. If it's some kind of advertisement for an exhibit, there would be an announcement but there isn't."

"Oh, but what else can it be? Are you sure?"—Hannah makes a point of checking the envelope, which is empty.

Wife of the house, mother. In this role Hannah is quick, deft, competent, earnest. A helpmeet to the husband and a model to the children, not a stricken woman resisting the first twinges of headache pain, nausea at the realization that her lover has so exposed her.

Conor has been clamoring to see what Daddy has brought home but it turns out to be disappointing, no sharks or giant squid that he can recognize. Nor does Katya see anything in the negative.

"Ismelda?—give a look."

Ismelda is preoccupied with kitchen work—(clearing up after the children's evening meal, completing preparations for the adult meal to come)—but Wes insists upon showing her the negative at which she merely glances before looking quickly away, laughing nervously as if she suspects that Mr. Jarrett is joking with her as often, to her discomfort, and at the most inopportune times, he does.

Not looking in Hannah's direction. Not meeting Hannah's eye.

Blackmail. How could I not have known.

How could I have been such a fool . . .

Hannah is stunned, the revelation is so blunt, so clear.

Lying awake through the night. Stinging red ants crawling over her body.

In loathing of herself ever having imagined that Y.K. had loved her. *Her!*

In delusion, an unspeakable happiness. Truly she'd believed. But how was it possible, she'd *believed*?

Y.K. has power over her now, Hannah understands. She can't just refuse to see the man, to answer her telephone. She will have to call him.

Terrifying to Hannah, to consider the likelihood that Y.K. has much worse, more obscene negatives of her. She doesn't doubt that he'd recorded having sex with her, his own identity obscured . . .

It would be the collapse of her marriage. Wes would win custody of the children.

All of Far Hills would know, and despise her.

She wonders: *Had* he drugged her? She'd drunk wine with him. He'd poured wine into her glass. Each time, she'd lost control, had had no idea how much time was passing, like one trapped in a dream.

But she does remember waking in the pigsty of the bed, naked, very groggy, as helpless as a sea creature lacking a spine, prized out of its shell and vulnerable to any predator.

Better if he'd killed her. Extinguished her. The pillow over her face, fingers tightening around her throat. The pleasure this man whom she scarcely knew has given her has been indistinguishable from the most excruciating pain, a part of her had hated it, yet she'd been haunted by the memory of what he'd made her feel, mesmerized.

Hannah obliterated, utterly. Was that her deepest desire, to not *be*?

She feels a despairing sort of desire for Y.K., even now. If he were here. If he lowered his weight upon her, forcing himself into her, laughing at her distress.

You like this. You know you do: this.

But no! Hannah is appalled by the adulterous acts she'd committed, so recklessly.

Appalled by her body, that betrays her. For Hannah's body is not *her*.

A solution would be: death.

. . . sees herself wraithlike removing the gun from the bedside table drawer so quietly that Wes, sleeping a few inches away, is not disturbed and in utter silence in the most courageous and selfless gesture of her life positioning the snub-nose barrel against her head touching the tremulous blue vein at the right temple, shutting her eyes as a child might do as she summons the strength to pull the trigger . . .

Her eyes spring open, she has fallen asleep. Thinking: What of Katya and Conor? Their lives would be ruined if their mother killed herself and especially in such a way—blood, brain matter, bits of bone splattered against a wall in a lurid pattern of self-display.

Better mortification, shame, the loss of the children, than the children's lives ruined because of their mother.

Better the contempt of her husband and of all of Far Hills, than ruining the children's lives.

Through the interminable night as Wes sleeps beside her in the massive bed, his back to her as if in another dimension, as distant as another galaxy. Hannah's thoughts race like tires spinning in mud. Not an inch's progress, no matter how the tires spin, yet she is exhausted.

At dawn slipping from the bed to descend the stairs in the still-darkened house, to locate the *strange thing,* the mysterious negative, where Wes had tossed it on a kitchen counter out of annoyance the night before, and finally boredom.

In the unnatural silence of the sleeping house Hannah examines the negative another time, hoping she will see that she'd been mistaken, there is no ghostly figure hidden inside the swirls and smudges, but indeed yes, the outline of the slovenly female body leaps at once to her eye, unmistakable.

What a joke! But so ugly, this revelation of sexual squalor, idiocy.

Her heart beats weakly as if it might cease. Oh, such a fool! And yet, such (lost) happiness.

For there is no denying: Y.K., deceiving Hannah, intent upon exploiting her, blackmailing her, nonetheless had made her deliriously happy. Given her a reason to *be.*

That is the final, unspeakable shame, she can never share with another living being. That, in spite of all she knows of her lover now, she recalls him with that sensation of sick, sinking helplessness that is the most profound experience of her emotional life.

And now, she must find another reason to live. To continue to live. A mission. To save herself, and the children. To save the life of her husband who has ceased loving her.

She takes the negative away with her, upstairs. As if it were a precious document. How fortunate that Wes lost interest in it and won't miss it, has likely forgotten it as if indeed it had been tossed out negligently with the trash.

· · ·

Phone ringing at the other end, in an empty room.

Hannah faint with dread, gripping the receiver against her ear.

Later in the day, late midmorning. Hannah is (blessedly, briefly) alone in the house. No one to overhear! Ismelda has gone shopping and won't return for ninety minutes at the earliest.

When it seems that the ringing will cease, a recording will switch on, the phone is brusquely answered: "Yes?"

Hannah has drawn breath to speak but cannot. She hears herself trying not to sob, choking.

"This is you? Mrs. Jar-rett?"

To her surprise Y.K. is sounding bemused, sardonic, not furious as Hannah has feared.

The intonation of *Mrs. Jar-rett* is almost playful, teasing.

He tells her that it's good that she has called him, she had better not try to cut him out of her life ever again.

"You understand what a mistake that would be, Hannah? Yes?"

"I—I don't know . . ."

"Yes, you *know*. You've seen the evidence. That's an example of what I can provide your husband. If you doubt me, I'll send him another negative, he won't have trouble identifying."

Hannah listens, helpless. She should beg Y.K. for mercy but will not.

"I want to see you tomorrow. That's not negotiable. If you have an 'appointment,' break it. I want a first installment. Let's say just under ten thousand dollars. Nine thousand, nine hundred, ninety-nine dollars. That's chump change for the Jarretts. We'll take it from there. We'll see how it works out. Marriage isn't out of the question. We'll see."

Nine thousand, nine hundred, ninety-nine dollars? *Marriage?* Hannah listens appalled.

In his bemused voice instructing her: She will come to the hotel room the next day at four, she will bring ten thousand dollars less one dollar in cash, predominantly hundred-dollar bills.

Adding he isn't asking for ten thousand dollars because if she withdraws ten thousand from a savings account, the bank will have to report it to the feds. But she can withdraw nine thousand, nine hundred, ninety-nine dollars. No problem.

But she can't, Hannah says. Without Wes knowing . . .

"Not my problem," Y.K. says. "Find a way."

Hannah protests: But he is blackmailing her!

Y.K. laughs. "Call it what you will, darling. Could be, you owe me."

Hannah is weeping, helpless.

Y.K. says: "I'm hanging up now."

Unbelievably, the connection is broken. And when Hannah calls back the phone rings, rings.

Tormenting her, not answering the phone until the fifth or sixth ring and then lifting the receiver, in mocking silence.

Plaintively Hannah asks how can she give him ten thousand dollars in cash without Wes knowing about it . . . At the end of the month, when the bank sends a statement to him, he will know.

"Fuck that," Y.K. says. "You've got money of your own."

Hannah tries to think: Does she have money of her own? Investments?

Joint investments with Wes, but nothing of her own. She is sure.

"Sell the pearls."

The *pearls*?

"Sell the pearls, the pink pearls you were showing off the other day. Bring me the money."

Hannah stammers she wouldn't know where to sell her pearls . . .

Y.K. gives her an address on Gratiot. Downtown. Tells her just go there. He'll call the jeweler, say she'll be there in the morning. He will take a commission—"What the pearls are worth, he'll give you half."

She can't sell her grandmother's pearls!—Hannah protests but Y.K. laughs, saying sure she can sell the pearls, she can sell anything she owns, if somebody is willing to buy it. As long as she turns up with ten thousand dollars minus one dollar.

Anyway, Y.K. asks, cruelly, why'd she wear the pearls to show him, what was the point?

Hannah tries to recall. *Why* had she worn her grandmother's pink-toned pearls to meet her lover at Lone Lake Park . . .

To make myself beautiful to you. To make you love me more.

Y.K. says, sneering: "You wore the pearls for me, darling. You wanted me to want the pearls, because the pearls are you. So now I want them. Sell them."

Hannah tries to explain that the pearls aren't real pearls, only just cultured pearls, she has no idea what they are worth . . .

"So find out. That's up to you." Adding, "They looked like good quality to me. A pearl necklace could be thirty thousand or more, depending."

Thirty thousand! Hannah doesn't think this can be possible.

But Y.K. is sounding bored with the subject. Telling Hannah to find out for herself. Bring him the money. Tomorrow at four. He's hanging up now.

Hannah cries: "Wait! Don't hang up . . ."

She pleads with him: Let her bring the pearls to him, he can have them. She will just give the necklace to him.

Y.K. says, "No! I don't want the fucking pearls, I want the money. The first installment. Ten thousand is a bargain. If you miss the deadline tomorrow it's fifteen thousand the next day. I don't have proof of ownership, I can't sell the pearls. It's up to you to sell them. Fuck I'm going to get fingerprinted to sell your necklace, you could call the police saying they were stolen."

Y.K. is becoming more exasperated as he speaks. His earlier sardonic poise drops away like a mask. Telling Hannah that she should think also about the plans they'd been making. Maybe she's forgotten, *he* hasn't.

She'd brought her children to him. She'd wanted him to meet her children, she'd boasted of her beautiful children, Christ!—she'd wanted him to *want* her children.

So now, he *wants* her children.

But more immediately: Hannah needs to look into increasing her husband's life insurance. She needs Wes's signature, it can't be done without the signature. *He* could maybe sign the signature, if she provides some samples.

So when she comes to the hotel tomorrow with the ten thousand dollars she should bring the life insurance policy. So that he can look it over. However much the policy is for, say it's five hundred thousand, she will have to produce a plausible argument for raising it. Eight hundred thousand, that's a first step.

Hannah is too shocked to reply. Y.K. laughs: "No. That will be the second step, darling. The first step is the pearls."

Hannah begins to sob uncontrollably. Telling him she'd loved him. She'd loved him, and believed him . . .

"Jesus!"—Y.K. laughs. "How stupid can you be, to imagine that I'd loved *you*."

There's no woman he gives a fuck about, he tells her, and if there was, not likely it would be *her*.

"But—I believed you . . . I loved you."

A plaintive piteous voice: Hannah has lost all control, all dignity, weeping like a child whose heart is broken, for whom there is no hope.

Should've thought of that before she betrayed him, Y.K. says disdainfully—"That was the mistake."

Hannah hears the dial tone, he has hung up a second time.

Zink Jewelers Estate & Loan

You make your own luck. It isn't handed to you on a silver platter, kids.
    Joker Daddy laughs, winks. His voice is a caress that chills like melting ice in a trickle inside your clothes where no one can see it.

Late morning, Hannah drives into Detroit, to search out Zink Jewelers Estate & Loan at 2997 Gratiot near Huron.

Difficult to find a parking place on Gratiot Avenue. This part of Detroit, far downtown on the east side, is old, rundown, not familiar to Hannah who is forced to circle the block, rerouted onto narrow one-way streets, thwarted by double-parked delivery trucks. Waiting at an intersection for a very long light, Hannah nervously locks all the doors of the gleaming-white Buick Riviera sedan that draws eyes to it, if but fleetingly.

How like a foreign country here, near the Eastern Market. African American Detroit bordering East Asian Detroit. Walking hurriedly along Gratiot, Hannah sees only dark-skinned pedestrians, thinks they may be Indian, Pakistani, Lebanese, hears fragments of indecipherable speech.

She has become invisible: almost literally, no one *sees* her. For these others know, by the color of her skin, that Hannah is no one of their acquaintance, no one who could possibly matter to them.

True, some of the men glance casually at her. She dreads to see scorn but sees instead carefully composed impassive faces.

Oh but why do they not *care*? Hannah is beautifully dressed: for beauty is armor. Black cashmere coat, new lizard-skin shoes, and about her head a Dior silk scarf to keep her hair from whipping in the wind.

But why was Mrs. Jarrett there, on Gratiot Avenue, at Huron? At that hour of the day?

Not where she died but where the body was found. That is the mystery.

Zink Jewelers is one of very few businesses still open along this block of Gratiot, near Huron; a much smaller establishment than Hannah has expected, heavily fortified with an iron grating across its front window and a door similarly barricaded, which seems to be locked.

Hannah tugs at the door. She is close to tears, she has come *so far.*

"Hello? Is anyone here?"—her voice is plaintive, querulous.

All that she can see inside is shadowy, cave-like. At the rear, a light—but no visible human presence.

Glittery merchandise in the front window, heaped like cheap baubles—jewelry, wristwatches, silver trays, trophies. A double strand of white pearls . . . Hannah feels a wave of despair, futility.

How easily she might have saved herself. But how blind she was!

Hannah is sure that Y.K. said he'd call the jeweler on her behalf. He can't have failed to do this, he wants money from her . . .

About to turn away in defeat Hannah sees a figure materializing out of the interior gloom like ectoplasm: a stout anemone-like shape, bulbous torso and fattish ferret face, eyes behind harlequin glasses flat-glaring like reflectors. A finger, a hand, floating as if bodiless, jabs impatiently as if to signal Hannah—to what, she isn't sure.

Only now, Hannah notices a small sign beside the door: RING TO ENTER.

Abashed, Hannah rings the doorbell.

A loud buzzer, a *click,* and the door is unlocked. Still, the door is so heavy that Hannah can hardly pull it open.

No one comes to her assistance. The figure in the harlequin glasses has vanished. How rude! Hannah steps inside the barely lit store.

This isn't a jewelry store as Hannah understands jewelry stores. Indeed it is also, or primarily, a pawnshop. The cluttered interior is not elegant, nor even very clean. There are too many display cases, oddly positioned at right angles to one another, as in a warehouse. Surfaces are layered in dust. The linoleum floor is sticky beneath the smooth soles of her high-heeled shoes.

The lighting is fluorescent, high overhead against a hammered-tin ceiling. No windows except the fortified front window through which a suety light is emitted. The air smells befouled, with cigarette smoke, dust, sorrow.

A mistake. It isn't too late: leave.

But Hannah has found her way here, she cannot turn back.

"Mrs. Jar-rett"—the name is uttered. Not a question but a statement in a flat incurious hoarse-husky voice.

So, Y.K. did call on her behalf! Her name is known here, at least.

Grateful, Hannah makes her way to a glass-topped cashier's counter, behind which a woman in harlequin glasses, with a fattish ferret face, is seated on a stool, cigarette in hand.

Hannah smiles, foolishly. She hadn't expected she would be waited on by a woman.

"Show me what you've got."

Not a smile of greeting. No small talk. Husky smoker's voice.

Self-consciously, reluctantly, like one disrobing before an impassive stranger Hannah removes the pearl necklace from a soft fabric bag, and spreads it open on the glass-topped counter which is as badly scratched as a much-used skating rink.

How beautiful the necklace is!—Hannah feels a twinge of guilt, and grief, that she must sell it.

A precious memento of her old, lost life as a girl. Though (in fact) Hannah has rarely given the necklace a thought in twenty years.

The woman in the harlequin glasses grunts a minimal sort of interest, somewhere below admiration or enthusiasm. Eagerly Hannah explains: These are antique pearls given to her by her grandmother . . .

Antique! Grandmother! Hannah can hear Y.K.'s jeering laughter.

The woman examines the pearls, frowning. Hannah is concerned, the woman is handling the pearls so roughly.

In a plastic ashtray at her elbow is a cigarette emitting a stream of smoke that makes Hannah's eyes water.

"ID with your picture, please."

Hannah provides a Michigan driver's license with a miniature photo of herself taken several years ago. The woman examines it, glancing from the photo to Hannah, and back again, as if in doubt.

Hannah laughs nervously. "I'm under some strain right now, I don't look like myself . . ."

There is a pause. Hannah expects the woman to respond sympathetically but she says only: "Hands. Here."

Brusquely Hannah is fingerprinted, each of her fingers and both of her thumbs, pressed on an inkpad, then on stiff white paper, with surprising strength by the woman.

"But these are my pearls," Hannah protests, "do you think that I've stolen them? They were my grandmother's."

"State law."

Hannah stares at her ink-stained hands, dismayed. The woman in the harlequin glasses nudges a box of tissues in her direction.

Without a word of explanation the woman takes Hannah's necklace away, deeper into the interior of the store, to a heavyset figure at a worktable in the rear, presumably the appraiser.

Amid the general gloom of the store the appraiser's worktable is lit with a concentrated light from a crook-necked lamp.

An older, obese person: Zink?

But why does this person not at least glance in her direction, Hannah wonders. Why are he and the woman both so incurious, so rude. Hannah has journeyed *so far*.

In Far Hills, Hannah wouldn't be treated with such indifference. A mile away at the Renaissance Plaza, in any of the boutique stores, in the Renaissance Grand Hotel, Hannah Jarrett would be treated with respect.

She has begun to perspire inside the chic cashmere coat. Watching the appraiser furtively. Not wanting to betray her anxiety. *They will substitute fake pearls for my pearls. This is how it's done, when you are a fool.*

Hannah has been wiping her ink-stained hands on tissues, without great success. She has a horror of smearing ink on her clothing, which will appear to be mere grime. She forces herself to breathe normally. Her eyes, sensitive and bloodshot from hours of weeping, and another sleepless night, water from the woman's cigarette smoke.

Her face aches from, evidently, smiling.

A lifetime of smiling and no one cares for her. Can't these strangers see, Hannah's heart is broken?

How stupid could you be to imagine I'd loved you.

The scorn in his voice. The contempt.

He'd never loved her, he'd tricked and exploited her. The crudest kind of sex he'd inflicted upon her, desperate Hannah chose to interpret as *love*.

Even his gentler lovemaking, Hannah understands was pretense. Those kisses. His hands framing her face . . .

You have come to dwell in my heart, Hannah.

Yet: Even now in Zink Jewelers where *he* has sent her, to humiliate her, Hannah is thinking, But he must have meant it! Some of it.

Yes, she is sure, recalling. Y.K. had truly desired her, she had not been mistaken—surely.

Sexual desire in the male can't be faked, fraudulent. The man's intense sexual pleasure, the jolt of it, she'd witnessed, as if it were her own.

A small pulse of hope stirs, even now. For certainly Y.K. had desired her. She imagines him framing her face in his hands and assuring her gravely—*Of course I didn't mean it, darling. I was testing you.*

And her children: He has called them beautiful, he has said he wants to be their father.

Impossible for Y.K. not to love them, Hannah thinks. He seems to have no children of his own. She'd seen how he'd looked at Conor, and at Katya. As he'd looked at her, many times.

How could you doubt me, Hannah? You must know I've always loved you.

She is sure, he'd loved her more than he'd ever loved Marlene Reddick. He'd desired *her*.

If she brings the money to him, as he'd requested. He'd been hurt by the way she pulled Conor away from him at the entrance to the filthy men's restroom in the park, this will be Hannah's opportunity to make reparation. He will probably not accept the money. Ten thousand dollars is nothing to him! Just a token, a gesture. As a cornered animal will bare its throat to the predator, in the hope that the predator will not tear it out.

He will laugh at her, and kiss her, and call her darling; he will lead her to the glass-topped table by the window where a bottle of red wine awaits them. He will lead her into the other room, the bedroom—that place of reconciliation.

Mirrors, edged with zinc. On a bureau top a heavy urn meant to replicate a Grecian urn, in which copper flowers, branches have been arranged.

Yet: Hannah is terrified, her husband will be murdered.

As Christina and Harold Rusch were murdered for their money, so, too, Wes Jarrett will be murdered.

When it's the right time for me to meet your husband, that will be arranged.

With mounting unease Hannah has been watching the appraiser at the rear of the store as he examines the pearl necklace beneath intense white light. He is an older man, obese, with a blunt, hairless skull. His neck is lost in fatty folds. Tenderly he peers at the necklace through an eyeglass, his heavy face is soft with a sensuous sort of concentration. This professional appraiser will respect her, Hannah thinks.

Close by the appraiser is an antique birdcage on a pedestal, made of delicately carved wood, with much Victorian filigree. Inside are several small birds—canaries?—fluttering about. Hannah realizes that she has been hearing faint birdsong she'd assumed was music from a radio. And scurrying about the floor at the appraiser's feet, indeed clambering about his thick thighs, there is something white, fretful . . . White rats? Tame rats? Hannah stares in disbelief. But the appraiser behaves as if nothing is out of the ordinary, like the woman with the harlequin glasses who has resumed work with an adding machine.

"Mrs. Jar-rett?"—the appraiser lifts his large somber head without exactly looking at Hannah. "Come here, please."

Please. Hannah feels absurdly grateful, to be addressed so politely.

But it isn't so easy to approach the appraiser, Hannah discovers. The woman at the cashier's counter offers Hannah no assistance, she is forced to make her way around the end of the counter, and along a narrow aisle between display cases, to arrive at the appraiser's worktable at the very rear of the store. Here are open shelves heaped with tagged jewelry, a row of padlocked filing cabinets, a wall safe directly behind the appraiser.

Hannah's stumbling approach has excited the canaries—yellow-feathered, cream-colored, red-orange—which are flitting about in their filigreed cage, emitting sharp little cries. And the white rats, at least a dozen of them, beautiful sleek creatures with pink, inflamed-looking eyes and twitching noses and hairless pink tails, blink at Hannah with avid interest.

Do you recognize us? Guess!

Hannah shudders, and laughs. An eerie sensation comes over her, as of an imminent revelation, like a metal flower opening in her brain.

"Shh! Shh! Behave yourselves!"—the appraiser chides the chittering birds and the curious rats. "We have a *customer*."

Hannah is feeling hopeful. The appraiser must admire her antique necklace, she thinks; for surely not every visitor to Zink Jewelers is allowed into this private part of the store.

Close up, Hannah sees that the appraiser is an attractive man in his sixties, despite his obesity, bumpy hairless skull, and liver-spotted skin. Indeed, he reminds her of her kindly therapist Dr. T__.

His eyes are small yet silvery-luminous behind the thick lenses of his bifocals; his heavy jaws are clean-shaven, and his fingernails are unusually large, very clean. He wears a dandyish madras vest, Hannah wonders if he'd purchased it at the Eastern Market across the street. (Or, no: He has a family, one of his devoted daughters gave him the vest, as a birthday gift for a man difficult to please, for he has everything he wants, indeed more than anyone could want, from the treasure trove of Zink Jewelers Estate & Loan.) Coatless, he wears a long-sleeved white cotton dress shirt with a starched collar. His cuff links are onyx. As the appraiser examines her pearls in his oddly intimate way, drawing the necklace slowly and sensuously across his thick lips, one of the sleek white rats that has been lolling in his lap stands, placing its claws on the tabletop, and peers impishly at Hannah.

Those pink, inflamed eyes! The twitching nose, smelling *her*.

Hannah feels hairs stir at the nape of her neck, as with a curious sort of recognition; but again, the uncanny sensation fades.

At last, the appraiser touches the necklace with his tongue, that seems to Hannah unusually large, moist, a living thing.

"Oh!"—Hannah cries, involuntarily; it's as if a light electric shock has rippled through her.

"Well, my dear! Mrs. Jar-rett! You see, you have come to me very late."

"What—what do you mean?" Hannah is unnerved by the elderly man peering at her with his silvery eyes, over the tops of his bifocals.

"You have neglected these pearls, dear. You need to wear pearls often. You should know, pearls require human warmth, intimacy, to maintain their beauty. Their being. Spinoza said, 'All things desire to persist in their being.' Pearls are not diamonds, dear. If left alone, they lose heart. They lose hope. Like all of us, they become brittle and begin to die."

Hannah stands abashed, contrite. Yet, she retains a glimmer of hope, that the pearls are of some worth.

"I realize they aren't 'natural' pearls. I realize that they are only 'cultured' . . ."

The appraiser laughs at her, not unkindly. To Hannah's surprise he tells her that indeed the pearls are not cultured but natural—"But, you see, they have begun to lose their luster. They have begun to lose hope. They are at the start of their decline, like a love that has gone wrong."

Hannah is astonished: *Natural* pearls? Her grandmother had owned, and had left to her, a necklace of *natural pearls*?

"Why have you not worn these pearls more often, Mrs. Jar-rett? Did you think they were unfashionable, 'old'?"

Hannah tries to think. She has no idea. She owns so many other necklaces, so many pairs of earrings, bracelets, most of them newly purchased, stylish and expensive costume jewelry, she'd never given the antique pearls much thought.

"They are not 'chic'—'sexy.' Is that it?"

Hannah feels her face heat, embarrassed. Has the elderly gentleman actually uttered the word *sexy*? In relation to her grandmother's pearls?

He adds: "There is a small diamond clasp, too. Very tasteful."

"I—I—yes, but I wasn't sure if—the stones might not be diamonds . . ."

"Yes, they are diamonds. But very small: one-quarter carat."

Hannah is conscious of the appraiser contemplating her with an unnerving sort of familiarity, like an older relative. She is still hopeful that, if he likes her, as he seems to be liking her, he will offer a good price for the necklace.

Impulsively she asks: "Are you a friend of Y.K., Mr. Zink?"

" 'Zink'—but who is 'Mr. Zink'?"

"Aren't you—Mr. Zink?"

"No, dear. I am not. I am a longtime, faithful employee of Morris Zink—but, to be truthful, I have not seen Morris Zink in a long time. Nor have I spoken with him. He lives in Grosse Pointe, in one of those grand old lakeside estates. He owns many jewelry stores, pawnshops in Detroit and vicinity. He communicates with his employees through intermediaries—if, indeed, he is still alive. It may be a son and heir who is 'Zink' now." The appraiser pauses, nudging away a needily affectionate white rat that has been burrowing beneath his arm. "And I have never heard of—did you say '*Why-kay*'?"

"But I thought he'd called you. Y.K. I think his name is—Yaakel Keinz. Didn't he call? To say that I was coming?" Hannah tries not to sound dismayed, disappointed.

"*Did* he? I'm not familiar with the name. Yaakel Keinz?"

Doubtfully the appraiser pronounces this name, giving it a strongly foreign inflection. Hannah feels a stab of vertigo as if the sticky linoleum floor is tilting beneath her feet.

"He—he's a businessman. He comes to Detroit every few weeks on—on business . . ." Hannah's voice trails off, weakly.

"He isn't a Black Hebrew Israelite—is he?" The appraiser looks alarmed.

"He—he's American. He was born in America."

"I doubt that, my dear. They are anti-Semites, you know. They are not *Jews*."

The appraiser shakes his heavy lips, disapproving. Hannah has no idea what he is talking about.

"He—isn't *Black*. His skin color is—is—not *black* . . ."

"Of course not. Not *evidently*." Then, thoughtfully: "The name—Yaakel Keinz—is a Hebrew name, I believe. But it's likely an appropriated name. The man could be a Russian agent—a contemporary anarchist—one who *destabilizes*."

Hannah shakes her head, confused. She has no idea what the appraiser is talking about.

She has no idea who her lover is—the man whom she believes to be *her lover*.

Nor has she any idea why she is here, in this airless subterranean place, in the late morning of an overcast winter day. And only the vaguest idea where she is.

"These people are deadly, my dear. Their tactics are ruthless. They insinuate themselves into the lives of 'real' people and eviscerate them from within. These are the most insidious terrorist attacks against Americans—'white' Americans—that are not correctly identified . . ."

Seeing that Hannah is baffled, and frightened, the appraiser drops the subject.

He informs Hannah that her pearls are indeed natural South Sea pearls, not well aged, with a clasp of small diamonds.

"Seven thousand, cash."

Seven thousand! Hannah is crushed. Does this mean that the pearl necklace is only worth approximately fourteen thousand dollars?

Hannah protests: "But—if those are real pearls—"

"You have neglected them, dear. You are a shallow person, perhaps. Probably the pearls have been forgotten in a drawer, you haven't worn them in years. Then, something happens in your life, something that calls into question your life, and so you turn back for help, you 'reach' for—something that is lost to you, you'd taken for granted. Your grandmother gave you the pearls? Well, then—you see—your grandmother is lost to you. The resale value of pearls isn't great, unlike diamonds. Do you have diamonds you'd like sell? Necklace, earrings? Rings?" Sharp-eyed, the appraiser is looking frankly at Hannah's fingers.

Hannah is overwhelmed by the appraiser's words, that seem to her both kindly and chiding, intimate and accusing. She had thought the man was her friend . . .

No time to go elsewhere for a second appraisal. In her agitated state Hannah dreads driving in the city. And she doesn't dare bring jewelry to an appraiser in the Far Hills vicinity, the news might get back to someone who knows her.

Impossible to give up her rings, Hannah thinks. Wes would notice.

(*Would* Wes notice? She could sell the engagement ring, which is a sizable diamond of several carats; she could replace it, in this very store perhaps, with a zircon or even a rhinestone ring, and Wes would never notice.)

"My dear, the offer is seven thousand, cash. Take it or leave it."

Several white rats on the worktable are regarding Hannah with impertinent interest. She feels a ticklish sensation—a warm-skinned rat nips at her ankle with its sharp teeth, as if teasing. "Oh!"—Hannah kicks at it, shocked.

The appraiser laughs, but cautions: "My dear, don't provoke them: They may appear tame, and they are very charming, but they are wild creatures, and they can *bite*."

Hannah examines her ankle: There is a tiny run in the sheer nylon stocking but her skin doesn't appear to be broken.

"Seven thousand, dear. But in two minutes, it will be six thousand."

Hannah means to say vehemently *No thank you*. Instead, she hears herself say *Yes*.

"Yes?—to seven thousand, cash?"

"Y-yes."

It is unnaturally warm in the cave-like interior, though neither the appraiser nor the woman with the harlequin glasses seems to notice. As if somewhere close by there is a beating heart, the heat of a furnace . . .

"Very sensible, dear. For one who has neglected a treasure."

Hannah rubs ruefully at her ankle, which has begun to itch. Alert and avid the pink-eyed white rats regard her as if they fear retaliation from her.

Even as the corpulent appraiser turns in his swivel chair to open the wall safe, to count out cash for Hannah, she hears herself protest— "Wait: *no*."

She has changed her mind, she tells him. This is all a mistake.

Suddenly desperate to get the necklace back as she'd been desperate to run after Y.K. and Conor, seize Conor's hand and reclaim him, at the entrance to the men's restroom in the park.

The appraiser isn't so incensed as Y.K. had been but he isn't amused.

But he is a gentleman: "Are you sure, dear? If you walk out of here with the necklace, then change your mind and return, the price will have dropped by fifteen hundred dollars."

He is laughing at her, Hannah thinks. She all but snatches the necklace from the appraiser's hands, slips it into her handbag. She has lost or forgotten the little cloth bag, left on the cashier's counter.

"Let me out, please. Unlock the door, please. *Let me out*."

Hannah makes her way with some difficulty to the front of the cluttered store. Barely she can see daylight through the barred front window overlooking Gratiot Avenue.

Frantically, Hannah pushes at the door. It is locked, unmovable, and then, with a *click!* unlocked, presumably by the woman in the harlequin glasses.

Ah, out on the street!—wide windswept Gratiot Avenue where the air has turned cold, hostile, with a mineral smell. A faint white sun glowers like a barely throbbing heart.

"For Sale"

Slowly like a woman in a dream from which she is in terror of waking Hannah drives home to Far Hills on the John C. Lodge Expressway.

Slowly, for wind from the river shakes the gleaming-white sedan.

Slowly in the right-hand lane, for Hannah is very tired.

Death rattling the windows of the sedan. But canny Hannah has locked all the doors . . .

Slowly and painstakingly for she must calculate how to live the rest of her life.

I am sorry, I could not sell my grandmother's pearls. I don't have the money to give you.

Please forgive me! Please don't punish me for loving you.

Like rushing water vehicles swing out to pass the white sedan in a turbulent stream. Drivers sound their horns, annoyed at Hannah's slow speed.

I am a wounded person, please don't wound me further.

Distracted by rushing thoughts. But grateful, she didn't sell her grandmother's pearls.

Natural pearls! South Sea pearls. Hannah is ashamed, she'd undervalued the gift from her grandmother, whom she had not loved enough.

Too young, too self-absorbed at the time, to realize.

She will withdraw nine thousand, nine hundred dollars from the Far Hills bank, she will provide the final hundred herself, out of her wallet. Too risky, to withdraw nine thousand, nine hundred and ninety-nine dollars, not a good idea.

Except: She will have to ask for the money in cash, in large denominations: one-hundred-dollar bills.

No choice, otherwise Y.K. will destroy her.

(But will the bank allow such a large withdrawal from a joint account? Will they call Wes even as Hannah stands foolishly waiting at the teller's window?)

Futile to beg the man for mercy. Indeed Y.K. is a terrorist, he has laughed at Hannah's distress.

Hannah is approaching Eight Mile Road, Detroit city limits. Approximately halfway to Far Hills. A wave of despair engulfs her, she has no idea what she will do to save herself, and the children.

Suicide. A solace.

But no: Kill him.

Helpless at the thought. Hannah cannot kill another person, Hannah cannot even kill herself.

An accidental death, on the expressway.

No one to blame, she is innocent.

A strong gust of wind shakes the car. Easily Hannah could lose control of the car, slam into a concrete wall . . .

But no, this doesn't happen. Hannah maintains control driving (slowly) in the right-hand lane like an invalid.

Her punishment is: continuing. As herself.

Suddenly she worries: Has she left the pearl necklace behind? She isn't sure.

Had she taken the necklace from the appraiser, had she slipped it into her handbag? Try as she will, Hannah cannot remember.

Her ankle itches, a stinging sensation. *That* she recalls, the damned white rat nipping at her with its sharp teeth.

"Oh, God. No."

She has left the pearl necklace behind—her grandmother's necklace. She is stricken with a sick, sinking sensation.

If she returns now to Zink Jewelers, if she has left the necklace there, if she changes her mind another time, to sell the necklace—how low will the price have dropped?

Braking the car to a jolting stop on the shoulder of the highway. A dangerous move, reckless, Hannah hasn't thought to signal. Vehicles rush past her irritably sounding their horns.

Hannah is scarcely aware. She is desperate suddenly. She has lost all clarity of mind. Her memory has shattered like a mirror. Rummaging through her handbag, cannot find the pearls, turns the damned handbag upside down so that its contents fall onto the passenger seat—wallet, tissues, comb, small hairbrush, ticket stubs, ballpoint pen, lipstick tube that falls onto the floor and rolls beneath the seat . . . Hannah lifts the handbag to stare into it, her eyes fill with tears of frustration, grief; she has lost the precious pearls after all, or they have been stolen from her. Shaking the handbag harder until at last the necklace falls out, for of course it has been there all along.

Careless of her to have simply shoved the necklace into her handbag, loose! A necklace worth thousands of dollars, given to Hannah by the only person who'd ever loved her, whom Hannah has virtually forgotten.

The appraiser had seen into Hannah's soul, as Dr. T__ had seen into her soul: *shallow.* She writhes with shame, recalling.

But here, here is the necklace! Not warm pearls but icy cold. What relief!

Recalling how the appraiser dared to draw the pearls across his thick lips, licking them with his immense tongue.

At least, Hannah's panic has subsided. A retreating tide drawing Hannah's strength away with it, she can barely keep her eyes open.

So tired! Exhausted. As if a narcotic has swept over her.

Fumbles to return most of the items, including the pearls, to the handbag, sinking then into a dazed sleep behind the wheel of the car cradling the handbag in her arms like an infant.

. . .

"Ma'am!"—a sharp rapping at the window beside Hannah's head.

Her head has been lolling on her shoulders, her mouth has drooped open. A strand of saliva on her chin.

Embarrassed, Hannah is wakened at once. A uniformed Detroit police officer is rapping on her window, ordering her to lower it.

Hannah complies, hurriedly. The officer asks, Is she ill? Has she been asleep? He frowns at her. He is not charmed by her. He glances into the rear of the car, as if someone might be hiding there. Dark glasses shield much of his hard-boned face, Hannah cannot see his eyes.

Hannah apologizes: She was overcome by fatigue, she has not been well lately, she has not been sleeping lately, she thought it would be wisest to pull over to the side of the freeway instead of falling asleep while driving.

A sensible explanation but the officer remains unconvinced. He might be a decade younger than Hannah, which is disconcerting; she is dismayed that he asks to see her driver's license and registration. "Have you been drinking, ma'am?"—his voice is barely civil.

Hannah insists, *no*. And this is true, Hannah has not been drinking, there is no trace of alcohol on her breath, this is her salvation.

"Have you been using a controlled substance?"

"A—what? No. I have not."

Thinking guiltily that possibly yes, there may be some trace of barbiturate in her bloodstream, but certainly not enough to affect her behavior so many hours later. And it's a prescription drug, she can prove it's legal . . .

The police officer examines the laminated card that is Hannah's driver's license, glancing from the miniature photograph to Hannah's strained face, and back again, with a look of—can it be suspicion? Pity?

Hannah laughs nervously: "I've been under a strain lately, I don't look like myself . . ."

"Are you in a condition to drive? Should I be calling 911?"

"No—no! I mean yes, I am in a condition to drive . . ."

"Did you faint? Are you short of breath? Can you breathe?"

"Of course I can breathe! I was sleepy but I am totally awake now and I am perfectly capable of driving the rest of the way home." Hannah is becoming incensed, indignant as the police officer scrutinizes the automobile registration. "Did I violate a law, officer? Is it against the law if, if you are driving your car and feeling very tired suddenly . . ."

Hannah worries that the police officer will search her car and find something incriminating of which she is totally unaware. He will search her handbag and discover the pearl necklace loose inside as if she'd shoplifted it . . .

Instead the officer makes a cursory examination of the cushiony backseat of the Buick which contains a child's safety seat and a few innocuous children's items like mittens, a jacket. Suddenly uninterested in Hannah, bored by the suburban mom, he doesn't trouble to search the trunk.

"Okay, ma'am. Stay awake and drive carefully."

Chastened, Hannah waits until the patrol car drives away, then eases out, warily, onto the expressway. Her heart is beating hard as if she has had a narrow escape.

If she'd been carrying Wes's revolver, what then! And *if* the police officer had demanded to see her handbag.

Back on the expressway Hannah notices that traffic has increased. Is this rush-hour traffic? It appears to be later in the day than Hannah would have expected. How long did she sleep? Has it been—*hours*?

The sun has begun to slant in the wintry sky, droplets of freezing rain have begun to strike her windshield, like spit.

Trying to see her wristwatch. Must be four at least.

The children will be home from school. Ismelda has picked them up. Safe at home. Afternoon naps.

Hannah is driving slowly, like one who has been wounded.

The police officer had not been interested in her. Not even mildly, as men have nearly always been interested in Hannah. Or perhaps he'd resented her.

The Far Hills address might have annoyed him. That Hannah had not smiled submissively to him might have annoyed him.

Though probably yes, without knowing it Hannah had smiled at the man.

For her face ached. Her mouth.

Please have mercy on me. Forgive me.

She'd begged Y.K. to forgive her. To not ruin her life.

To not ruin the lives of her children, who are innocent of their mother's adulterous deceit. To not murder her husband.

Though it seems likely, Hannah thinks. Inevitable: Wes will die.

First Wes, and then Hannah. If/when she and Y.K. are married. For it seems certain, they will be married if that is Y.K.'s wish.

Like Marlene Reddick, Hannah will *disappear*.

Has Hannah been with Y.K. this afternoon in his hotel suite? She seems to recall ascending in the glass cubicle of an elevator.

Her body aches from the man's punishing hands, the brute hungry mouth.

Her body is heavy with sorrow. Her body is weeping.

Bleeding from between her legs, where he'd hurt her with his fingers jammed up inside her.

Semen draining from her wounded vagina is cold, clotted like venom.

Did you not know? Semen is a kind of venom.

Hannah is feeling very strange. Sleeping behind the wheel of her car, head lolling on her shoulders, has left a crick in her neck, blurred vision. She feels as if someone has been slapping, pummeling her. The more she has cried out in pain, the more pain is directed at her. Her skin is becoming feverish. Her right ankle itches and stings as virulent microorganisms swarm into her bloodstream.

But she is headed home. After so long away. She could weep with joy at the prospect.

Grim November has vanished, already it is December. Already, Christmas carols are being played in stores and public places. In the glass cube of an elevator at the Renaissance Grand Hotel, a high-pitched tinkling rendition of "Jingle Bells." The holiday season will be a time of healing, reparation in the Jarrett household.

When Wes comes home in time for dinner, of course Hannah eats dinner with Wes. But when Wes is away, Hannah eats an early dinner with the children. And even when Wes is expected home, Hannah often sits at the table with the children, sipping a glass of wine.

This is pleasure: joining the children at their evening meal.

Unspeakable pleasure, Hannah will remember in the next life: joining the children at their evening meal, hearing them chatter about their day at school.

Virtually nothing of childish prattle can be remembered even a few hours afterward and yet: nothing is more precious to Mommy, than her children's prattle.

Perishable, and fading. Oh God help Hannah!

Mommy and Ismelda, preparing the meal in the kitchen. She sees them at a little distance, through the window of the kitchen door perhaps. Meatloaf is a favorite of the children: high-quality ground beef baked in the oven at 375 degrees. Heaped with ketchup that acquires a delicious crust when baked.

Hannah feels her mouth water, it has been a very long time since she has eaten.

Already nearing dusk. This day has passed with unnatural slowness, and then swiftness. Barely can Hannah recall trying to find a parking place on wide windswept Gratiot Avenue. The Buick Riviera is an absurdly large vehicle, so much less practical than the economy Ford Pinto.

The locked door, the jarring sound of the buzzer unlocking the door. Her name uttered out of the cave-like gloom: *Mrs. Jar-rett . . .*

Is it a consolation, your name is known? Your name has been recorded.

Beside the highway lights are beginning to come on. Headlights of oncoming traffic.

She is driving slowly. With caution. Her head feels bulky as if too many odd-sized thoughts have crowded inside it. Like the cluttered show window of Zink Jewelers where even beautiful jewelry resembles cheap baubles.

A throbbing in her ankle, where the fragile nylon stocking has been torn. A throbbing between her legs, where the fragile membrane has been torn.

He'd shoved his fingers into her. As a parting gesture.

"You like this"—he'd made her scream, in loathing of her screaming.

Driving on Ashtree Lane, a right turn onto Cradle Rock Road. Far Hills is a labyrinth of residential neighborhoods, many trees left intact, it is easy to become lost in its interiors. Even when Hannah is routed onto a detour she doesn't lose her way, her sense of direction. In another minute she is routed back onto Cradle Rock Road.

Badly she'd wanted to speak with Jill Hayden, to warn her. Or—badly she'd hoped that Jill Hayden could warn *her.*

Friends, at one time. Sister-friends. Hannah's heart aches, she so yearns for her *sister-friend.*

Then realizing, she is already home. So quickly.

But here is something strange: a FOR SALE sign on the front lawn. What is this?

And the house is unlighted. Every window darkened. Which is not possible because Ismelda and the children are certainly home.

Several downstairs rooms would be lighted. The kitchen, the TV room.

But a FOR SALE sign! This is surely a mistake.

(Has Wes put the property on the market without telling Hannah? Is that allowed? So far as Hannah knows, she is a co-owner of the property at 96 Cradle Rock Road.)

More in wonderment than in alarm Hannah turns the Buick sedan into the driveway. The setting is both familiar to her and not familiar. The freezing rain has become bits of ice, the front lawn is covered in frost. Delicate grass stubble, that looks as if it would break underfoot, like glass.

Here is another wrong thing: Hannah left the garage door open that morning when she'd left home but someone has shut it in the interval. Hannah can use the remote control to open the overhead door but the gadget, empowered by a battery, never works for her and so Wes will chide her, laugh at her: "Like this, Hannah!"—taking the remote from her and demonstrating how easy it is as the garage door rumbles up, or down.

In any case, Hannah can't locate the damned remote control. It isn't in its usual place in the pocket beside the driver's seat.

It must have been Ismelda who'd closed the garage door. Hoping to placate Wes, so often annoyed when Hannah has left the door open.

But it would be most unusual for Ismelda to shut the garage door when her employer Mrs. Jarrett isn't home (yet). Indeed, it would be impertinent for Ismelda to do such a thing.

The wind has ceased, even at the treetops. Everything has become very still.

Hannah feels a twinge of hope—*If time has stopped, too. I won't be left behind.*

Though she can see clearly that the house is darkened, and no one appears to be in the kitchen, still Hannah approaches the side entrance to the house, which leads into the kitchen, intending to unlock the door if the door is locked, but when she tries to insert her key into the lock, she cannot.

Hannah tries, tries again. The familiar key will not even fit into the lock.

"Hello? Ismelda? Where are you?"—she raps against the door.

Are they all at the rear of the house? Or—upstairs? The children are napping!—that is the explanation.

Hannah is beginning to be upset even as a part of her mind detaches coolly—*This is ridiculous, this is not happening. There is an obvious explanation.*

Has Wes discovered her affair with Y.K. and changed the locks on the doors?

Hannah tries to look through the window of the kitchen door but everything inside is dim, blurred.

She rings the doorbell. She knocks on the door. She is perspiring badly now inside the rumpled cashmere coat. The Dior silk scarf has slipped from her head and is lost. How is it possible, she'd left this house only a few hours ago and now it appears to be empty . . .

She will try the front door, which is rarely used. Visitors to the house who are not close friends will knock at the front door; others will enter by the side door into the bright homey kitchen.

Hannah's heels sink into the crusted gritty snow as she crosses the front lawn. She rings the doorbell at the front door, knocks on the heavy oak door until her knuckles ache. She peers through the narrow vertical windows beside the front door but can see nothing inside.

"Ismelda? This is Hannah—Mrs. Jarrett . . . Where are you? What is happening? Let me in."

No response. Silence inside. Hannah stands irresolute, beginning to cry, helplessly.

Should she break a window? But the alarm will go off . . .

Wes has done this, Hannah thinks wildly. Wes has stolen the house from her. The children. Of course: the (shrewd) husband has outmaneuvered the (trusting) wife.

Hadn't Y.K. warned Hannah: Don't let your husband know about us. Don't allow him to make the first step. Don't allow him to strike the first blow.

A husband can be a vengeful adversary.

On the front stoop of the darkened house Hannah stands unmoving as if paralyzed. Not knowing what to do or even what to think when she happens to see headlights approaching on the roadway, a neighbor returning home at dusk.

Houses on Cradle Rock Road are set apart from one another on three-acre lots and strategically built so that it's possible to look out all of the windows in the Jarretts' house without seeing a neighboring house. It's possible to be neighbors for years without knowing neighbors' names or what they look like.

As the neighbor stops his car to retrieve mail from the mailbox Hannah hurries across the front lawn to speak with him.

"Excuse me? Hello? I—I live here . . . I think you know me." But seeing that the man, a stranger, is staring at Hannah quizzically, without evident recognition, Hannah says, trying to keep her voice calm, "What has happened to the family who lives in this house, do you know? I see it's for sale."

The neighbor, middle-aged, polite, courteous, hair trimmed as short as Wes's hair, tells Hannah that, yes, the house is for sale, it's been for sale for a while: "I think the family moved away—a father and two young children."

"Moved away—where? What about the mother?"

"No mother. I think—people said—she'd disappeared."

" 'Disappeared'! But—where?"

The neighbor has removed his mail from the mailbox and shuts the box, thoughtfully. It's clear that he has no idea who Hannah is but is determined to be polite before climbing back into his car and driving up the driveway to his house.

"Now that I think of it, there was a nanny, too—with the father and children. From Guatemala, or the Philippines—one of those places. Our housekeeper might know her name."

"Bless Me, Father"

B *less me, Father. For I have sinned.*

No joke. He's in need of a priest. In need of confession. On his knees before his heart bursts, he dies like a dog, and goes to Hell.

Still feeling hurt, like shit, the woman hadn't reached out to him when he'd needed her.

Delivering flowers to her you'd think she'd think it was something special. *He* was something special. Can't just pretend there isn't some kind of *report* there. As people call *report*—a special connection.

He'd helped her when she was helpless, drove her home from the hotel in her own car when Hawkeye couldn't wait to get rid of her. Christ, he'd seen Mrs. J__ naked sprawled on her back like a slut. Seen her like nobody in her family has seen her. But he's forgiven that.

Mrs. J__ is a victim of Hawkeye like many others. *Trust* is the bait the coldhearted bastard catches them with.

The other time he'd arrived at her fancy house, no warning, she'd been a little surprised at first—(the look on her face!)—but let him inside and didn't call the cops, fed him a fantastic meal and gave him wine. *And drank with him.*

She'd cared for him. *She'd loved him.*

So he'd thought. But next time, delivering the Goddamned flowers, she hadn't seemed to know him. Looking at him like—like . . . he was *nobody to her.* Some asshole *delivery boy* delivering fucking flowers in a fucking wicker basket.

He'd killed a man! Christ.

That changed you forever in your heart.

Of course, Mikhail looks very different from Ponytail. He thinks so. She'd been shocked at the change in him. Sexy platinum-blond punk hair, like nobody in fucking Far Hills. That look on her face when she realized it wasn't Sid Vicious, it was *him*.

Driving south on Woodward after he'd delivered the flowers to her house. Heart racing like crazy.

He'd saved a kid *and* he'd killed a man. He'd saved the kid from the pervert he'd later killed.

If she knew. She'd be scared as hell of him but she'd respect him.

How's he going to tell her? He'd never hurt *her*.

Lies awake at night trying to think.

No more Ponytail, he'd cut off the hair. No more Mikey. They were losers, he's Mikhail now, sexy-cool. Mrs. J__ registered this, her eyes running over him like liquid.

If the maid hadn't been at the house. If Mrs. J__ had opened the door herself.

Oh. God. Is it you—Mikey?

Things would've gone differently, Mikhail smiles to think.

High on coke: Nostrils feel like parchment. Hot dry wires running up his nose into his brain. Terrific sensation but there's a trickle of something, inside the nostrils, feels like it starts far up inside the skull. Wipes his nose with the edge of his hand, comes away bright arterial blood.

That day after delivering the flowers he'd returned to Detroit driving south on Woodward. Sure it meant he had to stop for every fucking light but it spared him driving fast on the freeway in his nerved-up state. Good to avoid truckers driving eighteen-wheel rigs who'd fuck with a blond-punk kid in a Firebird hoping to scare the shit out of him and maybe succeed.

Which meant passing Saint Vincent's. The church and the Mission. Weathered red brick like streaked tears.

When it came so strong to him, he *had to* confess to a priest.

Could've been any priest anywhere in Detroit. Any priest who didn't know him. That was the special thing about the confessional, you just waited your turn, you went *in*.

Like, it wasn't *you* exactly. And it wasn't the priest, as a person.

But Mikhail knew, the priest would call the cops on him. Listen to the confession and pretend he could keep the secret but as soon as he could, the fucker would call the cops.

Must happen all the time. Lots of murders in Murder City, Detroit.

But (he's thinking) Father McKenzie would take pity on him.

Father McKenzie is his friend, he'd never betray him.

Also, Father McKenzie would be impressed with the sexy-punk look.

"Bless me, Father. For I have sinned"—Mikhail practices saying the words out loud, he has not said in a long time.

And in his velvety-soft voice, the voice of the confessional where you felt the other's nearness but could not see the other's face and so were spared shame, Father McKenzie would say, "And how long has it been since your last confession, my son?"

Thinking he might say *no*.

Except: You don't say *no* to Hawkeye.

Telling Mikhail he wants him at the hotel, in the suite, when the woman arrives with the first installment of what will be an endless succession of installments. Ten thousand to begin, but only to begin.

Hawkeye says she'd be selling some jewelry. He'd warned her not to withdraw ten thousand from a bank, the bank would have to report it to the feds. He's hoping to hell she actually listened.

Gravely Mikhail hears this. Never makes any comment, to anything Hawkeye tells him.

He's uneasy, Hawkeye confides in him so much more now than he had. And he's paying him more. Before he'd sent Mikhail out to expedite Bernard Rusch.

That is all over with, at least. Hawkeye never speaks of Rusch. News in the paper and on TV but Hawkeye isn't interested. Fuck he gives fuck all what's local news got to do with *him*?

Mikhail follows enough of it to see that police believe Rusch had killed himself, and that Rusch was Babysitter. So people are thinking—*The monster is dead.*

The consensus seems to be, Rusch killed his parents and the housekeeper.

Still there's people who think it was a "mob hit"—nothing to do with Bernard Rusch at all.

Mikhail wonders what Father McKenzie thinks about all this.

If Hawkeye has confided anything in him, considering their old connection.

"You'll stay in the back, in the bedroom," Hawkeye tells Mikhail, "you won't see the woman and she won't see you unless something goes wrong. If she has a breakdown like last time. Becomes hysterical, requires restraint."

So, there's the possibility, Mikhail might have to drive her home again, like the other time. Jesus!

"We want to keep her alive. Functioning. There's a lot invested in her, and there's the husband plus his family."

Laughing at the look on Mikhail's face, a kind of sick-excited look like a dog gazing at slabs of fresh bloody meat he's going to devour like crazy though (the dog knows) it's going to make him puke out his guts.

Joking: "At least you know where the cunt lives. No trouble finding her house."

Mikhail winces, tries to laugh. Not funny.

Hawkeye is *not funny*.

In Hawkeye's heart, *evil*.

"We might be married. Soon. If the way is cleared. I'll need you to do some expediting for that, too."

Only way Mikhail can do it, is *high*.

High like a kite, jittery waiting for Father McKenzie. Late afternoon, Friday, Saint Vincent's.

Actually there are two priests hearing confessions. Mikhail waits for Father McKenzie to be free.

"I am guilty of a mortal sin, Father."

Mikhail is hoarse, barely audible. Through the grating the priest listens with grave bowed head.

". . . killed a man, Father. I shot him dead. I—I shot him in the head . . ."

But Father McKenzie is hard of hearing now. Cups his hand to his ear, leans closer to the grating. Heavier than Mikhail recalls, and his face, once smooth-shaven and handsome like some old-time movie star, is ruddy, beefy.

Must be in his sixties. Overnight, *old*.

"My son, speak more clearly."

Speak *clearly*? Jesus!—there are people in nearby pews, waiting to enter the confessional. Obviously Father McKenzie hasn't heard a word Mikhail has said or, with the glaring platinum hair, hasn't recognized him through the grating.

Mikhail presses his mouth against the grating. Tries again, hoarse pleading voice like he's being strangled: "I—I killed a man, Father. You remember—Mister R__ . . ."

"Eh? What? Miser Earl—?"

Still the priest leans his head toward the grating, awkwardly. Grown so stout, he pants with the effort. A fold of flesh creases against turned-around white starched collar.

Mikhail is furious suddenly.

"He was your friend, Father. You remember: Mister R__. He had money. He brought you a bottle of Irish whiskey, we all drank it."

Mikhail's voice is louder, raw. Surely he has been heard by penitents in nearby pews and possibly by Father McKenzie who has frozen in his stooped posture, silent as if stunned.

Mikhail is remembering one of the boys telling how "Father Mac" made a sobbing sound when he came, like a rabbit being strangled. How disgusting it was. How you wanted to puke. How you *did* puke.

He'd been Mikey then, all this was news to him. "Father Mac" had never touched *him*.

Hiding his face in a boy's neck until it was very hot, damp from his panting, uncomfortable as hell. End up embarrassed for the priest, losing all his dignity as he did.

A *priest*! Christ.

Mikhail isn't remembering this, exactly. More like fragments of something broken he sees on the sidewalk, kicks around, it starts to form a picture.

Thinking, you're just a kid you don't know how to interpret adults who laugh in a high-pitched giggle. You expect an adult not to show such emotions.

A priest, in his priest's black clothing. Nothing like it—the long black cassock to the ankles . . . Watching Father McKenzie walk across the pavement, from the church to the residence hall. Watching him stride along the corridor—a *man*.

Remembering now, Mikhail feels like he's been punched in the gut. Could sob like hell, he has lost so much in his young life he will never regain.

He'd loved him. Christ! Might as well admit it.

On the other side of the grating Father McKenzie is breathing quickly, audibly like one who has been running clumsily. Squinting through the mesh at Mikhail, alarming to the penitent because it is not priestly protocol.

And the eyeballs glistening, as eyes never do in the confession.

Mikey! My God! Is that you! What have you done! You . . .

Mikhail whispers *I didn't mean to, Father! I was made to do it, I didn't have any choice.*

Like a guilty child. Fighting back tears.

What do you mean, you didn't have any choice? What—what are you saying?

He *made me do it. You know* . . .

Mikhail can't think of the name. Any name. He'd never called the man "Hawkeye" to Father McKenzie . . .

My son, you must come and see me. You have sinned, grievously. This is a terrible thing.

He has never seen the priest so shaken. Never heard him speaking in so halting and hushed a voice.

Can't take this. No more. Mikhail stumbles out of the confessional, blinking wildly.

In fucking *church*? This is where he is? In nearby pews strangers are waiting to take his place in the confessional, staring frankly at him.

Punk-blond boy with a blazing face, eyes like reflectors. Heart hammering so hard he has to press the heel of his hand against it.

Christ, he's left the door to the fucking confessional swinging open. Another thing you don't do.

At least, Father McKenzie hasn't hurriedly exited the confessional, he has remained inside. He isn't so alarmed that he is following Mikhail, which Mikhail wants to think is a good sign.

Outside in the wintry air Mikhail starts to feel calmer. It was a crazy thing to have risked, confessing to Father McKenzie like he had but hell: maybe the old man hadn't heard him so clearly, and wouldn't report him.

Like hell he's going to see Father McKenzie. No more of this shit! Best idea is to return to West Warren and crash. In his stash there's some barbiturates, put him out like a light.

Only if McKenzie calls Hawkeye, Mikhail is in trouble.

Sure, McKenzie will call him. You've made a mistake, asshole.

One fucking mistake after another, asshole. Jesus!

Hadn't been absolved of his sins, the confession is null and void.

The priest could hear his confession in private. That was a thing you could do.

He can still be forgiven for his sins, in the priest's private residence.

Or maybe murder the fucking old priest pervert like he should've done ten years ago.

My poor sweet boy, you have suffered.

Once they're alone together it rushes back to him: the room, the smell(s) of the room.

Venetian blind drawn shut over the window, heavy velvet drapery. Heavy mahogany furnishings. Carved ivory crucifix above the bed, ivory holy water font just inside the doorway.

Obstreperous. A bad boy. Must be punished.

Whiskey?—they will need it.

In smudged cut-glass tumblers, sweet amber liquid from a bottle kept in Father McKenzie's cabinet.

Mikhail remembers the unpronounceable name—*Laphroaig.* Never saw it anywhere else. *Select Single Malt. Scotch Whiskey.*

Muted light in the priest's bedroom. Pale beige lampshade, Father Mac would wrap a rose-colored light-woolen scarf around it. Mikhail remembers.

Rosy cast on all things. Narrow dead-white face, sexy stubbled jaw. Sure Mac could be sharp-tongued, cruel, but tender, too. And funny. *My obstreperous boy, how will you be punished?*

Depending on Father's mood, you didn't want to test him.

But then, you didn't want to test any priest. Any adult. *Adult* was a foreign country, a different language spoken there.

Kneeling on the carpet together. On the same side of the bed, shoulders touching.

How lean and handsome the priest was. And *young*—to be director of the Mission.

The old fags, in a flurry like hens flapping their wings. Saying how Father McKenzie looked like Clark Gable, did Mikey know who that was?

No. Yes. Some Hollywood actor, who knows. Who gives a shit this isn't some long-ago time this is now: 1977.

But now, it's fucked up. Not only is Father Mac *old*, not only is his hair thin and gray and he's gained twenty pounds around the middle, there's something wrong with him, a tremor in his left hand he's trying to hide so that Mikhail doesn't notice. Christ!

It comes back to Mikhail, someone he'd run into the other day on Cass told him that "Father Mac" had Parkinson's.

Parkinson's?—what the fuck is that?

Some kind of paralysis like polio. Like, he'll end up in a wheelchair.

Mikhail just laughed, this was too ridiculous. "Father Mac" wasn't the type for any fucking wheelchair.

Kneeling beside him now pretending not to notice the tremor. Shut his eyes. Like years ago, he's feeling an urge to murder the priest but at the same time to break down and cry in Mac's arms.

A priest's arms, in those dark priest sleeves, would give so much comfort . . . The surprise was, Father Mac was kind of lean yet his arms were ropey-muscled, strong. For a priest wearing a black skirt, weird how strong he was, or could become.

All right, son. Tell me what you did or think you did.

It wasn't what he'd *done*! Mikhail tries to explain.

What he'd been forced to do . . .

Noting how Father McKenzie doesn't ask *Forced to by who?*

Mikhail is breathing hard, can't catch his breath. The priest lays one of his hands on his.

Son, it's a terrible thing. Whatever it is. But it can't be undone by tears, you know.

That velvety voice, Mikhail recalls. If he shuts his eyes Father

McKenzie is his old self, you could expect a nice surprise, reward afterward. If you didn't ask for one.

Mikhail wonders if priests don't wear cassocks any longer. Maybe it's like the Latin mass, Mikhail doesn't actually remember but you heard about it from (older) people who'd missed it.

Father McKenzie has just come from hearing confessions over at the church but seems to be wearing just black trousers, a black shirt that fits his thickened abdomen tightly, not a cassock he'd be wearing for mass. Starched white collar. And the shiny black leather shoes, he'd used to shine for the priests, Mikey Kushel had been absurdly proud to be singled out for such an intimate task.

They'd give him the Black Cat shoeshine polish, the brushes. Set the shoes out for Mikey who was left (he remembers now, with a smirk) with black polish on his hands and under his nails, he'd had a hell of a time scrubbing off.

Wondering: Does Father McKenzie remember, too? That soft-cracking sound in his voice.

Nothing can be undone by tears, son. Tears are but self-pity.

Our savior on the cross, son. *He* didn't indulge in self-pity.

He'd looked like a movie star once but not now. Beneath his eyes the skin is creased and worn, tufts of hair grow in his ears and nostrils and the nostrils look wider like you could peer right inside his head. And that smell—a kind of old-man smell, deodorant that has sweated, and dried, and sweated again. And bedclothes, needing changing.

At least, the bed is decently made-up. Mikhail remembers that. The room is neat. Maroon velvet drapes drawn over the venetian blinds, somber, dark clothing hanging in the closet and shoes neatly arranged in a shoe bag attached to the back of the closet door. Because Father Mac had more pairs of shoes, better-quality shoes, than the other priests. Because (it was said) the McKenzie family had money.

A mirror, reflecting the crucifix as in a blaze of light extinguishing other objects. Carved ivory, glowed in the dim rosy light. Carved molding at the ceiling, oyster-white. Like some kind of halo.

There was a housekeeper for the residence, Mikhail wonders if it's the same one—Mrs. Laskey. Polish? Couldn't speak English but adored the priests and Father McKenzie the most.

They all adored Father Mac. They all feared Father Mac.

Mikhail swallows the fancy Scotch whiskey out of a tumbler needing to be washed. All this is flooding his brain.

Yes, he'd shot Mister R__. In the head, in the brain. Not his idea he'd been scared shitless.

He had given him a gun to use. Left it behind, the police would think the fucker killed himself.

Father McKenzie listens gravely. Mikhail would recall his surprise, that Father McKenzie was not so very surprised. Head bowed, fatty crease in his neck over the collar, offensive to Mikhail's eyes who wants to remember the priest as he'd been, not as he is. Father Mac gripping a glass, sweet-smelling amber liquid.

Mikhail will remember: Father Mac isn't asking him who'd sent him to shoot Mister R__ in the brain.

Nor asking him why Mister R__ had to be killed.

What Father McKenzie does pay heed to, Mikhail's bleached-blond hair, punk-style bristles. Sexier than the fucking ponytail, for sure.

And Mikhail informs him: He's not *Mikey* anymore, his name is *Mikhail.*

The priest is quiet. Thinking it over the way he holds the whiskey in his mouth for a beat, two beats, before swallowing it. The priest brain is like a sieve, some things shake through, of no consequence. Other things remain that are of consequence.

Mikhail sees the sidelong appraising look, familiar to him, too.

Feeling a sexual charge, in the groin. That sidelong look of an adult in a white clerical collar . . .

Mikhail explains: He'd had to cut his hair and get it bleached. He'd had to change his look. His name.

In case he was observed. On some surveillance tape.

Well, says Father McKenzie, sighing.

Mikhail waits for the priest to continue but that's all: Well.

Then, laying his hand on Mikhail's clenched hand. After a swallow of whiskey: My son, I am praying for both of us. And for Bernard. May God forgive him.

Him!—that fucker. Don't pray for *him,* Father.

Mikhail is hurt, aggrieved. An old stab of jealousy, he'd never outgrown.

In a raw young voice telling the priest: What I should have done is kill the bastard a lot earlier. The fucker. You should've sent me. I'd have done it for you, Father. After Michel. Why didn't you send me!

My son, no. Don't look back.

The whiskey has warmed both men. Glowing sensation, like the sun waning in the sky. Out on Woodward, late-afternoon traffic. Like a river, lulling. Maybe a nap: in Father Mac's arms. Christ he'd like that, so tired.

Father Mac does this thing he'd do sometimes, covers his face with his hands like his praying is so fierce it hurts. Mikhail can see just his lips finely shaped like a woman's lips moving.

God forgive us our sins. God we are in Your service. God instruct us. God we are empty vessels in Your hand. Amen.

Something is being lifted out of Mikhail's arms, a burden taken from him like a boulder so heavy it was breaking his spine.

Oh God: This is pleasure. Like those first strokes of a man's fingers, on his groin. Through his pants. He'd wanted to push the fingers away, he did push away, you did but then you didn't, or it was a later time and you'd been drinking the fancy whiskey, it was something that just happened and not your fault, God would understand.

That's how it is, Father McKenzie had told him, years ago. Nothing else matters in life, that's all that life is—who comes along . . .

Still it's a surprise, Mikhail has to smile, the priest has no more questions for him. As if possibly, Father McKenzie already knows as much as he needs to know about Mister R___ from another source.

Him, too?—should I kill *him*?

This question hovers in the air, unanswered. Father McKenzie doesn't have to ask who Mikhail means by *him.*

He doesn't say *yes,* but he doesn't say *no.*

Mikhail thinks—If I had permission to kill Mister R___, I will have permission to kill Hawkeye.

In the hotel suite, tomorrow. He will! Before Mrs. J__ arrives with the money.

With the money, or without. Let Mrs. J__ ring the doorbell, no one will answer.

She will go away, if there's no answer. Like a sleepwalker, stunned. Not a clue what has happened. Won't report to the front desk.

If Mikhail has permission and it seems maybe he does. How'd he do it? Crack the skull with something heavy, that urn in the hotel bedroom. Not a knife, too messy. Blood might soak through the carpet, leak through the floor, drip down through the ceiling of the room below.

Easily he can do it, come up quiet behind Hawkeye. Wait until the fucker is on the phone. Bring the urn down hard, crack the skull in an instant and the coldhearted bastard will fall like dead weight. Not even a cry.

This is pleasure: doing what you can do, why you were born. To save the innocent.

Mikhail tries to stand, his knees are weak. His face is streaked with tears, he's been crying like a little kid without realizing.

Meant to leave by now but instead he has climbed onto the bed as Father Mac has encouraged. Those pillows, he remembers—goose feathers—tight-packed like sausages about to burst. He'd never seen luxurious pillows like these.

Exactly how this has happened Mikhail has no idea. Just, crawling up onto the priest's bed, a good-sized bed for a single person. Lying very still atop the quilted coverlet hearing his breath come ragged.

In silence, but breathing audibly, Father McKenzie unties Mikhail's (waterstained, running) shoes, gently tugs them from Mikhail's feet, sets them on the carpet side by side, neatly. Always Mikhail has been embarrassed of his feet, like his hands, smaller than most other guys', and his cock, too, smaller. But just at first.

There was always that way about Father McKenzie—the unexpected. He could kneel before you but he could slap your face so hard tears flew out of your eyes. He could cry with you, relenting. He could cradle your feet in his hands, he could kiss your feet.

Washing the feet of the damned with his tears, our savior might do. Until the least of you, I will bless you.

But no: *unto the least of you.*

Climbing onto the bed beside Mikhail, bedsprings creaking beneath the middle-aged priest's weight. For his chest is fat, his thighs and belly. Crease of fat at the collar. Always the strangeness of Father Mac's thick pillows, where Mikey and the other boys had only cheap flat foam-rubber pillows on their beds. Never seen any bed with a fancy carved mahogany headboard like Father Mac's, had to be his own, special-shipped to the Mission.

Slow-easing his arm around Mikhail, at Mikhail's waist. Tentative at first, then more forcibly, embracing Mikhail from behind. The priest's face, his warm breath, a comfort, calming, against the nape of Mikhail's neck where hairs stir, pleasurably.

Good not to see the face. Up close faces confuse.

And Mikhail guesses, it's a comfort for Father Mac, too. Pressing the tremor-hand against Mikhail's chest, hard enough so it won't shake. So he can feel his heart beating, Mikhail thinks.

So weird! How life happens, he'd been ready to murder the God-damned pervert, all of them. Strangle this one with his two hands right here in this room, crack his skull against the wall and ram his knee against the fucker's trachea so Mrs. Laskey would discover him in the morning on the floor and his mouth open and she'd run screaming for help but it hasn't worked out that way, not today, tomorrow Mikhail vows he will expedite justice but not today, kind of just sleepy right now, maybe a little drunk.

That velvety voice. Soothing like Mikhail remembers. Nothing changed.

Son, you are safe here. You are safe with me.

God can't see in the dark, son. You remember.

Do Not Disturb

On the sixty-first floor of the hotel tower he awaits her.

She is the sole passenger in the elevator, which is a sleek glass cubicle rising rapidly and silently into the atrium as into the void.

Below, the crowded hotel lobby sinks away like a dream rapidly fading. Beside her, open floors and railings fly downward.

A sleek new way of *elevating,* so different from the larger, slower-moving, cumbersome elevators of her childhood.

In those elevators, there were likely to be uniformed operators who wore white gloves. In elevators like these, you are your own navigator.

Lingering in the elevator a faint aroma, is it cigar smoke?

It is December 1977. Smoking in the public areas of private hotels has not yet been banned.

She feels a thrill of vertigo, nausea. Cigar smoke as faint as memory. She shuts her eyes to steady herself.

Her sleek Italian leather handbag, she carries not slung from her right wrist but snug beneath her right arm, and steadied and supported by her left hand, for it is heavier than usual.

Still, the handbag is so positioned that its gleaming brass label shines outward—*Prada.*

By instinct, unconscious, vanity's gesture even on this day—*Prada.*

A large bag, perhaps large enough to be crammed with ten thousand dollars in large-denomination bills.

He must be led to think so, opening the door to her.

At the sixty-first floor the cubicle stops with a hiss and a jolt. The glass door slides open, Hannah has no choice but to step out. Something irrevocable has been decided, she has no choice.

Gripping the (heavy, bulky) handbag beneath her arm. *Has* she no choice?

You can still turn back.

If now, no one will know.

But her lover will know. He is expecting her. Ten thousand dollars. If she's a day late, fifteen thousand . . .

Hopeless, Hannah knows. No way for Hannah not to know, he has trapped her like a rat in a maze.

No matter how the rat makes its way through the maze, there is no way out of the maze.

No way except the death of the rat, or the death of the maze-maker.

Facing the row of elevators, a plate-glass window overlooking the riverfront, the river, a fierce white sun. Foreshortened view of Woodward Avenue far below, soundless traffic.

She'd been at the Far Hills bank that morning at nine. Waiting to see a teller. Sweating inside her beautiful flawless clothes. She'd made out the withdrawal slip, to present to the teller for a ridiculous figure: Nine thousand, nine hundred, ninety-nine dollars.

If she must speak her numbed lips had prepared *I would like to withdraw from this account . . .*

Before the (friendly, woman) teller she'd stood paralyzed. Too frightened to speak. At last turning aside, fleeing from the bank.

Impossible! The bank would call Wes, she was sure.

No choice. He is giving her no choice.

In the Prada bag, the Smith & Wesson Magnum. Always heavier than it appears.

Lifting the gun cautiously out of the drawer of the bedside table, her fingers icy cold, stiff. In terror that she will drop it, the gun will discharge, exactly the kind of "gun accident" that happens to persons unfamiliar with firearms, reckless persons, fools. But Hannah has no choice.

No idea how she will manage to remove the revolver from the handbag, in his hotel suite. How she will dare to lift, aim the barrel at *him*.

Not possible, she thinks. At the last moment she will grow faint, she will fail.

And if she misses? And if *he* wrenches the revolver from her.

He will beat her with it. He will beat, beat her face bloody, bruised. He will close his fingers around her neck . . .

How stupid could you be, to imagine that I'd loved you.

How stupid could you be, to imagine that you could kill me.

Her life has become a dream. Shimmering like the sun's reflection on a white wall. It is a mirage, it will pass. Yet, it will come again.

And yet, no matter how many times it has happened, it has never (yet) been *impossible.*

A sleepwalker making her slow careful way on stiletto heels along a windowless corridor. It is the curse of beauty, the stiletto heels. 6133, 6149, 6160 . . . So slowly do the numbers rise, Hannah begins to feel a thrill of relief, she will never arrive at 6183.

Faint odor of cigar smoke in her hair, in her nostrils that pinch with nausea so remote as to be merely residual, memory.

Joker Daddy. Buried deep in the marrow of her bones.

A costume she has chosen with care, white linen is always discreet, a silk shirt, red silk Dior scarf at her throat like the scarf worn by (very young) Audrey Hepburn in *Roman Holiday.*

Elegantly impractical stiletto heels, sinking into the carpet. If Hannah must turn and run, run desperately for her life, the tight-fitting shoes and the carpet will impede her.

One of those dreams in which she is a child again. She runs, runs. Her feet sink into something like sand, soft-seeming but not *soft.*

Never making any progress. Each time she has run.

Each time, *he* looms behind her. Daddy's strong hands threaten to seize her, lift her by her ribs . . .

Approaching 6183 she begins to shiver.

The nape of her neck rests against a stainless steel table, there is a drain just beneath. Her eyes stare open, unseeing. Only when your eyes are unseeing do you see *all.*

Yet, she presses on. In the Saint Laurent heels it is still December 1977, she has not yet entered the room for the final time. She is determined that she will come to the end of the riddle.

The brass plaque on the doorframe is 6183, each time it has been 6183.

She rings the doorbell. She listens.

Her heart beating very hard, she rings the bell again. She listens.

Hearing no one, nothing inside. And again ringing the bell, but now also knocking, hesitantly.

Yet still, no one. But he has been expecting her, Hannah thinks.

She wonders if this is a reprieve? He is not answering the door, perhaps he has departed.

He has decided to pity her. Forgive her and release her . . .

He has decided that he loves her, he cannot bear to hurt her. But he is angry with her, they've had a lover's quarrel. *He* will contact her.

Is this the correct door? Hannah checks again, yes: 6183. And there is the sign hanging from the doorknob, silver letters on lacquered black she has come to know so well—

PRIVACY PLEASE!
DO NOT DISTURB

ACKNOWLEDGMENTS

Babysitter was first published as a short story in *Ellery Queen* (2005); reprinted in *Horror: Best of the Year* (2006), and subsequently in *Sourland: Stories* (2010).

Excerpts from *Babysitter* were published in *Inque* (2021).